TELL ME A STORY

Charles Laughton

TELL ME A STORY

AN ANTHOLOGY

McGRAW-HILL BOOK COMPANY, INC.

New York   Toronto   London

"The Story Teller" from *The Short Stories of Saki* by H. H. Munro. Copyright 1930 by The Viking Press, Inc. Reprinted by permission of The Viking Press, Inc., New York, and John Lane The Bodley Head Limited.

"The Foghorn" and "Sun and Shadow" from *The Golden Apples of the Sun* by Ray Bradbury. Copyright 1952, 1953 by Ray Bradbury. Reprinted by permission of Doubleday & Company, Inc.

"The Fox and the Forest" from *The Illustrated Man* by Ray Bradbury. Copyright 1951 by Ray Bradbury. Reprinted by permission of Doubleday & Company, Inc.

"Oshidori" and "Mujina" from *The Selected Writings of Lafcadio Hearn*, edited by Henry Goodman, published by The Citadel Press.

"The Inexperienced Ghost," "The New Accelerator," "The Truth about Pyecraft" are from *Twelve Stories and a Dream* by H. G. Wells. Copyright 1905 by Charles Scribner's Sons, 1932 by H. G. Wells. Reprinted by permission of the publisher and the Executors of the Estate of H. G. Wells. Pages 216–221 are from *Meanwhile*. Copyright 1927 by H. G. Wells. Used by permission of the Executors of the Estate of H. G. Wells.

"Moonlight" and "Rose" from *The Complete Short Stories of Guy de Maupassant*, published by Doubleday & Company, Inc.

"The Standard of Living" from *The Portable Dorothy Parker*. Copyright 1928, 1944 by Dorothy Parker. Reprinted by permission of The Viking Press, Inc., New York.

"The Coming of Pan" from *Crock of Gold* by James Stephens. Copyright 1940 by The Macmillan Company. Used by permission of The Macmillan Company, New York, and The Macmillan Company of Canada Limited.

"Fairy Gifts" by Comte de Caylus from *Green Fairy Book*, edited by Andrew Lang, published by Longmans, Green and Co., Inc.

"The Shepherd's Daughter" from *The Daring Young Man on the Flying Trapeze and Other Stories* by William Saroyan. Copyright 1934 by The Modern Library, Inc. Reprinted by permission of Random House, Inc.

"Fable IX" and "The Sunday Zeppelin" from *The Saroyan Special*. Copyright 1948 by Harcourt, Brace and Company, Inc.

"A Worn Path," copyright 1945 by Eudora Welty. Reprinted from *A Curtain of Green* by Eudora Welty by permission of Harcourt, Brace and Company, Inc.

"The Secret Life of Walter Mitty" by James Thurber. Permission the author, © 1939 The New Yorker Magazine, Inc.

"The Little Girl and the Wolf" and "The Bear Who Let It Alone" by James Thurber. Permission the author, © 1939 The New Yorker Magazine, Inc.

"The Sea and the Shore" by James Thurber. Permission the author, © 1956 James Thurber. "The Peacelike Mongoose" and "The Daws on the Dial" by James Thurber. Permission the author, © 1956 The New Yorker Magazine, Inc.

"The Fable of the Wise Piker Who Had the Kind of Talk That Went" from *Forty Modern Fables* by George Ade. Copyright 1900, 1901 by Robert Howard Russell. "The Search for the Right House and How Mrs. Jump Had Her Annual Attack" from *People You Know* by George Ade. Copyright 1902, 1903 by Robert Howard Russell. Both used by permission of George Ade Davis.

"The Bedquilt" from *Hillsboro People*. Copyright 1915 by Henry Holt and Company, Inc. Copyright 1943 by Dorothy Canfield Fisher. By permission of the publishers.

"The Strength of God" and "The Teacher" from *Winesburg, Ohio* by Sherwood Anderson. Copyright 1919 by B. W. Huebsch, Inc., 1947 by Eleanor Copenhaver Anderson. Reprinted by permission of The Viking Press, Inc., New York.

"The Flight of Betsy Lane" from *The Country of the Pointed Firs* by Sarah Orne Jewett, published by Houghton Mifflin Company.

"Alone" from *The Web and the Rock* by Thomas Wolfe. Copyright 1939 by Maxwell Perkins as Executor. Reprinted by permission of Harper & Brothers.

"Paper Route" from *Look Homeward, Angel* by Thomas Wolfe. Copyright 1929 by Charles Scribner's Sons, 1957 by Edward C. Aswell and Fred W. Wolfe. Reprinted by permission of the publishers.

"Burning in the Night" from *You Can't Go Home Again* by Thomas Wolfe. Copyright 1940 by Maxwell Perkins as Executor. Reprinted by permission of Harper & Brothers.

"Tact," reprinted from *Mrs. Egg and Other Americans* by Thomas Beer, by permission of Alfred A. Knopf, Inc. Copyright 1947 by Alice Baldwin Beer.

"The Tremendous Adventures of Major Brown" from *The Club of Queer Trades* by G. K. Chesterton. Copyright 1903, 1904, 1905 by Harper & Brothers, 1933 by Gilbert Keith Chesterton. By permission of Miss D. E. Collins and A. P. Watt & Son.

"Big Trees" from *Big Trees* by Walter Fry and J. R. White. Copyright 1930, 1938 by the Board of Trustees of the Leland Stanford Junior University. Reprinted by permission of the publishers, Stanford University Press.

"Dusky Ruth," reprinted from *The Collected Tales of A. E. Coppard*, by permission of Alfred A. Knopf, Inc., and A. D. Peters. Copyright 1948 by A. E. Coppard.

"Just Like Little Dogs" from *Portrait of the Artist as a Young Dog* by Dylan Thomas. Copyright 1940 by New Directions, reprinted by permission of New Directions.

"The Elephant's Child" from *Just So Stories* by Rudyard Kipling. Reprinted by permission of Mrs. George Bambridge and Doubleday & Company, Inc.

Contents

Talking Horse Stories and Other Fables

Stories from Behind the Windowshades

Two Science-Fiction Stories

Tales of Derring-Do

Tales of Folly

Tall Stories

Life with a Capital "L"

Stained Glass and Stone

After-dinner Stories

In the Beginning

Stories of Belief

Endpiece

The Story Teller

As I am not an inventor of stories—I have many times tried to write very simple stories, but they all looked and sounded terrible the next morning—I have become a teller of stories.

I like stories better than anything else that is made by man. And the stories that I like best of all are those that have been told and retold before they were set down. These are the best stories, the stories that were told before they were written. This is so of the stories in the Bible. As an actor I quickly found that they are for the voice. There are places to go loud and places to go soft, and places to go fast and places to go slow. Any good reader is likely to go loud and soft and fast and slow in the same places all by himself.

I became a professional teller of stories in this way: I was under contract to M-G-M and I was earning a lot of money, and one day Elsa Lanchester, my wife, said to me, "You're impossible about the house. You're bad-tempered and snarl, and you bore me stiff."

Elsa does not speak like this all the time. She was indeed cross.

"You're an out-of-work man," she said. "Go out and work like a proper man."

Of course I was indignant. I went out and took a long walk along the beach at Santa Monica. Before I got back to the house I knew that, as usual, she was right. Acting in the movies was only using a tenth of my energy. The unused energy, as it always does, was churning inside me and turning me bad. I think I was also bad-tempered because it was during the war. At that time I was still a British citizen. I had been told by the British Consul in Los Angeles to remain where I was, and I was feeling guilty because I was not contributing what I could to the war.

So one day I met a couple of wounded men, who were visiting the cameraman in the still photography department at Universal, and I asked them what they did of an evening in the hospital and they said, "Nothing." I asked them if they'd be interested in anybody coming and reading to them a couple of times a week for an hour or so. They said they would—so I had a full occupation.

I read Dickens, Aesop, Shakespeare, Walt Whitman, de Maupassant, James Thurber, Hans Christian Andersen, Washington Irving, and most of the other writers you will find in this book. One day I picked up a Bible, and they protested. They did not want to hear anything from a dull book. The Bible was not dull to me, but I had to prove to them that it was not dull. I used every trick that I had learned and they liked it and asked for more. We had a pleasant time.

There is something about reading aloud to a group of people, however scarred, that turns them into children. These men would sit and listen to fairy stories. They found a reflection of their sufferings, which they had thought to be unique, in the tragedies of Shakespeare, and felt better. I lost my actor's nerves. The whole affair is one of the good memories of my life.

So we had to read in a larger and larger room at the hospital, and one day when I went home I told Elsa that I thought people wanted to be read to, so eventually I found myself reading in public all over the United States. When I had finished the first tour and went back home, Elsa said, "You look very tired—and fifteen years younger!"

Here, then, is a collection of stories that I have not been able to get out of my mind over the years. Few stories stick; some stories I have remembered so little that I have got to the end of them again before recognizing that I have read them before.

I have been asked how you learn to read aloud. In the hospitals I taught many men to read love poems to their wives, Mother Goose stories to their children. They would first of all start by imitating my English accent, and they would make recordings of their voices, but I quickly stopped that. I got them reading stories to their friends which they themselves liked—for the secret of learning to be a good reader is just that: to read something you love to someone you love, and practice and practice and practice till you don't have to pin them down any longer.

I would like to become the man who knows all the stories, who has on his back a bag of stories as bottomless as Santa Claus's bag of toys. That can never be because no man will ever know all the stories. When I go into a good bookstore or a library, I often feel sad when I see the shelves of books of all kinds that I know I will never be able to enjoy. I think of all the wonderful tales that I will never know and I wish I could live to be a thousand years old.

The Story Teller

SAKI

Once I was asked to go to read at a girls' school and, as I hadn't read at a girls' school before, being curious, I went. I read to them in a large hall with a carpet on the floor and heavy oak furniture around, and all these lovely young creatures were draped on window seats, oak tables, chiffoniers, and, of course, on the floor. One or two even sat on chairs. There was a pretty girl two or three girls from me on the floor who winked at me. As the teacher was standing beside me I gave no sign, but when the teacher wasn't looking, I winked back. I asked her if I had seen her before and she said I had. We had been on a radio show together for some charity. After I had read to them I was having tea and, as far as I remember, watercress sandwiches in the English style in the faculty room, and I said to one of the teachers, "Who was the pretty girl who winked at me?"

"Shirley Temple," she said, so the next day I sent her a telegram saying NEXT TIME I COME TO YOUR SCHOOL PLEASE DON'T WEAR A BEARD.

Where is the place to hide a leaf: in the forest? Where is the place to hide a pebble: on the beach? Where do you hide Shirley Temple: among a lot of other pretty girls of the same age?

So before the reading the teacher—who, by the way, was very nice—got up and said something like this:

"We have the great honor to have with us today the great and inspired talent of Mr. Charles Laughton to help you to understand the great writings of Shakespeare and Dickens." And so on. She didn't intend it, but her remarks had the effect of making all the girls hate me.

I had figured something of the sort might happen, so I brought along this little story, which is against teachers, to read. After it, I could have read from the Holy Scriptures in the original Aramaic and it wouldn't have made any difference. They would still have liked me and listened. It was

3

*a mean trick to play, but if the reader ever gets in a jam like
that, I advise him to use it.*

*You may have gathered that I have put this story first in
this book to take you off your guard.*

It was a hot afternoon and the railway carriage was correspondingly
sultry. The occupants of the carriage were a small girl and a smaller
girl and a small boy. An aunt belonging to the children occupied
the compartment. Most of the aunt's remarks seemed to begin with
"Don't," and nearly all of the children's remarks began with "Why?"
The bachelor said nothing out loud.

"Don't, Cyril, don't," exclaimed the aunt, as the small boy began
smacking the cushions of the seat, producing a cloud of dust at each
blow.

"Come and look out the window," she added.

The child moved reluctantly to the window. "Why are those sheep
being driven out of that field?" he asked.

"I expect they are being driven to another field where there is
more grass," said the aunt weakly.

"But there is lots of grass in that field," protested the boy; "there's
nothing else but grass there. Aunt, there's lots of grass in that field."

"Perhaps the grass in the other field is better," suggested the aunt
fatuously.

"Why is it better?" came the swift inevitable question.

The frown on the bachelor's face was deepening to a scowl.

The smaller girl created a diversion by beginning to recite "On
the Road to Mandalay." She only knew the first line. She repeated
it over and over again, "On the road to Mandalay" . . .

"Come over here and listen to a story," said the aunt.

The children moved listlessly toward the aunt's end of the carriage.
She began a story about a little girl who was good, and who made
friends with everyone on account of her goodness, and was finally
saved from a mad bull by a number of rescuers who admired her
moral character.

"Wouldn't they have saved her if she hadn't been good?" demanded the bigger of the small girls. It was exactly the question that
the bachelor had wanted to ask.

"Well, yes," admitted the aunt lamely, "but I don't think they
would have run quite so fast to her help if they had not liked her
so much."

"It's the stupidest story I've ever heard," said the bigger of the
small girls, with immense conviction.

"I didn't listen after the first bit, it was so stupid," said Cyril.

The smaller girl made no actual comment on the story, but she had long ago recommenced a murmured repetition of her favored line.

"You don't seem to be a success as a storyteller," said the bachelor suddenly from his corner.

"Perhaps *you* would like to tell them a story," was the aunt's retort.

"Tell us a story," demanded the bigger of the small girls.

"Once upon a time," began the bachelor, "there was a little girl called Bertha, who was extraordinarily good."

The children's momentarily-aroused interest began at once to flicker.

"She did all that she was told, she was always truthful, she kept her clothes clean, learned her lessons perfectly, and was polite in her manners."

"Was she pretty?" asked the bigger of the small girls.

"Not as pretty as any of you," said the bachelor, "but she was horribly good."

There was a wave of reaction in favor of the story; the word horrible in connection with goodness was a novelty that commended itself.

"She was so good," continued the bachelor, "that she won several medals for goodness, which she always wore, pinned onto her dress. There was a medal for obedience, another medal for punctuality, and a third for good behavior. They were large metal medals and they clanked against one another as she walked. No other child in the town where she lived had as many as three medals, so that everybody knew that she must be an extra good child."

"Horribly good," quoted Cyril.

"Everybody talked about her goodness and the Prince of the country got to hear about it, and he said that as she was so very good she might be allowed once a week to walk in his park, which was just outside the town. It was a beautiful park, and no children were ever allowed in it, so it was a great honor for Bertha to be allowed to go there."

"Were there any sheep in the park?" demanded Cyril.

"No," said the bachelor, "there were no sheep."

"Why weren't there any sheep?" came the inevitable question arising out of that answer.

The aunt permitted herself to smile, which might almost have been described as a grin.

"There were no sheep in the park," said the bachelor, "because the Prince's mother had once had a dream that her son would either be killed by a sheep or else by a clock falling on him. For that reason the Prince never kept a sheep in his park or a clock in his palace."

The aunt suppressed a gasp of admiration.

"Was the Prince killed by a sheep or a clock?" asked Cyril.

"He is still alive, so we can't tell whether the dream will come true," said the bachelor unconcernedly; "anyway, there were no sheep in the park, but there were lots of little pigs running all over the place."

"What color were they?"

"Black with white faces, white with black spots, black all over, grey with white patches, and some were white all over."

The storyteller paused to let a full idea of the park's treasures sink into the children's imaginations; then he resumed.

"Bertha was rather sorry to find that there were no flowers in the park. She had promised her aunts, with tears in her eyes, that she would not pick any of the kind Prince's flowers, and she had meant to keep her promise, so of course it made her feel silly to find that there were no flowers to pick."

"Why weren't there any flowers?"

"Because the pigs had eaten them all," said the bachelor promptly. "The gardeners had told the Prince that you couldn't have pigs and flowers, so he decided to have pigs and no flowers."

There was a murmur of approval at the excellence of the Prince's decision. So many people would have decided the other way.

Bertha walked up and down and enjoyed herself immensely and thought to herself: "If I were not so extraordinarily good I should not have been allowed to come into this beautiful park and enjoy all that there is to be seen in it," and her three medals clanked against one another as she walked and helped to remind her how very good she really was. Just then an enormous wolf came prowling into the park to see if it could catch a fat little pig for supper.

"What color was it?" asked the children, amid an immediate quickening of interest.

"Mud-color all over, with a black tongue and pale grey eyes that gleamed with unspeakable ferocity. The first thing that it saw in the park was Bertha. Her pinafore was so spotlessly white and clean it could be seen from a great distance. Bertha saw the wolf and saw that it was stealing towards her, and she began to wish that she had never been allowed to come into the park. She ran as hard as she could, and the wolf came after her with huge leaps and bounds. She managed to reach a shrubbery of myrtle bushes and she hid herself in one of the thickest of the bushes. The wolf came sniffing among the branches, its black tongue lolling out of its mouth and its pale grey eyes glaring with rage. Bertha was terribly frightened, and thought to herself: 'If I had not been so extraordinarily good I should have been safe in the town at this moment.' However, the scent of the myrtle was so strong that the wolf could not sniff out where Bertha was hiding, so he thought he might as well go off and catch a little pig instead. Bertha was trembling very much at having the wolf prowling and sniffing so near her, and as she trembled, the medal for obedience clanked against the medals for good conduct and punctuality. The wolf was just moving away when he heard the sound of the medals clanking and stopped to listen; they clanked again in a bush quite near him. He dashed into the bush, his pale grey eyes gleaming with ferocity and triumph, and dragged Bertha out and devoured her to the last morsel. All that was left of her were her shoes, bits of clothing, and the three medals for goodness."

"Were any of the little pigs killed?"

"No, they all escaped."

"The story began badly," said the smaller of the small girls, "but it had a beautiful ending."

"It is the most beautiful story that I ever heard," said the bigger of the small girls, with immense decision.

"It is the *only* beautiful story I have ever heard," said Cyril.

A dissentient opinion came from the aunt.

"A most improper story to tell to young children! You have undermined the effect of years of careful teaching."

"At any rate," said the bachelor, collecting his belongings preparatory to leaving the carriage, "I kept them quiet for ten minutes, which was more than you were able to do."

Haunting Stories

Sometimes we are haunted by a phrase of music, sometimes by a passage in a beautiful painting, often by a story.

The Foghorn

RAY BRADBURY

*The first haunting story is by a friend of mine, Ray Brad-
bury. He is a wonderful fellow—shining, pink, and healthy—
who comes to our swimming pool with his wife and kids.
As you probably know, he writes very popular science-fiction
stories (you will find one of them later in this book, on
page 223) about men traveling at incredible speeds through
space. He himself suffers horribly in an automobile if it
goes more than thirty miles per hour and will not, for anything, go up in an airplane. He is a jolly and rollicking fellow
with a fiendish imagination, as you will read.*

Out there in the cold water, far from land, we waited every night for
the coming of the fog, and it came, and we oiled the brass machinery
and lit the fog light up in the stone tower. Feeling like two birds in
the gray sky, McDunn and I sent the light touching out, red, then
white, then red again, to eye the lonely ships. And if they did not see
our light, then there was always our Voice, the great deep cry of our
Fog Horn shuddering through the rags of mist to startle the gulls
away like decks of scattered cards and make the waves turn high
and foam.

"It's a lonely life, but you're used to it now, aren't you?" asked
McDunn.

"Yes," I said. "You're a good talker, thank the Lord."

"Well, it's your turn on land tomorrow," he said, smiling, "to
dance the ladies and drink gin."

"What do you think, McDunn, when I leave you out here alone?"

"On the mysteries of the sea." McDunn lit his pipe. It was a
quarter past seven of a cold November evening, the heat on, the
light switching its tail in two hundred directions, the Fog Horn
bumbling in the high throat of the tower. There wasn't a town for
a hundred miles down the coast, just a road which came lonely
through dead country to the sea, with few cars on it, a stretch of
two miles of cold water out to our rock, and rare few ships.

"The mysteries of the sea," said McDunn thoughtfully. "You

know, the ocean's the biggest damned snowflake ever? It rolls and swells a thousand shapes and colors, no two alike. Strange. One night, years ago, I was here alone, when all of the fish of the sea surfaced out there. Something made them swim in and lie in the bay, sort of trembling and staring up at the tower light going red, white, red, white across them so I could see their funny eyes. I turned cold. They were like a big peacock's tail, moving out there until midnight. Then, without so much as a sound, they slipped away, the million of them was gone. I kind of think maybe, in some sort of way, they came all those miles to worship. Strange. But think how the tower must look to them, standing seventy feet above the water, the God-light flashing out from it, and the tower declaring itself with a monster voice. They never came back, those fish, but don't you think for a while they thought they were in the Presence?"

I shivered. I looked out at the long gray lawn of the sea stretching away into nothing and nowhere.

"Oh, the sea's full." McDunn puffed his pipe nervously, blinking. He had been nervous all day and hadn't said why. "For all our engines and so-called submarines, it'll be ten thousand centuries before we set foot on the real bottom of the sunken lands, in the fairy kingdoms there, and know *real* terror. Think of it, it's still the year 300,000 Before Christ down under there. While we've paraded around with trumpets, lopping off each other's countries and heads, they have been living beneath the sea twelve miles deep and cold in a time as old as the beard of a comet."

"Yes, it's an old world."

"Come on. I got something special I been saving up to tell you."

We ascended the eighty steps, talking and taking our time. At the top, McDunn switched off the room lights so there'd be no reflection in the plate glass. The great eye of the light was humming, turning easily in its oiled socket. The Fog Horn was blowing steadily, once every fifteen seconds.

"Sounds like an animal, don't it?" McDunn nodded to himself. "A big lonely animal crying in the night. Sitting here on the edge of ten billion years calling out to the Deeps, I'm here, I'm here, I'm here. And the Deeps do answer, yes, they do. You been here now for three months, Johnny, so I better prepare you. About this time of year," he said, studying the murk and fog, "something comes to visit the lighthouse."

"The swarms of fish like you said?"

"No, this is something else. I've put off telling you because you might think I'm daft. But tonight's the latest I can put it off, for if my calendar's marked right from last year, tonight's the night it comes. I won't go into detail, you'll have to see it yourself. Just sit down there. If you want, tomorrow you can pack your duffel and take the motorboat in to land and get your car parked there at the dinghy pier on the cape and drive on back to some little inland town and keep your lights burning nights, I won't question or blame you. It's happened three years now, and this is the only time anyone's been here with me to verify it. You wait and watch."

Half an hour passed with only a few whispers between us. When we grew tired waiting, McDunn began describing some of his ideas to me. He had some theories about the Fog Horn itself.

"One day many years ago a man walked along and stood in the sound of the ocean on a cold sunless shore and said, 'We need a voice to call across the water, to warn ships; I'll make one. I'll make a voice like all of time and all of the fog that ever was; I'll make a voice that is like an empty bed beside you all night long, and like an empty house when you open the door, and like trees in autumn with no leaves. A sound like the birds flying south, crying, and a sound like November wind and the sea on the hard, cold shore. I'll make a sound that's so alone that no one can miss it, that whoever hears it will weep in their souls, and hearths will seem warmer, and being inside will seem better to all who hear it in the distant towns. I'll make me a sound and an apparatus and they'll call it a Fog Horn and whoever hears it will know the sadness of eternity and the briefness of life.' "

The Fog Horn blew.

"I made up that story," said McDunn quietly, "to try to explain why this thing keeps coming back to the lighthouse every year. The Fog Horn calls it, I think, and it comes. . . ."

"But—" I said.

"Sssst!" said McDunn. "There!" He nodded out to the Deeps.

Something was swimming toward the lighthouse tower.

It was a cold night, as I have said; the high tower was cold, the light coming and going, and the Fog Horn calling and calling through the raveling mist. You couldn't see far and you couldn't see plain, but there was the deep sea moving on its way about the night earth, flat and quiet, the color of gray mud, and here were the two of us alone in the high tower, and there, far out at first, was a ripple, followed by a wave, a rising, a bubble, a bit of froth. And then, from the surface of the cold sea came a head, a large head, dark-colored, with immense eyes, and then a neck. And then—not a body—but more neck and more! The head rose a full forty feet above the water on a slender and beautiful dark neck. Only then did the body, like a little island of black coral and shells and crayfish, drip up from the subterranean. There was a flicker of tail. In all, from head to tip of tail, I estimated the monster at ninety or a hundred feet.

I don't know what I said. I said something.

"Steady, boy, steady," whispered McDunn.

"It's impossible!" I said.

"No, Johnny, *we're* impossible. *It's* like it always was ten million years ago. *It* hasn't changed. It's *us* and the land that've changed, become impossible. *Us!*"

It swam slowly and with a great dark majesty out in the icy waters, far away. The fog came and went about it, momentarily erasing its shape. One of the monster eyes caught and held and flashed back our immense light, red, white, red, white, like a disk held high and sending a message in primeval code. It was as silent as the fog through which it swam.

"It's a dinosaur of some sort!" I crouched down, holding to the stair rail.

"Yes, one of the tribe."

"But they died out!"

"No, only hid away in the Deeps. Deep, deep down in the deepest Deeps. Isn't *that* a word now, Johnny, a real word, it says so much: the Deeps. There's all the coldness and darkness and deepness in the world in a word like that."

"What'll we do?"

"Do? We got our job, we can't leave. Besides, we're safer here than in any boat trying to get to land. That thing's as big as a destroyer and almost as swift."

"But here, why does it come *here?*"

The next moment I had my answer.

The Fog Horn blew.

And the monster answered.

A cry came across a million years of water and mist. A cry so anguished and alone that it shuddered in my head and my body. The monster cried out at the tower. The Fog Horn blew. The monster roared again. The Fog Horn blew. The monster opened its great toothed mouth and the sound that came from it was the sound of the Fog Horn itself. Lonely and vast and far away. The sound of isolation, a viewless sea, a cold night, apartness. That was the sound.

"Now," whispered McDunn, "do you know why it comes here?"

I nodded.

"All year long, Johnny, that poor monster there lying far out, a thousand miles at sea, and twenty miles deep maybe, biding its time, perhaps it's a million years old, this one creature. Think of it, waiting a million years; could *you* wait that long? Maybe it's the last of its kind. I sort of think that's true. Anyway, here come men on land and build this lighthouse, five years ago. And set up their Fog Horn and sound it and sound it out toward the place where you bury yourself in sleep and sea memories of a world where there were thousands like yourself, but now you're alone, all alone in a world not made for you, a world where you have to hide.

"But the sound of the Fog Horn comes and goes, comes and goes, and you stir from the muddy bottom of the Deeps, and your eyes open like the lenses of two-foot cameras and you move, slow, slow, for you have the ocean sea on your shoulders, heavy. But that Fog Horn comes through a thousand miles of water, faint and familiar, and the furnace in your belly stokes up, and you begin to rise, slow, slow. You feed yourself on great slakes of cod and minnow, on rivers of jellyfish, and you rise slow through the autumn months, through September when the fogs started, through October with more fog and the horn still calling you on, and then, late in November, after pressurizing yourself day by day, a few feet higher every hour, you are near the surface and still alive. You've got to go slow; if you surfaced all at once you'd explode. So it takes you all of three months to surface, and then a number of days to swim through the cold waters to the lighthouse. And there you are, out there, in the night, Johnny, the biggest damn monster in creation. And here's the lighthouse calling to you, with a long neck like your neck sticking way up out of the water, and a body like your body, and, most important of all, a voice like your voice. Do you understand now, Johnny, do you understand?"

The Fog Horn blew.

The monster answered.

I saw it all, I knew it all—the million years of waiting alone, for someone to come back who never came back. The million years of isolation at the bottom of the sea, the insanity of time there, while the skies cleared of reptile-birds, the swamps dried on the continental lands, the sloths and saber-tooths had their day and sank in tar pits, and men ran like white ants upon the hills.

The Fog Horn blew.

"Last year," said McDunn, "that creature swam round and round, round and round, all night. Not coming too near, puzzled, I'd say. Afraid, maybe. And a bit angry after coming all this way. But the next day, unexpectedly, the fog lifted, the sun came out fresh, the sky was as blue as a painting. And the monster swam off away from the heat and the silence and didn't come back. I suppose it's been brooding on it for a year now, thinking it over from every which way."

The monster was only a hundred yards off now, it and the Fog Horn crying at each other. As the lights hit them, the monster's eyes were fire and ice, fire and ice.

"That's life for you," said McDunn. "Someone always waiting for someone who never comes home. Always someone loving some thing more than that thing loves them. And after a while you want to destroy whatever that thing is, so it can't hurt you no more."

The monster was rushing at the lighthouse.

The Fog Horn blew.

"Let's see what happens," said McDunn.

He switched the Fog Horn off.

The ensuing minute of silence was so intense that we could hear our hearts pounding in the glassed area of the tower, could hear the slow greased turn of the light.

The monster stopped and froze. Its great lantern eyes blinked. Its mouth gaped. It gave a sort of rumble, like a volcano. It twitched its head this way and that, as if to seek the sounds now dwindled off into the fog. It peered at the lighthouse. It rumbled again. Then its eyes caught fire. It reared up, threshed the water, and rushed at the tower, its eyes filled with angry torment.

"McDunn!" I cried. "Switch on the horn!"

McDunn fumbled with the switch. But even as he flicked it on, the monster was rearing up. I had a glimpse of its gigantic paws, fishskin glittering in webs between the finger-like projections, clawing at the tower. The huge eye on the right side of its anguished head glittered before me like a caldron into which I might drop, screaming. The tower shook. The Fog Horn cried; the monster cried. It seized the tower and gnashed at the glass, which shattered in upon us.

McDunn seized my arm. "Downstairs!"

The tower rocked, trembled, and started to give. The Fog Horn and the monster roared. We stumbled and half fell down the stairs. "Quick!"

We reached the bottom as the tower buckled down toward us. We ducked under the stairs into the small stone cellar. There were a thousand concussions as the rocks rained down; the Fog Horn stopped abruptly. The monster crashed upon the tower. The tower fell. We knelt together, McDunn and I, holding tight, while our world exploded.

Then it was over, and there was nothing but darkness and the wash of the sea on the raw stones.

That and the other sound.

"Listen," said McDunn quietly. "Listen."

We waited a moment. And then I began to hear it. First a great vacuumed sucking of air, and then the lament, the bewilderment, the loneliness of the great monster, folded over and upon us, above us, so that the sickening reek of its body filled the air, a stone's thickness away from our cellar. The monster gasped and cried. The tower was gone. The light was gone. The thing that had called to it across a million years was gone. And the monster was opening its mouth and sending out great sounds. The sounds of a Fog Horn, again and again. And ships far at sea, not finding the light, not seeing anything, but passing and hearing late that night, must've thought: There it is, the lonely sound, the Lonesome Bay horn. All's well. We've rounded the cape.

And so it went for the rest of that night.

The sun was hot and yellow the next afternoon when the rescuers came out to dig us from our stoned-under cellar.

"It fell apart, is all," said Mr. McDunn gravely. "We had a few bad knocks from the waves and it just crumbled." He pinched my arm.

There was nothing to see. The ocean was calm, the sky blue. The only thing was a great algaic stink from the green matter that covered the fallen tower stones and the shore rocks. Flies buzzed about. The ocean washed empty on the shore.

The next year they built a new lighthouse, but by that time I had a job in the little town and a wife and a good small warm house that glowed yellow on autumn nights, the doors locked, the chimney puffing smoke. As for McDunn, he was master of the new lighthouse, built to his own specifications, out of steel-reinforced concrete. "Just in case," he said.

The new lighthouse was ready in November. I drove down alone one evening late and parked my car and looked across the gray waters and listened to the new horn sounding, once, twice, three, four times a minute far out there, by itself.

The monster?

It never came back.

"It's gone away," said McDunn. "It's gone back to the Deeps. It's learned you can't love anything too much in this world. It's gone into the deepest Deeps to wait another million years. Ah, the poor thing! Waiting out there, and waiting out there, while man comes and goes on this pitiful little planet. Waiting and waiting."

I sat in my car, listening. I couldn't see the lighthouse or the light standing out in Lonesome Bay. I could only hear the Horn, the Horn, the Horn. It sounded like the monster calling.

I sat there wishing there was something I could say.

Oshidori

LAFCADIO HEARN

Of all the pretty stories of lovers killing themselves for love, this has touched me the most.

Lafcadio Hearn, who wrote it, was a remarkable man. He was very small and got an inferiority complex living among tall people, so he went to live in Japan where people were the same size. Before that he was a newspaperman in Cincinnati and New Orleans.

His words are jeweled, and no wonder, for he would work endlessly changing and rearranging them. He once wrote in a letter to a friend of his:

"For me words have colour, form, character; they have faces, ports, manners, gesticulations; they have moods, humours, eccentricities;—they have tints, tones, personalities. I am affected by the whispering of words, the rustling of the procession of letters ... the pouting of words, the frowning and fuming of words, the weeping, the raging and racketing and rioting of words, the noisomeness of words, the tenderness or hardness, the dryness or juiciness of words, —the interchange of values in the gold, the silver, the brass and the copper of words."

When you have read this story of his, reread the last seven lines. The story is extremely simple and its effect could only have been achieved with the utmost care.

There was a falconer and hunter, named Sonjo, who lived in the district called Tamura-no-Go, of the province of Mutsu. One day he went out hunting, and could not find any game. But on his way home, at a place called Akanuma, he perceived a pair of oshidori [1] (mandarin-ducks), swimming together in a river that he was about to cross. To kill oshidori is not good; but Sonjo happened to be very hungry, and he shot at the pair. His arrow pierced the male: the female escaped into the rushes of the farther shore, and disappeared. Sonjo took the dead bird home, and cooked it.

[1] From ancient time, in the Far East, these birds have been regarded as emblems of conjugal affection.

That night he dreamed a dreary dream. It seemed to him that a beautiful woman came into his room, and stood by his pillow, and began to weep. So bitterly did she weep that Sonjo felt as if his heart were being torn out while he listened. And the woman cried to him: "Why—oh! why did you kill him?—of what wrong was he guilty? ... At Akanuma we were so happy together—and you killed him! ... What harm did he ever do you? Do you even know what you have done?—oh! do you know what a cruel, what a wicked thing you have done? ... Me too you have killed—for I will not live without my husband! ... Only to tell you this I came." ... Then again she wept aloud—so bitterly that the voice of her crying pierced into the marrow of the listener's bones;—and she sobbed out the words of this poem:

> Hi kerureba
> Sasoeshi mono wo—
> Akanuma no
> Makomo no kure no
> Hitori-ne zo uki!

At the coming of twilight I invited him to return with me—! Now to sleep alone in the shadow of the rushes of Akanuma— ah! what misery unspeakable! [2]

And after having uttered these verses she exclaimed: "Ah, you do not know—you cannot know what you have done! But to-morrow when you go to Akanuma, you will see—you will see...." So saying, and weeping very piteously, she went away.

When Sonjo awoke in the morning, this dream remained so vivid in his mind that he was greatly troubled. He remembered the words: "But to-morrow, when you go to Akanuma, you will see—you will see." And he resolved to go there at once, that he might learn whether his dream was anything more than a dream.

So he went to Akanuma; and there, when he came to the river-bank, he saw the female oshidori swimming alone. In the same moment the bird perceived Sonjo; but, instead of trying to escape, she swam straight toward him, looking at him the while in a strange fixed way. Then, with her beak, she suddenly tore open her own body, and died before the hunter's eyes....

Sonjo shaved his head, and became a priest.

---

[2] There is a pathetic double meaning in the third verse; for the syllables composing the proper name Akanuma (Red Marsh) may also be read as akanu-ma signifying "the time of our inseparable (or delightful) relation." So the poem can also be thus rendered: "When the day began to fail, I had invited him to accompany me ...! Now, after the time of that happy relation, what misery for the one who must slumber alone in the shadow of the rushes!" The makomo is a sort of large rush, used for making baskets.

The Nightingale

HANS CHRISTIAN ANDERSEN

*Hans Andersen is one of the best of all storytellers. He is
supposed to have told his stories to children before he wrote
them. Most have a rather cruel twist to them. This one has
not.*

*Hans Christian Andersen was not very successful with
women. He was ugly, and one day he fell in love with the
great and famous singer Jenny Lind, and this story of the
nightingale which sang so naturally, as against the formal
singers of the day, is in praise of the singing of Jenny Lind.
So, in a way, it is a love story.*

In China, as you know, the Emperor is a Chinaman, and all the
people around him are Chinamen too. It is many years since the
story I am going to tell you happened, but that is all the more reason
for telling it, lest it should be forgotten. The Emperor's palace was
the most beautiful thing in the world; it was made entirely of the
finest porcelain, very costly, but at the same time so fragile that it
could only be touched with the very greatest care. There were the
most extraordinary flowers to be seen in the garden; the most beautiful ones had little silver bells tied to them, which tinkled perpetually,
so that one should not pass the flowers without looking at them.
Every little detail in the garden had been most carefully thought out,
and it was so big, that even the gardener himself did not know where
it ended. If one went on walking, one came to beautiful woods with
lofty trees and deep lakes. The wood extended to the sea, which was
deep and blue, deep enough for large ships to sail up right under the
branches of the trees. Among these trees lived a nightingale, which
sang so deliciously, that even the poor fisherman, who had plenty
of other things to do, lay still to listen to it, when he was out at night
drawing in his nets. "Heavens, how beautiful it is!" he said, but then
he had to attend to his business and forgot it. The next night when
he heard it again he would again exclaim, "Heavens, how beautiful
it is!"

Travellers came to the Emperor's capital, from every country in the world; they admired everything very much, especially the palace and the gardens, but when they heard the nightingale they all said, "This is better than anything!"

When they got home they described it, and the learned ones wrote many books about the town, the palace and the garden; but nobody forgot the nightingale, it was always put above everything else. Those among them who were poets wrote the most beautiful poems, all about the nightingale in the woods by the deep blue sea. These books went all over the world, and in course of time some of them reached the Emperor. He sat in his golden chair reading and reading, and nodding his head, well pleased to hear such beautiful descriptions of the town, the palace and the garden. "But the nightingale is the best of all," he read.

"What is this?" said the Emperor. "The nightingale? Why, I know nothing about it. Is there such a bird in my kingdom, and in my own garden into the bargain, and I have never heard of it? Imagine my having to discover this from a book!"

Then he called his gentleman-in-waiting, who was so grand that when any one of a lower rank dared to speak to him, or to ask him a question, he would only answer "P," which means nothing at all.

"There is said to be a very wonderful bird called a nightingale here," said the Emperor. "They say that it is better than anything else in all my great kingdom! Why have I never been told anything about it?"

"I have never heard it mentioned," said the gentleman-in-waiting. "It has never been presented at court."

"I wish it to appear here this evening to sing to me," said the Emperor. "The whole world knows what I am possessed of, and I know nothing about it!"

"I have never heard it mentioned before," said the gentleman-in-waiting. "I will seek it, and I will find it!" But where was it to be found? The gentleman-in-waiting ran upstairs and downstairs and in and out of all the rooms and corridors. No one of all those he met had ever heard anything about the nightingale; so the gentleman-in-waiting ran back to the Emperor, and said that it must be a myth, invented by the writers of the books. "Your Imperial Majesty must not believe everything that is written; books are often mere inventions, even if they do not belong to what we call the black art!"

"But the book in which I read it is sent to me by the powerful Emperor of Japan, so it can't be untrue. I will hear this nightingale; I insist upon its being here to-night. I extend my most gracious protection to it, and if it is not forthcoming, I will have the whole court trampled upon after supper!"

"Tsing-pe!" said the gentleman-in-waiting, and away he ran again, up and down all the stairs, in and out of all the rooms and corridors; half the court ran with him, for they none of them wished to be trampled on. There was much questioning about this nightingale, which was known to all the outside world, but to no one at court. At last they found a poor little maid in the kitchen. She said, "Oh heavens, the nightingale? I know it very well. Yes, indeed it can sing. Every evening I am allowed to take broken meat to my poor sick mother: she lives down by the shore. On my way back, when I am tired, I rest awhile in the wood, and then I hear the nightingale. Its song brings the tears into my eyes; I feel as if my mother were kissing me!"

"Little kitchen-maid," said the gentleman-in-waiting, "I will procure you a permanent position in the kitchen, and permission to see the Emperor dining, if you will take us to the nightingale. It is commanded to appear at court to-night."

Then they all went out into the wood where the nightingale usually sang. Half the court was there. As they were going along at their best pace a cow began to bellow.

"Oh!" said a young courtier, "there we have it. What wonderful power for such a little creature; I have certainly heard it before."

"No, those are the cows bellowing; we are a long way yet from the place." Then the frogs began to croak in the marsh.

"Beautiful!" said the Chinese chaplain, "it is just like the tinkling of church bells."

"No, those are the frogs!" said the little kitchen-maid. "But I think we shall soon hear it now!"

Then the nightingale began to sing.

"There it is!" said the little girl. "Listen, listen, there it sits!" and she pointed to a little grey bird up among the branches.

"Is it possible?" said the gentleman-in-waiting. "I should never have thought it was like that. How common it looks! Seeing so many grand people must have frightened all its colours away."

"Little nightingale!" called the kitchen-maid quite loud, "our gracious Emperor wishes you to sing to him!"

"With the greatest of pleasure!" said the nightingale, warbling away in the most delightful fashion.

"It's just like crystal bells," said the gentleman-in-waiting. "Look at its little throat, how active it is. It is extraordinary that we have never heard it before! I am sure it will be a great success at court!"

"Shall I sing again to the Emperor?" said the nightingale, who thought he was present.

"My precious little nightingale," said the gentleman-in-waiting, "I have the honour to command your attendance at a court festival to-night, where you will charm his gracious majesty the Emperor with your fascinating singing."

"It sounds best among the trees," said the nightingale, but it went with them willingly when it heard that the Emperor wished it.

The palace had been brightened up for the occasion. The walls and the floors, which were all of china, shone by the light of many thousand golden lamps. The most beautiful flowers, all of the tinkling kind, were arranged in the corridors; there was hurrying to and fro, and a great draught, but this was just what made the bells ring; one's ears were full of the tinkling. In the middle of the large reception-room, where the Emperor sat, a golden rod had been fixed, on which the nightingale was to perch. The whole court was assembled, and the little kitchen-maid had been permitted to stand behind the door, as she now had the actual title of cook. They were all dressed in their best; everybody's eyes were turned toward the little grey bird at which the Emperor was nodding. The nightingale sang delightfully, and the tears came into the Emperor's eyes, nay they rolled down his cheeks; and then the nightingale sang more beautifully than ever, its notes touched all hearts. The Emperor was charmed, and said the nightingale should have his gold slipper to wear round its neck. But the nightingale declined with thanks; it had already been sufficiently rewarded.

"I saw tears in the eyes of the Emperor; that is my richest reward. The tears of an Emperor have a wonderful power! God knows I am sufficiently recompensed!" and then it again burst into its sweet heavenly song.

"That is the most delightful coquetting I have ever seen!" said the ladies, and they took some water into their mouths to try and make the same gurgling when any one spoke to them, thinking so to equal the nightingale. Even the lackeys and the chamber-maids announced that they were satisfied, and that is saying a great deal; they are always the most difficult people to please. Yes, indeed, the nightingale had made a sensation. It was to stay at court now, and to have its own cage, as well as liberty to walk out twice a day, and once in the night. It always had twelve footmen, with each one holding a ribbon which was tied round its leg. There was not much pleasure in an outing of that sort.

The whole town talked about the marvellous bird, and if two people met, one said to the other "Night," and the other answered "Gale," and then they sighed, perfectly understanding each other. Eleven cheesemongers' children were called after it, but they had not got a voice among them.

One day a large parcel came for the Emperor; outside was written the word "Nightingale."

"Here we have another new book about this celebrated bird," said the Emperor. But it was no book; it was a little work of art in a box, an artificial nightingale, exactly like the living one, but it was studded all over with diamonds, rubies and sapphires.

When the bird was wound up it could sing one of the songs the real one sang, and it wagged its tale, which glittered with silver and gold. A ribbon was tied round its neck on which was written, "The Emperor of Japan's nightingale is very poor compared to the Emperor of China's."

Everybody said, "Oh, how beautiful!" And the person who brought the artificial bird immediately received the title of Imperial Nightingale-Carrier in Chief.

"Now, they must sing together; what a duet that will be!"

Then they had to sing together, but they did not get on very well, for the real nightingale sang in its own way, and the artificial one could only sing waltzes.

"There is no fault in that," said the music-master; "it is perfectly in time and correct in every way!"

Then the artificial bird had to sing alone. It was just as great a success as the real one, and then it was so much prettier to look at; it glittered like bracelets and breast-pins.

It sang the same tune three and thirty times over, and yet it was not tired; people would willingly have heard it from the beginning again, but the Emperor said that the real one must have a turn now— but where was it? No one had noticed that it had flown out of the open window, back to its own green woods.

"But what is the meaning of this?" said the Emperor.

All the courtiers railed at it, and said it was a most ungrateful bird.

"We have got the best bird, though," said they, and then the artificial bird had to sing again, and this was the thirty-fourth time that they heard the same tune, but they did not know it thoroughly even yet, because it was so difficult.

The music-master praised the bird tremendously, and insisted that it was much better than the real nightingale, not only as regarded the outside with all the diamonds, but the inside too.

"Because, you see, my ladies and gentlemen, and the Emperor before all, in the real nightingale you never know what you will hear, but in the artificial one everything is decided beforehand! So it is, and so it must remain, it can't be otherwise. You can account for things, you can open it and show the human ingenuity in arranging the waltzes, how they go, and how one note follows upon another!"

"Those are exactly my opinions," they all said, and the music-master got leave to show the bird to the public next Sunday. They were also to hear it sing, said the Emperor. So they heard it, and all became as enthusiastic over it as if they had drunk themselves merry on tea, because that is a thoroughly Chinese habit.

Then they all said "Oh," and stuck their forefingers in the air and nodded their heads; but the poor fisherman who had heard the real nightingale said, "It sounds very nice, and it is very like the real one, but there is something wanting, we don't know what." The real nightingale was banished from the kingdom.

The artificial bird had its place on a silken cushion, close to the Emperor's bed: all the presents it had received of gold and precious jewels were scattered round it. Its title had risen to be "Chief Imperial Singer of the Bed-Chamber," in rank number one, on the left side; for the Emperor reckoned that side the important one, where the heart was seated. And even an emperor's heart is on the left side. The music-master wrote five-and-twenty volumes about the artificial bird; the treatise was very long and written in all the most difficult Chinese characters. Everybody said they had read and understood it, for otherwise they would have been reckoned stupid, and then their bodies would have been trampled upon.

Things went on in this way for a whole year. The Emperor, the court, and all the other Chinamen knew every little gurgle in the song of the artificial bird by heart; but they liked it all the better for this, and they could all join in the song themselves. Even the street boys sang "zizizi" and "cluck, cluck, cluck," and the Emperor sang it too.

But one evening when the bird was singing its best, and the Emperor was lying in bed listening to it, something gave way inside the bird with a "whizz." Then a spring burst, "whirr" went all the wheels, and the music stopped. The Emperor jumped out of bed and sent for his private physicians, but what good could they do? Then they sent for the watchmaker, and after a good deal of talk and examination he got the works to go again somehow; but he said it would have to be saved as much as possible, because it was so worn out, and he could not renew the works so as to be sure of the tune. This was a great blow! They only dared to let the artificial bird sing once a year, and hardly that; but then the music-master made a little speech, using all the most difficult words. He said it was just as good as ever, and his saying it made it so.

Five years now passed, and then a great grief came upon the nation, for they were all very fond of their Emperor, and he was ill and could not live, it was said. A new Emperor was already chosen, and people stood about in the street, and asked the gentleman-in-waiting how their Emperor was going on.

"P," answered he, shaking his head.

The Emperor lay pale and cold in his gorgeous bed, the courtiers thought he was dead, and they all went off to pay their respects to their new Emperor. The lackeys ran off to talk matters over, and the chamber-maids gave a great coffee-party. Cloth had been laid down in all the rooms and corridors so as to deaden the sound of footsteps, so it was very, very quiet. But the Emperor was not dead yet. He lay stiff and pale in the gorgeous bed with its velvet hangings and heavy golden tassels. There was an open window high above him, and the moon streamed in upon the Emperor, and the artificial bird beside him. The poor Emperor could hardly breathe, he seemed to have a weight on his chest, he opened his eyes, and then he saw that it was Death sitting upon his chest, wearing his golden crown. In one hand he held the Emperor's golden sword, and in the other his imperial banner. Round about, from among the folds of the velvet hangings, peered many curious faces: some were hideous, others gentle and pleasant. They were all the Emperor's good and bad deeds, which now looked him in the face when Death was weighing him down.

"Do you remember that?" whispered one after the other; "Do you remember this?" and they told him so many things that the perspiration poured down his face.

"I never knew that," said the Emperor. "Music, music, sound the great Chinese drums!" he cried, "that I may not hear what they are saying." But they went on and on, and Death sat nodding his head, just like a Chinaman, at everything that was said.

"Music, music!" shrieked the Emperor. "You precious little golden bird, sing, sing! I have loaded you with precious stones, and even hung my own golden slipper round your neck; sing, I tell you, sing!"

But the bird stood silent; there was nobody to wind it up, so of course it could not go. Death continued to fix the great empty sockets of his eyes upon him, and all was silent, so terribly silent.

Suddenly, close to the window, there was a burst of lovely song; it was the living nightingale, perched on a branch outside. It had heard of the Emperor's need, and had come to bring comfort and hope to him. As it sang the faces round became fainter and fainter, and the blood coursed with fresh vigour in the Emperor's veins and through his feeble limbs. Even Death himself listened to the song and said, "Go on, little nightingale, go on!"

"Yes, if you give me the gorgeous golden sword; yes, if you give me the imperial banner; yes, if you give me the Emperor's crown."

And Death gave back each of these treasures for a song, and the nightingale went on singing. It sang about the quiet churchyard, where the roses bloom, where the elder flower scents the air, and where the fresh grass is ever moistened anew by the tears of the mourner. This song brought to Death a longing for his own garden, and, like a cold grey mist, he passed out of the window.

"Thanks, thanks!" said the Emperor; "you heavenly little bird, I know you! I banished you from my kingdom, and yet you have charmed the evil visions away from my bed by your song, and even Death away from my heart! How can I ever repay you?"

"You have rewarded me," said the nightingale. "I brought the tears to your eyes, the very first time I ever sang to you, and I shall never forget it! Those are the jewels which gladden the heart of a singer;— but sleep now, and wake up fresh and strong! I will sing to you!"

Then it sang again, and the Emperor fell into a sweet refreshing sleep. The sun shone in at his window, when he woke refreshed and well; none of his attendants had yet come back to him, for they thought he was dead, but the nightingale still sat there singing.

"You must always stay with me!" said the Emperor. "You shall only sing when you like, and I will break the artificial bird into a thousand pieces!"

"Don't do that!" said the nightingale, "it did all the good it could! Keep it as you have always done! I can't build my nest and live in this palace, but let me come whenever I like, then I will sit on the branch in the evening, and sing to you. I will sing to cheer you and to make you thoughtful too; I will sing to you of the happy ones, and of those that suffer too. I will sing about the good and the evil, which are kept hidden from you. The little singing bird flies far and wide, to the poor fisherman, and the peasant's home, to numbers who are far from you and your court. I love your heart more than your crown, and yet there is an odour of sanctity round the crown too! I will come, and I will sing to you!—But you must promise me one thing!"

"Everything!" said the Emperor, who stood there in his imperial robe which he had just put on, and he held the sword heavy with gold upon his heart.

"One thing I ask you! Tell no one that you have a little bird who tells you everything; it will be better so!"

Then the nightingale flew away. The attendants came in to see after their dead Emperor, and there he stood, bidding them "Good morning!"

Tales of Haunting

Ghost stories, along with fairy stories, have gone out of fashion. Perhaps it is because psychiatrists have been busy telling us that dreams, which are the stuff of fairy stories and ghost stories, come from unsatisfied longings or from indigestion or hallucinatory mushrooms, or are the result of the writer's having been neglected as a child.

At any rate we have instead science-fiction stories and psychological horror stories of the Tennessee Williams–Truman Capote school which, in fact, are much the same kind of thing. In form, most of these stories are similar to the old-fashioned ghost story.

All three of the stories I have chosen follow the classic technique. They start with a passage of very ordinary factual reportage and, having gotten you nice and comfortable, pull the supernatural trick at the end.

The Inexperienced Ghost

H. G. WELLS

This next story by Wells is one of my favorite ghost stories, with a good, snap, "oomey" ending. I can hear his voice telling it now!

The scene amidst which Clayton told his last story comes back very vividly to my mind. There he sat, for the greater part of the time, in the corner of the authentic settle by the spacious open fire, and Sanderson sat beside him smoking the Broseley clay that bore his name. There was Evans, and that marvel among actors, Wish, who is also a modest man. We had all come down to the Mermaid Club that Saturday morning, except Clayton, who had slept there over-night—which indeed gave him the opening of his story. We had golfed until golfing was invisible; we had dined, and we were in that mood of tranquil kindliness when men will suffer a story. When Clayton began to tell one, we naturally supposed he was lying. It may be that indeed he was lying—of that the reader will speedily be able to judge as well as I. He began, it is true, with an air of matter-of-fact anecdote, but that we thought was only the incurable artifice of the man.

"I say!" he remarked, after a long consideration of the upward rain of sparks from the log that Sanderson had thumped, "you know I was alone here last night?"

"Except for the domestics," said Wish.

"Who sleep in the other wing," said Clayton. "Yes. Well—" He pulled at his cigar for some little time as though he still hesitated about his confidence. Then he said, quite quietly, "I caught a ghost!"

"Caught a ghost, did you?" said Sanderson. "Where is it?"

And Evans, who admires Clayton immensely and has been four weeks in America, shouted, "*Caught* a ghost, did you, Clayton? I'm glad of it! Tell us all about it right now."

Clayton said he would in a minute, and asked him to shut the door.

He looked apologetically at me. "There's no eavesdropping of course, but we don't want to upset our very excellent service with any rumours of ghosts in the place. There's too much shadow and

oak panelling to trifle with that. And this, you know, wasn't a regular
ghost. I don't think it will come again—ever."

"You mean to say you didn't keep it?" said Sanderson.

"I hadn't the heart to," said Clayton.

And Sanderson said he was surprised.

We laughed, and Clayton looked aggrieved. "I know," he said,
with the flicker of a smile, "but the fact is it really *was* a ghost, and
I'm as sure of it as I am that I am talking to you now. I'm not joking.
I mean what I say."

Sanderson drew deeply at his pipe, with one reddish eye on Clayton, and then emitted a thin jet of smoke more eloquent than many
words.

Clayton ignored the comment. "It is the strangest thing that has
ever happened in my life. You know I never believed in ghosts or
anything of the sort, before, ever; and then, you know, I bag one in a
corner; and the whole business is in my hands."

He meditated still more profoundly and produced and began to
pierce a second cigar with a curious little stabber he affected.

"You talked to it?" asked Wish.

"For the space, probably, of an hour."

"Chatty?" I said, joining the party of the sceptics.

"The poor devil was in trouble," said Clayton, bowed over his cigar-
end and with the very faintest note of reproof.

"Sobbing?" someone asked.

Clayton heaved a realistic sigh at the memory. "Good Lord!" he
said; "yes." And then, "Poor fellow! yes."

"Where did you strike it?" asked Evans, in his best American
accent.

"I never realised," said Clayton, ignoring him, "the poor sort of
thing a ghost might be," and he hung us up again for a time, while
he sought for matches in his pocket and lit and warmed to his cigar.

"I took an advantage," he reflected at last.

We were none of us in a hurry. "A character," he said, "remains
just the same character for all that it's been disembodied. That's
a thing we too often forget. People with a certain strength or fixity
of purpose may have ghosts of a certain strength and fixity of purpose
—most haunting ghosts, you know, must be as one-idea'd as mono-
maniacs and as obstinate as mules to come back again and again.
This poor creature wasn't." He suddenly looked up rather queerly,
and his eye went round the room. "I say it," he said, "in all kindliness,
but that is the plain truth of the case. Even at the first glance he
struck me as weak."

He punctuated with the help of his cigar.

"I came upon him, you know, in the long passage. His back was towards me and I saw him first. Right off I knew him for a ghost. He was transparent and whitish; clean through his chest I could see the glimmer of the little window at the end. And not only his physique but his attitude struck me as being weak. He looked, you know, as though he didn't know in the slightest whatever he meant to do. One hand was on the panelling and the other fluttered to his mouth. Like —*so!*"

"What sort of physique?" said Sanderson.

"Lean. You know that sort of young man's neck that has two great flutings down the back, here and here—so! And a little, meanish head with scrubby hair and rather bad ears. Shoulders bad, narrower than the hips; turndown collar, ready-made short jacket, trousers baggy and a little frayed at the heels. That's how he took me. I came very quietly up the staircase. I did not carry a light, you know—the candles are on the landing table and there is that lamp—and I was in my list slippers, and I saw him as I came up. I stopped dead at that —taking him in. I wasn't a bit afraid. I think that in most of these affairs one is never nearly so afraid or excited as one imagines one would be. I was surprised and interested. I thought, 'Good Lord! Here's a ghost at last! And I haven't believed for a moment in ghosts during the last five-and-twenty years.' "

"Um," said Wish.

"I suppose I wasn't on the landing a moment before he found out I was there. He turned on me sharply, and I saw the face of an immature young man, a weak nose, a scrubby little moustache, a feeble chin. So for an instant we stood—he looking over his shoulder at me—and regarded one another. Then he seemed to remember his high calling. He turned round, drew himself up, projected his face, raised his arms, spread his hands in approved ghost fashion—came towards me. As he did so his little jaw dropped, and he emitted a faint, drawn-out 'Boo.' No, it wasn't—not a bit dreadful. I'd dined. I'd had a bottle of champagne, and being all alone, perhaps two or three—perhaps even four or five—whiskies, so I was as solid as rocks and no more frightened than if I'd been assailed by a frog. 'Boo!' I said. 'Nonsense. You don't belong to *this* place. What are you doing here?'

"I could see him wince. 'Boo—oo,' he said.

" 'Boo—be hanged! Are you a member?' I said; and just to show I didn't care a pin for him I stepped through a corner of him and made to light my candle. 'Are you a member?' I repeated, looking at him sideways.

"He moved a little so as to stand clear of me, and his bearing became crestfallen. 'No,' he said, in answer to the persistent interrogation of my eye; 'I'm not a member—I'm a ghost.'

" 'Well, that doesn't give you the run of the Mermaid Club. Is there anyone you want to see, or anything of that sort?' And doing it as steadily as possible for fear that he should mistake the careless-ness of whisky for the distraction of fear, I got my candle alight. I turned on him, holding it. 'What are you doing here?' I said.

"He had dropped his hands and stopped his booing, and there he stood, abashed and awkward, the ghost of a weak, silly, aimless young man. 'I'm haunting,' he said.

" 'You haven't any business to,' I said in a quiet voice.

" 'I'm a ghost,' he said, as if in defence.

" 'That may be, but you haven't any business to haunt here. This is a respectable private club; people often stop here with nursemaids and children, and, going about in the careless way you do, some poor little mite could easily come upon you and be scared out of her wits. I suppose you didn't think of that?'

" 'No, sir,' he said, 'I didn't.'

" 'You should have done. You haven't any claim on the place, have you? Weren't murdered here, or anything of that sort?'

" 'None, sir; but I thought as it was old and oak-panelled—'

" 'That's *no* excuse,' I regarded him firmly. 'Your coming here is a mistake,' I said, in a tone of friendly superiority. I feigned to see if I had my matches, and then looked up at him frankly. 'If I were you I wouldn't wait for cock-crow—I'd vanish right away.'

"He looked embarrassed. 'The fact *is*, sir—' he began.

" 'I'd vanish,' I said, driving it home.

" 'The fact is, sir, that—somehow—I can't.'

" 'You *can't?*'

" 'No, sir. There's something I've forgotten. I've been hanging about here since midnight last night, hiding in the cupboards of the empty bedrooms and things like that. I'm flurried. I've never come haunting before, and it seems to put me out.'

" 'Put you out?'

" 'Yes, sir. I've tried to do it several times, and it doesn't come off. There's some little thing has slipped me, and I can't get back.'

"That, you know, rather bowled me over. He looked at me in such an abject way that for the life of me I couldn't keep up quite the high hectoring vein I had adopted. 'That's queer,' I said, and as I spoke I fancied I heard someone moving about down below. 'Come into my room and tell me more about it,' I said. I didn't, of course, understand this, and I tried to take him by the arm. But, of course, you might as well have tried to take hold of a puff of smoke! I had forgotten my number, I think; anyhow, I remember going into several bedrooms—it was lucky I was the only soul in that wing—until I saw my traps. 'Here we are,' I said, and sat down in the armchair; 'sit down and tell me all about it. It seems to me you have got yourself into a jolly awkward position, old chap.'

"Well, he said he wouldn't sit down; he'd prefer to flit up and down the room if it was all the same to me. And so he did, and in a little while we were deep in a long and serious talk. And presently, you know, something of those whiskies and sodas evaporated out of me, and I began to realise just a little what a thundering rum and weird business it was that I was in. There he was, semi-transparent— the proper conventional phantom, and noiseless except for his ghost of a voice—flitting to and fro in that nice, clean, chintz-hung old bedroom. You could see the gleam of the copper candlesticks through him, and the lights on the brass fender, and the corners of the framed engravings on the wall, and there he was telling me all about this wretched little life of his that had recently ended on earth. He hadn't a particularly honest face, you know, but being transparent, of course, he couldn't avoid telling the truth."

"Eh?" said Wish, suddenly sitting up in his chair.

"What?" said Clayton.

"Being transparent—couldn't avoid telling the truth—I don't see it," said Wish.

"I don't see it," said Clayton, with inimitable assurance. "But it *is* so, I can assure you nevertheless. I don't believe he got once a nail's breadth off the Bible truth. He told me how he had been killed—he went down into a London basement with a candle to look for a leakage of gas—and described himself as a senior English master in a London private school when that release occurred."

"Poor wretch!" said I.

"That's what I thought, and the more he talked the more I thought it. There he was, purposeless in life and purposeless out of it. He talked of his father and mother and his schoolmaster, and all who had ever been anything to him in the world, meanly. He had been too sensitive, too nervous; none of them had ever valued him properly or understood him, he said. He had never had a real friend in the world, I think; he had never had a success. He had shirked games and failed examinations. 'It's like that with some people,' he said; 'whenever I got into the examination-room or anywhere everything seemed to go.' Engaged to be married of course to another over-sensitive person, I suppose—when the indiscretion with the gas escape ended his affairs. 'And where are you now?' I asked. 'Not in—?'

"He wasn't clear on that point at all. The impression he gave me was of a sort of vague, intermediate state, a special reserve for souls too non-existent for anything so positive as either sin or virtue. I don't know. He was much too egotistical and unobservant to give me any clear idea of the kind of place, kind of country, there is on the Other Side of Things. Wherever he was, he seems to have fallen in with a set of kindred spirits: ghosts of weak Cockney young men, who were on a footing of Christian names, and among these there was certainly a lot of talk about 'going haunting' and things like that. Yes—going haunting! They seemed to think 'haunting' a tremendous adventure, and most of them funked it all the time. And so primed, you know, he had come."

"But really!" said Wish to the fire.

"These are the impressions he gave me, anyhow," said Clayton, modestly. "I may, of course, have been in a rather uncritical state, but that was the sort of background he gave to himself. He kept flitting up and down, with his thin voice going—talking, talking about his wretched self, and never a word of clear, firm statement from first to last. He was thinner and sillier and more pointless than if he had been real and alive. Only then, you know, he would not have been in my bedroom here—if he *had* been alive. I should have kicked him out."

"Of course," said Evans, "there *are* poor mortals like that."

"And there's just as much chance of their having ghosts as the rest of us," I admitted.

"What gave a sort of point to him, you know, was the fact that he did seem within limits to have found himself out. The mess he had made of haunting had depressed him terribly. He had been told it would be a 'lark'; he had come expecting it to be a 'lark,' and here it was, nothing but another failure added to his record! He proclaimed himself an utter out-and-out failure. He said, and I can quite believe it, that he had never tried to do anything all his life that he hadn't made a perfect mess of—and through all the wastes of eternity he never would. If he had had sympathy, perhaps— He paused at that, and stood regarding me. He remarked that, strange as it might seem to me, nobody, not anyone, ever, had given him the amount of sympathy I was doing now. I could see what he wanted straight away, and I determined to head him off at once. I may be a brute, you know, but being the Only Real Friend, the recipient of the confidences of one of these egotistical weaklings, ghost or body, is beyond my physical endurance. I got up briskly. 'Don't you brood on these things too much,' I said. 'The thing you've got to do is to get out of this—get out of this sharp. You pull yourself together and *try*.' 'I can't,' he said. 'You try,' I said, and try he did."

"Try!" said Sanderson. "*How?*"

"Passes," said Clayton.

"Passes?"

"Complicated series of gestures and passes with the hands. That's how he had come in and that's how he had to get out again. Lord! what a business I had!"

"But how could *any* series of passes—" I began.

"My dear man," said Clayton, turning on me and putting a great emphasis on certain words, "you want *everything* clear. I don't know *how*. All I know is that you *do*—that *he* did, anyhow, at least. After a fearful time, you know, he got his passes right and suddenly disappeared."

"Did you," said Sanderson slowly, "observe the passes?"

"Yes," said Clayton, and seemed to think. "It was tremendously queer," he said. "There we were, I and this thin vague ghost, in that silent room, in this silent, empty inn, in this silent little Friday-night town. Not a sound except our voices and a faint panting he made when he swung. There was the bedroom candle, and one candle on the dressing-table alight, that was all—sometimes one or other would flare up into a tall, lean, astonished flame for a space. And queer things happened. 'I can't,' he said; 'I shall never—!' And suddenly he sat down on a little chair at the foot of the bed and began to sob and sob. Lord! what a harrowing, whimpering thing he seemed!

" 'You pull yourself together,' I said, and tried to pat him on the back, and . . . my confounded hand went through him! By that time, you know, I wasn't nearly so—massive as I had been on the landing. I got the queerness of it full. I remember snatching back my hand out of him, as it were, with a little thrill, and walking over to the dressing-table. 'You pull yourself together,' I said to him, 'and try.' And in order to encourage and help him I began to try as well."

"What!" said Sanderson, "the passes?"

"Yes, the passes."

"But—" I said, moved by an idea that eluded me for a space.

"This is interesting," said Sanderson, with his finger in his pipe-bowl. "You mean to say this ghost of yours gave way—"

"Did his level best to give away the whole confounded barrier? *Yes.*"

"He didn't," said Wish; "he couldn't. Or you'd have gone there too."

"That's precisely it," I said, finding my elusive idea put into words for me.

"That *is* precisely it," said Clayton, with thoughtful eyes upon the fire.

For just a little while there was silence.

"And at last he did it?" said Sanderson.

"At last he did it. I had to keep him up to it hard, but he did it at last—rather suddenly. He despaired, we had a scene, and then he got up abruptly and asked me to go through the whole performance, slowly, so that he might see. 'I believe,' he said, 'if I could *see* I should spot what was wrong at once.' And he did. '*I* know,' he said. 'What do you know?' said I. '*I* know,' he repeated. Then he said, peevishly, 'I *can't* do it, if you look at me—I really *can't*; it's been that, partly, all along. I'm such a nervous fellow that you put me out.' Well, we had a bit of an argument. Naturally I wanted to see; but he was as obstinate as a mule, and suddenly I had come over as tired as a dog —he tired me out. 'All right,' I said, '*I* won't look at you,' and turned towards the mirror, on the wardrobe, by the bed.

"He started off very fast. I tried to follow him by looking in the looking-glass, to see just what it was had hung. Round went his arms and his hands, so, and so, and so, and then with a rush came to the last gesture of all—you stand erect and open out your arms—and so, don't you know, he stood. And then he didn't! He didn't! He wasn't! I wheeled round from the looking-glass to him. There was nothing! I was alone, with the flaring candles and a staggering mind. What had happened? Had anything happened? Had I been dreaming? . . . And then, with an absurd note of finality about it, the clock upon the landing discovered the moment was ripe for striking *one*. So!— Ping! And I was as grave and sober as a judge, with all my champagne and whisky gone into the vast serene. Feeling queer, you know— confoundedly *queer!* Queer! Good Lord!"

He regarded his cigar-ash for a moment. "That's all that happened," he said.

"And then you went to bed?" asked Evans.

"What else was there to do?"

I looked Wish in the eye. We wanted to scoff, and there was some-thing, something perhaps in Clayton's voice and manner, that ham-pered our desire.

"And about these passes?" said Sanderson.

"I believe I could do them now."

"Oh!" said Sanderson, and produced a pen-knife and set himself to grub the dottel out of the bowl of his clay.

"Why don't you do them now?" said Sanderson, shutting his pen-knife with a click.

"That's what I'm going to do," said Clayton.

"They won't work," said Evans.

"If they do—" I suggested.

"You know, I'd rather you didn't," said Wish, stretching out his legs.

"Why?" asked Evans.

"I'd rather he didn't," said Wish.

"But he hasn't got 'em right," said Sanderson, plugging too much tobacco into his pipe.

"All the same, I'd rather he didn't," said Wish.

We argued with Wish. He said that for Clayton to go through those gestures was like mocking a serious matter. "But you don't believe—?" I said. Wish glanced at Clayton, who was staring into the fire, weighing something in his mind. "I do—more than half, anyhow, I do," said Wish.

"Clayton," said I, "you're too good a liar for us. Most of it was all right. But that disappearance ... happened to be convincing. Tell us, it's a tale of cock and bull."

He stood up without heeding me, took the middle of the hearth-rug, and faced me. For a moment he regarded his feet thoughtfully, and then for all the rest of the time his eyes were on the opposite wall, with an intent expression. He raised his two hands slowly to the level of his eyes and so began. . . .

Now, Sanderson is a Freemason, a member of the lodge of the Four Kings, which devotes itself so ably to the study and elucidation of all the mysteries of Masonry past and present, and among the students of this lodge Sanderson is by no means the least. He followed Clayton's motions with a singular interest in his reddish eye. "That's not bad," he said, when it was done. "You really do, you know, put things together, Clayton, in a most amazing fashion. But there's one little detail out."

"I know," said Clayton. "I believe I could tell you which."

"Well?"

"This," said Clayton, and did a queer little twist and writhing and thrust of the hands.

"Yes."

"That, you know, was what *he* couldn't get right," said Clayton. "But how do *you*—?"

"Most of this business, and particularly how you invented it, I don't understand at all," said Sanderson, "but just that phase—I do." He reflected. "These happen to be a series of gestures—connected with a certain branch of esoteric Masonry— Probably you know. Or else— *How?*" He reflected still further. "I do not see I can do any harm in telling you just the proper twist. After all, if you know, you know; if you don't, you don't."

"I know nothing," said Clayton, "except what the poor devil let out last night."

"Well, anyhow," said Sanderson, and placed his church-warden very carefully upon the shelf over the fireplace. Then very rapidly he gesticulated with his hands.

"So?" said Clayton, repeating.

"So," said Sanderson, and took his pipe in hand again.

"Ah, *now*," said Clayton, "I can do the whole thing—right."

He stood up before the waning fire and smiled at us all. But I think there was just a little hesitation in his smile. "If I begin—" he said.

"I wouldn't begin," said Wish.

"It's all right!" said Evans. "Matter is indestructible. You don't think any jiggery-pokery of this sort is going to snatch Clayton into the world of shades. Not it! You may try, Clayton, so far as I'm concerned, until your arms drop off at the wrists."

"I don't believe that," said Wish, and stood up and put his arm on Clayton's shoulder. "You've made me half believe in that story somehow, and I don't want to see the thing done."

"Goodness!" said I, "here's Wish frightened!"

"I am," said Wish, with real or admirably feigned intensity. "I believe that if he goes through these motions right he'll *go*."

"He'll not do anything of the sort," I cried. "There's only one way out of this world for men, and Clayton is thirty years from that. Besides . . . And such a ghost! Do you think—?"

Wish interrupted me by moving. He walked out from among our chairs and stopped beside the table and stood there. "Clayton," he said, "you're a fool."

Clayton, with a humorous light in his eyes, smiled back at him. "Wish," he said, "is right and all you others are wrong. I shall go. I shall get to the end of these passes, and as the last swish whistles through the air, Presto!—this hearthrug will be vacant, the room will be blank amazement, and a respectably dressed gentleman of fifteen stone will plump into the world of shades. I'm certain. So will you be. I decline to argue further. Let the thing be tried."

"No," said Wish, and made a step and ceased, and Clayton raised his hands once more to repeat the spirit's passing.

By that time, you know, we were all in a state of tension—largely because of the behavior of Wish. We sat all of us with our eyes on Clayton—I, at least, with a sort of tight, stiff feeling about me as though from the back of my skull to the middle of my thighs my body had been changed to steel. And there, with a gravity that was imperturbably serene, Clayton bowed and swayed and waved his hands and arms before us. As he drew towards the end one piled up, one tingled in one's teeth. The last gesture, I have said, was to swing the arms out wide open, with the face held up. And when at last he swung out to this closing gesture I ceased even to breathe. It was ridiculous, of course, but you know that ghost-story feeling. It was after dinner, in a queer, old shadowy house. Would he, after all—?

There he stood for one stupendous moment, with his arms open and his upturned face, assured and bright, in the glare of the hanging lamp. We hung through that moment as if it were an age, and then came from all of us something that was half a sigh of infinite relief and half a reassuring "No!" For visibly—he wasn't going. It was all nonsense. He had told an idle story, and carried it almost to conviction, that was all!...And then in that moment the face of Clayton changed.

It changed. It changed as a lit house changes when its lights are suddenly extinguished. His eyes were suddenly eyes that were fixed, his smile was frozen on his lips, and he stood there still. He stood there, very gently swaying.

That moment, too, was an age. And then, you know, chairs were scraping, things were falling, and we were all moving. His knees seemed to give, and he fell forward, and Evans rose and caught him in his arms....

It stunned us all. For a minute I suppose no one said a coherent thing. We believed it, yet could not believe it.... I came out of a muddled stupefaction to find myself kneeling beside him, and his vest and shirt were torn open, and Sanderson's hand lay on his heart....

Well—the simple fact before us could very well wait our convenience; there was no hurry for us to comprehend. It lay there for an hour; it lies athwart my memory, black and amazing still, to this day. Clayton had, indeed, passed into the world that lies so near to and so far from our own, and he had gone thither by the only road that mortal man may take. But whether he did indeed pass there by that poor ghost's incantation, or whether he was stricken suddenly by apoplexy in the midst of an idle tale—as the coroner's jury would have us believe—is no matter for my judging; it is just one of those inexplicable riddles that must remain unsolved until the final solution of all things shall come. All I certainly know is that, in the very moment, in the very instant, of concluding those passes, he changed, and staggered, and fell down before us—dead!

Mujina

LAFCADIO HEARN

*The Japanese are very given to stories and paintings and plays
and prints of ghosts.*
"Mujina" is a little jewel.

On the Akasaka road, in Tokyo, there is a slope called Kii-no-kuni-
zaka—which means the Slope of the Province of Kii. I do not know
why it is called the Slope of the Province of Kii. On one side of this
slope you see an ancient moat, deep and very wide, with high green
banks rising up to some place of gardens;—and on the other side
of the road extend the long and lofty walls of an imperial palace.
Before the era of street-lamps and jinrikishas, this neighborhood was
very lonesome after dark; and belated pedestrians would go miles
out of their way rather than mount the Kii-no-kuni-zaka, alone, after
sunset.

All because of a Mujina that used to walk there.

The last man who saw the Mujina was an old merchant of the
Kyobashi quarter, who died about thirty years ago. This is the story,
as he told it:

One night, at a late hour, he was hurrying up the Kii-no-kuni-zaka,
when he perceived a woman crouching by the moat, all alone, and
weeping bitterly. Fearing that she intended to drown herself, he
stopped to offer her any assistance or consolation in his power. She
appeared to be a slight and graceful person, handsomely dressed;
and her hair was arranged like that of a young girl of good family.
"O-jochu," [1] he exclaimed, approaching her—"O-jochu, do not cry
like that! . . . Tell me what the trouble is; and if there be any way
to help you, I shall be glad to help you." (He really meant what he
said; for he was a very kind man.) But she continued to weep—
hiding her face from him with one of her long sleeves. "O-jochu," he
said again, as gently as he could—"please, please listen to me! . . .
This is no place for a young lady at night! Do not cry, I implore
you!—only tell me how I may be of some help to you!" Slowly she

[1] O-jochu (honorable damsel)—a polite form of address used in speaking to a
young lady whom one does not know.

42

rose up, but turned her back to him, and continued to moan and sob behind her sleeve. He laid his hand lightly upon her shoulder, and pleaded: "O-jochu!—O-jochu!—O-jochu! ... Listen to me, just for one little moment! ... O-jochu!—O-jochu!" ... Then that O-jochu turned round, and dropped her sleeve, and stroked her face with her hand;—and the man saw that she had no eyes or nose or mouth— and he screamed and ran away.

Up Kii-no-kuni-zaka he ran and ran; and all was black and empty before him. On and on he ran, never daring to look back; and at last he saw a lantern, so far away that it looked like the gleam of a firefly; and he made for it. It proved to be only the lantern of an itinerant soba-seller,[2] who had set down his stand by the road-side; but any light and any human companionship was good after that experience; and he flung himself down at the feet of the soba-seller, crying out, "Aa!—aa!!—aa!!!" ...

"Kore! kore!" roughly exclaimed the soba-man. "Here! what is the matter with you? Anybody hurt you?"

"No—nobody hurt me," panted the other—"only ... Aa! aa!" ...

"—Only scared you?" queried the peddler, unsympathetically. "Robbers?"

"Not robbers—not robbers," gasped the terrified man. ... "I saw ... I saw a woman—by the moat;—and she showed me ... Aa! I cannot tell you what she showed me!" ...

"He! Was it anything like THIS that she showed you?" cried the soba-man, stroking his own face—which therewith became like unto an Egg. ... And, simultaneously, the light went out.

[2] Soba is a preparation of buckwheat, somewhat resembling vermicelli.

Story Paintings

For some time I did not know what to call this category. I tried "Picture-book Stories," "Pictures in the Fire," "Picture Stories"— and they sounded too much like Life magazine. These are stories that I always see when I read them, and I do not see them as photographs but as paintings or lithographs or colored prints, and I think "Story Paintings" is about as near as I can get.

Moonlight

GUY DE MAUPASSANT

*This beautiful and famous little story of de Maupassant is
here because of the breathless moment when the abbé opens
the door and sees the landscape painted with the moon. By
the way, it is said that Debussy wrote his famous piece
"Clair de Lune" after having read this story.*

The Abbé Marignan, as soldier of the Church, bore his fighting title
well. He was a tall, thin priest, very fanatical, with an ecstatic but
upright soul. All his beliefs were fixed, without ever wavering. He
thought that he understood God thoroughly, that he penetrated His
designs, His wishes, His intentions.

When he promenaded with great strides in the garden of his little
country parsonage, sometimes a question rose in his mind: "Why
did God make that?" And in fancy taking the place of God, he
searched obstinately, and nearly always found the reason. It is not
he who would have murmured in a transport of pious humility, "O
Lord, thy ways are past finding out!" He said to himself, "I am the
servant of God; I ought to know the reason of what He does, or to
divine it if I do not."

Everything in nature seemed to him created with an absolute and
admirable logic. The "Wherefore" and the "Because" were always
balanced. The dawns were made to render glad your waking, the
days to ripen the harvests, the rains to water them, the evenings to
prepare for sleeping, and the nights dark for sleep.

Only did he hate women; he hated them instinctively. He often
repeated the words of Christ, "Woman, what have I to do with
thee?" and he added, "One would almost say that God himself was
ill-pleased with this particular work of his hands." She was the
temptress who had ensnared the first man.

He had often felt women's tenderness attach itself to him, and
though he knew himself to be unassailable, he grew exasperated at
that need of loving which quivered always in their hearts.

God, to his mind, had only created woman to tempt man and to
test him. She should not be approached without the precautions you

would take near a trap. She was indeed, just like a trap, with her arms extended and her lips open towards a man.

He had some indulgence for nuns, rendered harmless by their vow; but he treated them harshly notwithstanding, because living at the bottom of their chained up hearts he sensed this eternal tenderness, which poured out to him, although he was a priest.

He was conscious of it, of that accursed tenderness, in their docility, in the softness of their voices when they spoke to him, in their lowered eyes, and in the meekness of their tears when he reproved them roughly.

And he shook his cassock on issuing from the doors of the convent, and he went off with long strides, as though he had fled some danger.

He had a niece who lived with her mother in a little house near by. He was bent on making her a sister of charity. She was pretty and hare-brained, and a great tease. When the abbé sermonized, she laughed; when he was angry at her, she kissed him vehemently, pressing him to her heart, while he would seek involuntarily to free himself from this embrace, which notwithstanding, made him taste a certain sweet joy, awaking deep within him that sensation of fatherhood which slumbers in every man.

Often he talked to her of God, of his God, walking beside her along the foot-paths through the fields. She hardly listened, and looked at the sky, the grass, the flowers with a joy of living which could be seen in her eyes. Sometimes she rushed forward to catch some flying creature, and bringing it back, would cry: "Look, my uncle, how pretty it is; I should like to kiss it." And this necessity to "kiss flies," or lilac berries, worried, irritated, and revolted the priest, who saw, even in that, the ineradicable tenderness which ever springs at the hearts of women.

And now one day the sacristan's wife, who kept house for the Abbé Marignan, told him, very cautiously, that his niece had a lover! He experienced a dreadful emotion, and he stood choked, with the soap all over his face, being in the act of shaving.

When he found himself able to think and speak once more, he cried: "It is not true; you are lying, Melanie!" But the peasant woman put her hand on her heart: "May our Lord judge me if I am lying, Monsieur le Curé. I tell you she goes to him every evening as soon as your sister is in bed. They meet each other beside the river. You have only to go there between ten o'clock and midnight, and see for yourself."

He ceased scratching his chin, and he paced the room violently. When he tried to begin his shaving again, he cut himself three times. All day long he remained silent, swollen with anger. To his priestly

zeal against the power of love was added the moral indignation of a
father, a teacher, of a keeper of souls, who has been deceived, robbed,
tricked by a child. He had the choking sensation which parents feel
when their daughter announces that she has chosen a husband without them and in spite of their advice.

After his dinner, he tried to read a little, but he could not settle;
he grew angrier and angrier. When it struck ten, he took his cane, a
formidable club which he always carried when he had to go out at
night to visit the sick. He clutched it in his solid, countryman's fist
and made threatening circles with it in the air. Then suddenly he
brought it down upon a chair and smashed its back.

He opened the door to go out but stopped upon the threshold,
surprised by the splendour of a wonderful moonlit night. Now since
he was a man of poetic spirit he felt himself suddenly distracted by
the serene beauty of the moonlit night.

In his garden, bathed with soft brilliance, his rows of slender fruit
trees threw their slender shadows across his path while the huge
honeysuckle on the wall exhaled such a powerful perfume it seemed
to be the living breath of this clear summer night.

He began to breathe deep, drinking the air as drunkards drink
their wine, and he walked slowly, ravished, astounded, and almost
forgetting his niece.

As soon as he came into the open country he stopped to take in
the whole plain, inundated by this caressing radiance, drowned in the
tender and languishing charm of the lovely night. Continually
the frogs repeated their short metallic notes, and the distant night-
ingales mingled with the seduction of the Moonlight that fitful music
which brings no thoughts but dreams, that light and vibrant melody
which is composed for kisses.

The abbé walked on, his courage failing, he knew not why. He
felt enfeebled, and suddenly exhausted; he had a desire to rest, to
pause, to praise God in all His works.

Down there, following the bank of the river, wound a line of
poplars. On and about the banks, wrapping all the watercourse with
a kind of light, transparent cotton was a fine mist, a white vapour,
which the moon-rays crossed, and silvered.

The priest paused again, his soul shaken by a strong and growing
emotion. And a doubt, a vague uneasiness, seized him; one of those
questions which he sometimes put to himself, occurred to him.

Why had God done this? If the night is made for sleep, for un-
consciousness, for forgetfulness of everything, why, then, make it
fairer than the day, sweeter than the dawns and the sunsets? And
this calm seductive star, more poetic than the sun, shedding its
quieter rays perhaps designed to reveal things too shy, too mysterious

for the light of common day. And, too, why was the most gifted of songsters not asleep like the rest? Why did he set himself to singing in the troubling dark?

Why this half-veil over the world? Why this heart ache, this stripping of the soul, this languor of the body? Why this parade of beauty when man never sees it for he is asleep? For whom was this sublime spectacle intended, this flood of poetry poured from heaven to earth?

And the abbé did not understand at all.

But now, along the edge of the field appeared two shadows walking side by side under the arched roof of the trees, in the glittering mist.

The man was the taller, and had his arm about the woman's, and from time to time he kissed her on the forehead. Suddenly they gave life to the landscape, which enveloped them like a divine frame made expressly for them. They seemed, these two, like one being, the being for whom this calm and silent night was made, and they came towards the priest, the answer, the living answer, vouchsafed by his Master, to his question.

He stood stock still, overwhelmed, with a beating heart and he thought he saw something biblical in the scene before him like the love of Ruth and Boaz, the fulfillment of the will of God in one of those noble stories in the Holy Book. Through his head began to run the canticles of the Song of Songs. The calls, the sighs, and the gusts of passion of that sublime poem which burns with love.

And he said to himself, "God has created such nights as this to transfigure the earthly loves of man."

He withdrew before this enlaced couple advancing arm in arm. It was his niece of course. He wondered if he had not been about to disobey God. For God must indeed permit love, since He provides for it a setting of such holy splendour.

And he fled from the scene in a maze, almost ashamed, as if he had trespassed in a temple where he had no right to be found.

The Standard of Living

DOROTHY PARKER

This delightful affair of Dorothy Parker's is always associated for me with the look on people's faces when they peer into the window of Van Cleef and Arpels, a very expensive jewelers on the woman's half-mile on Fifth Avenue, New York.

This elegant half-mile of women's shops between 50th and 59th Streets is a fine place to be on a crisp morning just before Christmas with the women in their fur coats, their eyes sparkling and their noses slightly reddened at the ends, and everybody in a high and holiday shopping mood.

Once when I was with J. B. Priestley on a hotel terrace overlooking this section, he said to me, "If the women of America were properly 'looked after,' this wouldn't exist."

I am forced to misquote Mr. Priestley. He did not say "looked after." The word he used was more direct.

At any rate, the story could make a beautiful cover for The New Yorker magazine.

Annabel and Midge came out of the tea room with the arrogant slow gait of the leisured, for their Saturday afternoon stretched ahead of them. They had lunched, as was their wont, on sugar, starches, oils, and butter-fats. Usually they ate sandwiches of spongy new white bread greased with butter and mayonnaise; they ate thick wedges of cake lying wet beneath ice cream and whipped cream and melted chocolate gritty with nuts. As alternates, they ate patties, sweating beads of inferior oil, containing bits of bland meat bogged in pale, stiffening sauce; they ate pastries, limber under rigid icing, filled with an indeterminate yellow sweet stuff, not still solid, not yet liquid, like salve that has been left in the sun. They chose no other sort of food, nor did they consider it. And their skin was like the petals of wood anemones, and their bellies were as flat and their flanks as lean as those of young Indian braves.

Annabel and Midge had been best friends almost from the day that Midge had found a job as stenographer with the firm that employed Annabel. By now, Annabel, two years longer in the stenographic department, had worked up to the wages of eighteen dollars and fifty cents a week; Midge was still at sixteen dollars. Each girl lived at home with her family and paid half her salary to its support.

The girls sat side by side at their desks, they lunched together every noon, together they set out for home at the end of the day's work. Many of their evenings and most of their Sundays were passed in each other's company. Often they were joined by two young men, but there was no steadiness to any such quartet; the two young men would give place, unlamented, to two other young men, and lament would have been inappropriate, really, since the newcomers were scarcely distinguishable from their predecessors. Invariably the girls spent the fine idle hours of their hot-weather Saturday afternoons together. Constant use had not worn ragged the fabric of their friendship.

They looked alike, though the resemblance did not lie in their features. It was in the shape of their bodies, their movements, their style, and their adornments. Annabel and Midge did, and completely, all that young office workers are besought not to do. They painted their lips and their nails, they darkened their lashes and lightened their hair, and scent seemed to shimmer from them. They wore thin, bright dresses, tight over their breasts and high on their legs, and tilted slippers, fancifully strapped. They looked conspicuous and cheap and charming.

Now, as they walked across to Fifth Avenue with their skirts swirled by the hot wind, they received audible admiration. Young men grouped lethargically about newsstands awarded them murmurs, exclamations, even—the ultimate tribute—whistles. Annabel and Midge passed without the condescension of hurrying their pace; they held their heads higher and set their feet with exquisite precision, as if they stepped over the necks of peasants.

Always the girls went to walk on Fifth Avenue on their free afternoons, for it was the ideal ground for their favorite game. The game could be played anywhere, and indeed, was, but the great shop windows stimulated the two players to their best form.

Annabel had invented the game; or rather she had evolved it from an old one. Basically, it was no more than the ancient sport of what-would-you-do-if-you-had-a-million-dollars? But Annabel had drawn a new set of rules for it, had narrowed it, pointed it, made it stricter. Like all games, it was the more absorbing for being more difficult.

Annabel's version went like this: You must suppose that somebody dies and leaves you a million dollars, cool. But there is a condition to the bequest. It is stated in the will that you must spend every nickel of the money on yourself.

There lay the hazard of the game. If, when playing it, you forgot and listed among your expenditures the rental of a new apartment for your family, for example, you lost your turn to the other player. It was astonishing how many—and some of them among the experts, too—would forfeit all their innings by such slips.

It was essential, of course, that it be played in passionate serious-ness. Each purchase must be carefully considered and, if necessary, supported by argument. There was no zest to playing it wildly. Once Annabel had introduced the game to Sylvia, another girl who worked in the office. She explained the rules to Sylvia and then offered her the gambit "What would be the first thing you'd do?" Sylvia had not shown the decency of even a second of hesitation. "Well," she said, "the first thing I'd do, I'd go out and hire somebody to shoot Mrs. Gary Cooper, and then . . ." So it is to be seen that she was no fun.

But Annabel and Midge were surely born to be comrades, for Midge played the game like a master from the moment she learned it. It was she who added the touches that made the whole thing cozier. According to Midge's innovations, the eccentric who died and left you the money was not anybody you loved, or, for the matter of that, anybody you even knew. It was somebody who had seen you somewhere and had thought, "That girl ought to have lots of nice things. I'm going to leave her a million dollars when I die." And the death was to be neither untimely nor painful. Your benefactor, full of years and comfortably ready to depart, was to slip softly away during sleep and go right to heaven. These embroideries permitted Annabel and Midge to play their game in the luxury of peaceful consciences.

Midge played with a seriousness that was not only proper but ex-treme. The single strain on the girls' friendship had followed an an-nouncement once made by Annabel that the first thing she would buy with her million dollars would be a silver-fox coat. It was as if she had struck Midge across the mouth. When Midge recovered her breath, she cried that she couldn't imagine how Annabel could do such a thing—silver-fox coats were so common! Annabel defended her taste with the retort that they were not common, either. Midge then said that they were so. She added that everybody had a silver-fox coat. She went on, with perhaps a slight loss of head, to declare that she herself wouldn't be caught dead in silver fox.

For the next few days, though the girls saw each other as con-stantly, their conversation was careful and infrequent, and they did not once play their game. Then one morning, as soon as Annabel entered the office, she came to Midge and said she had changed her mind. She would not buy a silver-fox coat with any part of her million dollars. Immediately on receiving the legacy, she would select a coat of mink.

Midge smiled and her eyes shone. "I think," she said, "you're doing absolutely the right thing."

Now, as they walked along Fifth Avenue, they played the game anew. It was one of those days with which September is repeatedly cursed; hot and glaring, with slivers of dust in the wind. People drooped and shambled, but the girls carried themselves tall and walked a straight line, as befitted young heiresses on their afternoon promenade. There was no longer need for them to start the game at its formal opening. Annabel went direct to the heart of it.

"All right," she said. "So you've got this million dollars. So what would be the first thing you'd do?"

"Well, the first thing I'd do," Midge said, "I'd get a mink coat." But she said it mechanically, as if she were giving the memorized answer to an expected question.

"Yes," Annabel said. "I think you ought to. The terribly dark kind of mink." But she, too, spoke as if by rote. It was too hot; fur, no matter how dark and sleek and supple, was horrid to the thoughts.

They stepped along in silence for a while. Then Midge's eye was caught by a shop window. Cool, lovely gleamings were there set off by chaste and elegant darkness.

"No," Midge said, "I take it back. I wouldn't get a mink coat the first thing. Know what I'd do? I'd get a string of pearls. Real pearls."

Annabel's eyes turned to follow Midge's.

"Yes," she said, slowly. "I think that's a kind of a good idea. And it would make sense, too. Because you can wear pearls with anything."

Together they went over to the shop window and stood pressed against it. It contained but one object—a double row of great, even pearls clasped by a deep emerald around a little pink velvet throat.

"What do you suppose they cost?" Annabel said.

"Gee, I don't know," Midge said. "Plenty, I guess."

"Like a thousand dollars?" Annabel said.

"Oh, I guess like more," Midge said. "On account of the emerald."

"Well, like ten thousand dollars?" Annabel said.

"Gee, I wouldn't even know," Midge said.

The devil nudged Annabel in the ribs. "Dare you to go in and price them," she said.

"Like fun!" Midge said.

"Dare you," Annabel said.

"Why, a store like this wouldn't even be open this afternoon," Midge said.

"Yes, it is so, too," Annabel said. "People just came out. And there's a doorman on. Dare you."

"Well," Midge said. "But you've got to come too."

They tendered thanks, icily, to the doorman for ushering them into the shop. It was cool and quiet, a broad, gracious room with paneled walls and soft carpet. But the girls wore expressions of bitter disdain, as if they stood in a sty.

A slim, immaculate clerk came to them and bowed. His neat face showed no astonishment at their appearance.

"Good afternoon," he said. He implied that he would never forget it if they would grant him the favor of accepting his soft-spoken greeting.

"Good afternoon," Annabel and Midge said together, and in like freezing accents.

"Is there something—?" the clerk said.

"Oh, we're just looking," Annabel said. It was as if she flung the words down from a dais.

The clerk bowed.

"My friend and myself merely happened to be passing," Midge said, and stopped, seeming to listen to the phrase. "My friend here and myself," she went on, "merely happened to be wondering how much are those pearls you've got in your window."

"Ah, yes," the clerk said. "The double rope. That is two hundred and fifty thousand dollars, Madam."

"I see," Midge said.

The clerk bowed. "An exceptionally beautiful necklace," he said. "Would you care to look at it?"

"No, thank you," Annabel said.

"My friend and myself merely happened to be passing," Midge said.

They turned to go; to go, from their manner, where the tumbrel awaited them. The clerk sprang ahead and opened the door. He bowed as they swept by him.

The girls went on along the Avenue and disdain was still on their faces.

"Honestly!" Annabel said. "Can you imagine a thing like that?"

"Two hundred and fifty thousand dollars!" Midge said. "That's a quarter of a million dollars right there!"

"He's got his nerve!" Annabel said.

They walked on. Slowly the disdain went, slowly and completely as if drained from them, and with it went the regal carriage and tread. Their shoulders dropped and they dragged their feet; they bumped against each other, without notice or apology, and caromed away again. They were silent and their eyes were cloudy.

Suddenly Midge straightened her back, flung her head high, and spoke, clear and strong.

"Listen, Annabel," she said. "Look. Suppose there was this terribly rich person, see? You don't know this person, but this person has seen you somewhere and wants to do something for you. Well, it's a terribly old person, see? And so this person dies, just like going to sleep, and leaves you ten million dollars. Now, what would be the first thing you'd do?"

The Coming of Pan

JAMES STEPHENS

*It would be inaccurate to say that this next passage from a
great book reminds me of a picture, for actually it reminds
me of a statue of the god Pan I have seen somewhere. It is
a little bronze either in the British Museum, the Naples
Museum, the Vatican in Rome, or the Louvre. I can only
see the statue; I cannot remember where I have seen it.*

*This is a passage from The Crock of Gold, a book by an
Irishman about leprechauns and pots of gold and the god
Pan and Irish country people. I believe I'm correct in saying
that the musical Finian's Rainbow came from a theme in
The Crock of Gold.*

*I put the story here as it has a startling and beautiful idea
in it which you will recognize as a truth and feel better. For
another thing, it is written in lovely Irish English.*

*I met James Stephens once at a party in London many
years ago. He was a little man, but he wanted to meet me
and I wanted to meet him, and we sat on the same sofa
together and had nothing whatever to say to each other.
I was shy because I had read his books, and he was shy
because he had seen me on the stage.*

*I have some vague memory of his face; I associate the spirit
I saw in his eyes with the spirit of the god Pan in this extract
from his book. Anyway, that is how I remember it.*

...One morning she lay among the long, warm grasses. She watched
a bird who soared and sang for a little time, and then it sped swiftly
away down the steep air and out of sight in the blue distance. After
a few moments she knew it was not a bird. No bird's song had that
consecutive melody, for their themes are as careless as their wings.
She sat up and looked about her, but there was nothing in sight.

She could not find her goats anywhere although for a long time
she searched. They came to her at last of their own accord, and they
were more wildly excited than she had ever seen them before. Even
the cows forsook their solemnity and broke into awkward gambols

56

around her. As she walked home that evening a strange elation taught her feet to dance.

The following day she heard the music again, faint and thin, wonderfully sweet and as wild as the song of a bird, but it was a melody which no bird would adhere to. A theme was repeated again and again. There was something in it that set her heart beating. It was personal to her.

On that day she did not see anybody either. She drove her charges home in the evening listlessly and the beasts also were very quiet.

When the music came again and when the tune was ended she saw a figure rise from the fold of a little hill. The sunlight was gleaming from his arms and shoulders but the rest of his body was hidden by the bracken and he did not look at her as he went away playing softly on a double pipe.

The next day he did look at her. He stood waist-deep in greenery fronting her squarely. She had never seen so strange a face before. His hair was a cluster of brown curls, his nose was little and straight, and his wide mouth drooped sadly at the corners. His sad eyes and mouth almost made her weep.

Then he went mincingly away. As he went he lifted the slender double reed to his lips and blew a few careless notes.

The next day he fronted her as before, looking down to her eyes from a short distance. He played for only a few moments, and then he came to her. When he left the bracken the girl suddenly clapped her hands against her eyes affrighted. There was something different, terrible about him. The upper part of his body was beautiful, but the lower part. . . . She dared not look at him again. She would have risen and fled away but she feared he might pursue her, and the thought of such a chase and the inevitable capture froze her blood. The thought of anything behind us is always terrible. The sound of pursuing feet is worse than the murder from which we fly—So she sat still and waited but nothing happened. At last, desperately, she dropped her hands. He was sitting on the ground a few paces from her. His legs were crossed; they were shaggy and hoofed like the legs of a goat; but she would not look at these because of his wonderful, sad, grotesque face. Gaiety is good to look upon and an innocent face is delightful to our souls, but no woman can resist sadness or weakness and ugliness she dare not resist. Her nature leaps to be the comforter. It is her reason. It exalts her to an ecstasy wherein nothing but the sacrifice of herself has any proportion. Men are not fathers by instinct but by chance, but women are mothers beyond thought, beyond instinct, which is the father of thought. Motherliness, pity, self-sacrifice—these are the charges of her primal cell, and not even the discovery that men are comedians, liars, and egotists will wean her from this. As she looked at the pathos of his face she repudiated the hideousness of his body. The beast which is in men is glossed by women; it is his childishness, the destructive energy inseparable from youth and high spirits, and it is always forgiven by women, often forgotten, sometimes, and not rarely, cherished and fostered.

After a few moments of this silence he placed the reed to his lips and played a plaintive little air, and then he spoke to her in a strange voice, coming like a wind from distant places.

"What is your name, Shepherd Girl?" said he.

"Caitilin, Ingin Ni Murrachu," she whispered.

"Daughter of Murrachu," said he, "I have come from a far place where there are high hills. The men and maidens who follow their flocks in that place know me and love me for I am the Master of the Shepherds. They sing and dance and are glad when I come to them in the sunlight; but in this country no people have done any reverence to me. The shepherds fly away when they hear my pipes in the pastures; the maidens scream in fear when I dance to them in the meadows. I am very lonely in this strange country. You also, though you danced to the music of my pipes, have covered your face against me and made no reverence."

"I will do whatever you say if it is right," said she.

"You must not do anything because it is right, but because it is your wish. Right is a word, and wrong is a word, but the bee flies to the flower and the seed goes abroad and is happy. Is that right, Shepherd Girl? It is wrong also. I come to you because the bee goes to the flower—it is wrong! If I did not come to you to whom would I go? There is no right and no wrong but only the will of the gods."

"I am afraid of you," said the girl.

"You fear me because my legs are shaggy like the legs of a goat. Look at them well, O Maiden, and know that they are indeed the legs of a beast and then you will not be afraid any more. Do you not love beasts? Surely you should love them for they yearn to you humbly or fiercely, craving your hand upon their heads as I do. If I were not fashioned thus I would not come to you because I would not need you. Man is a god and a brute, and when he forsakes the brute upon which he stands then there will be no more men and no more women and the immortal gods will blow this world away like smoke."

"I don't know what you want me to do," said the girl.

"I want you to want me. I want you to forget right and wrong; to be as happy as the beasts, to live to the depths of your nature as well as to the heights. Wondrous deep are the depths, very fertile in the lowest deep. There are stars there, also, brighter than the stars on high. The name of the heights is Wisdom and the name of the depths is Love. Wisdom is the spirit and the wings of the spirit. Love is the shaggy beast that goes down. Wisdom is righteous and clean, but Love is unclean and holy. I sing of the beast and the descent: the great unclean purging itself in fire: the thought that is not born in the measure or the ice or the head, but in the feet and the hot blood and the pulse of fury. The Crown of Life is not lodged in the sun: the wise gods have buried it deeply where the thoughtful will not find it, nor the good: but the Gay Ones, the Adventurous Ones, the Careless Plungers, they will bring it to the wise and astonish them. They will be noble because of our desire for them. Come away with me, Shepherd Girl, through the fields, and we will be careless and happy, and we will leave thought to find us when it can, for that is the duty of thought, and it is more anxious to discover us than we are to be found."

So Caitilin Ni Murrachu arose and went with him through the fields, and she did not go with him because of love, nor because his words had been understood by her, but only because he was naked and unashamed.

Fairy Gifts

COMTE DE CAYLUS

The Comte de Caylus, who was born at the end of the seventeenth century, was an honored and scholarly archaeologist and collector of antiquities. He wrote volumes about the ancient and great civilizations of Europe and the Mediterranean, but he also set down this lovely fairy tale. It makes me think of the picture of any father who, loving his daughter, takes her on his knee and tells her this story, with its gentle warning about beauty and wit, because he wanted her to grow up to be nicer than anybody else's daughter.

I'm sure that is why the Comte de Caylus wrote it.

People's surroundings often reflect their minds and dispositions. Perhaps that is why the Flower Fairy lived in a lovely palace, with the most delightful garden, full of flowers and trees and fountains and fishponds and everything nice. The fairy herself was so kind and charming everybody loved her. All the young princes and princesses who formed her court were as happy as the day was long, simply because they were near her. They came to her when they were quite tiny and never left until they were grown up and had to go away into the great world. When that time came she gave to each whatever gift was asked of her.

The fairy loved the Princess Sylvia with all her heart. She had nearly reached the age when the gifts were bestowed. However, the fairy had a great wish to know how the other princesses, who had left her, were prospering. Before the time came for Sylvia to go away, she resolved to send her to some of them. So one day her chariot drawn by butterflies was made ready, and the fairy said:

"Sylvia, I am going to send you to the court of Iris. She will receive you with pleasure for my sake as well as for your own. In two months you may come back to me and tell me what you think of her."

Sylvia was very unwilling to go away but, as the fairy wished it, she said nothing. When the two months were over she stepped joyfully into the butterfly chariot and could not get back quickly enough to the Flower Fairy, who for her part was equally delighted to see her again.

60

"Now, child," said she, "tell me what you found."

"You sent me, madam," answered Sylvia, "to the court of Iris, on whom you had bestowed the gift of beauty. She never tells anyone that it was your gift, though she often speaks of your kindness in general. It seemed her loveliness, which fairly dazzled me at first, had caused her to forget her other gifts or graces. In allowing herself to be seen, she appeared to think she was doing all that could be required. Unfortunately, she became seriously ill and though she presently recovered, her beauty is entirely gone. She hates the very sight of herself and is in despair. She entreated me to tell you what had happened and to beg you, in pity, to restore her beauty. Indeed, she does need it terribly, for all the things in her that were tolerable and even agreeable, when she was so pretty, seem quite different now she is ugly. It is so long since she thought of using her mind or her natural cleverness, I really do not think she has any left now. She is quite aware of all this herself, so you may imagine how unhappy she is and how earnestly she begs for your aid."

"You have told me what I wanted to know," cried the fairy, "but alas! I cannot help her. My gifts can be given but once."

Some time passed in all the usual delights of the Flower Fairy's palace. She sent for Sylvia again and told her she was to stay for a while with the Princess Daphne. Accordingly the butterflies whisked her off and set her down in a strange kingdom. But she had only been there a very little time before a wandering butterfly brought a message from her to the fairy, begging that she might be sent for as soon as possible, and before very long she was allowed to return to the Flower Fairy's palace.

"Ah, madam," cried she, "what a place you sent me to that time!"

"Why, what was the matter?" asked the fairy. "Daphne was one of the princesses who asked for the gift of eloquence, if I remember rightly."

"And very ill the gift of eloquence becomes a woman," replied Sylvia, with an air of conviction. "It is true she speaks well and her expressions are well chosen, but she never leaves off talking. And, though at first one may be amused, one ends by being wearied to death. Above all things she loves any assembly for settling the affairs of her kingdom, for on those occasions she can talk and talk without fear of interruption. But the moment it is over she is ready to begin again about anything or nothing, as the case may be. Oh, I cannot tell you how glad I was to come away."

The fairy smiled at Sylvia. After allowing her a little time to recover she sent her to the court of the Princess Cynthia, where she left her for three months. At the end of that time Sylvia came back to her with all the joy and contentment one feels at being once more beside a dear friend. The fairy, as usual, was anxious to hear what she thought of Cynthia, who had always been amiable, and to whom she had given the gift of pleasing.

"I thought at first," said Sylvia, "that she must be the happiest princess in the world. She had a thousand suitors who vied with one another in their efforts to please and gratify her. Indeed, I had nearly decided I would ask for a similar gift."

"Have you changed your mind, then?" interrupted the fairy.

"Yes, indeed, madam," replied Sylvia, "and I will tell you why. The longer I stayed the more I saw Cynthia was not really happy. In her desire to please everyone she ceased to be sincere and degenerated into a mere coquette, and the charms and fascinations exercised upon all who approached her were valueless. So in the end her suitors ceased to care for them, and went away disdainfully."

"I am pleased with you, child," said the fairy. "Enjoy yourself here for a while and presently you shall go to Phyllida."

Sylvia could not make up her mind at all what she should ask for herself, and the time was drawing very near. Before very long the fairy sent her to Phyllida and waited for her report.

"I reached her court safely," said Sylvia. "She received me with much kindness and immediately began to exercise that brilliant wit you had bestowed upon her. I confess I was fascinated by it and for a week thought nothing could be more desirable. The time passed like magic, so great was the charm of her society. But like the gift of pleasing, it cannot really give satisfaction. I wearied of what had so delighted me at first, and perceived more and more plainly it is impossible to be constantly smart and amusing without being frequently ill-natured and too apt to turn all things, even the most serious, into mere occasions for a brilliant jest."

The fairy in her heart agreed with Sylvia, and felt pleased with herself for having brought her up so well. But now the time came for Sylvia to receive her gift and all her companions were assembled. The fairy stood in their midst and in the usual manner asked what she would take with her into the great world.

Sylvia paused for a moment, and then answered, "A quiet spirit." And the fairy granted her request.

This lovely gift makes life a constant happiness to its possessor and to all who are brought in contact with her. She has all the beauty of gentleness and contentment in her sweet face. If at times it seems less lovely through some chance grief or disquietude, the hardest thing one ever hears said is:

"Sylvia's dear face is pale today. It grieves one to see her so."

When, on the contrary, she is gay and joyful the sunshine of her presence rejoices all who have the happiness of being near her.

The Shepherd's Daughter

WILLIAM SAROYAN

This is a story about an old lady who brought a story with
her from Armenia to teach a lesson in California. I have
never known the people of the vineyards around Fresno,
about whom William Saroyan has written this and many
other stories, although I have often driven through this
California countryside. But I do know the people of the
vineyards in the Napa Valley, for I made a movie called
They Knew What They Wanted in the Napa Valley and
I got to know them and their stories and their dances.

The people in William Saroyan's stories are generally of
Armenian extraction, but in the Napa Valley the people are
mostly Italian. I have often been moved to see a people
bringing their old traditions to the new country. You can
often tell the different nationalities by the way they trim their
vines and by the kinds of shrubs and flowers they plant about
their doors.

It is the opinion of my grandmother, God bless her, that all men
should labor, and at the table, a moment ago, she said to me: You
must learn to do some good work, the making of some item useful
to man, something out of clay, or out of wood, or metal, or cloth.
It is not proper for a young man to be ignorant of an honorable
craft. Is there anything you can make? Can you make a simple
table, a chair, a plain dish, a rug, a coffee pot? Is there anything
you can do?

And my grandmother looked at me with anger.

I know, she said, you are supposed to be a writer, and I suppose
you are. You certainly smoke enough cigarettes to be anything, and
the whole house is full of smoke, but you must learn to make solid
things, things that can be used, that can be seen and touched.

There was a king of the Persians, said my grandmother, and he
had a son, and this boy fell in love with a shepherd's daughter. He
went to his father and he said, My lord, I love a shepherd's daughter,
and I would have her for my wife. And the king said, I am king

and you are my son and when I die you shall be king, how can it be that you would marry the daughter of a shepherd? And the son said, My Lord, I do not know but I know that I love this girl and would have her for my queen.

The king saw that his son's love for the girl was from God, and he said, I will send a message to her. And he called a messenger to him and he said, Go to the shepherd's daughter and say that my son loves her and would have her for his wife. And the messenger went to the girl and he said, The king's son loves you and would have you for his wife. And the girl said, What labor does he do? And the messenger said, Why, he is the son of the king; he does no labor. And the girl said, He must learn to do some labor. And the messenger returned to the king and spoke the words of the shepherd's daughter.

The king said to his son, The shepherd's daughter wishes you to learn some craft. Would you still have her for your wife? And the son said, Yes, I will learn to weave straw rugs. And the boy was taught to weave rugs of straw, in patterns and in colors and with ornamental designs, and at the end of three days he was making very fine straw rugs, and the messenger returned to the shepherd's daughter, and he said, These rugs of straw are the work of the king's son.

And the girl went with the messenger to the king's palace, and she became the wife of the king's son.

One day, said my grandmother, the king's son was walking through the streets of Bagdad, and he came upon an eating place which was so clean and cool that he entered it and sat at a table.

This place, said my grandmother, was a place of thieves and murderers, and they took the king's son and placed him in a large dungeon where many great men of the city were being held, and the thieves and murderers were killing the fattest of the men and feeding them to the leanest of them, and making sport of it. The king's son was of the leanest of the men, and it was not known that he was the son of the king of the Persians, so his life was spared, and he said to the thieves and murderers, I am a weaver of straw rugs and these rugs have great value. And they brought him straw and asked him to weave and in three days he weaved three rugs, and he said, Carry these rugs to the palace of the king of the Persians, and for each rug he will give you a hundred gold pieces of money. And the rugs were carried to the palace of the king, and when the king saw the rugs he saw that they were the work of his son and he took the rugs to the shepherd's daughter and he said, These rugs were brought to the palace and they are the work of my son who is lost. And the shepherd's daughter took each rug and looked at it closely and in the design of each rug she saw in the written language of the Persians a message from her husband, and she related this message to the king.

And the king, said my grandmother, sent many soldiers to the place of the thieves and murderers, and the soldiers rescued all the captives and killed all the thieves and murderers, and the king's son was returned safely to the palace of his father, and to the company of his wife, the little shepherd's daughter. And when the boy went into the palace and saw again his wife, he humbled himself before her and he embraced her feet, and he said, My love, it is because of you that I am alive, and the king was greatly pleased with the shepherd's daughter.

Now, said my grandmother, do you see why every man should learn an honorable craft?

I see very clearly, I said, and as soon as I earn enough money to buy a saw and a hammer and a piece of lumber I shall do my best to make a simple chair or a shelf for books.

Noah

THE BOOK OF GENESIS
Chapters 6–9, extracts

I think this is the best picture story ever written. Noah talking to God, the dove in the window in the Ark, the rainbow, and the immense long shots of God talking to Noah toward the end of the story are pictures which were impressed upon us in childhood and will stay with us forever.

And it came to pass when men began to multiply on the face of the
      earth,
That God saw
That the wickedness of man was great in the earth and that every
      imagination of the thoughts of his heart was only evil
Continually.
And it repented the Lord that he had made man on the earth and
      it grieved him
At his heart.

But
Noah
Found grace in the eyes of the Lord. Noah was a just man.
And God said unto Noah,
"The end of all flesh is come before me;
For the earth is filled with violence through them.
Make thee an ark
Of gopher wood;
Rooms shalt thou make in the ark,
And shalt pitch it within and without with pitch.
And this is the fashion which thou shalt make it of;
The length of the ark shall be three hundred cubits,
The breadth of it fifty cubits
And the height of it thirty cubits.
A window shalt thou make in the ark
And the door of the ark shalt thou make in the side thereof;

66

With lower and second and third stories
Shalt thou make it.
"And behold, I,
Even I,
Do bring a flood of waters upon the earth.
But thou
Shalt come into the ark,
Thou
And thy sons
And thy wife
And thy sons' wives with thee.
And of every living thing of all flesh,
Two of every sort,
Shalt thou bring into the ark,
To keep them alive;
They shall be male and female.
And take thou unto thee of all food that is eaten,
And it shall be for food for thee and for them."

Thus did Noah,
According to all that God commanded him,
So did he.

And the Lord said unto Noah;
"Come thou and all thy house
Into the ark.
And I will cause it to rain upon the earth forty days and forty nights."

In the selfsame day
Entered
Noah
And Shem and Ham and Japeth, the sons of Noah,
And Noah's wife and the three wives of his sons with them
Into the ark,
They,
And every beast
After his kind,
And all the cattle
After their kind,
And every creeping thing that creepeth upon the earth
After his kind,
And every fowl
After his kind,
Every bird of every sort.
And they went in unto Noah,

Two and two,
Into the ark.
And the Lord
Shut him in.

The same day,
Were all the fountains of the great deep broken up
And the windows of heaven were opened.
And the waters increased and bare up the ark, and it was lifted up
      above the earth.
And the waters prevailed exceedingly upon the earth;
And all the high hills that were under the whole heaven were
      covered.
Fifteen cubits upward did the waters prevail;
And the mountains were covered.
And all in whose nostrils was the breath of life, of all that was on
      the dry land,
Died.
And Noah only remained alive.
And they that were with him in the ark.
And God remembered Noah,
And every living thing and all the cattle that was with him in the
      ark;
And God made a wind to pass over the earth
And the waters assuaged
The fountains also of the deep
And the windows of heaven were stopped,
And the rain from heaven was restrained,
And the waters returned from off the earth continually;
And the ark rested
Upon the mountains of Ararat.

And it came to pass that Noah
Opened
The window of the ark, which he had made;
And he sent forth a dove from him to see if the waters were abated
      from off the face of the ground,
But the dove found no rest for the sole of her foot,
And she returned unto the ark;
Then he put forth his hand
And took her and pulled her in unto him into the ark.
And he stayed yet another seven days;
And again he sent forth the dove out of the ark;
And the dove came in to him in the evening,

And, lo,
In her mouth was an olive leaf pluckt off;
So Noah knew that the waters were abated from off the earth.
And he stayed yet other seven days;
And sent forth the dove;
Which returned not again unto him any more.

And Noah removed the covering of the ark
And looked
And behold the face of the ground was dry.
And God spoke unto Noah, saying,
"Go forth of the ark, thou and thy wife, and thy sons and thy sons'
    wives with thee. Bring forth with thee every living thing that
    is with thee, of all flesh, that they may breed abundantly in
    the earth."
And Noah went forth,
And his sons
And his wife
And his sons' wives with him,
Every beast,
And every fowl,
And whatsoever creepeth upon the earth,
After their kinds,
Went forth out of the ark.

And Noah builded an altar unto the Lord; and offered burnt offerings
    on the altar.
And the Lord smelled a sweet savour;
And the Lord said in his heart
I will not again curse the ground any more for man's sake;
For the imagination of man's heart is evil from his youth.
While the earth remaineth,
Seed-time
And harvest,
And cold
And heat,
And summer
And winter,
And day
And night,
Shall not cease.

And God spoke unto Noah and to his sons with him, saying,
"And I,

Behold,
I establish my covenant with you
And with your seed after you;
And with every living creature that is with you.
Neither shall all flesh be cut off any more by the waters of a flood;
Neither shall there be any more flood to destroy the earth."
And God said;
"This is the token
Of the covenant which I make between me and you.
I do set my bow in the cloud,
And it shall be for a token
Of a covenant between me and the earth.
And it shall come to pass,
When I bring a cloud over the earth,
That the bow shall be seen in the cloud.
And I will look upon it,
That I may remember
The everlasting covenant between God and every living creature of
    all flesh that is upon the earth."

A Worn Path

EUDORA WELTY

This story reminds me of the paintings of a Negro called Horace Pippin, who painted highly colored pictures of his people which are of a simplicity that moves me almost to tears. I have one of Horace Pippin's paintings at home and I got it in the following way.

I knew a man who has since died called Dr. Albert Barnes, who lived near Philadelphia. Dr. Barnes made what is undoubtedly one of the greatest collections of paintings in existence—Renoirs and Cezannes and Rousseaus and Matisses and that whole school. I do not think anybody can truly say that he has seen and understood the great Impressionist school of painting until he has seen the Barnes collection.

One day, sometime in the thirties, I had just arrived in New York and I was being given a welcoming party, and somebody said, "Old Barnes wants to see you."

I said, "Let's go and see old Barnes."

I had no idea who I was about to meet. We went to his apartment in the old Ritz Tower, and he got me in a corner away from the rest of the people and was complimentary about my acting. I am, in fact, rather shy about that sort of thing and fished around to change the subject. There was a painting by Raoul Dufy on the wall, and I said, "That's a beautiful Dufy."

His tone immediately changed and he said, "What do you know about paintings?"

I said that paintings meant more to me than music. He said, "What paintings have you looked at?"

I told him that in London, when things were rough, I would go to the National Gallery for consolation.

"What paintings did you look at?" said he.

I described three or four that I went back to time and again.

"You must see my paintings," he said.

"I can't," I said. "I have to leave for Hollywood in the morning."

"Who are you working for?"

"For Irving Thalberg."

"Get Irving Thalberg on the phone," he said to his secretary. I was about to make Mutiny on the Bounty, and Irving Thalberg told me he didn't want me for a few days. At this time I did not know who Dr. Barnes was and that it was difficult to get to see his paintings.

An automobile came for me in the morning and drove me down to Merion, Pennsylvania.

The Barnes gallery stands in a fine garden run by Mrs. Barnes, who is no mean horticulturist, and there it was, for all the world, like some kind of church, with a house to one side like the bishop's residence.

The great doors of the gallery opened wide. I went in. In the middle of the gallery stood Dr. Barnes, and behind him there was a series of large windows looking out into the garden, with no paintings on that wall. "Look at these," he said, "and tell me which of them you like."

I turned around. On the opposite wall hung a large percentage of the great paintings of the Impressionist school, paintings that I had never hoped to see. I stayed there that night. I got to know him well and I have been there many times since.

One day in Hollywood I got a telegram from him saying, IF YOU READ YOU HAVE BOUGHT A PAINTING, KEEP YOUR FOOL MOUTH SHUT. What he meant was he had wandered into a little gallery in Philadelphia and seen the paintings of Horace Pippin, so he had bought one for himself and one for me and got hold of a publicity man to publicize the fact that Dr. Barnes and Charles Laughton had bought Horace Pippin. That week there was a photograph of my painting in Time magazine with Horace Pippin standing beside it and a story about Dr. Barnes. Horace Pippin sold out his entire exhibition.

Dr. Barnes, I think anybody who knows about Impressionist paintings will admit, had the most sensitive eye of any man then living. He was tagged "the terrible-tempered Dr. Barnes" because he did not tolerate people whom he did not like looking at his paintings. But, as you will gather from this anecdote, he was by no means an unkind or unthoughtful man.

Anyway, "A Worn Path" by Eudora Welty makes me think of the paintings of Horace Pippin.

It was December—a bright frozen day in the early morning. Far out in the country there was an old Negro woman with her head tied in a red rag, coming along a path through the pinewoods. Her name was Phoenix Jackson. She was very old and small and she walked slowly in the dark pine shadows, moving a little from side to side in her steps, with the balanced heaviness and lightness of a pendulum in a grandfather clock. She carried a thin, small cane made from an umbrella, and with this she kept tapping the frozen earth in front of her. This made a grave and persistent noise in the still air, that seemed meditative like the chirping of a solitary little bird.

She wore a dark striped dress reaching down to her shoe tops, and an equally long apron of bleached sugar sacks, with a full pocket: all neat and tidy, but every time she took a step she might have fallen over her shoelaces, which dragged from her unlaced shoes. She looked straight ahead. Her eyes were blue with age. Her skin had a pattern all its own of numberless branching wrinkles and as though a whole little tree stood in the middle of her forehead, but a golden color ran underneath, and the two knobs of her cheeks were illumined by a yellow burning under the dark. Under the red rag her hair came down on her neck in the frailest of ringlets, still black, and with an odor like copper.

Now and then there was a quivering in the thicket. Old Phoenix said, "Out of my way, all you foxes, owls, beetles, jack rabbits, coons and wild animals! . . . Keep out from under these feet, little bob-whites . . . Keep the big wild hogs out of my path. Don't let none of those come running my direction. I got a long way." Under her small black-freckled hand her cane, limber as a buggy whip, would switch at the brush as if to rouse up any hiding things.

On she went. The woods were deep and still. The sun made the pine needles almost too bright to look at, up where the wind rocked. The cones dropped as light as feathers. Down in the hollow was the mourning dove—it was not too late for him.

The path ran up a hill. "Seem like there is chains about my feet, time I get this far," she said, in the voice of argument old people keep to use with themselves. "Something always take a hold of me on this hill—pleads I should stay."

After she got to the top she turned and gave a full, severe look behind her where she had come. "Up through pines," she said at length. "Now down through oaks."

Her eyes opened their widest, and she started down gently. But before she got to the bottom of the hill a bush caught her dress.

Her fingers were busy and intent, but her skirts were full and long, so that before she could pull them free in one place they were caught in another. It was not possible to allow the dress to tear. "I in the thorny bush," she said. "Thorns, you doing your appointed work. Never want to let folks pass, no sir. Old eyes thought you was a pretty little *green* bush."

Finally, trembling all over, she stood free, and after a moment dared to stoop for her cane.

"Sun so high!" she cried, leaning back and looking, while the thick tears went over her eyes. "The time getting all gone here."

At the foot of this hill was a place where a log was laid across the creek.

"Now comes the trial," said Phoenix.

Putting her right foot out, she mounted the log and shut her eyes. Lifting her skirt, leveling her cane fiercely before her, like a festival figure in some parade, she began to march across. Then she opened her eyes and she was safe on the other side.

"I wasn't as old as I thought," she said.

But she sat down to rest. She spread her skirts on the bank around her and folded her hands over her knees. Up above her was a tree in a pearly cloud of mistletoe. She did not dare to close her eyes, and when a little boy brought her a plate with a slice of marble-cake on it she spoke to him. "That would be acceptable," she said. But when she went to take it there was just her own hand in the air.

So she left that tree, and had to go through a barbed-wire fence. There she had to creep and crawl, spreading her knees and stretching her fingers like a baby trying to climb the steps. But she talked loudly to herself: she could not let her dress be torn now, so late in the day, and she could not pay for having her arm or her leg sawed off if she got caught fast where she was.

At last she was safe through the fence and risen up out in the clearing. Big dead trees, like black men with one arm, were standing in the purple stalks of the withered cotton field. There sat a buzzard.

"Who you watching?"

In the furrow she made her way along.

"Glad this not the season for bulls," she said, looking sideways, "and the good Lord made his snakes to curl up and sleep in the winter. A pleasure I don't see no two-headed snake coming around that tree, where it come once. It took a while to get by him, back in the summer."

She passed through the old cotton and went into a field of dead corn. It whispered and shook and was taller than her head. "Through the maze now," she said, for there was no path.

Then there was something tall, black, and skinny there, moving before her.

At first she took it for a man. It could have been a man dancing in the field. But she stood still and listened, and it did not make a sound. It was as silent as a ghost.

"Ghost," she said sharply, "who be you the ghost of? For I have heard of nary death close by."

But there was no answer—only the ragged dancing in the wind.

She shut her eyes, reached out her hand, and touched a sleeve. She found a coat and inside that an emptiness, cold as ice.

"You scarecrow," she said. Her face lighted. "I ought to be shut up for good," she said with laughter. "My senses is gone. I too old. I the oldest people I ever know. Dance, old scarecrow," she said, "while I dancing with you."

She kicked her foot over the furrow, and with mouth drawn down, shook her head once or twice in a little strutting way. Some husks blew down and whirled in streamers about her skirts.

Then she went on, parting her way from side to side with the cane, through the whispering field. At last she came to the end, to a wagon track where the silver grass blew between the red ruts. The quail were walking round like pullets, seeming all dainty and unseen.

"Walk pretty," she said. "This the easy place. This the easy going."

She followed the track, swaying through the quiet bare fields, through the little strings of trees silver in their dead leaves, past cabins silver from weather, with the doors and windows boarded shut, all like old women under a spell sitting there. "I walking in their sleep," she said, nodding her head vigorously.

In a ravine she went where a spring was silently flowing through a hollow log. Old Phoenix bent and drank. "Sweet-gum makes the water sweet," she said, and drank more. "Nobody know who made this well, for it was here when I was born."

The track crossed a swampy part where the moss hung as white as lace from every limb. "Sleep on, alligators, and blow your bubbles." Then the track went into the road.

Deep, deep the road went down between the high green-colored banks. Overhead the live-oaks met, and it was as dark as a cave.

A black dog with a lolling tongue came up out of the weeds by the ditch. She was meditating, and not ready, and when he came at her she only hit him a little with her cane. Over she went in the ditch, like a little puff of milkweed.

Down there, her senses drifted away. A dream visited her, and she reached her hand up, but nothing reached down and gave her a pull. So she lay there and presently went to talking. "Old woman," she said to herself, "that black dog come up out of the weeds to stall you off, and now there he sitting on his fine tail, smiling at you."

A white man finally came along and found her—a hunter, a young man, with his dog on a chain.

"Well, Granny!" he laughed. "What are you doing there?"

"Lying on my back like a June-bug waiting to be turned over, mister," she said, reaching up her hand.

He lifted her up, gave her a swing in the air, and set her down. "Anything broken, Granny?"

"No sir, them old dead weeds is springy enough," said Phoenix, when she had got her breath. "I thank you for your trouble."

"Where do you live, Granny?" he asked, while the two dogs were growling at each other.

"Away back yonder, sir, behind the ridge. You can't even see it from here."

"On your way home?"

"No sir, I going to town."

"Why, that's too far! That's as far as I walk when I come out myself, and I get something for my trouble." He patted the stuffed bag he carried, and there hung down a little closed claw. It was one of the bob-whites, with its beak hooked bitterly to show it was dead. "Now you go on home, Granny!"

"I bound to go to town, mister," said Phoenix. "The time come around."

He gave another laugh, filling the whole landscape. "I know you old colored people! Wouldn't miss going to town to see Santa Claus!"

But something held old Phoenix very still. The deep lines in her face went into a fierce and different radiation. Without warning, she had seen with her own eyes a flashing nickel fall out of the man's pocket onto the ground.

"How old are you, Granny?" he was saying.

"There is no telling, mister," she said, "no telling."

Then she gave a little cry and clapped her hands and said, "Git on away from here, dog! Look! Look at that dog!" She laughed as if in admiration. "He ain't scared of nobody. He a big black dog." She whispered, "Sic him!"

"Watch me get rid of that cur," said the man. "Sic him, Pete! Sic him!"

Phoenix heard the dogs fighting, and heard the man running and throwing sticks. She even heard a gunshot. But she was slowly bending forward by that time, further and further forward, the lids stretched down over her eyes, as if she were doing this in her sleep. Her chin was lowered almost to her knees. The yellow palm of her hand came out from the fold of her apron. Her fingers slid down and along the ground under the piece of money with the grace and care they would have in lifting an egg from under a setting hen. Then she slowly straightened up, she stood erect, and the nickel was in her apron pocket. A bird flew by. Her lips moved. "God watching me the whole time. I come to stealing."

The man came back, and his own dog panted about them. "Well, I scared him off that time," he said, and then he laughed and lifted his gun and pointed it at Phoenix.

She stood straight and faced him.

"Doesn't the gun scare you?" he said, still pointing it.

"No, sir, I seen plenty go off closer by, in my day, and for less than what I done," she said, holding utterly still.

He smiled, and shouldered the gun. "Well, Granny," he said, "you must be a hundred years old, and scared of nothing. I'd give you a dime if I had any money with me. But you take my advice and stay home, and nothing will happen to you."

"I bound to go on my way, mister," said Phoenix. She inclined her head in the red rag. Then they went in different directions, but she could hear the gun shooting again and again over the hill.

She walked on. The shadows hung from the oak trees to the road like curtains. Then she smelled wood-smoke, and smelled the river, and she saw a steeple and the cabins on their steep steps. Dozens of little black children whirled around her. There ahead was Natchez shining. Bells were ringing. She walked on.

In the paved city it was Christmas time. There were red and green electric lights strung and crisscrossed everywhere, and all turned on in the daytime. Old Phoenix would have been lost if she had not distrusted her eyesight and depended on her feet to know where to take her.

She paused quietly on the sidewalk where people were passing by. A lady came along in the crowd, carrying an armful of red-, green-, and silver-wrapped presents; she gave off perfume like the red roses in hot summer, and Phoenix stopped her.

"Please, missy, will you lace up my shoe?" She held up her foot.

"What do you want, Grandma?"

"See my shoe," said Phoenix. "Do all right for out in the country, but wouldn't look right to go in a big building."

"Stand still then, Grandma," said the lady. She put her packages down on the sidewalk beside her and laced and tied both shoes tightly.

"Can't lace 'em with a cane," said Phoenix. "Thank you, missy. I doesn't mind asking a nice lady to tie my shoe, when I gets out on the street."

Moving slowly and from side to side, she went into the big building, and into a tower of steps, where she walked up and around and around until her feet knew to stop.

She entered a door, and there she saw nailed up on the wall the document that had been stamped with the gold seal and framed in the gold frame, which matched the dream that was hung up in her head.

"Here I be," she said. There was a fixed and ceremonial stiffness over her body.

"A charity case, I suppose," said the attendant who sat at the desk before her.

But Phoenix only looked above her head. There was sweat on her face, the wrinkles in her skin shone like a bright net.

"Speak up, Grandma," the woman said. "What's your name? We must have your history, you know. Have you been here before? What seems to be the trouble with you?"

Old Phoenix only gave a twitch to her face as if a fly were bothering her.

"Are you deaf?" cried the attendant.

But then the nurse came in.

"Oh, that's just old Aunt Phoenix," she said. "She doesn't come for herself—she has a little grandson. She makes these trips just as regular as clockwork. She lives away back off the Old Natchez Trace." She bent down. "Well, Aunt Phoenix, why don't you just take a seat? We won't keep you standing after your long trip." She pointed.

The old woman sat down, bolt upright in the chair.

"Now, how is the boy?" asked the nurse.

Old Phoenix did not speak.

"I said, how is the boy?"

But Phoenix only waited and stared straight ahead, her face very solemn and withdrawn into rigidity.

"Is his throat any better?" asked the nurse. "Aunt Phoenix, don't you hear me? Is your grandson's throat any better since the last time you came for the medicine?"

With her hands on her knees, the old woman waited, silent, erect and motionless, just as if she were in armor.

"You mustn't take up our time this way, Aunt Phoenix," the nurse said. "Tell us quickly about your grandson, and get it over. He isn't dead, is he?"

At last there came a flicker and then a flame of comprehension across her face, and she spoke.

"My grandson. It was my memory had left me. There I sat and forgot why I made my long trip."

"Forgot?" The nurse frowned. "After you came so far?"

Then Phoenix was like an old woman begging a dignified forgiveness for waking up frightened in the night. "I never did go to school, I was too old at the Surrender," she said in a soft voice. "I'm an old woman without an education. It was my memory fail me. My little grandson, he is just the same, and I forgot it in the coming."

"Throat never heals, does it?" said the nurse, speaking in a loud, sure voice to old Phoenix. By now she had a card with something written on it, a little list. "Yes. Swallowed lye. When was it?—January—two-three years ago—"

Phoenix spoke unasked now. "No, missy, he not dead, he just the same. Every little while his throat begin to close up again, and he not able to swallow. He not get his breath. He not able to help himself. So the time come around, and I go on another trip for the soothing medicine."

"All right. The doctor said as long as you came to get it, you could have it," said the nurse. "But it's an obstinate case."

"My little grandson, he sit up there in the house all wrapped up, waiting by himself," Phoenix went on. "We is the only two left in the world. He suffer and it don't seem to put him back at all. He got a sweet look. He going to last. He wear a little patch quilt and peep out holding his mouth open like a little bird. I remembers so plain now. I not going to forget him again, no, the whole enduring time. I could tell him from all the others in creation."

"All right." The nurse was trying to hush her now. She brought her a bottle of medicine. "Charity," she said, making a check mark in a book.

Old Phoenix held the bottle close to her eyes, and then carefully put it into her pocket.

"I thank you," she said.

"It's Christmas time, Grandma," said the attendant. "Could I give you a few pennies out of my purse?"

"Five pennies is a nickel," said Phoenix stiffly.

"Here's a nickel," said the attendant.

Phoenix rose carefully and held out her hand. She received the nickel and then fished the other nickel out of her pocket and laid it beside the new one. She stared at her palm closely, with her head on one side.

Then she gave a tap with her cane on the floor.

"This is what come to me to do," she said. "I going to the store and buy my child a little windmill they sells, made out of paper. He going to find it hard to believe there such a thing in the world. I'll march myself back where he waiting, holding it straight up in this hand."

She lifted her free hand, gave a little nod, turned around, and walked out of the doctor's office. Then her slow step began on the stairs, going down.

Daydreams

I think you will find that if you describe one of your daydreams it will sound funny. Daydreams are usually about what you want to be and are not, something you desire and do not have.

Elsa dragged me into a store once. She wanted to buy a hat. There were a bunch of women pulling faces in mirrors as they were trying on hats and, of course, when they turned away from the mirrors, they stopped pulling faces and they didn't look the same at all. They looked much nicer and the hats looked worse. And I suddenly knew what had often puzzled me about women's hats in restaurants, and I started to laugh and I had to leave.

We don't have many men's mustaches these days, but men always shape their mustaches as they want to present themselves to the world. I'm sure they pull faces in the mirror, too, and when they relax and forget the mustache is there, it doesn't fit any more, like the women's hats. There is the matter of Hitler's historic mustache. I never could understand why the German people trusted a man with a mustache like that. However, I kept on saying that it could not last.

The Secret Life of Walter Mitty

JAMES THURBER

I put this famous and perhaps overprinted story of James Thurber's first to lead you to the others.

"We're going through!" The Commander's voice was like thin ice breaking. He wore his full-dress uniform, with the heavily braided white cap pulled down rakishly over one cold gray eye. "We can't make it, sir. It's spoiling for a hurricane, if you ask me." "I'm not asking you, Lieutenant Berg," said the Commander. "Throw on the power light! Rev her up to 8,500! We're going through!" The pounding of the cylinders increased; ta-pocketa-pocketa-pocketa-*pocketa-pocketa*. The Commander stared at the ice forming on the pilot window. He walked over and twisted a row of complicated dials. "Switch on No. 8 auxiliary!" he shouted. "Switch on No. 8 auxiliary!" repeated Lieutenant Berg. "Full strength in No. 3 turret!" shouted the Commander. "Full strength in No. 3 turret!" The crew, bending to their various tasks in the huge, hurtling eight-engined Navy hydroplane, looked at each other and grinned. "The Old Man'll get us through," they said to one another. "The Old Man ain't afraid of hell!" . . .

"Not so fast! You're driving too fast!" said Mrs. Mitty. "What are you driving so fast for?"

"Hmm?" said Walter Mitty. He looked at his wife, in the seat beside him, with shocked astonishment. She seemed grossly unfamiliar, like a strange woman who had yelled at him in a crowd. "You were up to fifty-five," she said. "You know I don't like to go more than forty. You were up to fifty-five." Walter Mitty drove on toward Waterbury in silence, the roaring of the SN202 through the worst storm in twenty years of Navy flying fading in the remote, intimate airways of his mind. "You're tensed up again," said Mrs. Mitty. "It's one of your days. I wish you'd let Dr. Renshaw look you over."

Walter Mitty stopped the car in front of the building where his wife went to have her hair done. "Remember to get those overshoes while I'm having my hair done," she said. "I don't need overshoes," said Mitty. She put her mirror back into her bag. "We've been through all that," she said, getting out of the car. "You're not a young man any longer." He raced the engine a little. "Why don't you wear your gloves? Have you lost your gloves?" Walter Mitty reached in a pocket and brought out the gloves. He put them on, but after she had turned and gone into the building and he had driven on to a red light, he took them off again. "Pick it up, brother!" snapped a cop as the light changed, and Mitty hastily pulled on his gloves and lurched ahead. He drove around the streets aimlessly for a time, and then he drove past the hospital on his way to the parking lot.

...."It's the millionaire banker, Wellington McMillan," said the pretty nurse. "Yes?" said Walter Mitty, removing his gloves slowly. "Who has the case?" "Dr. Renshaw and Dr. Benbow, but there are two specialists here, Dr. Remington from New York and Dr. Pritchard-Mitford from London. He flew over." A door opened down a long, cool corridor and Dr. Renshaw came out. He looked distraught and haggard. "Hello, Mitty," he said. "We're having the devil's own time with McMillan, the millionaire banker and close personal friend of Roosevelt. Obstreosis of the ductal tract. Tertiary. Wish you'd take a look at him." "Glad to," said Mitty.

In the operating room there were whispered introductions: "Dr. Remington, Dr. Mitty. Dr. Pritchard-Mitford, Dr. Mitty." "I've read your book on streptothricosis," said Pritchard-Mitford, shaking hands. "A brilliant performance, sir." "Thank you," said Walter Mitty. "Didn't know you were in the States, Mitty," grumbled Remington. "Coals to Newcastle, bringing Mitford and me up here for a tertiary." "You are very kind," said Mitty. A huge, complicated machine, connected to the operating table, with many tubes and wires, began at this moment to go pocketa-pocketa-pocketa. "The new anesthetizer is giving way!" shouted an interne. "There is no one in the East who knows how to fix it!" "Quiet, man!" said Mitty, in a low, cool voice. He sprang to the machine, which was now going pocketa-pocketa-queep-pocketa-queep. He began fingering delicately a row of glistening dials. "Give me a fountain pen!" he snapped. Someone handed him a fountain pen. He pulled a faulty piston out of the machine and inserted the pen in its place. "That will hold for ten minutes," he said. "Get on with the operation." A nurse hurried over and whispered to Renshaw, and Mitty saw the man turn pale. "Coreopsis has set in," said Renshaw nervously. "If you would take over, Mitty?" Mitty looked at him and at the craven figure of Benbow, who drank, and at the grave, uncertain faces of the two great specialists. "If you wish," he said. They slipped a white gown on him; he adjusted a mask and drew on thin gloves; nurses handed him shining ...

"Back it up, Mac! Look out for that Buick!" Walter Mitty jammed on the brakes. "Wrong lane, Mac," said the parking-lot attendant, looking at Mitty closely. "Gee. Yeh," muttered Mitty. He began cautiously to back out of the lane marked "Exit Only." "Leave her sit there," said the attendant. "I'll put her away." Mitty got out of the car. "Hey, better leave the key." "Oh," said Mitty, handing the man the ignition key. The attendant vaulted into the car, backed it up with insolent skill, and put it where it belonged.

They're so damn cocky, thought Walter Mitty, walking along Main Street; they think they know everything. Once he had tried to take his chains off, outside New Milford, and he had got them wound around the axles. A man had had to come out in a wrecking car and unwind them, a young, grinning garage-man. Since then Mrs. Mitty always made him drive to a garage to have the chains taken off. The next time, he thought, I'll wear my right arm in a sling; they won't grin at me then. I'll have my right arm in a sling and they'll see I couldn't possibly take the chains off myself. He kicked at the slush on the sidewalk. "Overshoes," he said to himself, and he began looking for a shoe store.

When he came out into the street again, with the overshoes in a box under his arm, Walter Mitty began to wonder what the other thing was his wife had told him to get. She had told him twice, before they set out from their house for Waterbury. In a way he hated these weekly trips to town—he was always getting something wrong. Kleenex, he thought, Squibb's, razor blades? No. Toothpaste, toothbrush, bicarbonate, carborundum, initiative and referendum? He gave it up. But she would remember it. "Where's the what's-its-name?" she would ask. "Don't tell me you forgot the what's-its-name." A newsboy went by shouting something about the Waterbury trial.

. . . "Perhaps this will refresh your memory." The District Attorney suddenly thrust a heavy automatic at the quiet figure on the witness stand. "Have you ever seen this before?" Walter Mitty took the gun and examined it expertly. "This is my Webley-Vickers 50.80," he said calmly. An excited buzz ran around the courtroom. The judge rapped for order. "You are a crack shot with any sort of firearms, I believe?" said the District Attorney, insinuatingly. "Objection!" shouted Mitty's attorney. "We have shown that the defendant could not have fired the shot. We have shown that he wore his right arm in a sling on the night of the fourteenth of July." Walter Mitty raised his hand briefly and the bickering attorneys were stilled. "With any known make of gun," he said evenly, "I could have killed Gregory Fitzhurst at three hundred feet *with my left hand*." Pandemonium broke loose in the courtroom. A woman's scream rose above the bedlam and suddenly a lovely, dark-haired girl was in Walter Mitty's arms. The District Attorney struck at her savagely. Without rising from his chair, Mitty let the man have it on the point of the chin. "You miserable cur!". . .

"Puppy biscuit," said Walter Mitty. He stopped walking and the buildings of Waterbury rose up out of the misty courtroom and surrounded him again. A woman who was passing laughed. "He said 'Puppy biscuit,' " she said to her companion. "That man said 'Puppy biscuit' to himself." Walter Mitty hurried on. He went into an A. & P., not the first one he came to but a smaller one farther up the street. "I want some biscuit for small, young dogs," he said to the clerk. "Any special brand, sir?" The greatest pistol shot in the world thought a moment. "It says 'Puppies Bark for It' on the box," said Walter Mitty.

His wife would be through at the hairdresser's in fifteen minutes, Mitty saw in looking at his watch, unless they had trouble drying it; sometimes they had trouble drying it. She didn't like to get to the hotel first; she would want him to be there waiting for her as usual. He found a big leather chair in the lobby, facing a window, and he put the overshoes and the puppy biscuit on the floor beside it. He picked up an old copy of *Liberty* and sank down into the chair. "Can Germany Conquer the World Through the Air?" Walter Mitty looked at the pictures of bombing planes and of ruined streets.

. . ."The cannonading has got the wind up in young Raleigh, sir," said the Sergeant. Captain Mitty looked up at him through tousled hair. "Get him to bed," he said wearily. "With the others. I'll fly alone." "But you can't, sir," said the sergeant anxiously. "It takes two men to handle that bomber and the Archies are pounding hell out of the air. Von Richtman's circus is between here and Saulier." "Somebody's got to get that ammunition dump," said Mitty. "I'm going over. Spot of brandy?" He poured a drink for the sergeant and one for himself. War thundered and whined around the dugout and battered at the door. There was a rending of wood and splinters flew through the room. "A bit of a near thing," said Captain Mitty carelessly. "The box barrage is closing in," said the sergeant. "We only live once, Sergeant," said Mitty, with his faint, fleeting smile. "Or do we?" He poured another brandy and tossed it off. "I never see a man could hold his brandy like you, sir," said the sergeant. "Begging your pardon, sir." Captain Mitty stood up and strapped on his huge Webley-Vickers automatic. "It's forty kilometers through hell, sir," said the sergeant. Mitty finished one last brandy. "After all," he said softly, "what isn't?" The pounding of the cannon increased; there was the rat-tat-tatting of machine guns, and from somewhere came the menacing pocketa-pocketa-pocketa of the new flame-throwers.

Walter Mitty walked to the door of the dugout humming "Auprès de Ma Blonde." He turned and waved to the sergeant. "Cheerio!" he said. . . .

Something struck his shoulder. "I've been looking all over this hotel for you," said Mrs. Mitty. "Why do you have to hide in this old chair? How did you expect me to find you?" "Things close in," said Walter Mitty vaguely. "What?" Mrs. Mitty said. "Did you get the what's-its-name? The puppy biscuit? What's in that box?" "Overshoes," said Mitty. "Couldn't you have put them on in the store?" "I was thinking," said Walter Mitty. "Does it ever occur to you that I am sometimes thinking?" She looked at him. "I'm going to take your temperature when I get you home," she said.

They went out through the revolving doors that made a faintly derisive whistling sound when you pushed them. It was two blocks to the parking lot. At the drugstore on the corner she said, "Wait here for me. I forgot something. I won't be a minute." She was more than a minute. Walter Mitty lighted a cigarette. It began to rain, rain with sleet in it. He stood up against the wall of the drugstore, smoking. . . . He put his shoulders back and his heels together. "To hell with the handkerchief," said Walter Mitty scornfully. He took one last drag on his cigarette and snapped it away. Then, with that faint, fleeting smile playing about his lips, he faced the firing squad; erect and motionless, proud and disdainful, Walter Mitty the Undefeated, inscrutable to the last.

The Barber's Tale
of His Fifth Brother

THE ARABIAN NIGHTS

This dream of grandeur comes from The Arabian Nights. Like most daydreams it is sexual. I had a plan once of doing it as part of a reading program—wandering away from the center of the stage, a spotlight following me, and sitting with my back against the proscenium arch.

This is also a form of the story I once did in a film called If I Had a Million, where I was a poor clerk and blew a raspberry at the boss after I had inherited a million dollars.

There is a story attached to that: the English censor would not pass the raspberry, so we had to put the set up again and try substitutes for the raspberry, like "Phooey!" and "Yaaah!" and "Nerrrts!" All of them seemed very unfunny; there is no substitute for a lusty raspberry. Lubitsch was in despair, so I said to him, "I've got an idea. I'd like to try something."

Lubitsch said, "Roll 'em!"

And so I raised two fingers with an upward motion and whistled through my teeth like an errand boy. We all laughed and thought it was a waste of film because no board of censorship would pass that particular gesture. However, the English censor, who was Lord Somebody at that time, was uneducated in the meaning of such matters and he did pass it. I knew the audience would understand, so I concealed myself in the back of the Empire Theatre in London where the film was running for the first time. I think I am correct in saying that the audience did not stop laughing for ten minutes.

My fifth brother Al-Nashshar, O Commander of the Faithful, was a beggar. Now when our father, who was an old man sickened and died, he left us seven hundred coppers whereof each son took his hundred; and my fifth brother bethought him to lay his hundred

88

out on glassware of all sorts and turn an honest penny on its price. So he bought a hundred coppers worth of glassware and, putting it into a big tray, sat down to sell it on a bench at the foot of a wall against which he leant back. As he sat with the tray before him he fell to musing and said to himself, "Know, O my good self, that my principal invested in this glassware, is a hundred coppers. I will assuredly sell it for two hundred, with which I will forthright buy other glass and make by it four hundred; nor will I cease to sell and buy on this wise, till I have gotten four thousand and soon find myself the master of much money. With these coins I will buy merchandise and jewels and perfumes and gain great profit on them; till, Allah willing, I will make my capital into an hundred thousand. Then I will purchase a fine house with white slaves and eunuchs and horses; and I will eat and drink and disport myself; nor will I leave a singing man or a singing woman in the city, but I will summon them to my palace and make them perform before me. And when, Inshallah! my capital shall have become one hundred thousand pieces of silver, I will send out marriage-brokeresses to require for me in wedlock the daughters of Kings and Ministers of State; and I will demand to wife the eldest daughter of the Prime Minister; for it hath reached me that she is perfect in beauty and prime in loveliness and rare in accomplishments. I will give a marriage settlement of one thousand pieces of silver; and, if her father consent, well: but if not I will take her by force from under his very nose. When she is safely home in my house, I will buy ten little eunuchs and for myself a robe of the robes of Kings and Sultans; and get me a saddle of gold and a bridle set thick with gems of price. Then I will mount with the slaves preceding me and surrounding me, and I will make the round of the city whilst the folk salute me and bless me; after which I will repair to the Minister (he that is father of the girl), with armed white slaves before and behind me and on my right and on my left. When he sees me, the Minister stands up, and seating me in his own place sits down much below me. Now I have with me two eunuchs carrying purses, each containing a thousand pieces of silver; and of these I deliver to him the thousand, his daughter's marriage-settlement, and make him a free gift of the other thousand, that he may have reason to know my generosity and liberality and my greatness of spirit and the littleness of the world in my eyes. And for ten words he addresses to me I answer him two. Then back I go to my house, and if one come to me on the bride's part, if he bring me a gift, I give it back to him and refuse to accept it, that they may learn what a proud spirit is mine. Thus I establish my rank and status. When this is done I appoint her wedding night and adorn my house showily! gloriously! And as the time for parading the bride is come,

I don my finest attire and sit down on a mattress of gold brocade, propping up my elbow with a pillow, and turning neither to the right nor to the left; but looking only straight in front for the haughtiness of my mind and the gravity of my understanding. And there before me stands my wife in her raiment and ornaments, lovely as the full moon; and I, in my loftiness and dread lordliness, will not glance at her till those present say to me, "O our lord and our master, thy wife, thy handmaid, standeth before thee; vouch-safe her one look for standing wearieth her." Then they kiss the ground before me many times; whereupon I raise my eyes and cast at her one single glance and turn my face earthwards again. Then they bear her off to the bride-chamber, and I arise and change my clothes for a far finer suit; and, when they bring in the bride the second time, I deign not to throw her a look till they have begged me many times; after which I glance at her out of the corner of one eye, and then bend down my head. Thereupon I order one of my eunuchs to bring me a bag of five hundred pieces of silver which I give as largesse to the tirewomen present and bid them one and all to lead me to the bride-chamber. When they leave me alone with her I neither look at her nor speak to her, but lie by her side with my face to the wall showing my contempt, that each and every man may again remark how high and haughty I am. Presently her mother comes in to me; and kissing my head and hand, says to me, "Oh my lord, look upon thine hand-maiden who longs for thy favour; so heal her broken spirit!" I give her no answer; and when she sees this she rises and busses my feet many times and says, "O my lord, in very sooth my daughter is a beautiful maid, who hath never known man; and if thou show her this backwardness and aversion, her heart will break; so do thou incline to her and speak to her and soothe her mind and spirit." Then she rises and fetches a cup of wine; says to her daughter, "Take it and hand it to thy lord." But as she approaches me I leave her standing between my hands and sit, propping my elbow on a round cushion with gold thread, leaning lazily back, and without looking at her in the majesty of my spirit, so that she may deem me indeed a Sultan and a mighty man. Then she says to me, "O my lord, do not refuse to take the cup from the hand of thine handmaid, for verily I am thy bondswoman." But I do not speak to her and she presses me, saying, "There is no help but that thou drink it"; and she puts it to my lips. Then I shake my fist in her face and kick her with my foot thus. So he let out with his toe and knocked over the tray of glass-ware which fell to the ground and, falling from the bench, all that was on it was broken to bits.

Rendezvous with M____ M____

CASANOVA

I think Casanova must have dreamed up all his adventures.
He wrote his memoirs when he was an old man, and I'm
sure he was dreaming about his life as he would have liked
it to have been. No man could be that potent!

This was pointed out to me by Elsa, who read the whole
twelve volumes and was moved to hysteria. She said that I
wasn't to worry, that any woman would know that he was
boasting.

If you read it out loud in the accents of the fashionable
type of stage or movie star of the moment, you will get the
idea. I have never dared to risk it in public because I would
laugh all the way through it myself.

There is nothing, there can be nothing dearer to a thinking being
than life; yet the man who tries to enjoy it is the man who practises
the difficult art of shortening life, of driving it fast.

Perfectly certain that M____ M____ would keep her word, I
went to her hotel at ten o'clock in the morning, and she joined me
in the parlour as soon as I was announced.

"Good heavens!" she exclaimed, "are you ill?"

"No, but I may as well look so, for the expectation of happiness
wears me out. I have lost sleep and appetite, and, if my felicity were
to be deferred, my life would be the forfeit."

"There shall be no delay, dearest; but how impatient you are!
Let us sit down. Here is the key of my casino. You will find some
persons in it, because we must be served; but nobody will speak to
you, and you need not speak to anyone. You must be masked, and
you must not go there till two hours after sunset—mind, not before.
Then go up the stairs opposite the street door, and at the top of those
stairs you will see by the light of a lamp a green door which you will
open to enter the apartment, which you will find lighted. You will
find me in the second room, and, in case I should not be there, you
will wait for me a few minutes; you may rely upon my being punctual.
You can take off your mask in that room and make yourself com-

fortable; you will find some books and a good fire."

The description could not be clearer; I kissed the hand which was giving me the key of that mysterious temple.

In the evening, at the time named by her, I repaired to the casino, and, obeying all her instructions, I reached a sitting-room in which I found my new conquest dressed in a most elegant costume. The room was lighted up by girandoles, which were reflected by the looking-glasses and by four splendid candlesticks placed on a table covered with books. I threw myself at her feet to show her my deep gratitude, and I kissed with rapture her beautiful hands. As a lover, respectful, tender, but bold, enterprising, certain of victory, I blended delicately the gentleness of my proceedings with the ardent fire which was consuming me, and stealing the most voluptuous kisses from the most beautiful mouth, I felt as if my soul would burst from my body.

She said to me, "My dear, I have an appetite which promises to do honour to the supper; are you able to keep me good company?"

"Yes," I said, knowing well what I could do in that line, "yes, I can."

She rang the bell, and a woman, middle-aged, but well dressed and respectable-looking, laid out a table for two persons, she then placed on another table close by all that was necessary to enable us to do without attendance, and she brought, one after the other, eight different dishes in Sèvres porcelain placed on silver heaters. It was a delicate and plentiful supper.

We drank nothing but burgundy and champagne. She dressed the salad cleverly and quickly, and in everything she did I had to admire the graceful ease of her manners.

It was near midnight; we had made an excellent supper, and we were near a good fire. Besides, I was in love with a beautiful woman, and, thinking that time was precious, I became very pressing; but she resisted.

"Be satisfied for this time, dearest, and learn from me how to practise abstinence; we shall be happier another time. When I have gone, if you have nothing to hurry you, you can rest here." M——— M——— kissed me warmly and tenderly and said to me, "I expect to see you the day after tomorrow. Tell me, my love, where will you wait for me, two hours after the setting of the sun?"

"Could I not wait for you at your casino?"

"No."

"I will wait for you in St. John and St. Paul's Square behind the pedestal of the statue."

"Farewell."

Pleased without being satisfied, I went to bed and slept soundly until noon.

I left the casino without seeing anyone.

I had five rooms, furnished in the most elegant style, and everything seemed to be calculated for love, pleasure and good cheer. The service of the dining-room was made through a sham window in the wall, provided with a dumb-waiter revolving upon itself and fitting the window so exactly that masters and servants could not see each other. The drawing-room was decorated with magnificent looking-glasses, crystal chandeliers, girandoles in gilt and bronze and a splendid pier-glass placed on a chimney of white marble; the walls were covered with small squares of real china, representing little Cupids; elegant and very comfortable sofas were placed on every side. Next to it was an octagonal room, the walls, the ceiling and the floor of which were entirely covered with splendid Venetian glass, arranged in such a manner as to reflect on all sides. Close by was a beautiful alcove with two secret outlets; on the right, an elegant dressing-room; on the left, a boudoir with a bath in Carrara marble. Everywhere the wainscots were embossed in ormolu or painted with flowers and arabesques.

After I had given my orders for all the chandeliers to be filled with wax candles and the finest linen to be provided wherever necessary, I ordered a most delicate and sumptuous supper for two, without regard to expense, and especially the most exquisite wines. I then took possession of the key of the principal entrance and warned the master that I did not want to be seen by anyone when I came in or went out.

I was at the place of meeting one hour before the time appointed, and, although the night was cold, I did not feel it. Precisely as the hour struck, I saw a two-oared gondola reach the shore and a mask come out of it, speak a few words to the gondolier and take the direction of the statue. My heart was beating quickly, but, seeing that it was a man, I avoided him and regretted not having brought my pistols. The mask, however, turning round the statue, came up to me with outstretched hands; I then recognized my angel, who was amused at my surprise and took my arm.

I found everything in good order; we went upstairs and I threw off my mask and my disguise; but M_____ M_____ took delight in walking about the rooms and examining every nook of the charming place in which she was received. She was surprised at the almost magic spell which, although she remained motionless, showed her lovely person in a thousand different manners. Her multiplied portraits, reproduced by the looking-glasses and the numerous candles disposed for that purpose, offered to her sight a spectacle entirely new to her and from which she could not withdraw her eyes. Sitting down on a stool, I contemplated her elegant person with rapture. A coat of rosy velvet, embroidered with gold spangles, a vest to match, embroidered likewise in the richest fashion, breeches of black satin, diamond buckles, a solitaire of great value on her little finger, and on the other hand a ring—such was her toilet. Her black lace mask was remarkable for its fineness and the beauty of the design. To enable me to see her better, she stood before me. I looked in her pockets, in which I found a gold snuffbox, a sweetmeat-box adorned with pearls, a gold case, a splendid opera glass, handkerchiefs of the finest cambric, soaked rather than perfumed with the most precious essences. I examined attentively the richness and the workmanship of her two watches, her chains, her trinkets, brilliant with diamonds.

After the supper, which she found excellent, she made some punch, and she was a very good hand at it. But I felt my impatience growing stronger every moment, and I said, "Recollect that we have only seven hours before us."

"You reason better than Socrates," she answered.

After drinking a cup of coffee, we went out.

I saw her safe in her gondola, and then I went to bed. Ten hours of profound sleep restored me to my usual state of vigour.

Alone

THOMAS WOLFE

*As to this piece by Thomas Wolfe, what boy in his teens
has not been through this in his spotty period? This excerpt
is from The Web and the Rock, and I select it—with his
wonderful description of Broadway—because I feel much
the same about that part of the world myself.*

*"Alone" makes you sigh for your lost youth, when you
were certain of the world and knew all of the things you were
going to accomplish, and you were sure that you were right
and all older people were wrong, when you knew just how
you were going to order your life as against the tangled mess
other people had made of their lives around you.*

Heigh-ho!

Why was he so unhappy? Where had it come from—this fury of
unrest and longing, terrific speed and smashing movement that went
nowhere?

Each day they swarmed into the brutal stupefaction of a million
streets, were hurled like vermin through the foul, fetid air of roaring
tunnels.

At night they rushed out again with the idiot and unwearied
pertinacity of a race that was damned and lost, to seek new pleasures
and sensations that, when found, filled them with weariness, bore-
dom, and horror of the spirit.

And for what? For what? To drive the huge exasperation of their
weary bodies, their tortured nerves, their bewildered, overladen hearts,
back to those barren, furious avenues of night again. To embrace
again the painted shell of the old delusion, hurling themselves on-
ward towards that huge, sterile shine and glitter of the night as feverishly as if some great reward of fortune, love, or living joy was waiting
for them there.

For what? For what? What was the reward of all this frenzied
searching? To be shone on lividly by the lights of death, to walk with
jaunty swagger and knowing wink past all the gaudy desolations of
the hot-dog, fruit-drink stands, past the blazing enticements, the

trickster's finery of the eight-foot hole-in-the-wall shops, and to cram their dead grey jaws in the gaudy restaurants with the lifeless husks of dead grey food. Proudly to thrust their way into the lurid maws, the dreary, impotent escapes, the feeble, half-hid nastiness of the moving picture shows, and then to thrust and swagger it upon the streets again. To know nothing, yet to look with knowing looks upon the faces of their fellow nighttime dead, to look at them with sneering lips and scornful faces, and with hard, dark, slimy eyes, and jeering tongues. Each night to see and be seen—oh, priceless triumph! —displaying the rich quality of their wit, the keen humor of their fertile minds, with such gems of repartee as:

"Jesus!"

"Ho-ly Chee!"

"Oh, yeah?"

"Yeah!"

"Wich guy?"

"Dat guy! Nah—not him! Duh otheh guy!"

"Dat guy? Je-sus! Is dat duh guy yuh mean?"

"Wich guy?"

"Duh guy dat said he was a friend of yours."

"A friend of mine! Je-sus! Who said he was a friend of mine?"

"He said so."

"G'wan! Where d'yah get dat stuff? Dat son-of-a-bitch ain't no friend of mine!"

"No?"

"No."

"Holy Chee!"

"Je-sus!"

Oh, to hurl that stony gravel of their barren tongues forever, forever, with a million million barren repetitions into the barren ears of their fellow dead men! And then, having prowled the streets again in that ancient, fruitless, and unceasing quest, having hugged the husks of desolation to the bone, to be hurled back into their cells again, as furiously as they had come!

Oh, dear friends, is that not the abundant life of glory, power, and wild, exultant joy, the great vision of the shining and enchanted city?

At other times his mood would change, and he would walk the swarming streets for hours at a time and find in the crowds that thronged about him nothing but delight, the promise of some glorious adventure. At such a time he would sink himself wholly and exultantly into the city's life. The great crowds stirred him with a feeling of ecstasy and anticipation. With senses unnaturally absorptive, he drank in every detail of the mighty parade, forever alert for the pretty face and seductive figure of a woman. Every woman with a well-shaped leg, or with a strong, attractive, sexual energy in her appearance, was invested at once with the glamorous robe of beauty, wisdom, and romance which he threw around her.

He had a hundred unspoken meetings and adventures in a day. Each passed and was lost in the crowd, and the brevity of that meeting and departure pierced him with an intolerable sense of pain and joy, of triumph and of loss. Into each lovely mouth he put words of tenderness and understanding. A sales girl in a department store became eloquent and seductive with poignant and beautiful speech; the vulgar, loose mouth of an Irish waitress uttered enchanted music for him when it spoke. In these adventures of his fancy, it never occurred to him that he would have any difficulty in winning the admiration of these beauties—that he was nothing but an ungainly youth, with small features, large shoulders, legs too short, a prowling, simian look about the out-thrust head, and an incredible length of flailing arms. No: instead he cut a very handsome and heroic figure in these fantasies, and dreamed of an instant marriage of noble souls, of an immediate and tremendous seduction, ennobled by a beautiful and poetic intensity of feeling.

Sometimes, in these golden fantasies, it was a great lady who yielded herself to him—a lady rich, twenty-four or five years of age (for he could not stand them younger than he was), and widowed recently from an old man that she did not love but had been forced to marry by some bitter constraint and hard occasion dear. The circumstances of his meeting with her varied from repelling with a single annihilating blow of the fist the proffered violence of some Irish thug, to finding quite by accident in the gutter, already half obscured by the dead leaves of Autumn, a wallet or a mesh-bag containing not only ten or twenty thousand dollars in bank notes of huge denominations, but also a rope of pearls, some loose, uncut gems, an emerald of great size mounted on a ring, and a number of stocks or bonds, together with letters of the most valuable and distressing privacy. This form of meeting he preferred to any other, for, although it deprived him of heroism, it enabled him to show equivalent virtues of honesty and manly dignity. Also by means of it he could pay his way.

Thus, having picked up the bag on a lonely walk in Central Park, he would see at once the value of its contents—so huge as to make even a modest reward a substantial thing—and, thrusting it quickly into his pocket, he would go at once, though by a rather circuitous route which he had all planned out, to his room, where carefully and exactly he would itemize everything upon the back of an envelope, noting that the initials upon the clasp agreed with the name upon the visiting card he should find within.

This done, he would summon a taxicab and drive at once and at great speed to the indicated address. It would be a modest house in the East Sixties, or again it would be a large, grim pile on Fifth Avenue. He preferred the modest house, high storied, but with a narrow façade, not glaringly obtrusive, but almost gloomily mellow and dark. The furnishings would be masculine, the house still bearing the mark of its dead master's character—walnut and mahogany, with heavy, worn leather cushions on the chairs. To the right of the entrance hall would be the library, a gloomy room in walnut, completely lined up to its high ceiling with ten or fifteen thousand books save for the interstices of recessed, narrow windows.

Having arrived before the house, he would dismiss the taxicab and mount the steps. The door would be opened by a maid, a well-made girl of twenty-one or two, who obviously bathed frequently, and who wore expensive black silk stockings—which her mistress gave her—on her heavy but shapely legs. Smiling, she would usher him into the library, pausing, before she went to inform her mistress, to poke up the glowing coals in a small grate, revealing as she bent before him, the heavy white flesh of her under leg, just above the knee, where her garters of ruffled green silk (probably a gift from her mistress) furrowed deeply into the smooth column of her thigh. Then she would depart, one side of her face prettily flushed by the heat, casting him a swift and provocative glance as she went, while he grew conscious of the rhythmical undulations of her heavy breasts.

Presently he would hear the maid's low voice upstairs, and the nervous, irritable voice of another woman:

"Oh, who is it? Some young man? Tell him I can't see him today! I'm much too upset by this whole affair!"

Ablaze with fierce but righteous anger at this unhandsome return for his labor and honesty, he would stride to the foot of the stairway in time to find the maid descending, and to address her in a proud, harsh voice, not loud but almost metallic—a voice of great carrying power.

"Tell your mistress that it is imperative she give me the honor of her attendance. If I am intruding here, it is certainly against my will, and at a cost of considerable anxiety, care, and labor to myself. But I have information concerning a loss she may have sustained, which I believe may be of the greatest interest to her."

He would get no further. There would be a sharp cry above, and she would come down the stairs regardless of safety, her tense face very pale, her voice almost stricken. She would seize him so fiercely with her small, strong hands that she made a white circle around his wrists, speaking in a tone that was no more than a trembling breath:

"What is it? You must tell me at once, do you hear? Have you found it?"

Gently, soothingly, but with implacable firmness, he would answer:

"I have found something which may be your property. But so serious are the possibilities of this matter, to me, that I must ask you first of all to submit yourself to a few questions that I am going to ask you."

"Anything—anything you like!"

"You have suffered a loss. Describe that loss—the time and the place."

"I lost a silver mesh-bag two days ago between 8:20 and 8:35 in the morning, while riding in Central Park, just back of the Museum. The bag had been put in the right-hand pocket of my riding jacket; it was dislodged during my ride."

"Describe as carefully and exactly as you can the contents of the bag."

"There were $16,400 in bank notes—140 hundred dollar bills, the rest in fifties and twenties. There was also a necklace with a platinum clasp, containing ninety-one pearls of graduated size, the largest about the size of a large grape; a plain gold ring set with a diamond-shaped emerald—"

"Of what size?"

"About the size of a lump of sugar. There were, in addition, eight Bethlehem Steel stock certificates, and, what I value most of all, several letters written by friends and business associates to my late husband, which contain matter of the most private sort."

Meanwhile he would be checking the list off, envelope in hand. Now he would say quietly, taking the bag from his pocket and presenting it to her:

"I think you will find your property intact."

Seizing the bag with a cry, she would sink quickly upon a leather divan, opening it with trembling fingers and hastily counting through the contents. He would watch her with nervous constraint, conscious of the personal risk he took, the unanswerable suspicion that might be attached to him if everything was not there. But everything would be!

Finally looking up, her voice filled with fatigue and unutterable relief, she would say:

"Everything is here! Everything! Oh! I feel as if I had been born again!"

Bowing coldly and ironically, he would answer:

"Then, madam, you will pardon me the more willingly if I leave you now to enjoy the first happy hours of your childhood alone."

And, taking his battered but adventurous-looking old hat from a table, he would start for the door. She would follow immediately and interrupt his passage, seizing him again by the arms in her excitement:

"No, you *shall not* go yet. You shall *not* go until you tell me what your name is. What is your name? You *must* tell me your name!"

Very coldly he would answer:

"The name would not matter to you. I am not known yet. I am only a poor writer."

She would see, of course, from his ragged clothing—the same suit he was now wearing—that he was neither a wealthy nor fashionable person, but she would also see, from the great sense of style with which his frame carried these rags, as if indifferent or unconscious of them, that there was some proud royalty of nature in him that had no need of worldly dignities. She would say:

"Then, if you are a poor writer, there is one thing I can do—one very small return I can make for your splendid honesty. You must accept the reward that I have offered."

"*Reward?*" He would say in an astounded tone. "Is there a *reward?*"

"Five thousand dollars. I—I—hope—if you wouldn't mind—" she would falter, frightened by the stern frown on his forehead.

"I accept, of course," he would answer, harshly and proudly. "The service I rendered was worth it. I am not ashamed to take my wage. At any rate, it is better invested in me than it would be among a group of Irish policemen. Let me congratulate you on what you have done today for the future of art."

"I am so glad—so happy—that you'll take it—that it will be of any help to you. Won't you come to dinner tonight? I want to talk to you."

He would accept.

Before he left they would have opportunity to observe each other more closely. He would see that she was rather tall for a woman— about five feet six or seven inches, but giving the impression of being somewhat taller. She would have a heavy weight of rather blondish hair, but perhaps with a reddish tint in it, also—perhaps it would be the color of very pale amber. It would be piled compactly and heavily upon her head, so as to suggest somewhat a molten or malleable weight, and it would be innumerably various with little winking lights.

This weight would rest like a heavy coronal above a small, delicately-moulded face, remarkably but not unhealthily pale, and saved from unpleasant exoticism by the rapid and boyish daring of its movements, a smile like a flick of golden light across a small, full, incredibly sensitive mouth—a swift, twisted smile, revealing small, milk-white, but not too even teeth. The face would usually be cast in an intense, slightly humorous earnestness. Her conversation would be boyishly direct and sincere, delivered half while looking seriously at the auditor, and half with the eyes turned thoughtfully away; at the conclusion of each remark, however, the eyes, of a luminous blue-grey depth, a catlike health and sensuousness, would steal thievishly sideways up to the face of the listener.

She would be dressed in a close-fitting blouse of knitted green silk, with pockets into which she occasionally thrust her small, brown, competent hands (unjeweled). Her breasts would not be like the slow rich melons of the maid, but eager and compact—each springing forward lithely and passionately, their crisp and tender nozzles half defined against the silk. She would wear a short, straight skirt of blue serge; her long, graceful legs would be covered with silk hose; her small feet sheathed in velvet shoes clasped by old buckles.

Before he left, she would tell him that he must come as often as he liked—daily, if possible—to use the library: it was rarely used now, and that he might have it all to himself. He would depart, the door being closed behind him by the voluptuous and softly smiling maid.

Then, in a fever of excitement and rapt contemplation, he would walk, a furnace of energy, through the streets and up the broad promenade in the middle of Central Park. It would be a slate-colored day in late Autumn, dripping with small, cold rain, pungent with smoke, and as inchoate as Spring with unknown prophecy and indefinable hope. A few lone, wet, withered leaves would hang from bare boughs; occasionally he would burst into a bounding run, leaping high in the air and tearing with tooth or hand at some solitary leaf.

Finally, late in the afternoon, he would become conscious of delightful physical exhaustion, which, ministered by the golden wine of his fancy, could easily be translated into voluptuous ease, just as the flesh of certain fowl becomes more dainty when slightly old. Then turning towards Lexington Avenue, his face chill with beaded rain, he would take the subway to Fourteenth Street, go home to his room, enjoy the soaking luxury of a hot bath, shave, put on clean underwear, socks, shirt, and tie; and then wait with trembling limbs and a heart thudding with strong joy for the impending meeting.

Then, at half-past eight, he would present himself at her door again. The rain would fall coldly and remotely from bare branches, and from all the eaves. The first floor of the house would be dark, but behind drawn curtains the second floor would be warm with mellow light. Again the maid would open the door for him, leading him past the dark library, up the broad, carpeted stairs, where a single dim lamp was burning at the landing. He would follow, not too close, but a step or two behind, in order to watch the pleasant rhythm of her hips and the slipping back and forth of her rather tight skirt up her comely but somewhat heavy legs.

At the top of the stairs, waiting to greet him, the lady would be waiting. Taking him quickly by the hand with a warm, momentary pressure, and drawing him slightly towards her, she led the way into the living room, probably without saying a word, but with only the liquid stealth of the eyes. There would be none of that cold, remote, well-bred iciness of courtesy that chills and freezes up the warm glow of affection, such as "I'm so glad you could come!" or "It's so nice of you to come"—they would have begun almost instantly with a natural and casual intimacy, full of dignity and ease and beauty.

The boyishness of her morning garb and manner would have disappeared entirely. In unadorned but costly evening dress, of heavy, pearl-colored silk, with silver hose, and black, jeweled slippers, she would reveal an unsuspected maturity, depth of breast, and fullness of limb. Her sloping shoulders, round, firm arms, and long throat in which a pulse would be beating slowly and warmly, in that light would be pearl-tinted, suffused, however, with a delicate bone color.

The living room would be a high, spacious room, masculine in its dimensions, but touched by her delicate taste, as the library had not been, into a room which was, although not frillishly, obviously, or offensively so, feminine.

There would be a huge divan, a chaise-longue, several large, deep chairs, luxuriously upholstered and covered with a dull, flowered pattern of old satin. A warm, bright fire of coals would be burning in a hearth of small dimensions, with a sturdy and sensible alignment of shovels, pokers, and tongs to one side, their brass very highly polished, and with no revolting antiquey-ness of pseudo-Revolutionary bed warmers. The mantel would be an unadorned piece of creamy marble; above, extending the entire distance to the ceiling, there would be an eighteenth-century French mirror, with a simple gilded border, somewhat mottled with small brown patches at the lower edges. The sole object upon the mantel would be an ornate, gilded, eighteenth-century clock, very feminine and delicate. All of the furniture would have strong but delicate proportions. There would be a table behind the divan—a round leaf of polished walnut. Scattered about its surface would be several periodicals and magazines: a copy of *The Dial*, *Vanity Fair*, which he might pick up without comment, tossing them back carelessly with a slight ironical lifting of the eyebrows, copies of *The Century*, *Harper's*, and *Scribner's*, but none of

The Atlantic Monthly. There would also be copies of *Punch*, of *Sketch, The Tatler,* or sporting and dramatic magazines, filled with pictures of hunt and chase, and many small photographs showing members of the English aristocracy, gaunt, toothy men and women, standing, talking, tailored into squares and checks with the toes of their large feet turned inwards, or caught walking, with their open mouths awry, and an arm or leg cutting angularly the air, with such legends below as, "Captain McDingle and the Lady Jessica Houndsditch caught last week enjoying a chat at the Chipping-Sodbury Shoot."

On a small table at one end of the divan there would be materials for making various kinds of cocktails and iced drinks—a rich, squat bottle of mellow rum, a bottle of Kentucky Bourbon whiskey matured for more than twenty years in oaken casks, and pungent gin, faintly nostalgic with orange bitters. There would be as well a cocktail shaker, a small bucket of cracked ice, and dishes of olives and salted almonds.

After drinking a chill and heady liquor, infused with her own certain intoxication, he would have another, his senses roused to controlled ecstasy, his brain leaping with a fiery and golden energy. Then they would go in to dinner.

The dining room, on the same floor, would be in semi-darkness, save for the golden light that bathed a round table, covered with a snowy and capacious cover, and two small, shaded lamps upon a huge buffet, gleaming with glassware, and various bottles containing whiskey, wines, liqueurs, vermouth, and rum. They would be attended at table by the maid. There would be only one other servant, the cook, a middle-aged New Hampshire woman, who had added to her native art things she had learned when the family had spent the Summer on Cape Cod, or in Paris, where the lady would have lived for several years. In the daytime there would be a man as well, who tended the furnace and did the heavier chores.

This would be all the service. The estate would not be unhappily and laboriously wealthy, extending into several millions of dollars: there would only be seven or eight hundred thousand dollars, solidly founded in tax-free bonds, yielding an annual income of twenty or twenty-five thousand, the whole intention and purpose of the fortune being total expenditure of the income for simple luxury.

The dishes would be few in number; the food would be man's food, simply and incomparably cooked. They would begin with a heavy tomato soup, the color of mahogany, or with a thick pea soup of semi-solid consistency, or with a noble dish of onion soup with a solid crust of toasted bread and cheese upon it, which she had made herself. There would be no fish, but, upon a huge silver platter, a thick sirloin or porterhouse, slightly charred and printed with the grid at the edges and center. Small pats of butter previously mixed with chopped mint and a dash of cinnamon would be dissolving visibly upon its surface. She would carve the steak into tender three-inch strips, revealing the rich, juicy, but not pasty, red of its texture. Then she would help his plate to mealy fried potatoes and tender, young boiled onions, exfoliating their delicate and pungent skins evenly at the touch of a fork. She would cover them with a rich butter sauce, touched with paprika.

There would be as well a salad—a firm heart of lettuce, or an artichoke, or, better still, crisp white endive. She would prepare the dressing in a deep mixing bowl, cutting small fragments of mint or onion into the vinegar, oil, and mustard to give it pungency. Finally, there would be deep-dish apple pie, spiced with nutmeg and cinnamon, and gummed with its own syrups along its crisped, wavy crust; this would be served with a thick hunk of yellow American cheese. They would have also a large cup of strong, fragrant coffee, with heavy cream. He would watch the cream coil through the black surface like thick smoke, changing finally into mellow brown. He would say little during the course of the meal. He would eat his food decently, but with enthusiastic relish, looking up from time to time to find her eyes fastened upon him with a subtly humorous and yet tender look.

Later, in the living room, they would sit before the fire, he in a deep upholstered chair, she on the chaise-longue, where they would have small cups of black coffee, a glass of green Chartreuse, or of Grand Marnier, and cigarettes. He would smoke fragant, toasted, loose-drawing Lucky Strikes; she would smoke Melachrinos. From time to time she would move her limbs slightly, and her silken calves, sliding gently apart or together, would cause an audible and voluptuous friction.

There would be little other sound save the enveloping and quieting drip of rain from eaves and boughs, a brief gaseous spurt from the red coals, and the minute ticking of the little clock. From time to time he would hear the maid clearing the table in the dining room. Presently she would appear, ask if anything more was wanted, say good-night, and mount the stairs to her room on the top floor. Then they would be left alone.

They would begin to talk at first, if not with constraint, at least with some difficulty. She would speak of her education—in a convent —of her life abroad, of stupid and greedy parents, now dead, of her great devotion to an aunt, a wise and kindly woman, her only friend against her family in her difficult youth, and of her marriage at twenty to a man in his late forties, good, devoted, but vacant of any interest for her. He had died the year before.

Then she would ask him about his life, his home, his childhood, his age, and his ambition. Then he would talk, at first in short spurts and rushes. At length, language bursting like a torrent at the gates of speech, he would make a passionate avowal of what he had done, believed, felt, loved, hated, and desired, of all he wanted to do and be. Then he would light another cigarette, get up restlessly before the fire, sit down again beside her on the chaise-longue, and take her hand in a natural and casual way, at which she would give a responsive squeeze to his. Then, throwing his cigarette into the grate, he would put his arms around her quite naturally and easily, and kiss her, first for about forty seconds upon the mouth, then in a circle upon the cheeks, eyes, forehead, nose, chin, and throat, about the place where the pulse was beating. After this, he would gently insinuate his hand into her breasts, beginning near the deep and fragrant channel that parted them. Meanwhile, she would ruffle his hair gently and stroke his face with her delicate fingers. Their passion would have them chained in a silent drunkenness; she would submit to every action of his embrace without thought of resistance.

Lying beside her now, wound in her long arms, he would pass his hand along her silken, swelling hips, down the silken seam of her calf, and gently up her thigh below her skirt, lingering for a moment upon the tender, heavy flesh of her under leg. Then he would loosen one breast over the neck of her gown, holding its tender weight and teat gently and lovingly in one hand. The nipples of her firm breasts would not be leathery, stained brown, and flaccid, like those of a woman who has borne children; they would end briefly in a tender pink bud, as did those of the ladies in old French paintings—those of Boucher, for example.

Then he would lift her arms, observing the delicate silken whorls and screws of blonde hair in the arm pits. He would kiss and perhaps bite her tender shoulder haunch, and smell the pungent but not unpleasant odor, already slightly moist with passion. And this odor of an erotic female would have neither the rank stench of a coarse-bodied woman, nor some impossible and inhuman bouquet, disgusting to a healthy taste. It would be delicately vulgar: the odor of a healthy woman and a fine lady, who has not only been housed, clothed, fed, and attended with the simple best, but has been derived from ancestral loins similarly nourished, so that now the marrow of her bones, the substance of her flesh, the quality of her blood, the perspiration of her skin, the liquor of her tongue, the moulding of her limbs— all the delicate joinings and bindings of ligament and muscle, and the cementing jellies, the whole incorporate loveliness of her body— were of rarer, subtler, and more golden stuff than would be found elsewhere the world over.

And lying thus, warmed by the silent, glowing coals, he would perform on her the glorious act of love. He would dedicate to her the full service of his love and energy, and find upon her mouth double oblivion.

Later, reviving slowly, he would lie in her embrace, his head heavily sunk upon her neck, feel the slow, unsteady respiration of her breast, and hear, his senses somewhat drugged, the faint, incessant beating of the rain.

And he would stay with her that night, and on many nights thereafter. He would come to her in the darkness, softly and quietly, although there was no need for silence, conscious that in the dark there was waiting a central energy of life and beauty; in the darkness they would listen to the million skipping feet of rain.

Shortly after this night, he would come and live with her in the house. This would be all right because he would insist on paying for his board. He would pay, against all protests, fifteen dollars a week, saying:

"This is all I can afford—this is what I would pay elsewhere. I could not eat and drink and sleep as I do here, but I could live. Therefore, take it!"

His days would be spent in the library. There he would do stupendous quantities of reading, going voraciously and completely through those things he desired most to know, but effecting combinations, mélanges, woven fabrics of many other books, keeping a piled circle about him and tearing chunks hungrily from several at random.

The library would be based solidly, first, on five or six thousand volumes, which would cover excellently but not minutely the range of English and American literature. There would be standard editions of Thackeray, the Cruikshank and Phiz Dickenses, Meredith, James, Sir Walter Scott, and so on. In addition to the well-known literature of the Elizabethans, such as Shakespeare, the handy Mermaid collection of the dramatists, and the even more condensed anthologies with Jonson's *Volpone*, *The Alchemist*, and *Bartholomew Fair*, Dekker's *Shoemaker's Holiday*, Chapman's *Bussy d'Ambois*, there would be several hundred of the lesser-known plays, bad, silly, and formless as they were, but filled with the bawdy, beautiful, and turbulent speech of that time.

There would be prose pamphlets, such as the romances after Bandello of Robert Greene, the dramatist, or his quarrel with Gabriel Harvey, or his confessions, Dekker's *Guls Horne-booke*, the remnant of Jonson's *Sad Shepherd*, his *Underwoods*. There would be such books as Coleridge's *Anima Poetae*, the *Biographia Literaria*, *The Table Talk of S. T. C.*, and the sermons of the Puritan divines, particularly of Jonathan Edwards. There would be books of voyages, Hakluyt, Purchas, Bartram's *Travels in North America*.

And there would be facsimile reproductions of all the scientific manuscripts of Leonardo da Vinci, the great *Codice Atlantico*, written backwards and reversed across the page, scribbled with hundreds of drawings, including his flying machines, canals, catapults, fire towers, spiral staircases, anatomical dissections of human bodies, diagrams of the act of copulation while standing erect, researches in the movement of waves, fossilized remains, sea shells on a mountain side, notes on the enormous antiquity of the world, the leafless and blasted age of the earth which he put in the background of his paintings—as he did in Mona Lisa. With the aid of mirrors and of Italian grammars and dictionaries, he would spell out the words and translate them, using as a guide the partial deciphering already made by a German. Then, in his spare moments between writing novels, he would show how Leonardo regarded painting only as a means of support for his investigation into all movement, all life, and was only incidentally an artist and an engineer, and how what he was really doing was tracing with a giant's brush the map of the universe, showing the possibility of Man becoming God.

There would also be books of anatomical drawings, besides those of Leonardo, of the fifteenth and sixteenth centuries, showing ladies lying on divans, gazing wistfully through their open bellies at their entrails, and maps out of the medieval geographers, compounded of scraps of fact, hypothesis, and wild imaginings, with the different quarters of the sea peopled by various monsters, some without heads, but with a single eye and with a mouth between the shoulders.

Then there would be some of those books that Coleridge "was deep in" at the time he wrote *The Ancient Mariner*, such as Iamblichus, Porphyry, Plotinus, Josephus, Jeremy Taylor, "the English Metaphysicum"—the whole school of the neoplatonists; all the works that could be collected on the histories of demons, witches, fairies, elves, gnomes, witches' sabbaths, black magic, alchemy, spirits—all the Elizabethans had to say about it, particularly Reginald Scott; and all the works of Roger Bacon; all legends and books of customs and superstition whatever, and works of quaint and learned lore, Burton's *Anatomy of Melancholy*, Frazer's *Golden Bough*, *The Encyclopædia Britannica*, in which, when he was tired of other reading, he could plunge luxuriously—picking out first the plums, such as Stevenson on Bérenger, or Theodore Watts-Dunton on poetry, or Carlyle, if any of him was left, on various things, or Swinburne on Keats, Chapman, Congreve, Webster, Beaumont and Fletcher.

He would have the *Magnalia* of Cotton Mather, the *Voyages of*

Dr. Syntax, with illustrations, Surtees' sporting novels. He would have the complete works of Fielding, Smollett, Sterne, and Richardson, and everything of Daniel Defoe's he could lay his hands on. He would have the entire corpus of Greek and Latin literature, so far as it might be obtained in Loeb's library and in the coffee-colored india paper Oxford classical texts, with footnotes and introduction all in Latin, as well as cross-references to all the manuscripts. And he would have several editions each of the *Carmina* of Catullus (with Lamb's translations and settings to verse); Plato, with Jowett's great rendering—in particular, of the *Apology* and the *Phaedo*; the histories of Herodotus, and in general all lying and entertaining histories and voyages whatever, as Strabo, Pausanias, Froissart, Josephus, Holinshed, Marco Polo, Swift, Homer, Dante, Xenophon in his *Anabasis*, Chaucer, Sterne, Voltaire in his voyage to England, *With Stanley in Africa*, Baron Munchausen.

There would be as well the Oxford and Cambridge University texts of the poets, with other editions when lacking for men like Donne, Crashaw, Herbert, Carew, Herrick, Prior. And in the drama there would be several hundred volumes besides the Elizabethans, including everyone from the early Greeks to the liturgical plays of the Middle Ages, to the great periods in France, Germany, Spain, Italy, Scandinavia, Russia, including all newer dramatists of the art theatre —Ibsen, Shaw, Chekhov, Benavente, Molnar, Toller, Wedekind, the Irish, Pirandello, O'Neill, Sardou, Romains, including others from the Bulgarian, Peruvian, and Lithuanian never heard of. There would also be complete bound editions of *Punch, Blackwood's, Harper's Weekly, L'Illustration, The Police Gazette, The Literary Digest,* and *Frank Leslie's Illustrated Weekly.*

Walled by these noble, life-giving books, he would work furiously throughout the day, drawing sustenance and courage, when not reading them, from their presence. Here in the midst of life, but of life flowing in regular and tranquil patterns, he could make his rapid and violent sorties into the world, retiring when exhausted by its tumult and fury to this established place.

And at night again, he would dine with rich hunger and thirst, and, through the hours of darkness, lie in the restorative arms of his beautiful mistress. And sometimes at night when the snow came muffling in its soft fall all of the noises of the earth and isolating them from all its people, they would stand in darkness, only a dying flicker of coal fire behind them, watching the transforming drift and flurry of white snow outside.

Thus, being loved and being secure, working always within a circle of comfort and belief, he would become celebrated as well. And to be loved and to be celebrated—was there more than this in life for any man?

After the success of his first book, he would travel, leaving her forever steadfast, while he drifted and wandered like a ghost around the world, coming unknown, on an unplanned journey, to some village at dusk, and finding there a peasant woman with large ox eyes. He would go everywhere, see everything, eating, drinking, and devouring his way across the earth, returning every year or so to make another book.

He would own no property save a small lodge with thirty acres of woodland, upon a lake in Maine or New Hampshire. He would not keep a motor—he would signal a taxi whenever he wanted to go anywhere. His clothing, laundry, personal attentions, and, when he was alone at the lodge, his cooking, would be cared for by a negro man, thirty-five years old, black, good-humored, loyal, and clean.

When he was himself thirty or thirty-five years old, having used up and driven out all the wild frenzy and fury in him by that time, or controlled it somehow by flinging and batting, eating and drinking and whoring his way about the world, he would return to abide always with the faithful woman, who would now be deep-breasted and steadfast like the one who waited for Peer Gynt.

And they would descend, year by year, from depth to depth in each other's spirit; they would know each other more completely than two people ever had before, and love each other better all the time. And as they grew older, they would become even younger in spirit, triumphing above all the weariness, dullness, and emptiness of youth. When he was thirty-five he would marry her, getting on her blonde and fruitful body two or three children. He would wear her love like a most invulnerable target over his heart. She would be the heart of his desire, the well of all his passion. He would triumph over the furious welter of the days during the healing and merciful nights: he would be spent, and there would always be sanctuary for him; weary, a place of rest; sorrowful, a place of joy.

So was it with him during that year. So was it with him that year when he was twenty-three years old, and when he walked the pavements of the city—a beggar and a king.

Has it been otherwise with any man?

Later on George Webber meets his true love and it is all very different from his dreams. Here are a few beautiful lines expressing his discovery.

Mrs. Esther Jack was fair; she was fair, she had the flower face; it was October, nineteen twenty-five, and dark time was flowing by her like a river.

Shall we save one face from the million faces? Shall we keep one moment from the adyts of lost time? Was no love living in the wilderness, and was there nothing but the snarl and jungle of the streets, the rasp and driven fury of the town? No love? Was no love living in the wilderness, and was there nothing but unceasing dying and begetting, birth, growth, pollution, and the cat's great snarl for blood and honey? Was there no love?

We shall scorn scorners, curse revilers, mock at mockers. Have they grown wise on dust and slum? Do they speak truly because their tongues are bitter? Have they seen clearly because their eyes are blind? Is there no gold because the sands are yellow? It is not true. They'll build great bridges yet and taller towers. But a vow has lasted where a wall has fallen: a word has been remembered where a city perished; and faith has lived when flesh grew rotten.

Mrs. Jack was fair; she was fair, she had dove's eyes; and in all the world there was no one like her.

Stories from the Magazines

Have you ever thought what treasure must lie buried in the back issues of magazines?

I had a friend named Albert Brush who, alas, died. He used to do all my research. I owe him a great debt, for he introduced me to many fields of literature. He was always talking about the stories in the back issues of The Saturday Evening Post. He introduced me to the work of Thomas Beer.

I would like to say something about Albert Brush. He was a little man who wrote poetry and was content to live a quiet and obscure life, and he had real knowledge. In spite of the fact that he had no money, I always thought of him as a very rich man, for he owned Dickens and Shakespeare and Jane Austen and Proust and the Russian novelists. He did not own any of the books himself, for he would read them and give them away and if he wanted to read them again he would either borrow them or buy them in old tattered copies. But there they were, alive and kicking, when so often they remain in people's houses on their shelves. (There is a house in Hollywood where they do not even have the books, only their backs, like stage props to make a decoration on the bookshelves.)

For Albert Brush it was the same with painting and sculpture and prints. He always lived in one room, and a small room at that, but there was always something astonishingly beautiful in it. He would nose around and find something at an auction or an obscure shop, absorb it, sell it, and buy something else. He did not have the kind of knowledge that people have who win fabulous amounts of money on television quiz shows. When I have watched these shows, I have always felt that the people on them know nothing at all. Their minds appear to be crammed with nothing but surface statistics, and I have thought there can be room for nothing else in them, even for love.

Albert Brush could never have appeared on such programs, or even have held down a job as an official librarian or a teacher. There were so many things he had not read, but he had more deep knowledge of books and paintings by far than any man I have known.

Tact

THOMAS BEER

Thomas Beer was a writer for The Saturday Evening Post. *He wrote seven books, one of which I have read—and a very good book it is, too—*The Mauve Decade. *He also wrote countless short stories, but he was ashamed of the short stories. He thought they were trashy. They indeed are not.*

An author or a composer or a painter—or an actor, for that matter—will often turn against his most popularly accepted work. I understand it was unwise to mention The Nutcracker Suite *to Tchaikovsky, and in my modest way I'm a little tired of hearing about Captain Bligh. But that does not mean you should avoid listening to "The Dance of the Sugarplum Fairy" or seeing* Mutiny on the Bounty *or reading about Mrs. Egg and her family.*

This story makes me think of Iowa and Ohio and Illinois and the other Middle Western states, and the people by whom I have been entertained when I have been on a reading tour. By the way, I think "Tact" would make a really good movie.

"You make me sick," said Mrs. Egg. She spoke with force. Her three daughters murmured, "Why, mamma!" A squirrel ran up an apple tree that shaded the veranda; a farm hand turned from weeding the mint bed by the garage. Mrs. Egg didn't care. Her chins shook fiercely. She ate a wafer, emptied her glass of iced tea, and spread her little hands with their buried rings on the table.

"You make me sick, girls," she said. "Dammy's been home out of the Navy precisely one year, seven weeks, an' two days, an' a month hasn't passed but what one of you've been 'phonin' me from town about what he had or ain't done unbecomin' to a boy that's engaged to Edith Sims! I don't know why you girls expect a boy that was champion heavyweight wrestler of the Atlantic Fleet an' stands six foot five inches in his shoes to get all thrilled over bein' engaged. A person that was four years in the Navy an' went clean to Japan has naturally been in love before, and—"

"Mamma!"

Mrs. Egg ate another sugar wafer and continued relentlessly "—ain't likely to get all worked up over bein' engaged to a seventeen-year-old girl who can't cook any better than a Cuban, on his own say-so." She mused: "As for his takin' Edith Sims out drivin' in over-alls and a shirt, Adam John Egg is the best-lookin' person in this family and you know it. You three girls are the sent'mentalest women in the state of Ohio and I don't know how your husbands stand it. My gee! D'you expect Dammy to chase this girl around heavin' roses at her like a fool in a movie?" She panted and peered into the iced-tea pitcher, then aimed an affable bawl at the kitchen door. "Benjamina! I'd be awful obliged if you'd make up some more iced tea, please. Dammy'll be through pickin' peaches soon and he's usually thirsty about four o'clock."

The new cook came down the long veranda. The daughters stared at this red-haired girl, taller than their tall selves. Benjamina lifted the vacant pitcher and carried it silently away. Her slim height vanished into the kitchen and the oldest daughter whispered, "Mercy, mamma, she's almost as tall as Dammy!"

"She's just six feet," said Mrs. Egg with deliberate clarity meant to reach Benjamina, "but extremely graceful, I think. My gee! It's perfectly embarrassin' to ask a girl as refined as that to clear the table or dust. She went through high school in Cleveland and can read all the French in the cookbook exactly as if it made sense. It's a pleasure to have such a person in the house."

The second daughter leaned forward and said, "Mamma, that's another thing! I do think it's pretty—untactful of Dammy to take this girl's brother around in the car and introduce him to Edith Sims and her folks as if—"

"I think it was extremely sensible," Mrs. Egg puffed. "Hamish is a very int'restin' boy, and has picked up milkin' remarkably when he's only been here a week, and Dammy's taught him to sem'phore, or whatever that wiggling-your-arms thing is called. And he appreciates Dammy a lot." The plate of sugar wafers was stripped to crumbs. Mrs. Egg turned her flushed face and addressed the unseen: "Benjamina, you might bring some more cookies when the tea's ready, and some of those cup cakes you made this mornin'. Dammy ate five of them at lunch."

Benjamina answered, "Yes, Mrs. Egg" in her slow fashion.

"Mamma," said the oldest daughter, "it's all right for you to say that Dammy is absolutely perfect, but the Simses are the most refined people in town, and it does look disgraceful for Dammy not to dress up *a little* when he goes there, and he's got all those beautiful tailor-made clothes from New York."

Mrs. Egg patiently drawled, "Fern, that's an awful uninterestin' remark. Dammy looks exactly like a seal in an aquarium when he's dressed up, his things fit so smooth; but a boy that was four years in the Navy and helps milk a hundred and twenty-seven cows twice a day, besides mendin' all the machinery on the place, is *not* called upon to dress up evenings to go see a girl he's known all his life. He's twenty-two years and nine weeks old, an' capable of managin' his own concerns. —Thank you, Benjamina," she told the red-haired girl as the fresh pitcher clinked on the table and the cup cakes gleamed in yellow charm beside it. "I do hate to trouble you on such a hot day."

Benjamina smiled nicely and withdrew. Mrs. Egg ate one of the cup cakes and thought it admirable. She broke out, "My gee! There's another thing! You girls keep actin' as if Dammy wasn't as smart as should be! On the other hand, he drove up to Cleveland and looked at the list of persons willin' to work in the country and didn't waste time askin' the agency questions, but went round to Benjamina's flat and ate some choc'late cake. Then he loaded her and Hamish into the car and brought 'em down, all between six in the mornin' and twelve at night. I've had eight days of rest an' comfort since! My gee! Your papa's the second biggest dairyman in this state, but that don't keep me in intell'gent cooks!"

The three young matrons sighed. Mrs. Egg considered them for a moment over her glass, and sniffed, "Mercy! This has been a pleasant afternoon!"

"Mamma," said the first-born, "you can't very well deny that Dammy's awful careless for an engaged man. He ought to've got a ring for Edith Sims when he was home at Christmas and the engagement came off. And—"

Mrs. Egg lost patience. She exclaimed, "Golden Jerusalem! Dammy got engaged at Judge Randolph's party the night before he went back to Brooklyn to his ship! My gee! I never heard such idiotic nonsense. You girls act as if Edith Sims—whose ears are much too big even if she does dress her hair low—was too good for Adam Egg! She's a nice child, an' her folks are nice and all the rest of it! —Dammy," she panted as the marvel appeared, "here's the girls!"

Adam came up the veranda with a clothes basket of peaches on his right shoulder. He nodded his black head to his sisters and put the basket noiselessly down. Then he blew smoke from both nostrils of his bronze small nose and rubbed its bridge with the cigarette. He seldom spoke. Mrs. Egg filled a glass with iced tea and Adam began to absorb this pensively. His sisters cooed and his mother somewhat forgave them. They had sense enough to adore Adam, anyhow. In hours of resolute criticism Mrs. Egg sometimes admitted that Adam's nose was too short. He was otherwise beyond praise.

His naked dark shoulders rippled and convulsed as he stooped to gather three cup cakes. A stained undershirt hid some of his terrific chest and his canvas trousers hung beltless on his narrow hips. Mrs. Egg secretly hoped that he would change these garments before he went to call on Edie Sims. The three cup cakes departed through his scarlet mouth into his insatiable system of muscles, and Adam lit his next cigarette. Smoke surged in a tide about his immovable big eyes. He looked at the road beyond the apple trees, then swung and made swift, enigmatic gestures with his awesome arms to young Hamish Saunders, loitering by the garage. Hamish responded with more flappings of his lesser arms and trotted down the grass. A letter carrier approached the delivery box at the gates of the monstrous farm.

"What did you sem'phore to Hamish, lamb?" Mrs. Egg asked.

Adam said "Mail" and sat down on the floor.

He fixed a black stare on the pitcher and Mrs. Egg filled his glass. Muscles rose in ovals and ropes under the hairless polish of his arm as he took the frail tumbler. His hard throat stirred and his short feet wriggled in moccasins of some soiled soft leather, indicating satisfaction. Mrs. Egg beamed. Benjamina made tea perfectly. She must tactfully tell the girl that Adam liked it. No female could hear that fact without a thrill.

"Package for you," said young Hamish, bounding up the steps. He gave Adam a stamped square box, announced "I signed for it," and retired shyly from the guests to read a post card. He was a burly lad of sixteen, in a shabby darned jersey and some outgrown breeches of Adam's. Mrs. Egg approved of him; he appreciated Adam.

The marvel tore the box to pieces with his lean fingers and got out a flat case of velvet. Two rings glittered in its satin lining. Adam contemplated the diamond of the engagement ring and the band of gold set with tiny brilliants which would forever nail Edith Sims to his perfections. His sisters squealed happily. Mrs. Egg thought how many pounds of Egg's A1 Butter were here consumed in vainglory and sighed gently. But she drawled, "My gee, Dammy! Nobody can poss'bly say you ain't got good taste in jewelry, anyhow," and shot a stare of fierce pride at her daughters. They rose. She knew that the arrival of these gauds would be known in Ilium forthwith. She said "Well, good evenin', girls," and affably accepted their kisses.

Adam paid no attention to the going of the oldest daughter's motor car; he was staring at the rings, and the blank brown of his forehead was disturbed by some superb and majestic fancy current under the dense smoothness of his jet hair. Hamish Saunders came shyly to peep at the gems and stooped his curly red head. The boy had large gray eyes, like those of his sister, and her hawk nose, which Mrs. Egg thought patrician.

"Hamish, you ain't had any tea yet, lamb. Dammy's left some. Benjamina puts in exactly sugar enough, an' I never heard of mint in iced tea before. It's awful interestin'."

Hamish soberly drank some tea and asked Adam, "Want the motor bike, Mr. Egg?"

Adam nodded. The boy went leaping down the flagged walk to the garage and busily led Adam's red motorcycle back to the veranda steps. Then he gazed with reverence at Adam's shoulders, felt his own right biceps, and sadly walked off toward the barns. The herd of the Egg Dairy Company was an agitation of twinkling horns and multicolored hides in the white-fenced yard. The ten hired men were sponging their hands at the model washstand by the colossal water tower's engine house. Mrs. Egg ate the last cup cake and looked at the town of Ilium, spread in a lizard of trees on the top of a long slope. The motor containing her female offspring was sliding into the main street. The daughters would stop at the Sims house to tell the refined Edith that her engagement ring had come.

Mrs. Egg pursed her lips courageously and said, "Dammy, you might change your duds, dear, before you take Edith her sol'taire. It's a kind of a formal occasion, sort of."

The giant pronounced lazily the one syllable "Bunk," and turned his face toward his mother. Then he said, "You've got awful pretty hands, mamma."

"Mercy, Dammy," Mrs. Egg panted, flushing. Her prodigiousness shook in the special chair of oak under the blow of this compliment. She tittered, "Well, your papa—I do hope it ain't so hot in Chicago —used to say so before I got stout."

Adam blew a snake of smoke from his left nostril and surprised her with a whole sentence. He drawled, "Was a oiler on the *Nevada* that sung a song about pale hands, pink-tipped like some kind of a flower, mamma."

"Mercy," said Mrs. Egg, "I know that song! A person sang it at the Presbyterian supper in 1910 when the oysters were bad, and some people thought it wasn't correct for a church party, bein' a pretty passionate kind of song. It was awful popular for a while after that. —Benjamina would know, her papa havin' kept a music store. I'll ask her. Help me up, lamb."

Adam arose and took his mother kindly out of her chair with one motion. Mrs. Egg passed voluminously over the sill into the kitchen and addressed her superior cook.

"There's a sent'mental kind of song that Dammy's interested in which is about some gump lovin' a woman's pale hands beside the shallow Marne or some such place."

Benjamina brushed back her blazing hair with both slender hands and looked at the rosy nails. " 'Pale Hands,' I think— No, it's the Kashmir love song. It used to be sung a great deal."

Adam said "Thanks" in the doorway.

Then he turned, jamming the jewel case into his pocket, and lounged down the steps. His shoulders gleamed like oiled wood. He picked a handful of peaches from the basket, which would have burdened two mortals, and split one in his terrible fingers. He ate a peach absently and threw the red stone at a roaming chicken, infamously busy in the nasturtiums. Mrs. Egg leaned on the side of the door. A slight nervousness made her reach for the radishes that Benjamina was cleaning. Radishes always stimulated Mrs. Egg. She ate two and hoped that Edith Sims wouldn't happen to look at Adam's back. The undershirt showed both shoulder blades and most of the sentiment "Damn Kaiser Bill" tattooed in pink across Adam. It seemed indecorous at the moment of betrothal, and Mrs. Egg winced.

Then she wondered. Adam took another peach and pressed it in a hand. Its blood welled over his shoulder and smeared the rear of the shirt brilliantly. He scrubbed it thoroughly into the back of his cropped hair and massaged his flat abdomen with a second fruit. After some study he kicked his feet out of the moccasins and doubled down in his fluid manner to rub both insteps with black grease from valves of the motorcycle. Then he signaled contentment by a prolonged pouring of smoke from his mouth, gave his mother a glance as he tucked the cast moccasins into the fork of the apple tree, and fled down the driveway with a coughing of his machine's engine, barefoot, unspeakably soiled and magnificently shimmering with peach blood.

"Oh, Lord!" said Mrs. Egg.

Benjamina looked up from the radishes and asked "What did you say?"

Mrs. Egg meditated, eating a radish. Adam had favored Benjamina with some notice in these ten days, and his approval of her cooking was manifest. He had even eaten veal goulash, a dish that he usually declined. The girl was a lady, anyhow. Mrs. Egg exploded.

"Benjamina, Dammy's up to somethin'! His sisters keep tellin' me he ain't tactful, either! My gee! He simply washed himself in peach juice and went off to give Edith Sims her engagement ring! And left his moc'sins in the apple tree where he always used to put his cigarettes when his papa didn't think he was old enough to smoke. But heaven knows, I can't see that anything ever hurt Dammy! He's always been the neatest boy that ever lived, and had all his clothes made when he was in the Navy. It's perfectly true that he ain't dressed respectable once since he got home. Mercy, the other day

he went in to see Edith in a half a khaki shirt that he'd been usin'
to clean the garage floor with!"

Benjamina pared a radish with a flutter of her white fingers and
asked, "How long have they been engaged, Mrs. Egg?"

"He had ten days' liberty, a year ago Christmas, and was home. It
perfectly upset me, because Dammy hadn't ever paid any attention
to the child. They got engaged at a dance Judge Randolph gave. It
was extremely sudden," Mrs. Egg pondered, "although the Simses are
very refined folks and Edith's a nice girl. All this year Edie's been
with her aunt in Washington, going to school.—A boy who was
four years in the Navy naturally ought to know when he's in love or
not. But men do fall in love in the most accidental manner, Benjamina! They don't seem to have any intentions of it. My gee! A man
who takes to runnin' after a girl for her money is within my compre-
hensions, or because she's good-lookin'. But what most men marry
most women for is beyond me. I'm forty-six years of age," she said,
"but I still get surprised at things. I think I'll lie down.—Do you
man'cure your nails, or are they as pink as that all the time?"

"They're naturally pink," Benjamina said.

"They're awful pretty," Mrs. Egg yawned, pausing in her advance
to the door of the living room. Then it seemed guileful to increase
this praise. She added "Dammy was sayin' so," and strolled into the
living room, where twenty-five photographs of Adam stood on shelves
and tables.

She closed the door and stopped to eat a peppermint out of a
glass urn beside the phonograph's cabinet. Excitements worked in
her. She brushed a fly from the picture of Adam in wrestling tights
and sank on a vast couch. The leather cushions hissed, breathing out
air under her descent. She closed her eyes and brooded.—If Adam
wanted to annoy Edith Sims, he had chosen a means cleverly. The
girl was elaborate as to dress and rather haughty about clothes. She
had praised a shirt of Judge Randolph's second son before Adam
pointedly on Sunday at tea in the veranda. Perturbations and guesses
clattered in Mrs. Egg's mind. Then a real clatter in the kitchen
roused her.

"I milked three cows," said Hamish Saunders to his sister in a
loud and complacent voice.

Benjamina said less loudly but with vigor, "Hamish, you got a post
card! I saw you reading it! I told you not to write anyone where we'd
gone to. Now—"

Mrs. Egg knew that the boy was wiggling. He said, "Oh, I wrote
Tick Matthews. He won't tell Cousin Joe, Benjy."

"He'll tell his mother and she'll tell everyone in the building! I didn't want anyone to know where we'd gone to!"

Mrs. Egg sat up. In a little, the lad spoke with a sound of male determination. He spoke airily. His hands must be jammed into his pockets. He said, "Now, Cousin Joe ain't going to come runnin' down here after us, Benjy. You've gone off, so that ought to sort of show him you ain't going to marry him. I was asking Adam if there's any law that a person's guardian can make 'em live with him if they don't want to—"

"You told him!"

"I did not!"

The girl said, "Don't talk so loud, Hamish! Mrs. Egg's taking a nap upstairs. You told him!"

"I didn't tell him a thing! I said there was a guy I knew that had run off from his guardian and—"

Benjamina burst into queer, vexed laughter. She said, "You might as well have told him! The day he came to the flat he asked who else lived there besides us. Cousin Joe's pipes were all over the place. It—"

"Look here! There's a judge in this town, and Mrs. Egg or Adam would tell him we're not children or imbeciles or nothin'! If Cousin Joe came down here lookin' for us—" Presently he said with misery in each syllable, "Don't cry, Benjy.—But nothin'll happen.—Anyhow, you'll be twenty-one in October and the court'll give you our income, 'stead of payin' it to Cousin Joe.—Bet you a dollar it's more than he says it is!" He whistled seven notes of a bugle call and then whimpered, "Quit cryin', Benjy!"

"F-finish these radishes," Benjamina commanded; "I want to go brush my hair."

There was the light sound of her soles on the back stairs. Mrs. Egg lay down again, wishing that the urn of peppermints was within reach. In the kitchen Hamish said "Aw, hell!" and the chair by the table creaked as he slumped into it. He would pare radishes very badly, Mrs. Egg thought.

She now thought of Benjamina with admiration. Adam had seen the girl's name on a list of women willing to take service in the country, at a Cleveland agency. He had gone to interview Benjamina, Mrs. Egg gathered, because a cook on the U.S.S. *Nevada* had been named Saunders and the word looked auspicious. Accident, said Mrs. Egg to herself, was the dominant principle of life. She was much interested. Benjamina had taken proper steps to get away from an unpleasant guardian and should be shielded from any consequences. Certainly a girl who could cook to satisfy Adam wasn't to be given back to some nameless male in Cleveland, in a flat. Mrs. Egg abhorred flats. A man who would coop two children in a flat deserved no consideration. And Adam required gallons of peach butter for winter use. Mrs. Egg arose, stalked openly into the kitchen and addressed Hamish as an equal. She said, "Bub, you're an awful tactful boy, and have sense. Dammy said so himself. Honesty is my policy, an' I may as well say that I could hear all you were talkin' with Benjamina right now.—Who is this Cousin Joe you've run off from?"

Hamish cut a radish in two and wretchedly stammered, "H-he's dad's cousin. He's a louse!"

Mrs. Egg drawled, "My gee! That's a awful good description of your relation! Now, I haven't any intention to lose Benjamina when she's the best cook I ever had, an' you're not as bad at milkin' as you might be. If this person comes down here or makes any fuss I'll see to it that he don't get anywheres. So if Benjamina gets frightened you tell her that I'm goin' to look after this."

"Yes'm," said Hamish.

He looked at Mrs. Egg with an awe that was soothing. She beamed and strolled out of the kitchen. Descending the steps one by one, she came to the level walk of the dooryard and marched along it toward the barns. Mr. Egg was taking a holiday with his sister, married to a dyspeptic clergyman in Chicago, and it was her duty to aid Adam by surveying the cows. She entered the barnyard and rounded the corner of the cows' palace into a group of farm hands bent above a trotting of dice on the clay. Adam looked up from this sport and said "'Lo, mamma," cheerfully.

"My gee," Mrs. Egg faltered, regarding a pile of silver before his knees, "I never saw you win a cent at any game before, Dammy!"

The giant grinned, cast the dice, and raked three dollars toward him. His eyes were black lights. He announced, "This is my lucky day, mamma!" and all the worshipful youths chuckled as he stood away from her husband's hirelings. Then he lit a cigarette and consumed half of its length in an appalling suction. The smoke jetted from his nostrils in a flood. He patted Mrs. Egg's upper chin with a thumb and said, "She gave me the air, mamma!"

"What?"

"She told me to fly my kite! She's off me! She's goin' to marry Jim Randolph. It's all flooie.—I'd like a tub of champagne an' five fried hens for supper! Mamma," said Adam, "I ain't engaged to that girl any more!" Therewith he took all the silver from his pocket and sent it in a chiming shower up the roof of the cow barn. His teeth flashed between his parted lips and dimples invaded his brown cheeks. He swung his arms restlessly and his mother thought that he would break into a dance. Adam reflected, "It's hell what happens by accident, mamma. Was a bowl of punch in the lib'ry at that dance of Judge Randolph's Christmas time that'd knock the teeth out of a horse. Had six cups. Saw this girl's hand hangin' over the banisters when I was headin' for the front door. I kissed it. Mamma, there ain't any way of tellin' a girl in this town that you don't mean anything when you kiss her. They don't understand it."

A devastating admiration of her child made Mrs. Egg's heart cavort. His manners were sublime. He lit another cigarette and stated, "Well, that's all of that." Then, wearied with much speech, he was still.

"Mercy, Dammy! This is an awful relief! Your sisters have been holdin' forth about Edith Sims bein' much more refined than God all afternoon. I was gettin' kind of scared of her.—What's that phonograph plate, lamb?"

Adam didn't answer, but ripped the envelope from the grained disk, and Mrs. Egg saw, on the advertising, "Kashmiri Song." But her thought had sunk to a profound and cooling peace; there would be no more Edith Sims. She drawled, "Edith's pretty awful sedate, Dammy. I don't think she'd have the sand to run off from—a person she didn't like, or make her own livin'."

The giant flung up his arms and made certain gestures. Hamish Saunders came hurtling from the house for orders. Adam said, "Go get me some clothes, kid—white. And shoes 'n' a cake of soap. Then come swimmin'. Put this plate with the rest. Hustle!" He ground his nose with a fist, staring after the boy, then said, "Nice kid, mamma."

"Mercy, yes, Dammy! Dammy, it's pretty ridiculous to have Benjamina and the boy eat in the kitchen, and it takes tact to keep a nice girl like that contented. I think they'd better take their meals with us, sweetheart."

He nodded and strode off among the regular files of apple and pear trees toward the aimless riverlet that watered the farm. Mrs. Egg felt hunger stir in her bulk. She plucked an apple leaf and chewed its fragrant pulp, marching up the walk. Benjamina was soberly chopping the chickens for dinner into convenient bits.

Mrs. Egg applauded her performance, saying, "We'd better have 'em fried, I think. Dammy prefers it. And when you've got time you might go get one of those very big green bottles of pear cider down in the cellar, honey. It's awful explosive stuff and Hamish hadn't better drink any. And lay the table for four, because it's pretty lonely for Dammy eatin' with me steadily.—Edith Sims busted their engagement this afternoon, by the way, though it isn't at all important."

"Isn't it?"

Mrs. Egg refreshed herself with a bit of cracker from the table and drawled, "Not a bit, dearie. I've never heard of anybody's heart breakin' under the age of thirty over a busted engagement. Dammy's pretty much relieved, though too polite to say so, and Edith'll marry

Judge Randolph's second boy, who's a very nice kid and has curly hair, although his teeth stick out some. So it don't seem to matter except to my daughters, who'll want Dammy to go into full mourning and die of sorrow. They're tearful girls, but nice. Let me show you how Dammy likes tomatoes fried when they're done with the chicken."

"Mrs. Egg," said Benjamina, "you're—a remarkable person." The slim, pale fingers twisted themselves against her dull blue frock into the likeness of a frightened white moth. She went on, "You—you never get excited."

"My gee! I haven't any patience with excitement, Benjamina. Things either go right or they go wrong. In either case, it's no good foamin' at the mouth and tryin' to kick the roof off. I'm like Dammy. I prefer to be calm," said Mrs. Egg. "As for scatterin' rays of sunshine like a Sunday-school hymn, most people don't thank anyone to do so—nor me, when I have indigestion."

"I—I feel much calmer since I've been here," Benjamina said. "It was so hot in the flat in Cleveland, and noisy. And it's very kind of you to ask Hamish and me to eat with you and Mr. Egg."

Her hands had become steadfast. She smiled a little.

"It'll be much more sociable, honey," Mrs. Egg reflected. "Even if Dammy don't talk, he likes company, havin' been in the Navy where he had lots.—Where's the biscuit flour? There's time to make some before supper."

The kitchen dimmed and Benjamina's tall body dulled into a restful shadow. She moved without noise and her pleasant voice was low. Mrs. Egg devised biscuits in comfort and smelled Adam's cigarettes in the living room. Hamish came to stimulate the making of this meal by getting his large feet in the way, and Mrs. Egg was scolding him tranquilly when the phonograph loosed a series of lazy notes. Then it sang, fervidly, of pale hands that it had loved beside some strange name.

"It's that Kashmir business," said Mrs. Egg. "Open the door, bub, so's we can hear."

The music swelled as the door opened and a circle of smoke died in the kitchen. Mrs. Egg saw Adam as a white pillar in the gloom. The machine sobbed "Where are you now? Where are you now?" with an oily sadness.

"Real touching," Mrs. Egg mentioned.

A crashing of the orchestra intervened. Then the voice cried, "Pale hands, pink-tipped, like lotus flowers that—" The words jumbled into sounds. Mrs. Egg hungrily yawned. The tenor wailed, "I would have rather felt you on my throat, crushing out life, than waving me farewell!" and the girl stirred beside the doorway, her hands in motion.

The song expired with a thin noise of violins. Adam stopped the plate. An inexplicable silence filled the house, as if this stale old melody had wakened something that listened. Then Adam lit a cigarette.

"Supper near ready, mamma?"

"Pretty near, lamb," said Mrs. Egg.

Supper was pleasant. Hamish talked buoyantly of cows. He was impressed by their stupidity and their artless qualities. Benjamina gazed at the four candles with gray eyes and smiled at nothing. Adam ate fourteen hot biscuits and three mounds of an ice cream that held fresh raspberries. He stared at the ceiling gravely, and his white shirt tightened as he breathed out the first smoke above a cup of coffee.

Then he said, "We'll go to the movies. Get your hat, Miss Saunders."

"But the dishes aren't washed!" Benjamina exclaimed.

"The kid and I'll wash 'em," Adam vouchsafed.

Mrs. Egg yawned, "Go ahead, Benjamina," and watched the girl's hands flutter as she left the green dining room.

Adam blew a ring of smoke, which drooped, dissolving about a candle. He reached across the table for the coffee pot and filled his cup, then looked at Hamish.

"What's she scared of, Kid?"

"Cousin Joe," said Hamish presently. "He's—our guardian—wants to marry her. Y'see, we have some money from dad's store. Cousin Joe's a lawyer and the bank pays him the money."

"Lived with him in Cleveland?"

Hamish groaned, "You saw where we lived! Benjy couldn't keep the place lookin' decent. He knocked his pipe out wherever he sat. But Benjy'll be twenty-one in October and the bank'll pay her the money."

"An' this Joe's a sour plum?"

"Well," said Hamish, with the manner of last justice, "he can sing pretty well."

Mrs. Egg was thinking of bed at ten o'clock when the telephone rang and the anguished voice of her oldest daughter came pouring in from Ilium: "Mamma! Dammy's got that girl in a box at the movies!"

"I'm glad," said Mrs. Egg, "that they're sitting in a box. My gee! It's hot as I ever felt it for this time of year, Fern! Benjamina's such a large person that she—"

"Oh, mamma! And it's all over town that Edith Sims is going to marry—"

"I can't pretend that I'm either surprised or sorry, Fern. As for Dammy marryin' a girl he would have had to stoop over a yard to kiss after breakfast, it never seemed a just kind of arrangement to me, although I didn't want to criticize her. The Simses are nice folks—awful refined. Mercy, but don't Dammy look well in white pants?"

"Mamma! You simply haven't any heart!"

"I'll be forty-seven in December, Fern," said Mrs. Egg. "Good night."

She drowsily ascended to her cool bedroom, where a vacuum flask of iced lemonade stood with a package of oatmeal crackers on the bedside table. In the dark she lay listening to the obliging wind that now moved in the ten acres of orchard, and sometimes she chuckled, nibbling a cracker. Finally she slept, and was wakened by Adam's voice.

"Was it a nice picture, Dammy?"

"Fair. Where's that law dictionary dad got last year, mamma?"

"It's in the pantry, under the paraffin for the preserves, sweetheart."

"Thanks," said Adam, and his feet went softly away.

Mrs. Egg resumed her slumbers composedly, and woke on the first clash of milk pails in the barnyard. Day was clear. Adam could get in the rest of the peaches and paint the garage roof without discomfort. She ate a cracker, dressing, and went down the back stairs to find Benjamina grinding coffee in a white gown that set off color in her cheeks.

"Mercy," said Mrs. Egg, "but you're up real early!"

"I don't think it can be very healthy for Mr. Egg and Hamish to wait so long for breakfast," the girl said.

"The men's cook down at the bunkhouse always has coffee for Dammy. It's a sad time that Dammy can't get himself a meal around here, honey. But it's nice to have breakfast early. I think he's hungriest in the mornin'.'"

"Isn't he always hungry?"

"Always," Mrs. Egg assured her, beginning to pare chilled peaches; "and he likes your oatmeal, I notice. Bein' Scotch by descent, you understand the stuff. You've been here ten days, and it's remarkable how you've learned what Dammy likes. If he was talkative it wouldn't take so much intelligence. A very good way is to watch his toes. If they move he likes what he's eatin'. My gee! It was easy to tell when he was little and went barefooted. He's too tactful to complain about anything."

"He said, driving down from Cleveland, that he hated talking much," Benjamina murmured.

Adam's black head showed above his blue milking shirt in the barnyard. Mrs. Egg watched the tall girl's gray eyes quicken as she gazed down the wet grass. Morning mist fairly smoked from the turf and the boles of apple trees were moist. Hamish was lugging pails to the dairy valiantly.

"The high school here," said Mrs. Egg, "is very good for the size of the town, and Hamish will be perfectly comfortable in winters. You mustn't be alarmed by my husband when he comes back from Chicago. It's a nervous habit he has of winkin' his left eye. It don't mean a thing. I'll try to get hold of some girl that's reasonably intell'gent to do waitin' on table and dusting, which is not good for your hands."

"It's very nice here," Benjamina said, still looking at the barnyard.

Mrs. Egg decided that she was a beautiful creature. Her color improved breath by breath, and her face had the look of a goddess on a coin. The vast woman ate a peach and inspected this virgin hopefully. Then the pale hands shot to Benjamina's throat and she whirled from the window. Hamish tumbled through the door, his shoes smeared with milk and his mouth dragged into a gash of fright.

"It's Cousin Joe! He's gettin' out of a buggy at the gate!"

"Gracious!" said Mrs. Egg.

She rose and walked into the veranda, smoothing her hair. The man limping up from the white gates was tall and his shoulders seemed broad. He leaned on a cane. He wore a hat made of rough rings of straw. Mrs. Egg greatly disliked him at once, and went down the steps slowly, sideways. Adam was lounging up from the barnyard and some farmhands followed him in a clump of tanned faces. Light made their eyes flash. The woman sighed. There might be a deal of angry talk before she got rid of the lame person in black. He advanced and she awaited him under the apple tree below the steps. When he approached she saw that his hair was dull brown and sleek as he took off his hat.

"Mrs. Egg?"

"I am," said Mrs. Egg.

The man smoothly bowed. He was less than six feet tall, but burly and not pale. His mouth smiled charmingly. He glanced at Adam, smoking on the steps, and twirled the cane in his hand. He said, "My name's Hume. I'm an attorney. I'm the guardian of Benjamina and Hamish Saunders, my cousin's children. They're here, I understand?"

"I understand," Mrs. Egg drawled, "that you ain't much of a guardian, and they're better off here."

Adam's voice came over her shoulder, "They're goin' to stay here."

Cold sweat rose in Mrs. Egg's clenched hands. She turned and saw Adam's nostrils rigid, yellow on his bronze face. She said, "Go in to breakfast, Dammy. I'm talkin' to this person."

Adam might lose his temper. He must go away. She looked at him for a moment, and the farm hands made new shadows on the turf, approaching curiously. Then Adam turned and walked into the kitchen.

"We're wasting time," the man said, always smoothly. "Benjy's my ward and she's going back to Cleveland with me."

"I don't see as that follows, precisely," Mrs. Egg panted.

"The nearest justice would."

"Then you'd better get the nearest justice to say it," said Mrs. Egg, "because Benjamina's perfectly well off here. As for sendin' her back to Cleveland for you to make love at in a flat—my gee!"

She felt herself impolitic and tactless in saying this, but rage had mounted. Her chins were shaking. The man's clothes smelled of pipe smoke. His collar wasn't clean. He was a dog. The kitchen door slammed. She dreaded that Adam might lose his temper and thrash this fellow. The man looked over her head.

"Here," said Adam, "get out of the way, mamma, please! Let's settle this! Come ahead, Benj'mina. He can't hurt you." He was leading the girl down the steps by a hand. Smoke welled from his nostrils and his eyes had partly shut. He brought the white girl to face her cousin and said, "Now! My name's Adam Egg. Benjamina's married to me. Show him your rings, kid."

The farm hands gasped and an Irish lad shooped. Adam undid his brown fingers from the pale hand. The big diamond and the circlet of little stones blazed below the rosy nails. Mrs. Egg put her palm on her mouth and a scream was a pain in her throat. She hadn't seen Adam married! He threw away the cigarette by a red motion of his tongue and drawled, "Go back in the house, kid!"

The man clamped a hand on his cane and said, "Without my permission!"

"She's twenty," Adam grunted, his shoulders tremulous under the thin blue shirt, "so what you goin' to do?"

Then nothing happened. Benjamina walked up the steps and stood with an arm about Hamish at the top. A farm hand lit a pipe. Mrs. Egg's heart beat horribly with the pain of having missed Adam's wedding. The man's face was getting green. He was odious, completely. He said, "Their property stays in my control!"

"The hell with their property!"

Nothing happened. The man stood poking his cane into the turf and turning the thick end among grass blades. Hamish came down one step. Then the man backed and whirled up his cane.

Mrs. Egg shrieked "Dammy!" and bruised her lip with her teeth.

The heavy cane seemed to balance a long while against the sun. Adam stood. The thing fell across his right shoulder and broke with a cracking sound. The blue shirt tore and Benjamina screamed. Adam's whole length shook and his lips were gray for a second. He slung out both hands and caught the fellow's throat. He said, "Now! You've 'saulted me with a dangerous weapon, see? Now, get out of here! Here's your witnesses! You hit me! All I've got to do is walk you in to a judge and you'll get a year, see? That's law! Get out of this! I could kill you," he drawled, "an' I will if you ain't out the gates in one minute!"

His shoulders heaved. The shirt split down his back. The man went spinning in a queer rotation along the grass, like some collapsing toy. Adam stood with his hands raised, watching. The figure stumbled twice. Then it lurched toward the white gates in a full run, and the farm hands yelled. Adam dropped his hands and ripped the shirt from his shoulder. A band of scarlet had risen on the bronze of his chest. He said thickly, "Damn if he ain't a husky! Hey, Hamish, get me some iodine, will you?"

Benjamina ran down the steps and dragged the rings from her fingers. She babbled, "Oh! Oh, Adam! What did you let him strike you for? I'm so sorry!" She thrust the rings into one of his palms and cried, "You shouldn't have let him hit you! He's so strong!"

"What was I goin' to say if he said to show any weddin' certificate? If he hit me it was assault, an' I could get rid of him."

Mrs. Egg wailed, "Then you ain't married, Dammy?"

"No."

Adam leaned on the apple tree and stared at Benjamina, turning the rings in his hand. After a moment the girl flushed and walked away into the orchard of rustling boughs. A morning wind made the giant's torn shirt flap. He sent his eyes to the gaping hired men and drawled "What about those cows?"

Feet thudded off on the grass. Hamish came bounding down the steps with a bottle of iodine and a handkerchief.

"My gee, Dammy," said Mrs. Egg, grasping the bottle, "if your sisters have the nerve to say you're tactless after this I'll— Sit down, lamb! Oh, Dammy, how can you think as fast as that?"

Adam lit a cigarette and blew smoke through his nostrils. His face was again blank and undisturbed. He asked, "Peaches for breakfast?"

"Anything you want, lamb! Benjamina has oatmeal ready."

He clicked the rings in his hand and his feet wriggled in the moccasins. Then he said "Mamma," strangely.

"Yes, Dammy."

"Mamma, I've put Miss Saunders in a hell of a position, sayin' we're married."

"That's so, Dammy. It'll be all over town in no time."

Adam arose from the grass and examined his mother for a whole minute. His nostrils shook somewhat. He took the engagement ring from one palm and handed it to Hamish, ordering, "Kid, you go take that to your sister and tell her it's with my compliments. I hate talkin'."

The boy's red hair went flashing under the trees. Mrs. Egg watched him halt by his sister, who was wiping her eyes beside a trunk. They conferred. Soon Hamish turned about and began to make swift signs with his arms.

Adam said, "Good enough.—I guess I'll call her Ben." He lit his next cigarette and walked up the steps.

Mrs. Egg screamed, "Dammy! Ain't you goin' to go kiss her?"

Adam's eyes opened on his mother in alarm. He said, "I'm thirsty, mamma. And I've got to get a fresh shirt. Couldn't kiss anybody in this one. It wouldn't be polite."

Then he waved his cigarette to his new love and slammed the kitchen door behind him.

The Tremendous Adventures of Major Brown

G. K. CHESTERTON

> In England, until after the last war, there was a famous magazine called the Strand magazine. I remember reading the stories of G. K. Chesterton, Conan Doyle, and others in it.
>
> This one is by Chesterton, who is best known as the author of "The Innocence of Father Brown," "The Wisdom of Father Brown," etc., which, in my opinion, are the best detective stories ever written. Try sometime "Queer Feet" and "The Hammer of God" and "The Invisible Man" (not the H. G. Wells one, the Chesterton one). I think you will want to read the rest of them.
>
> I had some trouble finding this story, which I remember from my late teens. It is long, but mightily entertaining, and Chesterton is very skillful at throwing sand in your eyes and making it difficult to guess the ending.
>
> Apart from his books, of which I would particularly recommend Man Alive, he also wrote some hearty and funny poetry.

Rabelais, or his wild illustrator, Gustave Doré, must have had something to do with the designing of the things called flats in England and America. There is something entirely Gargantuan in the idea of economizing space by piling houses on top of each other, front doors and all. And in the chaos and complexity of those perpendicular streets anything may dwell or happen, and it is in one of them, I believe, that the inquirer may find the offices of the Club of Queer Trades. It may be thought at the first glance that the name would attract and startle the passer-by, but nothing attracts or startles in these dim, immense hives. The passer-by is only looking for his own melancholy destination of the Montenegro Shipping Agency or the London office of the *Rutland Sentinel*, and passes through the twilight passages as one passes through the twilight corridors of a dream.

If the thugs set up a Strangers' Assassination Company in one of the great buildings in Norfolk Street, and sent in a mild man in spectacles to answer inquiries, no inquiries would be made. And the Club of Queer Trades reigns in a great edifice hidden like a fossil in a mighty cliff of fossils.

The nature of this society, such as we afterwards discovered it to be, is soon and simply told. It is an eccentric and Bohemian club, of which the absolute condition of membership lies in this, that the candidate must have invented the method by which he earns his living. It must be an entirely new trade. The exact definition of this requirement is given in the two principal rules. First, it must not be a mere application or variation of an existing trade. Thus, for instance, the club would not admit an insurance agent simply because, instead of insuring men's furniture against being burned in a fire, he insured, let us say, their trousers against being torn by a mad dog. The principle (as Sir Bradcock Burnaby-Bradcock, in the extraordinarily eloquent and soaring speech to the club on the occasion of the question being raised in the Stormby Smith affair, said wittily and keenly) is the same. Secondly, the trade must be a genuine commercial source of income, the support of its inventor. Thus the club would not receive a man simply because he chose to pass his days collecting broken sardine tins, unless he could drive a roaring trade in them. Professor Chick made that quite clear. And when one remembers what Professor Chick's own new trade was, one doesn't know whether to laugh or cry.

The discovery of this strange society was a curiously refreshing thing; to realize that there were ten new trades in the world was like looking at the first ship or the first plough. It made a man feel what he should feel, that he was still in the childhood of the world. That I should have come at last upon so singular a body was, I may say without vanity, not altogether singular, for I have a mania for belonging to as many societies as possible. I may be said to collect clubs, and I have accumulated a vast and fantastic variety of specimens ever since. In my audacious youth I collected the Athenaeum. At some future day, perhaps, I may tell tales of some of the other bodies to which I have belonged. I will recount the doings of the Dead Man's Shoes Society (that superficially immoral, but darkly justifiable communion); I will explain the curious origin of the Cat and Christian, the name of which has been so shamefully misinterpreted; and the world shall know at least why the Institute of Typewriters coalesced with the Red Tulip League. Of the Ten Teacups, of course, I dare not say a word. The first of my revelations, at any rate, shall be concerned with the Club of Queer Trades, which, as I have said, was one of this class, one which I was almost bound to come across sooner or later, because of my singular hobby. The wild youth of the metropolis call me facetiously "The King of Clubs." They also called me "The Cherub," in allusion to the roseate and youthful appearance I have presented in my declining years. I only hope the spirits in the better world have as good dinners as I have. But the finding of the Club of Queer Trades has one very curious thing about it. The most curious thing about it is that it was not discovered by me; it was discovered by my friend Basil Grant, a stargazer, a mystic, and a man who scarcely stirred out of his attic.

Very few people knew anything of Basil; not because he was in the least unsociable, for if a man out of the street had walked into his rooms he would have kept him talking till morning. Few people knew him, because, like all poets, he could do without them; he welcomed a human face as he might welcome a sudden blend of color in a sunset; but he no more felt the need of going out to parties than he felt the need of altering the sunset clouds. He lived in a queer and comfortable garret in the roofs of Lambeth. He was surrounded by a chaos of things that were in odd contrast to the slums around him: old, fantastic books, swords, armor—the whole dust-hole of romanticism. But his face, amid all these quixotic relics, appeared curiously keen and modern—a powerful, legal face. And no one but I knew who he was.

Long ago as it is, every one remembers the terrible and grotesque scene that occurred in ———, when one of the most acute and forcible of the English judges suddenly went mad on the bench. I had my own view of that occurrence; but about the facts themselves there is no question at all. For some months, indeed for some years, people had detected something curious in the judge's conduct. He seemed to have lost interest in the law, in which he had been, beyond expression, brilliant and terrible as a K.C., and to be occupied in giving personal and moral advice to the people concerned. He talked more like a priest or a doctor, and a very outspoken one at that. The first thrill was probably given when he said to a man who had attempted a crime of passion: "I sentence you to three years' imprisonment, under the firm, and solemn, and God-given conviction that what you require is three months at the sea-side." He accused criminals from the bench, not so much of their obvious legal crimes, but of things that had never been heard of in a court of justice, monstrous egoism, lack of humor, and morbidity deliberately encouraged. Things came to a head in that celebrated diamond case in which the prime-minister himself, that brilliant patrician, had to come forward, gracefully and reluctantly, to give evidence against his valet. After the detailed life of the household had been thoroughly exhibited, the judge requested the premier again to step forward, which he did with quiet dignity. The judge then said, in a sudden, grating voice: "Get a new soul. That thing's not fit for a dog. Get a new soul." All this, of course, in the eyes of the sagacious, was premonitory of that melancholy and farcical day when his wits actually deserted him in open court. It was a libel case between two very eminent and powerful financiers, against both of whom charges of considerable defalcation were brought. The case was long and complex; the advocates were long and eloquent; but at last, after weeks of work and rhetoric, the time came for the great judge to give a summing-up; and one of his celebrated masterpieces of lucidity and pulverizing logic was eagerly looked for. He had spoken very little during the prolonged affair, and he looked sad and lowering at the end of it. He was silent for a few moments, and then burst into a stentorian song. His remarks (as reported) were as follows:

> Oh Rowty-owty tiddly-owty
> Tiddly-owty tiddly-owty
> Highty-ighty tiddly-ighty
> Tiddly-ighty ow.

He then retired from public life and took the garret in Lambeth.

I was sitting there one evening, about six o'clock, over a glass of that gorgeous Burgundy which he kept behind a pile of black-letter folios; he was striding about the room, fingering, after a habit of his, one of the great swords in his collection; the red glare of the strong fire struck his square features and his fierce gray hair; his blue eyes were even unusually full of dreams, and he had opened his mouth to speak dreamily, when the door was flung open, and a pale, fiery man, with red hair and a huge furred overcoat, swung himself panting into the room.

"Sorry to bother you, Basil," he gasped. "I took a liberty—made an appointment here with a man—a client—in five minutes—I beg your pardon, sir," and he gave me a bow of apology.

Basil smiled at me. "You didn't know," he said, "that I had a practical brother. This is Rupert Grant, Esquire, who can and does all there is to be done. Just as I was a failure at one thing, he is a success at everything. I remember him as a journalist, a house-agent, a naturalist, an inventor, a publisher, a school-master, a—what are you now, Rupert?"

"I am and have been for some time," said Rupert, with some dignity, "a private detective, and there's my client."

A loud rap at the door had cut him short, and, on permission being given, the door was thrown sharply open and a stout, dapper man walked swiftly into the room, set his silk hat with a clap on the table, and said, "Good-evening, gentlemen," with a stress on the last syllable that somehow marked him out as a martinet, military, literary, and social. He had a large head streaked with black and gray, and an abrupt black mustache, which gave him a look of fierceness which was contradicted by his sad, sea-blue eyes.

Basil immediately said to me, "Let us come into the next room, Gully," and was moving towards the door, but the stranger said:

"Not at all. Friends remain. Assistance possibly."

The moment I heard him speak I remembered who he was, a certain Major Brown I had met years before in Basil's society. I had forgotten altogether the black, dandified figure and the large, solemn head, but I remembered the peculiar speech, which consisted of only saying about a quarter of each sentence, and that sharply, like the crack of a gun. I do not know, it may have come from giving orders to troops.

Major Brown was a V.C., and an able and distinguished soldier, but he was anything but a warlike person. Like many among the iron men who recovered British India, he was a man with the natural belief and tastes of an old maid. In his dress he was dapper and yet demure; in his habits he was precise to the point of the exact adjustment of a teacup. One enthusiasm he had, which was of the nature of a religion—the cultivation of pansies. And when he talked about his collection his blue eyes glittered like a child's at a new toy, the eyes that had remained untroubled when the troops were roaring victory round Roberts at Candahar.

"Well, major," said Rupert Grant, with a lordly heartiness, flinging himself into a chair, "what is the matter with you?"

"Yellow pansies. Coal-cellar. P. G. Northover," said the major, with righteous indignation.

We glanced at each other with inquisitiveness. Basil, who had his eyes shut in his abstracted way, said, simply:

"I beg your pardon."

"Fact is. Street, you know, man, pansies. On wall. Death to me. Something. Preposterous."

We shook our heads gently. Bit by bit, and mainly by the seemingly sleepy assistance of Basil Grant, we pieced together the major's fragmentary but excited narration. It would be infamous to submit the reader to what we endured; therefore I will tell the story of Major Brown in my own words. But the reader must imagine the scene. The eyes of Basil closed as in a trance, after his habit, and the eyes of Rupert and myself getting rounder and rounder as we listened to one of the most astounding stories in the world from the lips of the little man in black, sitting bolt upright in his chair and talking like a telegram.

Major Brown was, I have said, a successful soldier, but by no means an enthusiastic one. So far from regretting his retirement on half-pay, it was with delight that he took a small, neat villa, very like a doll's house, and devoted the rest of his life to pansies and weak tea. The thought that battles were over when he had once hung up his sword in the little front hall (along with two patent stewpots and a bad water-color), and betaken himself instead to wielding the rake in his little sunlit garden, was to him like having come into a harbor in heaven. He was Dutch-like and precise in his taste in gardening, and had, perhaps, some tendency to drill his flowers like soldiers. He was one of those men who are capable of putting four umbrellas in the stand rather than three, so that two may lean one way and two another; he saw life like a pattern in a free-hand drawing-book. And assuredly he would not have believed, or even understood, any one who had told him that within a few yards of his brick paradise he was destined to be caught in a whirlpool of incredible adventures such as he had never seen or dreamed of in the horrible jungle or the heart of battle.

One certain bright and windy afternoon, the major, attired in his usual faultless manner, had set out for his usual constitutional. In crossing from one great residential thoroughfare to another, he happened to pass along one of those aimless-looking lanes which lie along the back-garden walls of a row of mansions, and which in their empty and discolored appearance give one an odd sensation as of being behind the scenes of a theatre. But mean and sulky as the scene might be in the eyes of most of us, it was not altogether so in the major's, for along the coarse gravel footway was coming a thing which was to him what the passing of a religious procession is to a devout person. A large, heavy man, with fish-blue eyes and a ring of irradiating red beard, was pushing before him a barrow which was ablaze with incomparable flowers. There were splendid specimens of almost every order, but the major's own favorite pansies predominated. The major stopped and fell into conversation, and then into bargaining. He treated the man after the manner of collectors and other mad men— that is to say, he carefully and with a sort of anguish selected the best roots from the less excellent, praised some, disparaged others, made a subtle scale ranging from a thrilling worth and rarity to a degraded insignificance, and then bought them all. The man was just pushing off his barrow when he stopped and came close to the major.

"I'll tell you what, sir," he said. "If you're interested in them things, you just get on to that wall."

"On the wall!" cried the scandalized major, whose conventional soul quailed within him at the thought of such fantastic trespass.

"Finest show of yellow pansies in England in that there garden, sir," hissed the tempter. "I'll help you up, sir."

How it happened no one will ever know, but that positive enthusiasm of the major's life triumphed over all its negative traditions, and with an easy leap and swing that showed that he was in no need of physical assistance, he stood on the wall at the end of the strange garden. The second after, the flapping of the frock-coat at his knees made him feel inexpressibly a fool. But the next instant all such trifling sentiments were swallowed up by the most appalling shock of surprise the old soldier had ever felt in all his bold and wandering existence. His eyes fell upon the garden, and there across a large bed in the centre of the lawn was a vast pattern of pansies; they were splendid flowers, but for once it was not their horticultural aspects that Major Brown beheld, for the pansies were arranged in gigantic capital letters so as to form the sentence

DEATH TO MAJOR BROWN

A kindly looking old man with white whiskers was watering them.

Brown looked sharply back at the road behind him; the man with the barrow had suddenly vanished. Then he looked again at the lawn with its incredible inscription. Another man might have thought he had gone mad, but Brown did not. When romantic ladies gushed over his V.C. and his military exploits, he sometimes felt himself to be a painfully prosaic person, but by the same token he knew he was incurably sane. Another man, again, might have thought himself a victim of a passing practical joke, but Brown could not easily believe this. He knew from his own quaint learning that the garden arrangement was an elaborate and expensive one; he thought it extravagantly improbable that any one would pour out money like water for a joke against him. Having no explanation whatever to offer, he admitted the fact to himself, like a clear-headed man, and waited as he would have done in the presence of a man with six legs.

At this moment the stout old man with white whiskers looked up, and the watering-can fell from his hand, shooting a swirl of water down the gravel path.

"Who on earth are you?" he gasped, trembling violently.

"I am Major Brown," said that individual, who was always cool in the hour of action.

The old man gaped helplessly like some monstrous fish. At last he stammered wildly, "Come down—come down here!"

"At your service," said the major, and alighted at a bound on the grass beside him, without disarranging his silk hat.

The old man turned his broad back and set off at a sort of waddling run towards the house, followed with swift steps by the major.

His guide led him through the back passages of a gloomy but gorgeously appointed house, until they reached the door of the front room. Then the old man turned with a face of apoplectic terror dimly showing in the twilight.

"For Heaven's sake," he said, "don't mention jackals."

Then he threw open the door, releasing a burst of red lamplight, and ran down-stairs with a clatter.

The major stepped into a rich, glowing room, full of red-copper and peacock and purple hangings, hat in hand. He had the finest manners in the world, and, though mystified, was not in the least embarrassed to see that the only occupant was a lady, sitting by the window, looking out.

"Madam," he said, bowing simply, "I am Major Brown."

"Sit down," said the lady; but she did not turn her head.

She was a graceful, green-clad figure, with fiery red hair and a flavor of Bedford Park. "You have come, I suppose," she said mournfully, "to tax me about the hateful title-deeds."

"I have come, madam," he said, "to know what is the matter—to know why my name is written across your garden. Not amicably, either."

He spoke grimly, for the thing had hit him. It is impossible to describe the effect produced on the mind by that quiet and sunny garden scene, the frame for a stunning and brutal personality. The evening air was still, and the grass was golden in the place where the little flowers he studied cried to Heaven for his blood.

"You know I must not turn round," said the lady; "every afternoon till the stroke of six I must keep my face turned to the street."

Some queer and unusual inspiration made the prosaic soldier resolute to accept these outrageous riddles without surprise.

"It is almost six," he said; and even as he spoke the barbaric copper clock upon the wall clanged the first stroke of the hour. At the sixth the lady sprang up and turned on the major one of the queerest and yet most attractive faces he had ever seen in his life—open and yet tantalizing, the face of an elf.

"That makes the third year I have waited," she cried. "This is an anniversary. The waiting almost makes one wish the frightful thing would happen once and for all."

And even as she spoke a sudden rending cry broke the stillness. From low down on the pavement of the dim street (it was already twilight) a voice cried out with a raucous and merciless distinctness:

"Major Brown, Major Brown, where does the jackal dwell?"

Brown was decisive and silent in action. He strode to the front door and looked out. There was no sign of life in the blue gloaming of the street, where one or two street lamps were beginning to light their lemon sparks. On returning he found the lady in green trembling.

"It is the end," she cried, with shaking lips; "it may be death for both of us. Whenever—"

But even as she spoke her speech was cloven by another hoarse proclamation from the dark street, again horribly articulate.

"Major Brown, Major Brown, how did the jackal die?"

Brown dashed out of the door and down the steps, but again he was frustrated; there was no figure in sight, and the street was far too long and empty for the shouter to have run away. Even the rational major was a little shaken as he returned at a certain time to the drawing-room. Scarcely had he done so than the terrific voice came:

"Major Brown, Major Brown, where did—"

Brown was in the street almost at a bound, and he was in time— in time to see something which at first glance froze the blood. The cries appeared to come from a decapitated head resting on the pavement.

The next moment the pale major understood. It was the head of a man thrust through the coal-hole in the street. The next moment, again, it had vanished, and Major Brown turned to the lady. "Where's your coal-cellar?" he said, and stepped out into the passage.

She looked at him with wild, gray eyes. "You will not go down," she cried, "alone, into the dark hole with that beast?"

"Is this the way?" replied Brown, and descended the kitchen stairs three at a time. He flung open the door of a black cavity and stepped in, feeling in his pocket for matches. As his right hand was thus occupied, a pair of great, slimy hands came out of the darkness, hands clearly belonging to a man of gigantic stature, and seized him by the back of the head. They forced him down, down in the suffocating darkness, a brutal image of destiny. But the major's head, though upside-down, was perfectly clear and intellectual. He gave quietly under the pressure until he had slid down almost to his hands and knees. Then, finding the knees of the invisible monster within a foot of him, he simply put out one of his long, bony, and skilful hands, and, gripping the leg by a muscle, pulled it off the ground, and laid the huge, living man with a crash along the floor. He strove to rise, but Brown was on top like a cat. They rolled over and over. Big as the man was, he had evidently now no desire but to escape; he made sprawls hither and thither to get past the major to the door, but that tenacious person had him hard by the coat-collar, and hung with the other hand to a beam. At length there came a strain in holding back this human bull, a strain under which Brown expected his hand to rend and part from the arm. But something else rent and parted—

and the dim, fat figure of the giant vanished out of the cellar, leaving the torn coat in the major's hand, the only fruit of his adventure and the only clew to the mystery. For when he went up and out at the front door the lady, the rich hangings, and the whole equipment of the house had disappeared. It had only bare boards and whitewashed walls.

"The lady was in the conspiracy, of course," said Rupert, nodding.

Major Brown turned brick-red. "I beg your pardon," he said. "I think not."

Rupert raised his eyebrows and looked at him for a moment, but said nothing. When next he spoke he asked:

"Was there anything in the pockets of the coat?"

"There was sevenpence halfpenny in coppers and a threepenny-bit," said the major, carefully; "there was a cigarette-holder, a piece of string, and this letter," and he laid it on the table. It ran as follows:

> Dear Mr. Plover,—I am annoyed to hear that some delay has occurred in the arrangements re Major Brown. Please see that he is attacked as per arrangement to-morrow. The coal-cellar, of course.
>
> Yours faithfully,
> P. G. Northover.

Rupert Grant was leaning forward listening with hawklike eyes. He cut in:

"Is it dated from anywhere?"

"No—oh yes!" replied Brown, glancing upon the paper—"14 Tanner's Court, North—"

Rupert sprang up and struck his hands together.

"Then why are we hanging here? Let's get along. Basil, lend me your revolver."

Basil was staring into the embers like a man in a trance; and it was some time before he answered:

"I don't think you'll need it."

"Perhaps not," said Rupert, getting into his fur coat. "One never knows. But going down a dark court to see criminals—"

"Do you think they are criminals?" asked his brother.

Rupert laughed stoutly. "Giving orders to a subordinate to strangle a harmless stranger in a coal-cellar may strike you as a very blameless experiment, but—"

"Do you think they wanted to strangle the major?" asked Basil, in the same distant and monotonous voice.

"My dear fellow, you've been asleep. Look at the letter."

"I am looking at the letter," said the mad judge, calmly; though, as a matter of fact, he was looking at the fire. "I don't think it's the sort of letter one criminal would write to another."

"My dear boy, you are glorious!" cried Rupert, turning round, with laughter in his bright blue eyes. "Your methods amaze me. Why, there *is* the letter. It *is* written, and it does give orders for a crime. You might as well say that the Nelson Column was not at all the sort of thing that was likely to be set up in Trafalgar Square."

Basil Grant shook all over with a sort of silent laughter, but did not otherwise move.

"That's rather good," he said; "but, of course, logic like that's not what is really wanted. It's a question of spiritual atmosphere. It's not a criminal letter."

"It is. It's a matter of fact," cried the other, in an agony of reasonableness.

"Facts," murmured Basil, like one mentioning some strange, far-off animals—"how facts obscure the truth. I may be silly—in fact, I'm off my head—but I never could believe in that man—what's his name, in those capital stories?—Sherlock Holmes. Every detail points to something, certainly; but generally to the wrong thing. Facts point in all directions, it seems to me, like the thousands of twigs on a tree. It's only the life of the tree that has unity and goes up—only the green blood that springs, like a fountain, at the stars."

"But what the deuce else can the letter be but criminal?"

"We have eternity to stretch our legs in," replied the mystic. "It can be an infinity of things. I haven't seen any of them—I've only seen the letter. I look at that, and say it's not criminal."

"Then what's the origin of it?"

"I haven't the vaguest idea."

"Then why don't you accept the ordinary explanation?"

Basil continued for a little to glare at the coals, and seemed collecting his thoughts in a humble and even painful way. Then he said:

"Suppose you went out into the moonlight. Suppose you passed through silent, silvery streets and squares until you came into an open and deserted space set with a few monuments, and you beheld one dressed as a ballet-girl dancing in the argent glimmer. And suppose you looked and saw it was a man disguised. And suppose you looked again and saw it was Lord Kitchener. What would you think?"

He paused a moment and went on:

"You could not adopt the ordinary explanation. The ordinary explanation of putting on singular clothes is that you look nice in them; you would not think that Lord Kitchener dressed up like a ballet-girl out of ordinary personal vanity. You would think it much more likely that he inherited a dancing madness from a great-grandmother, or had been hypnotized at a seance, or threatened by a secret society with death if he refused the ordeal. With Baden-Powell, say, it might be a bet—but not with Kitchener. I should know all that, because in my public days I knew him quite well. So I know that letter quite well, and criminals quite well. It's not a criminal's letter. It's all atmospheres." And he closed his eyes and passed his hand over his forehead.

Rupert and the major were regarding him with a mixture of respect and pity. The former said:

"Well, I'm going, anyhow, and shall continue to think—until your spiritual mystery turns up—that a man who sends a note recommending a crime—that is, actually a crime that is actually carried out, at least tentatively, is, in all probability, a little casual in his moral tastes. Can I have that revolver?"

"Certainly," said Basil, getting up. "But I am coming with you." And he flung an old cape or cloak round him and took a sword-stick from the corner.

"You!" said Rupert, with some surprise, "you scarcely ever leave your hole to look at anything on the face of the earth."

Basil fitted on a formidable old white hat.

"I scarcely ever," he said, with an unconscious and colossal arrogance, "hear of anything on the face of the earth that I do not understand at once, without going to see it."

And he led the way out into the purple night.

We four swung along the flaring Lambeth streets, across Westminster Bridge, and along the Embankment in the direction of that part of Fleet Street which contained Tanner's Court. The erect, black figure of Major Brown, seen from behind, was a quaint contrast to the houndlike stoop and flapping mantle of young Rupert Grant, who adopted, with childlike delight, all the dramatic poses of the detective of fiction. The finest among his many fine qualities was his boyish appetite for the color and poetry of London. Basil, who walked behind, with his face turned blindly to the stars, had the look of a somnambulist.

Rupert paused at the corner of Tanner's Court, with a quiver of delight at danger, and gripped Basil's revolver in his great-coat pocket.

"Shall we go in now?" he asked.

"Not get police?" asked Major Brown, glancing sharply up and down the street.

"I am not sure," answered Rupert, knitting his brows. "Of course, it's quite clear, the thing's all crooked. But there are three of us, and—"

"I shouldn't get the police," said Basil, in a queer voice. Rupert glanced at him and stared hard.

"Basil," he cried, "you're trembling. What's the matter—are you afraid?"

"Cold, perhaps," said the major, eying him. There was no doubt that he was shaking.

At last, after a few moments' scrutiny, Rupert broke into a curse.

"You're laughing," he cried. "I know that confounded, silent, shaky laugh of yours. What the deuce is the amusement, Basil? Here we are, all three of us, within a yard of a den of ruffians—"

"But I shouldn't call the police," said Basil. "We four heroes are quite equal to a host," and he continued to quake with his mysterious mirth.

Rupert turned with impatience and strode swiftly down the court, the rest of us following. When he reached the door of No. 14, he turned abruptly, the revolver glittering in his hand.

"Stand close," he said, in the voice of a commander. "The scoundrel may be attempting an escape at this moment. We must fling open the door and rush in."

The four of us cowered instantly under the archway, rigid, except for the old judge and his convulsion of merriment.

"Now," hissed Rupert Grant, turning his pale face and burning eyes suddenly over his shoulder, "when I say 'Four,' follow me with a rush. If I say 'Hold him,' pin the fellows down, whoever they are. If I say 'Stop,' stop. I shall say that if there are more than three. If they attack us I shall empty my revolver on them. Basil, have your sword-stick ready. Now—one, two, three, four!"

With the sound of the word the door burst open, and we fell into the room like an invasion, only to stop dead.

The room, which was an ordinary and neatly appointed office, appeared, at the first glance, to be empty. But on a second and more careful glance we saw, seated behind a very large desk with pigeon-holes and drawers of bewildering multiplicity, a small man with a black, waxed mustache and the air of a very average clerk, writing hard. He looked up as we came to a stand-still.

"Did you knock?" he asked, pleasantly. "I am sorry if I did not hear. What can I do for you?"

There was a doubtful pause, and then, by general consent, the major himself, the victim of the outrage, stepped forward.

The letter was in his hand, and he looked unusually grim.

"Is your name P. G. Northover?" he asked.

"That is my name," replied the other, smiling.

"I think," said Major Brown, with an increase in the dark glow of his face, "that this letter was written by you." And with a loud clap he struck open the letter on the desk with his clinched fist. The man called Northover looked at it with unaffected interest and merely nodded.

"Well, sir," said the major, breathing hard, "what about that?"

"What about it, precisely?" said the man with the mustache.

"I am Major Brown," said that gentleman, sternly.

Northover bowed. "Pleased to meet you, sir. What have you to say to me?"

"Say!" cried the major, loosing a sudden tempest; "why, I want this confounded thing settled. I want—"

"Certainly, sir," said Northover, jumping up, with a slight elevation of the eyebrows. "Will you take a chair for a moment?" And he pressed an electric bell just above him, which thrilled and tinkled in a room beyond. The major put his hand on the back of the chair offered him, but stood chafing and beating the floor with his polished boot.

The next moment an inner glass door was opened and a fair, weedy, young man in a frock-coat entered from within.

"Mr. Hopson," said Northover, "this is Major Brown. Will you please finish that thing for him I gave you this morning and bring it in?"

"Yes, sir," said Mr. Hopson, and vanished like lightning.

"You will excuse me, gentlemen," said the egregious Northover, with his radiant smile, "if I continue to work until Mr. Hopson is ready. I have some books that must be cleared up before I get away on my holiday to-morrow. And we all like a whiff of the country, don't we? Ha! ha!"

The criminal took up his pen with a childlike laugh, and a silence ensued—a placid and busy silence on the part of Mr. P. G. Northover; a raging silence on the part of everybody else.

At length the scratching of Northover's pen in the stillness was mingled with a knock at the door, almost simultaneous with the turning of the handle, and Mr. Hopson came in again with the same silent rapidity, placed a paper before his principal, and disappeared again.

The man at the desk pulled and twisted his spiky mustache for a few moments as he ran his eye up and down the paper presented to him. He took up his pen with a slight, instantaneous frown and altered something, muttering—"Careless." Then he read it again with the same impenetrable reflectiveness, and finally handed it to the frantic Brown, whose hand was beating the devil's tattoo on the back of the chair.

"I think you will find that all right, major," he said, briefly.

The major looked at it; whether he found it all right or not will appear later, but he found it like this:

Major Brown to P. G. Northover

	£	s.	d.
January 1, to account rendered	5	6	0
May 9, to potting and embedding of 200 pansies	2	0	0
To cost of trolley with flowers	0	15	0
To hiring of man with trolley	0	5	0
To hire of house and garden for one day	1	0	0
To furnishing of room in peacock curtains, copper ornaments, etc.	3	0	0
To salary of Miss Jameson	1	0	0
To salary of Mr. Plover	1	0	0
Total	£14	6	0

A remittance will oblige.

"What," said Mr. Brown, after a dead pause, and with eyes that seemed slowly rising out of his head. "What in Heaven's name is this?"

"What is it?" repeated Northover, cocking his eyebrow with amusement. "It's your account, of course."

"My account!" The major's ideas appeared to be in a vague stampede. "My account! And what have I got to do with it?"

"Well," said Northover, laughing outright, "naturally I prefer you to pay it."

The major's hand was still resting on the back of the chair as the words came. He scarcely stirred otherwise, but he lifted the chair bodily into the air with one hand and hurled it at Northover's head.

The legs crashed against the desk, so that Northover only got a blow on the elbow as he sprang up with clinched fists, only to be seized by the united rush of the rest of us. The chair had fallen clattering on the empty floor.

"Let me go, you scamps," he shouted. "Let me—"

"Stand still," cried Rupert, authoritatively. "Major Brown's action is excusable. The abominable crime you have attempted—"

"A customer has a perfect right," said Northover hotly, "to question an alleged overcharge, but, confound it all, not to throw furniture."

"What, in God's name, do you mean by your customers and overcharges?" shrieked Major Brown, whose keen feminine nature, steady in pain or danger, became almost hysterical in the presence of a long and exasperating mystery. "Who are you? I've never seen you or your insolent tomfool bills. I know one of your cursed brutes tried to choke me—"

"Mad," said Northover, gazing blankly round—"all of them mad. I didn't know they travelled in quartets."

"Enough of this prevarication," said Rupert; "your crimes are discovered. A policeman is stationed at the corner of the court. Though only a private detective myself, I will take the responsibility of telling you that anything you say—"

"Mad," repeated Northover, with a weary air.

And at this moment, for the first time, there struck in among them the strange, sleepy voice of Basil Grant.

"Major Brown," he said, "may I ask you a question?"

The major turned his head with an increased bewilderment.

"You?" he cried; "certainly, Mr. Grant."

"Can you tell me," said the mystic, with sunken head and lowering brow, as he traced a pattern in the dust with his sword-stick—"can you tell me what was the name of the man who lived in your house before you?"

The unhappy major was only faintly more disturbed by this last and futile irrelevancy, and he answered, vaguely:

"Yes, I think so; a man named Gurney something—a name with a hyphen—Gurney-Brown; that was it."

"And when did the house change hands?" said Basil, looking up sharply. His strange eyes were burning brilliantly.

"I came in last month," said the major.

And at the mere word the criminal Northover suddenly fell into his great office chair and shouted with a volleying laughter.

"Oh! it's too perfect—it's too exquisite," he gasped, beating the arms with his fists. He was laughing deafeningly; Basil Grant was laughing voicelessly; and the rest of us only felt that our heads were like weathercocks in a whirlwind.

"Confound it, Basil," cried Rupert, stamping. "If you don't want me to go mad and blow your metaphysical brains out, tell me what all this means?"

Northover rose.

"Permit me, sir, to explain," he said. "And, first of all, permit me to apologize to you, Major Brown, for a most abominable and unpardonable blunder, which has caused you menace and inconvenience, in which, if you will allow me to say so, you have behaved with astonishing courage and dignity. Of course you need not trouble about the bill. We will stand the loss." And, tearing the paper across, he flung the halves into the wastepaper basket and bowed.

Poor Brown's face was still a picture of distraction. "But I don't even begin to understand," he cried. "What bill? what blunder? what loss?"

Mr. P. G. Northover advanced in the centre of the room thoughtfully and with a great deal of unconscious dignity. On closer consideration there were apparent about him other things besides a screwed mustache, especially a lean, sallow face, hawklike, and not without a careworn intelligence. Then he looked up abruptly.

"Do you know where you are, major?" he said.

"God knows I don't," said the warrior, with fervor.

"You are standing," replied Northover, "in the office of the Adventure and Romance Agency, Limited."

"And what's that?" blankly inquired Brown.

The man of business leaned over the back of the chair and fixed his dark eyes on the other's face.

"Major," said he, "did you ever, as you walked along the empty street upon some idle afternoon, feel the utter hunger for something to happen—something, in the splendid words of Walt Whitman: 'Something pernicious and dread; something far removed from a puny and pious life; something unproved; something in a trance; something loosed from its anchorage, and driving free.' Did you ever feel that?"

"Certainly not," said the major, shortly.

"Then I must explain with more elaboration," said Mr. Northover, with a sigh. "The Adventure and Romance Agency has been started to meet a great modern desire. On every side, in conversation and in literature, we hear of the desire for a larger theatre of events—for something to waylay us and lead us splendidly astray. Now the man who feels this desire for a varied life pays a yearly or a quarterly sum to the Adventure and Romance Agency; in return, the Adventure and Romance Agency undertakes to surround him with startling and weird events. As a man is leaving his front door, an excited sweep approaches him and assures him of a plot against his life; he gets into a cab, and is driven to an opium den; he receives a mysterious telegram or a dramatic visit, and is immediately in a vortex of incidents. A very picturesque and moving story is first written by one of the staff of distinguished novelists who are at present hard at work in the adjoining room. Yours, Major Brown (designed by our Mr. Grigsby), I consider peculiarly forcible and pointed; it is almost a pity you did not see the end of it. I need scarcely explain further the monstrous mistake. Your predecessor in your present house, Mr. Gurney-Brown, was a subscriber to our agency, and our foolish clerks, ignoring alike the dignity of the hyphen and the glory of military rank, positively imagined that Major Brown and Mr. Gurney-Brown were the same person. Thus you were suddenly hurled into the middle of another man's story."

"How on earth does the thing work?" asked Rupert Grant, with bright and fascinated eyes.

"We believe that we are doing a noble work," said Northover, warmly. "It has continually struck us that there is no element in modern life that is more lamentable than the fact that the modern man has to seek all artistic existence in a sedentary state. If he wishes to float into fairyland, he reads a book; if he wishes to dash into the thick of battle, he reads a book; if he wishes to soar into heaven, he reads a book; if he wishes to slide down the banisters, he reads a book. We give him these visions, but we give him exercise at the same time, the necessity of leaping from wall to wall, of fighting strange gentlemen, of running down long streets from pursuers—all healthy and pleasant exercises. We give him a glimpse of that great morning world of Robin Hood or the knights-errant, when one great game was played under the splendid sky. We give him back his childhood, that godlike time when we can act stories, be our own heroes, and at the same instant dance and dream."

Basil gazed at him curiously. The most singular psychological discovery had been reserved to the end, for as the little businessman ceased speaking he had the blazing eyes of a fanatic.

Major Brown received the explanation with complete simplicity and good-humor.

"Of course; awfully dense, sir," he said. "No doubt at all, the scheme excellent. But I don't think—" He paused a moment and looked dreamily out of the window. "I don't think you will find me in it. Somehow, when one's seen—seen the thing itself, you know—blood and men screaming, one feels about having a little house and a little hobby; in the Bible, you know, 'There remaineth a rest.'"

Northover bowed. Then, after a pause, he said:

"Gentlemen, may I offer you my card. If any of the rest of you desire, at any time, to communicate with me, despite Major Brown's view of the matter—"

"I should be obliged for your card, sir," said the major, in his abrupt but courteous voice. "Pay for chair."

The agent of Romance and Adventure handed his card, laughing.

It ran, "P. G. Northover, B.A., C.Q.T., Adventure and Romance Agency, 14 Tanner's Court, Fleet Street."

"What on earth is 'C.Q.T.'?" asked Rupert Grant, looking over the major's shoulder.

"Don't you know?" returned Northover. "Haven't you ever heard of the Club of Queer Trades?"

"There seems to be a confounded lot of funny things we haven't heard of," said the little major, reflectively. "What's this one?"

"The Club of Queer Trades is a society consisting exclusively of people who have invented some new and curious way of making money. I was one of the earliest members."

"You deserve to be," said Basil, taking up his great white hat with a smile, and speaking for the last time that evening.

When they had passed out the Adventure and Romance agent

wore a queer smile as he trod down the fire and locked his desk up. "A fine chap, that major; when one hasn't a touch of the poet one stands some chance of being a poem. But to think of such a clockwork little creature of all people getting into the nets of one of Grigsby's tales!" and he laughed out aloud in the silence.

Just as the laugh echoed away, there came a sharp knock at the door. An owlish head, with dark mustaches, was thrust in, with deprecating and somewhat absurd inquiry.

"What! back again, major?" cried Northover, in surprise. "What can I do for you?"

The major shuffled feverishly into the room.

"It's horribly absurd," he said. "Something must have got started in me that I never knew before. But upon my soul I feel the most desperate desire to know the end of it all."

"The end of it all?"

"Yes," said the major, " 'Jackals,' and the title-deeds, and 'death to Major Brown.' "

The agent's face grew grave, but his eyes were amused.

"I am terribly sorry, major," said he, "but what you ask is impossible. I don't know any one I would sooner oblige than you; but the rules of the agency are strict. The adventures are confidential; you are an outsider; I am not allowed to let you know an inch more than I can help. I do hope you understand—"

"There is no one," said Brown, "who understands discipline better than I do. Thank you very much. Good-night."

And the little man withdrew for the last time.

He married Miss Jameson, the lady with the red hair and the green garments. She was an actress, employed (with many others) by the Romance Agency; and her marriage with the prim old veteran caused some stir in her languid and intellectualized set. She always replied very quietly that she had met scores of men who acted splendidly in the charades provided for them by Northover, but that she had only met one man who went down into a coal-cellar when he really thought it contained a murderer.

The major and she are living as happily as birds, in an absurd villa, and the former has taken to smoking. Otherwise he is unchanged— except, perhaps, there are moments when, alert and full of feminine unselfishness as the major is by nature, he falls into a trance of abstraction. Then his wife recognizes with a concealed smile, by the blind look in his blue eyes, that he is wondering what were the title-deeds, and why he was not allowed to mention jackals. But, like so many old soldiers, Brown is religious, and believes that he will realize the rest of those purple adventures in a better world.

Talking Horse Stories
and Other Fables

A fable is a short short story which has a moral. As most people detest being openly moralized at, most fables are put in the form of "talking horse stories" to make them palatable. At any rate, a writer of fables has to be especially careful to be amusing. Otherwise he will not be listened to. Fables in my view are almost the most skillful and amusing form of stories ever.

The first writer of fables was our old friend Aesop, and if you look at Aesop properly, you will find him a very funny man. I used to play a trick on audiences when I was reading fables. I would read a fable of James Thurber—and James Thurber is a very funny man and people know that he is a very funny man—and then I would read a fable of Aesop afterward. Having listened to Thurber, they did not get solemn on Aesop and laughed at him, too. This is what I have done with the fables in this book.

Maybe I shouldn't have exposed the trick before you read them.

The Little Girl and the Wolf

JAMES THURBER

The first one is Thurber's version of "Little Red Riding Hood," which he has turned into a fable. I don't know if you have ever noticed that most children's stories are sadistic. When I was a child, they used to scare the pants off me. "Little Red Riding Hood" scared me the most. If you remember it goes something like this:

Little Red Riding Hood is sent with a basket of food to her grandmother's cottage. She meets the Wicked Wolf in the forest. The Wicked Wolf finds out where she is going. Then he goes ahead of her, eats up grandmother (this sort of thing is enough to mark a child for life!), dresses up in grandmother's nightgown, and gets into bed. When Little Red Riding Hood gets in the cottage, she says, "What great big eyes you have, Grandmamma!" Then the person telling the story always put on a frightening voice, like ten Captain Blighs rolled into one, and pounced on you with "All the better to see you with, my dear!" The idea of the sadistic grownup was to make you jump, which you did.

Anyway, the story ends up with the Wicked Wolf eating up Red Riding Hood, after which you didn't sleep for a week because you didn't like the idea of being eaten up by the auntie or uncle who told you the story, because by this time you had figured that they were the Wicked Wolf—or at least that's what happened to me.

Here is James Thurber's modern version of the same tale.

One afternoon a big wolf waited in a dark forest for a little girl to come along carrying a basket of food to her grandmother. Finally a little girl did come along and she was carrying a basket of food. "Are you carrying that basket to your grandmother?" asked the wolf. The little girl said yes, she was. So the wolf asked her where her grandmother lived and the little girl told him and he disappeared into the wood.

When the little girl opened the door of her grandmother's house she saw that there was somebody in bed with a nightcap and night-gown on. She had approached no nearer than twenty-five feet from the bed when she saw that it was not her grandmother but the wolf, for even in a nightcap a wolf does not look any more like your grand-mother than the Metro-Goldwyn lion looks like Calvin Coolidge. So the little girl took an automatic out of her basket and shot the wolf dead.

MORAL: *It is not so easy to fool little girls nowadays as it used to be.*

The Bear Who Let It Alone

JAMES THURBER

In the woods of the Far West there once lived a brown bear who could take it or let it alone. He would go into a bar where they sold mead, a fermented drink made of honey, and he would have just two drinks. Then he would put some money on the bar and say, "See what the bears in the back room will have," and he would go home. But finally he took to drinking by himself most of the day. He would reel home at night, kick over the umbrella stand, knock down the bridge lamps, and ram his elbows through the windows. Then he would collapse on the floor and lie there until he went to sleep. His wife was greatly distressed and his children were very frightened.

At length the bear saw the error of his ways and began to reform. In the end he became a famous teetotaller and a persistent temperance lecturer. He would tell everybody that came to his house about the awful effects of drink, and he would boast about how strong and well he had become since he gave up touching the stuff. To demonstrate this, he would stand on his head and on his hands and he would turn cartwheels in the house, kicking over the umbrella stand, knocking down the bridge lamps, and ramming his elbows through the windows. Then he would lie down on the floor, tired by his healthy exercise, and go to sleep. His wife was greatly distressed and his children were very frightened.

MORAL: *You might as well fall flat on your face as lean over too far backward.*

The Widow and the Hen

AESOP

*They say that Aesop was a colored slave in ancient Greece
and that he was crippled. At one time in his career his master
was so delighted with the stories Aesop told that he released him from his slavery.*

*This little story is not a bad joke at all, considering that
it is two thousand five hundred or so years old.*

A Widow had a plump Hen who laid an egg every day, without fail.
The Widow thought to herself: If I give the Hen twice as much
barley, she will lay twice as many eggs. So she fed the Hen twice
a day. But after a few days, the Hen became so fat, that she stopped
laying eggs at all.

MORAL: *You can't bribe Nature.*

The House-Dog and the Wolf

AESOP

One night a hungry Wolf and a fat House-Dog met while roaming
through the woods. My, how fat and nice you look, said the Wolf.
You must get lots of good things to eat. As for me, I can hardly keep
from starving. Well, said the Dog, If you want to help guard the
Master's house with me, you'll get the same food I do. Fine, said
the Wolf, I'm with you! But just as they were starting off home,
the Wolf said: What is that thing around your neck? My collar,
said the Dog. What is it for? asked the Wolf. Oh, they chain me up
by it during the day, said the Dog. Good-bye, said the Wolf, I think
I'll keep to my present life.

MORAL: *Better a bone and liberty than plenty and a chain.*

The Sea and the Shore

JAMES THURBER

A pair of gibbous creatures, who had lived in the sea since time began, which hadn't been long before, were washed upon the shore one day and became the discoverers of land. "The light that never was!" exclaimed the female, lying on the sand in the sun.

"You're always seeing things that never were," grumbled the male. "You're always wanting things that aren't yet."

In the female, lying on the sand in the sun, a dim intuition and prescience began developing. She prefigured mistily things that would one day become rose-point lace and taffeta, sweet perfumes and jewelry. The male, who had a feeling only for wetness and wash, mumbled, "You're a little moist for things like that, a little moist and shapeless."

"I only need to lose a little amorphousness around the waist," she said. "It won't take more than a million years." And she began flobbering, almost imperceptibly, toward the scrubby brown growth beyond the sand and toward the sun. "Come on," she said. But the male had globbed back into the sea, and was gone.

A couple of eons later, the male, unable to get along alone, reappeared one day upon the shore. He noted with faint satisfaction that the female's shapelessness was beginning to take shape and had become almost shapely. He turned back toward the sea, but a mindless urge deep inside him took on the frail flicker of desire. Suddenly the sea seemed something less than satisfying. He turned about and began flobbering up the sand toward the female, who seemed certain to reach the greening undergrowth in another two thousand years. "Hey, Mag," he shouted. "Wait for baby!"

MORAL: *Let us ponder this basic fact about the human: Ahead of every man, not behind him, is a woman.*

The Two Pots

AESOP

Two Pots, one of earthenware, the other of brass, were carried down a river together in a flood. The Brass Pot urged the Earthen Pot to keep by his side, for their mutual protection. Thank you for your offer, said the Earthen Pot, But that is just what I'm afraid of; if you will only keep at a distance, I may float down in safety; but should we touch, I am sure to suffer.

MORAL: *Avoid powerful neighbors, for in a collision, the weakest goes down.*

The Miller, His Son, and the Donkey

AESOP

A Miller and his Son were taking their Donkey to market to sell him. They passed some laughing girls, who said to the boy: Silly, what is a Donkey good for? Why don't you ride on him? So the Miller told his Son to ride on the Donkey. They hadn't gone far along when they passed an old man, who grumbled: Look at that lazy boy! Letting his father walk while he rides! So the Miller got on the Donkey, and the Son walked. After a little way farther, they passed some women, who clacked: Lazy man! Riding in luxury while that poor boy trots along in the dust! So the Miller took his son up on the Donkey with him. As they got near town, a man saw them and shook his head: That poor little Donkey, he said, Carrying two big louts like you. You ought to be ashamed of yourselves! So the Miller and his Son got off the Donkey, and to prevent any further criticism they tied his legs together, got a long pole, and marched into town with the beast slung between them. As they crossed over the bridge the fishermen laughed at them for fools, the boy began to cry, the Donkey began to twist and kick, until the boy let go his end of the pole and the beast tumbled into the river.

MORAL: *If you try to please everyone you will end by pleasing no one.*

156

The Peacelike Mongoose

JAMES THURBER

In cobra country a mongoose was born one day who didn't want to fight cobras or anything else. The word spread from mongoose to mongoose that there was a mongoose who didn't want to fight cobras. If he didn't want to fight anything else, it was his own business, but it was the duty of every mongoose to kill cobras or be killed by cobras.

"Why?" asked the peacelike mongoose, and the word went around that the strange new mongoose was not only pro-cobra and anti-mongoose but intellectually curious and against the ideals and traditions of mongooseism.

"He is crazy," cried the young mongoose's father.

"He is sick," said his mother.

"He is a coward," shouted his brothers.

"He is a mongoosexual," whispered his sisters.

Strangers who had never laid eyes on the peacelike mongoose remembered that they had seen him crawling on his stomach, or trying on cobra hoods, or plotting the violent overthrow of Mongoosia.

"I am trying to use reason and intelligence," said the strange new mongoose.

"Reason is six-sevenths of treason," said one of his neighbors.

"Intelligence is what the enemy uses," said another.

Finally, the rumor spread that the mongoose had venom in his sting, like a cobra, and he was tried, convicted by a show of paws, and condemned to banishment.

MORAL: *Ashes to ashes, and clay to clay, if the enemy doesn't get you your own folks may.*

The Fable of the Wise Piker
Who Had the Kind of Talk
That Went

GEORGE ADE

*George Ade was a Chicago newspaperman at the turn of
the century, and people began to read him avidly and look
forward to his column. And as with many other newspaper-
men in American history, they found out later that he was
a fine writer and began to collect his stories in books. The
book that this comes from is called Forty Modern Fables
and is worth anybody's time and money.*

*You will notice that George Ade does not use the "talking
horse" technique as a blind. He uses the slang of his day,
which still has great charm, like the lamented El stations
in New York City.*

Once there was a man who wore a Six Hat and had a Head shaped
like an Egg Plant. He had not found time to sit down and absorb
Culture. Yet he had to go out and meet the high Mansard Foreheads.
Sometimes he found himself in the Front Room where every one
was expected to discuss Literature, Art, Music and the Difficulty of
getting good Kitchen Help.

This Man was a Pin-Head in a good many Respects, but he was
Wise as a Serpent.

This Man was what Edmund Clarence Stedman would call a
Piker. A Piker is one who gets into the Game on Small Capital and
Lets On to be holding back a huge Reserve. A Piker is usually Safe
when he sagatiates among the Well-Bred because they are too Polite
to call a Bluff.

A Piker always has his entire Stock of Goods in the Show Window.

When it came to Music, the Piker did not know the difference
between a Fugue and a Cantata. Such knowledge of Literature as he
could boast was picked up by reading the Posters in front of Book-
Stores. The average Katy-Did had about as much Art Education as

he could have Spread had it come to a Show-Down. He had as much
Business in an Assemblage of cultivated Chautauquans as a man with
a ragged $2.00 Bill would have in Wall Street. Yet he managed to
cut Figure Eights over the Thin Ice and he had the name of being
one of the Brainiest Gentlemen that ever accepted an Invitation to
the Evening Session of the Olympian Circle of Hens.

The Piker knew the Value of the Stock Phrase. And the way he
could raise a Dust and dodge out of a Tight Place was a little Bit
of All Right.

One evening the Piker went to call on Mrs. Hester Kazam, author
of many unpublished Poems, and the boss Diana of the Tuft-
Hunters. At the Kazam Home, which is rigged up with Red Blankets
and Green Lamps so as to be Oriental, he bumped into Henrietta
Hunter Haw, who will be remembered as the Young Lady who
poured at the Afternoon Reception to F. Hopkinson Smith.

Miss Haw reclined at half length in the Turkish Corner and asked
the Piker what he thought of Sienkiewicz. The Piker knew that he
had heard that name sprung somewhere before, but if he had tried
to Pronounce it, he would have gone to the Floor. He didn't know
whether Sienkiewicz was the author of "Lovers Once but Strangers
Now" or "The Gentleman from Arkansaw." However, he was not to
be Feazed. He knew the kind of Conversational Parsley that is
needed to Garnish a full-blown Intellectual Vacuum, and he passed
some of it to Henrietta.

He said he liked Sienk, so far as the Psychological Analysis was
concerned, but it sometimes occurred to him that there was a lack
of Insight and Broad Artistic Grasp.

That is the Style of Vapor calculated to keep a Young Woman
anchored right in the Turkish Corner and make her believe she has
met the Really and Truly Gazip.

The Piker unreeled a little more of the same kind. He said that
the Elaboration of Incident showed a certain Modicum of Skill, but
there was not enough Plus-Human Sympathy in the Coloring of the
Subtle Motives. When the Piker got rid of this he was always Relieved, for it is an Awful Thing to Memorize and carry around with
you.

Afterward Miss Haw went out and told her Girl Friends that the
Piker was Terrible Deep.

When they brought up Music, that was where the Piker lived. He
could get in early and stay late and never Trip himself up. He had
attended a couple of Concerts and at one time boarded with a Lady
who played the Autoharp.

One Evening when he was out with a few People who were such
Thorough Musicians that they seemed Sour about something all the

time, a Tall Man with a Low Collar asked him if he had heard that latest Thing by Tschaikowsky.

If he had made it Charles K. Harris, the Piker might have been with him. But he never turned a Hair.

"Impressive, isn't it?" he said, having learned how to Spar for Wind, without leaving an Opening.

"Yes, but it didn't get into me the way Vogner does," replied the Tall Party.

This was the Cue for the Piker to insert his Speech on Vogner.

He said he preferred Vogner any day in the Week on account of the distinct Appeal to the Intellectual Side and the Atmosphere of Mysticism, whatever that was. He said he couldn't listen to Vogner without going into a Cold Sweat and Chewing the Buttons off his Gloves, particularly if the Interpretation was made with a Broad and Comprehensive Virtuosity and such Mastery of Technique as to abolish all suggestion of the Intermediary and bring one into direct Communion with the Soul-Moods.

Then the Tall Man would know just as much about it as the Piker did.

Among the Acquaintances was a Lady named Wigley, who was Crazy about Art. In her Parlor she had one of her own Works entitled "Sunset on the Little Miami River," with a Frame that cost $26. It was Mrs. Wigley who read the Paper before the Raphael Suburbanites, setting forth that the Highest Effects could not be obtained by the Use of Crayon. She loved to hear the Piker cut loose about Art. Even when he got in over his Head she was right there swimming along after him and never missing a Stroke.

Mrs. Wigley was stuck on his Conversation because he said so many things that could be Thought About later on. Nearly every one who heard him went Home and Thought about what he had said and Wondered what he had been Driving at.

Mrs. Wigley had a Theory that an Artist who is any Good at all should be able to suggest through the Medium of Colors all that he or she felt and suffered during the Throes of Execution. So she called in the Piker to size up her Picture of the Little Miami River at Sundown and asked him what Emotion, if any, was stirred up within him as he gazed at the Effort. The Piker said it gave him a touch of Sadness. Then she knew he was a real Critic all right.

The Piker kept it up until after a while he began to think that possibly he was something of a Sassy Savant.

He was elected Director of a Museum and was invited to sit on the Platform at Lectures. And at last he departed this Life, with only a few Relatives and Intimate Friends being on to him.

MORAL: *For Parlor Use the Vague Generality is a Life-Saver.*

The Daws on the Dial

JAMES THURBER

A young jackdaw told his father that he was going to build his nest
on the minute hand of the town clock. "That's the most unthinkable
thing you ever thought of," said old John Daw. Young Jack was not
deterred. "We'll build our nest when the minute hand is level," he
said, "at a quarter of or a quarter after."

"Those who lives in castles in the air have nowhere to go but
down," the old Daw warned, but Jack and his mate built their nest
on the clock at a quarter after eight the next morning. At twenty
minutes after eight the nest slipped off the minute hand and fell
into the street below. "We didn't start early enough," the young
Daw told his father that evening. "Better never than late. We'll try
again tomorrow at a quarter after six."

"If at first you don't succeed, fail, fail again," said the elder Daw.
But he might as well have been talking to a gargoyle. Jack and his
mate stole some of the elder Daw's silverware and built their nest
again the following morning, and again it slipped off the minute
hand and fell into the street below.

That evening old John Daw had more to say to his reckless offspring. "To stick on a dial, you would need three feet, one of them
a rabbit's. Don't hang heavy on time's hands, just because it hangs
heavy on yours. Clockwise is not wise enough. Even the cyclone and
the merry-go-round know that much."

And again the young Daws did not listen, and again they swiped
some silverware from his parents' nest to furnish their own. This
time, those human beings known as municipal authorities were concealed in the clock tower, and, with brooms and yells and stones and
bells, they frightened the foolish Daws away from the clock and the
tower and the town.

That night old John Daw's mate counted her silverware and
sighed with dismay. "Gone, alas, with our youth, two spoons," she
said, "and half the knives, and most of the forks, and all of the
napkin rings."

"If I told him once, I told him a hundred times, 'Neither a
burglar nor a lender be,'" raged old John, "but I might as well have
been talking to a cast-iron lawn Daw." Not a word was heard from

the young Daws as the weeks went on. "No news is bad news," grumbled old John Daw. "They have probably built their nest this time on a wagon wheel, or inside a bell."

He was wrong about that. The young Daws had built their last nest in the muzzle of a cannon, and they heard only the first gun of a twenty-one-gun salute fired in honor of a visiting chief of state.

MORAL: *The saddest words of pen or tongue are wisdom's wasted on the young.*

The Shirt Collar

HANS CHRISTIAN ANDERSEN

Hans Andersen's story of the shirt collar is strictly a fable; that is, it is a short short story with a moral. And a very frightening one, too, not recommended for modern children. It is likely to give them traumas, guilt complexes, and all the rest of the modern diseases. It is, however, very well told and amusing enough for grownups. We can take it.

Once upon a time there was an elegant gentleman whose whole outfit consisted of a bootjack and a comb, but he also had the most wonderful shirt collar in the world, and it's about this shirt collar that we're to hear a story.

The collar had now arrived at an age when he began to think of getting married, and it so happened that in the wash he found himself next to a garter.

"My word!" exclaimed the collar. "I've never seen anyone so slender, so fine, so soft and so dainty as you. May I ask your name?"

"I won't tell you," said the garter.

"Where do you belong?" asked the collar.

But the garter was overcome with shyness and found it rather embarrassing to answer such a question.

"I should imagine that you're a belt," said the collar. "I mean a sort of inner belt. I quite realize that you're useful as well as ornamental, my pretty one."

"I forbid you to speak to me," said the garter. "I can't see that I've given you any encouragement."

"The mere fact of being so beautiful is encouragement enough," said the collar.

"Please don't come any nearer," said the garter. "You look so masculine."

"Well, after all, I'm an elegant gentleman," said the collar. "I own a bootjack and a comb." Now that was not true at all, for it was his master who owned them, but he was boasting.

"Keep your distance," said the garter. "I'm not accustomed to such familiarity."

"Prude!" said the collar.

At that very moment he was taken out of the wash-tub, starched, hung over a chair in the sun and laid on the ironing-board. Then the hot iron appeared on the scene.

"Honoured Madam," said the collar, "fascinating little widow, my blood is stirring within me. I shall never be the same again. You're taking the crease out of me! You're burning a hole in me! Oh!— will you be my wife?"

"Rag!" said the iron, and she passed haughtily over the collar, for she fancied she was a steam engine running on a railway track, pulling carriages behind her.

"Rag!" she said again.

The collar was a bit frayed at the edges, so the cutting-out scissors arrived to snip off the ends.

"Oh!" said the collar, "I can see you're a Premiere Danseuse. How magnificently you point your toes! I've never seen anything more fascinating. No one in the world can do that like you."

"I know," said the scissors.

"You really ought to be a countess," said the collar. "All I possess is an elegant gentleman, a bootjack, and a comb. Oh, if I only possessed an earldom!"

"As I live and breathe, he is proposing to me!" said the infuriated scissors, and gave him such a snip that he had to be scrapped.

"Now I shall have to propose to the comb," said the collar. "It's very remarkable how you keep all your teeth, my pretty one. Have you never thought of getting married?"

"Of course I have," said the comb. "Didn't you know that I'm engaged to the bootjack?"

"Engaged!" exclaimed the collar.

There was nobody left to propose to, and so he disdainfully turned his back on love-making.

A long time passed, and the collar found himself at the papermill in a box where there was a social gathering of rags; the upper ten on one side, and the rag-tag and bob-tail on the other, which is quite as it should be.

Everyone had a great deal to tell, but the collar had the most, for he was a consummate braggart.

"You've no idea how many sweethearts I've had," he said. "They would never give me a moment's peace. After all, I was a stiff and starched gentleman once. I had a bootjack and a comb that I never used. You should have seen me then—you should have seen me when I had a day off! Never shall I forget my first love. She was a belt, so lovely, so soft and charming! She threw herself into a wash-tub for my sake.—There was also a widow; she was red-hot for me, but I gave her the slip and she turned black again. Then there was a Premiere Danseuse. She gave me the cut which you can still see—a fiery minx she was! Even my own comb was mad about me, and lost all her teeth from unrequited love. Oh yes, I've had plenty of experiences like that. But the gart— I mean the belt who threw herself into the wash-tub, is the one I feel most sorry for. I've a great deal on my conscience; it's about time I was made into white paper."

And that is what actually happened. All the rags were made into white paper, but the collar became that very piece of white paper we see here, the very one on which this story is printed. And that was because he boasted so dreadfully of what he had never been. So let us remember not to behave like that, for who knows? One day we might land in the rag-bag, be made into a piece of white paper, and have our whole life's history, even the most intimate details, printed on the front, and so publish it abroad ourselves—just like the collar.

Fable IX

WILLIAM SAROYAN

Saroyan's delightful tale is not in the strictest sense a fable because it does not point a moral, rather the reverse.

It is more like a story of Balzac or Boccaccio and much less dull. I'm always trying to read the Droll Stories of Balzac and Boccaccio's tales and I always finish up by throwing them across the bedroom floor and picking up James Thurber or Thomas Wolfe or indeed Saroyan himself.

But I found "Fable IX" irresistible, so here it is.

The Tribulations of the Simple Husband Who Wanted Nothing More than to Eat Goose but was Denied this Delight by His Unfaithful Wife and Her Arrogant but Probably Handsome Lover.

A simple husband one morning took his wife a goose and said, Cook this bird for me; when I come home in the evening I shall eat it.

The wife plucked the bird, cleaned it, and cooked it. In the afternoon her lover came. Before going away he asked what food he could take with him to his friends. He looked into the oven and saw the roasted goose.

That is for my husband, the wife said.

I want it, the lover said. If you do not let me take it, I shall never love you again.

The lover went off with the goose.

In the evening the husband sat at the table and said, Bring me the goose.

What goose? the wife said.

The goose I brought you this morning, the husband said. Bring it to me.

Are you serious? the wife said. You brought me no goose. Perhaps you dreamed it.

Bring me the goose, the husband shouted.

The wife began to scream, saying, My poor husband has lost his mind. My poor husband is crazy. What he has dreamed he imagines has happened.

The neighbors came and believed the wife, so the husband said nothing and went hungry, except for bread and cheese and water.

The following morning the husband brought his wife another goose and said, Is this a goose?

Yes, the wife said.

Am I dreaming?—No.

Is this the goose's head?—Yes.

Wings?—Yes.

Feathers?—Yes.

All right, the husband said, cook it. When I come home tonight I'll eat it.

The wife cooked the goose. The lover came.

There is another goose today, he said. I can smell it.

You cannot take it, the wife said. I had a terrible scene with my husband last night, and again this morning. It is too much, I love you but you cannot have the goose.

Either you love me or you don't love me, the lover said. Either I take the goose or not.

So he took the goose.

Bring the goose, the husband said.

My poor husband, the wife screamed. He's stark raving mad. Goose, goose, goose. What goose? There is no goose. My poor, poor husband.

The neighbors came and again believed the wife.

The husband went hungry.

The following morning he bought another goose in the city. He hired a tall man to carry the goose on a platter on his head. He hired an orchestra of six pieces, and with the musicians in a circle around the tall man carrying the goose, he walked with them through the streets to his house, calling to his neighbors.

When he reached his house there were many people following him.

He turned to the people and said, Mohammedans, neighbors, the world, heaven above, fish in the sea, soldiers, and all others, behold, a goose.

He lifted the bird off the platter.

A goose, he cried.

He handed the bird to his wife.

Now cook the God Damned thing, he said, and when I come home in the evening I will eat it.

The wife cleaned the bird and cooked it. The lover came. There was a tender scene, tears, kisses, running, wrestling, more tears, more kisses, and the lover went off with the goose.

In the city the husband saw an old friend and said, Come out to the house with me tonight; the wife's roasting a goose; we'll take a couple of bottle of *rakki* and have a hell of a time.

So the husband and his friend went out to the house and the husband said, Have you cooked the goose?

Yes, the wife said. It's in the oven.

Good, the husband said. You were never really a bad wife. First, my friend and I will have a few drinks: then we will eat the goose.

The husband and his friend had four or five drinks and then the husband said, All right, bring the goose.

The wife said, There is no bread; go to your cousin's for bread; goose is no good without bread.

All right, the husband said.

He left the house.

The wife said to the husband's friend, My husband is crazy. There is no goose. He has brought you here to kill you with this enormous carving knife and this fork. You had better go.

The man went. The husband came home and asked about his friend and the goose.

Your *friend* has run off with the goose, the wife said. What kind of a friend do you call that, after I slave all day to cook you a decent meal?

The husband took the carving knife and the fork and began running down the street. At length in the distance he saw his friend running and he called out, Just a leg, my friend, that's all.

My God, the other said, he is truly crazy.

The friend began to run faster than ever. Soon the husband could run no more. He returned wearily to his home and wife. Once again he ate bread and cheese. After this plain food he began to drink *rakki* again.

As he drank, the truth began to come to him little by little, as it does through alcohol.

When he was very drunk he knew all about everything. He got up and quietly whacked his wife across the room.

If your lover's got to have a goose every day, he said, you could have told me. Tomorrow I will bring *two* of them. I get hungry once in a while myself, you know.

Stories from Behind
the Windowshades

I have traveled all over the United States on reading tours. Once I traveled 23,000 miles in thirteen weeks and played eighty-seven engagements. I suppose I have been at more places in the United States than any other actor before me and I have had so many pangs of regret: I always travel by automobile as I often go to places very difficult to get to by train or plane, and I have wanted to stop in rather than pass through little towns in Ohio and Pennsylvania and Vermont and the Carolinas and Louisiana and Texas.

But there was never time; I always had to make a date that night and all there was time for was a gas station and a hamburger stand. But I have learned what was going on in many of these places from stories that have been written about them, and I am grateful to their authors.

The Strength of God

AND

The Teacher

SHERWOOD ANDERSON

These stories are from one of my favorite American books, Winesburg, Ohio. I understand that when the book was first published it shocked people by its directness. It is now universally known as a masterpiece. In my mind's eye I can see the places with which I associate these two related stories.

The Strength of God

The Reverend Curtis Hartman was pastor of the Presbyterian Church of Winesburg, and had been in that position ten years. He was forty years old, and by his nature very silent and reticent. To preach, standing in the pulpit before the people, was always a hardship for him and from Wednesday morning until Saturday evening he thought of nothing but the two sermons that must be preached on Sunday. Early on Sunday morning he went into a little room called a study in the bell tower of the church and prayed. In his prayers there was one note that always predominated. "Give me strength and courage for Thy work, O Lord!" he plead, kneeling on the bare floor and bowing his head in the presence of the task that lay before him.

The Reverend Hartman was a tall man with a brown beard. His wife, a stout, nervous woman, was the daughter of a manufacturer of underwear at Cleveland, Ohio. The minister himself was rather a favorite in the town. The elders of the church liked him because he was quiet and unpretentious and Mrs. White, the banker's wife, thought him scholarly and refined.

The Presbyterian Church held itself somewhat aloof from the other churches of Winesburg. It was larger and more imposing and its minister was better paid. He even had a carriage of his own and on summer evenings sometimes drove about town with his wife.

Through Main Street and up and down Buckeye Street he went, bowing gravely to the people, while his wife, afire with secret pride, looked at him out of the corners of her eyes and worried lest the horse become frightened and run away.

For a good many years after he came to Winesburg things went well with Curtis Hartman. He was not one to arouse keen enthusiasm among the worshippers in his church but on the other hand he made no enemies. In reality he was much in earnest and sometimes suffered prolonged periods of remorse because he could not go crying the word of God in the highways and byways of the town. He wondered if the flame of the spirit really burned in him and dreamed of a day when a strong sweet new current of power would come like a great wind into his voice and his soul and the people would tremble before the spirit of God made manifest in him. "I am a poor stick and that will never really happen to me," he mused dejectedly and then a patient smile lit up his features. "Oh well, I suppose I'm doing well enough," he added philosophically.

The room in the bell tower of the church, where on Sunday mornings the minister prayed for an increase in him of the power of God, had but one window. It was long and narrow and swung outward on a hinge like a door. On the window, made of little leaded panes, was a design showing the Christ laying his hand upon the head of a child. One Sunday morning in the summer as he sat by his desk in the room with a large Bible opened before him, and the sheets of his sermon scattered about, the minister was shocked to see, in the upper room of the house next door, a woman lying in her bed and smoking a cigarette while she read a book. Curtis Hartman went on tiptoe to the window and closed it softly. He was horror stricken at the thought of a woman smoking and trembled also to think that his eyes, just raised from the pages of the book of God, had looked upon the bare shoulders and white throat of a woman. With his brain in a whirl he went down into the pulpit and preached a long sermon without once thinking of his gestures or his voice. The sermon attracted unusual attention because of its power and clearness. "I wonder if she is listening, if my voice is carrying a message into her soul," he thought and began to hope that on future Sunday mornings he might be able to say words that would touch and awaken the woman apparently far gone in secret sin.

The house next door to the Presbyterian Church, through the windows of which the minister had seen the sight that had so upset him, was occupied by two women. Aunt Elizabeth Swift, a grey competent-looking widow with money in the Winesburg National Bank, lived there with her daughter Kate Swift, a school teacher. The school teacher was thirty years old and had a neat trim-looking figure.

She had few friends and bore a reputation of having a sharp tongue. When he began to think about her, Curtis Hartman remembered that she had been to Europe and had lived for two years in New York City. "Perhaps after all her smoking means nothing," he thought. He began to remember that when he was a student in college and occasionally read novels, good, although somewhat worldly women, had smoked through the pages of a book that had once fallen into his hands. With a rush of new determination he worked on his sermons all through the week and forgot, in his zeal to reach the ears and the soul of this new listener, both his embarrassment in the pulpit and the necessity of prayer in the study on Sunday mornings.

Reverend Hartman's experience with women had been somewhat limited. He was the son of a wagon maker from Muncie, Indiana, and had worked his way through college. The daughter of the under-wear manufacturer had boarded in a house where he lived during his school days and he had married her after a formal and prolonged courtship, carried on for the most part by the girl herself. On his marriage day the underwear manufacturer had given his daughter five thousand dollars and he promised to leave her at least twice that amount in his will. The minister had thought himself fortunate in marriage and had never permitted himself to think of other women. He did not want to think of other women. What he wanted was to do the work of God quietly and earnestly.

In the soul of the minister a struggle awoke. From wanting to reach the ears of Kate Swift, and through his sermons to delve into her soul, he began to want also to look again at the figure lying white and quiet in the bed. On a Sunday morning when he could not sleep because of his thoughts he arose and went to walk in the streets. When he had gone along Main Street almost to the old Richmond place he stopped and picking up a stone rushed off to the room in the bell tower. With the stone he broke out a corner of the window and then locked the door and sat down at the desk before the open Bible to wait. When the shade of the window to Kate Swift's room was raised he could see, through the hole, directly into her bed, but she was not there. She also had arisen and had gone for a walk and the hand that raised the shade was the hand of Aunt Elizabeth Swift.

The minister almost wept with joy at this deliverance from the carnal desire to "peep" and went back to his own house, praising God. In an ill moment he forgot, however, to stop the hole in the window. The piece of glass broken out at the corner of the window just nipped off the bare heel of the boy standing motionless and looking with rapt eyes into the face of the Christ.

Curtis Hartman forgot his sermon on that Sunday morning. He

talked to his congregation and in his talk said that it was a mistake for people to think of their minister as a man set aside and intended by nature to lead a blameless life. "Out of my own experience I know that we, who are the ministers of God's word, are beset by the same temptations that assail you," he declared. "I have been tempted and have surrendered to temptation. It is only the hand of God, placed beneath my head, that has raised me up. As He has raised me so also will He raise you. Do not despair. In your hour of sin raise your eyes to the skies and you will be again and again saved."

Resolutely the minister put the thoughts of the woman in the bed out of his mind and began to be something like a lover in the presence of his wife. One evening when they drove out together he turned the horse out of Buckeye Street and in the darkness on Gospel Hill, above Waterworks Pond, put his arm about Sarah Hartman's waist. When he had eaten breakfast in the morning and was ready to retire to his study at the back of his house he went around the table and kissed his wife on the cheek. When thoughts of Kate Swift came into his head, he smiled and raised his eyes to the skies. "Intercede for me, Master," he muttered, "keep me in the narrow path intent on Thy work."

And now began the real struggle in the soul of the brown-bearded minister. By chance he discovered that Kate Swift was in the habit of lying in her bed in the evenings and reading a book. A lamp stood on a table by the side of the bed and the light streamed down upon her white shoulders and bare throat. On the evening when he made the discovery the minister sat at the desk in the study from nine until after eleven and when her light was put out stumbled out of the church to spend two more hours walking and praying in the streets. He did not want to kiss the shoulders and the throat of Kate Swift and had not allowed his mind to dwell on such thoughts. He did not know what he wanted. "I am God's child and He must save me from myself," he cried, in the darkness under the trees as he wandered in the streets. By a tree he stood and looked at the sky that was covered with hurrying clouds. He began to talk to God intimately and closely. "Please, Father, do not forget me. Give me power to go tomorrow and repair the hole in the window. Lift my eyes again to the skies. Stay with me, Thy servant, in his hour of need."

Up and down through the silent streets walked the minister and for days and weeks his soul was troubled. He could not understand the temptation that had come to him nor could he fathom the reason for its coming. In a way he began to blame God, saying to himself that he had tried to keep his feet in the true path and had not run about seeking sin. "Through my days as a young man and all through my life here I have gone quietly about my work," he declared. "Why now should I be tempted? What have I done that this burden should be laid on me?"

Three times during the early fall and winter of that year Curtis Hartman crept out of his house to the room in the bell tower to sit in the darkness looking at the figure of Kate Swift lying in her bed and later went to walk and pray in the streets. He could not understand himself. For weeks he would go along scarcely thinking of the school teacher and telling himself that he had conquered the carnal desire to look at her body. And then something would happen. As he sat in the study of his own house, hard at work on a sermon, he would become nervous and begin to walk up and down the room. "I will go out into the streets," he told himself and even as he let himself in at the church door he persistently denied to himself the cause of his being there. "I will not repair the hole in the window and I will train myself to come here at night and sit in the presence of this woman without raising my eyes. I will not be defeated in this thing. The Lord has devised this temptation as a test of my soul and I will grope my way out of darkness into the light of righteousness."

One night in January when it was bitter cold and snow lay deep on the streets of Winesburg Curtis Hartman paid his last visit to the room in the bell tower of the church. It was past nine o'clock when he left his own house and he set out so hurriedly that he forgot to put on his overshoes. In Main Street no one was abroad but Hop Higgins the night watchman and in the whole town no one was awake but the watchman and young George Willard, who sat in the office of the *Winesburg Eagle* trying to write a story. Along the street to the church went the minister, plowing through the drifts and thinking that this time he would utterly give way to sin. "I want to look at the woman and to think of kissing her shoulders and I am going to let myself think what I choose," he declared bitterly and tears came into his eyes. He began to think that he would get out of the ministry and try some other way of life. "I shall go to some city and get into business," he declared. "If my nature is such that I cannot resist sin, I shall give myself over to sin. At least I shall not be a hypocrite, preaching the word of God with my mind thinking of the shoulders and neck of a woman who does not belong to me."

It was cold in the room of the bell tower of the church on that January night and almost as soon as he came into the room Curtis Hartman knew that if he stayed he would be ill. His feet were wet from tramping in the snow and there was no fire. In the room in the house next door Kate Swift had not yet appeared. With grim determination the man sat down to wait. Sitting in the chair and gripping the edge of the desk on which lay the Bible he stared into the darkness thinking the blackest thoughts of his life. He thought of his wife and for the moment almost hated her. "She has always been ashamed of passion and has cheated me," he thought. "Man has a right to expect living passion and beauty in a woman. He has no right to forget that he is an animal and in me there is something that is Greek. I will throw off the woman of my bosom and seek other women. I will besiege this school teacher. I will fly in the face of all men and if I am a creature of carnal lusts I will live then for my lusts."

The distracted man trembled from head to foot, partly from cold, partly from the struggle in which he was engaged. Hours passed and a fever assailed his body. His throat began to hurt and his teeth chattered. His feet on the study floor felt like two cakes of ice. Still he would not give up. "I will see this woman and will think the thoughts I have never dared to think," he told himself, gripping the edge of the desk and waiting.

Curtis Hartman came near dying from the effects of that night of waiting in the church, and also he found in the thing that happened what he took to be the way of life for him. On other evenings when he had waited he had not been able to see, through the little hole in the glass, any part of the school teacher's room except that occupied by her bed. In the darkness he had waited until the woman suddenly appeared sitting in the bed in her white nightrobe. When the light was turned up she propped herself up among the pillows and read a book. Sometimes she smoked one of the cigarettes. Only her bare shoulders and throat were visible.

On the January night, after he had come near dying with cold and after his mind had two or three times actually slipped away into an odd land of fantasy so that he had by an exercise of will power to force himself back into consciousness, Kate Swift appeared. In the room next door a lamp was lighted and the waiting man stared into an empty bed. Then upon the bed before his eyes a naked woman threw herself. Lying face downward she wept and beat with her fists upon the pillow. With a final outburst of weeping she half arose, and in the presence of the man who had waited to look and to think thoughts the woman of sin began to pray. In the lamplight her figure, slim and strong, looked like the figure of the boy in the presence of the Christ on the leaded window.

Curtis Hartman never remembered how he got out of the church. With a cry he arose, dragging the heavy desk along the floor. The Bible fell, making a great clatter in the silence. When the light in the house next door went out he stumbled down the stairway and into the street. Along the street he went and ran in at the door of the *Winesburg Eagle*. To George Willard, who was tramping up and down in the office undergoing a struggle of his own, he began to talk half incoherently. "The ways of God are beyond human understanding," he cried, running in quickly and closing the door. He began to advance upon the young man, his eyes glowing and his voice ringing with fervor. "I have found the light," he cried. "After ten years in this town, God has manifested himself to me in the body of a woman." His voice dropped and he began to whisper. "I did not understand," he said. "What I took to be a trial of my soul was only a preparation for a new and more beautiful fervor of the spirit. God has appeared to me in the person of Kate Swift, the school teacher, kneeling naked on a bed. Do you know Kate Swift? Although she may not be aware of it, she is an instrument of God, bearing the message of truth."

Reverend Curtis Hartman turned and ran out of the office. At the door he stopped, and after looking up and down the deserted street, turned again to George Willard. "I am delivered. Have no fear." He held up a bleeding fist for the young man to see. "I smashed the glass of the window," he cried. "Now it will have to be wholly replaced. The strength of God was in me and I broke it with my fist."

The Teacher

Snow lay deep in the streets of Winesburg. It had begun to snow about ten o'clock in the morning and a wind sprang up and blew the snow in clouds along Main Street. The frozen mud roads that led into town were fairly smooth and in places ice covered the mud. "There will be good sleighing," said Will Henderson, standing by the bar in Ed Griffith's saloon. Out of the saloon he went and met Sylvester West the druggist stumbling along in the kind of heavy overshoes called arctics. "Snow will bring the people into town on Saturday," said the druggist. The two men stopped and discussed their affairs. Will Henderson, who had on a light overcoat and no overshoes, kicked the heel of his left foot with the toe of the right. "Snow will be good for the wheat," observed the druggist sagely.

Young George Willard, who had nothing to do, was glad because he did not feel like working that day. The weekly paper had been printed and taken to the post office on Wednesday evening and the snow began to fall on Thursday. At eight o'clock, after the morning train had passed, he put a pair of skates in his pocket and went up to Waterworks Pond but did not go skating. Past the pond and along a path that followed Wine Creek he went until he came to a grove of beech trees. There he built a fire against the side of a log and sat down at the end of the log to think. When the snow began to fall and the wind to blow he hurried about getting fuel for the fire.

The young reporter was thinking of Kate Swift who had once been his school teacher. On the evening before he had gone to her house to get a book she wanted him to read and had been alone with her for an hour. For the fourth or fifth time the woman had talked to him with great earnestness and he could not make out what she meant by her talk. He began to believe she might be in love with him and the thought was both pleasing and annoying.

Up from the log he sprang and began to pile sticks on the fire. Looking about to be sure he was alone he talked aloud pretending he was in the presence of the woman. "Oh, you're just letting on, you know you are," he declared. "I am going to find out about you. You wait and see."

The young man got up and went back along the path toward town leaving the fire blazing in the wood. As he went through the streets the skates clanked in his pocket. In his own room in the New Willard House he built a fire in the stove and lay down on top of the bed. He began to have lustful thoughts and pulling down the shade of the window closed his eyes and turned his face to the wall. He took a pillow into his arms and embraced it thinking first of the school teacher, who by her words had stirred something within him and later of Helen White, the slim daughter of the town banker, with whom he had been for a long time half in love.

By nine o'clock of that evening snow lay deep in the streets and the weather had become bitter cold. It was difficult to walk about. The stores were dark and the people had crawled away to their houses. The evening train from Cleveland was very late but nobody was interested in its arrival. By ten o'clock all but four of the eighteen hundred citizens of the town were in bed.

Hop Higgins, the night watchman, was partially awake. He was lame and carried a heavy stick. On dark nights he carried a lantern. Between nine and ten o'clock he went his rounds. Up and down Main Street he stumbled through the drifts trying the doors of the stores. Then he went into alleyways and tried the back doors. Finding all tight he hurried around the corner to the New Willard House and beat on the door. Through the rest of the night he intended to stay by the stove. "You go to bed. I'll keep the stove going," he said to the boy who slept on a cot in the hotel office.

Hop Higgins sat down by the stove and took off his shoes. When the boy had gone to sleep he began to think of his own affairs. He intended to paint his house in the spring and sat by the stove calculating the cost of paint and labor. That led him into other calculations. The night watchman was sixty years old and wanted to retire. He had been a soldier in the Civil War and drew a small pension. He hoped to find some new method of making a living and aspired to become a professional breeder of ferrets. Already he had four of the strangely shaped savage little creatures, that are used by sportsmen in the pursuit of rabbits, in the cellar of his house. "Now I have one male and three females," he mused. "If I am lucky by spring I shall have twelve or fifteen. In another year I shall be able to begin advertising ferrets for sale in the sporting papers."

The night watchman settled into his chair and his mind became a blank. He did not sleep. By years of practice he had trained himself to sit for hours through the long nights neither asleep nor awake. In the morning he was almost as refreshed as though he had slept.

With Hop Higgins safely stowed away in the chair behind the stove only three people were awake in Winesburg. George Willard was in the office of the *Eagle* pretending to be at work on the writing of a story but in reality continuing the mood of the morning by the fire in the wood. In the bell tower of the Presbyterian Church the Reverend Curtis Hartman was sitting in the darkness preparing himself for a revelation from God, and Kate Swift, the school teacher, was leaving her house for a walk in the storm.

It was past ten o'clock when Kate Swift set out and the walk was unpremeditated. It was as though the man and the boy, by thinking of her, had driven her forth into the wintry streets. Aunt Elizabeth Swift had gone to the county seat concerning some business in connection with mortgages in which she had money invested and would not be back until the next day. By a huge stove, called a base burner, in the living room of the house sat the daughter reading a book. Suddenly she sprang to her feet and, snatching a cloak from a rack by the front door, ran out of the house.

At the age of thirty Kate Swift was not known in Winesburg as a pretty woman. Her complexion was not good and her face was covered with blotches that indicated ill health. Alone in the night in the winter streets she was lovely. Her back was straight, her shoulders square and her features were as the features of a tiny goddess on a pedestal in a garden in the dim light of a summer evening.

During the afternoon the school teacher had been to see Dr. Welling concerning her health. The doctor had scolded her and had declared she was in danger of losing her hearing. It was foolish for Kate Swift to be abroad in the storm, foolish and perhaps dangerous.

The woman in the streets did not remember the words of the doctor and would not have turned back had she remembered. She was very cold but after walking for five minutes no longer minded the cold. First she went to the end of her own street and then across a

pair of hay scales set in the ground before a feed barn and into
Trunion Pike. Along Trunion Pike she went to Ned Winter's barn
and turning east followed a street of low frame houses that led over
Gospel Hill and into Sucker Road that ran down a shallow valley
past Ike Smead's chicken farm to Waterworks Pond. As she went
along, the bold, excited mood that had driven her out of doors passed
and then returned again.

There was something biting and forbidding in the character of
Kate Swift. Everyone felt it. In the schoolroom she was silent, cold,
and stern, and yet in an odd way very close to her pupils. Once in a
long while something seemed to have come over her and she was
happy. All of the children in the schoolroom felt the effect of her
happiness. For a time they did not work but sat back in their chairs
and looked at her.

With hands clasped behind her back the school teacher walked up
and down in the schoolroom and talked very rapidly. It did not seem
to matter what subject came into her mind. Once she talked to the
children of Charles Lamb and made up strange intimate little stories
concerning the life of the dead writer. The stories were told with the
air of one who had lived in a house with Charles Lamb and knew
all the secrets of his private life. The children were somewhat confused, thinking Charles Lamb must be someone who had once lived
in Winesburg.

On another occasion the teacher talked to the children of Ben-
venuto Cellini. That time they laughed. What a bragging, bluster-
ing, brave, lovable fellow she made of the old artist! Concerning him
also she invented anecdotes. There was one of a German music
teacher who had a room above Cellini's lodgings in the city of Milan
that made the boys guffaw. Sugars McNutts, a fat boy with red
cheeks, laughed so hard that he became dizzy and fell off his seat
and Kate Swift laughed with him. Then suddenly she became again
cold and stern.

On the winter night when she walked through the deserted snow-
covered streets, a crisis had come into the life of the school teacher.
Although no one in Winesburg would have suspected it, her life
had been very adventurous. It was still adventurous. Day by day as
she worked in the schoolroom or walked in the streets, grief, hope,
and desire fought within her. Behind a cold exterior the most extraordinary events transpired in her mind. The people of the town
thought of her as a confirmed old maid and because she spoke sharply
and went her own way thought her lacking in all the human feeling
that did so much to make and mar their own lives. In reality she was
the most eagerly passionate soul among them, and more than once,
in the five years since she had come back from her travels to settle

in Winesburg and become a school teacher, had been compelled to go out of the house and walk half through the night fighting out some battle raging within. Once on a night when it rained she had stayed out six hours and when she came home had a quarrel with Aunt Elizabeth Swift. "I am glad you're not a man," said the mother sharply. "More than once I've waited for your father to come home, not knowing what new mess he had got into. I've had my share of uncertainty and you cannot blame me if I do not want to see the worst side of him reproduced in you."

Kate Swift's mind was ablaze with thoughts of George Willard. In something he had written as a school boy she thought she had recognized the spark of genius and wanted to blow on the spark. One day in the summer she had gone to the *Eagle* office and finding the boy unoccupied had taken him out Main Street to the fair ground, where the two sat on a grassy bank and talked. The school teacher tried to bring home to the mind of the boy some conception of the difficulties he would have to face as a writer. "You will have to know life," she declared, and her voice trembled with earnestness. She took hold of George Willard's shoulders and turned him about so that she could look into his eyes. A passer-by might have thought them about to embrace. "If you are to become a writer you'll have to stop fooling with words," she explained. "It would be better to give up the notion of writing until you are better prepared. Now it's time to be living. I don't want to frighten you, but I would like to make you understand the import of what you think of attempting. You must not become a mere peddler of words. The thing to learn is to know what people are thinking about, not what they say."

On the evening before that stormy Thursday night, when the Reverend Curtis Hartman sat in the bell tower of the church waiting to look at her body, young Willard had gone to visit the teacher and to borrow a book. It was then the thing happened that confused and puzzled the boy. He had the book under his arm and was preparing to depart. Again Kate Swift talked with great earnestness. Night was coming on and the light in the room grew dim. As he turned to go she spoke his name softly and with an impulsive movement took hold of his hand. Because the reporter was rapidly becoming a man something of his man's appeal, combined with the winsomeness of the boy, stirred the heart of the lonely woman. A passionate desire to have him understand the import of life, to learn to interpret it truly and honestly, swept over her. Leaning forward, her lips brushed his cheek. At the same moment he for the first time became aware of the marked beauty of her features. They were both embarrassed, and to relieve her feeling she became harsh and domineering. "What's the use? It will be ten years before you begin to understand what I mean when I talk to you," she cried passionately.

On the night of the storm and while the minister sat in the church waiting for her Kate Swift went to the office of the *Winesburg Eagle*, intending to have another talk with the boy. After the long walk in the snow she was cold, lonely, and tired. As she came through Main Street she saw the light from the print shop window shining on the snow and on an impulse opened the door and went in. For an hour she sat by the stove in the office talking of life. She talked with passionate earnestness. The impulse that had driven her out into the snow poured itself out into talk. She became inspired as she sometimes did in the presence of the children in school. A great eagerness to open the door of life to the boy, who had been her pupil and who she thought might possess a talent for the understanding of life, had possession of her. So strong was her passion that it became something physical. Again her hands took hold of his shoulders and she turned him about. In the dim light her eyes blazed. She arose and laughed, not sharply as was customary with her, but in a queer, hesitating way. "I must be going," she said. "In a moment, if I stay, I'll be wanting to kiss you."

In the newspaper office a confusion arose. Kate Swift turned and walked to the door. She was a teacher but she was also a woman. As she looked at George Willard, the passionate desire to be loved by a man, that had a thousand times before swept like a storm over her body, took possession of her. In the lamplight George Willard looked no longer a boy, but a man ready to play the part of a man.

The school teacher let George Willard take her into his arms. In the warm little office the air became suddenly heavy and the strength went out of her body. Leaning against a low counter by the door she waited. When he came and put a hand on her shoulder she turned and let her body fall heavily against him. For George Willard the confusion was immediately increased. For a moment he held the body of the woman tightly against his body and then it stiffened. Two sharp little fists began to beat on his face. When the school teacher had run away and left him alone, he walked up and down in the office swearing furiously.

It was into this confusion that the Reverend Curtis Hartman protruded himself. When he came in George Willard thought the town had gone mad. Shaking a bleeding fist in the air, the minister proclaimed the woman George had only a moment before held in his arms an instrument of God bearing a message of truth.

George blew out the lamp by the window and locking the door of the print shop went home. Through the hotel office, past Hop Higgins lost in his dreams of the raising of ferrets, he went and up into his own room. The fire in the stove had gone out and he undressed in the cold. When he got into bed the sheets were like blankets of dry snow.

George Willard rolled about in the bed on which he had lain in the afternoon hugging the pillow and thinking thoughts of Kate Swift. The words of the minister, who he thought had gone suddenly insane, rang in his ears. His eyes stared about the room. The resentment, natural to the baffled male, passed and he tried to understand what had happened. He could not make it out. Over and over he turned the matter in his mind. Hours passed and he began to think it must be time for another day to come. At four o'clock he pulled the covers up about his neck and tried to sleep. When he became drowsy and closed his eyes, he raised a hand and with it groped about in the darkness. "I have missed something. I have missed something Kate Swift was trying to tell me," he muttered sleepily. Then he slept and in all Winesburg he was the last soul on that winter night to go to sleep.

The Bedquilt

DOROTHY CANFIELD FISHER

"The Bedquilt" is sentimental. It is about a gallant old lady, and I associate it with the paintings of Grandma Moses. She is a real, live gallant old lady. It is impossible to look at her paintings without feeling happy. They make me remember how I saw things when I was a child.

I think such stories as this bring us all comfort, for we all have to get old, we hope, and it is pleasant to reflect that when we do get old we may win out, too.

Of all the Elwell family Aunt Mehetabel was certainly the most unimportant member. It was in the New England days, when an unmarried woman was an old maid at twenty, at forty was everyone's servant, and at sixty had gone through so much discipline that she could need no more in the next world. Aunt Mehetabel was sixty-eight.

She had never for a moment known the pleasure of being important to anyone. Not that she was useless in her brother's family; she was expected, as a matter of course, to take upon herself the most tedious and uninteresting part of the household labors. On Mondays she accepted as her share, the washing of the men's shirts, heavy with sweat and stiff with dirt from the fields and from their own hard-working bodies. Tuesdays, she never dreamed of being allowed to iron anything pretty or even interesting, like the baby's white dresses or the fancy aprons of her young lady nieces. She stood all day pressing out a tiresome monotonous succession of dish-cloths and towels and sheets.

In preserving time she was allowed to have none of the pleasant responsibility of deciding when the fruit had cooked long enough, nor did she share in the little excitement of pouring the sweet-smelling stuff into the stone jars. She sat in a corner with the children and stoned cherries incessantly, or hulled strawberries until her fingers were dyed red to the bone.

The Elwells were not consciously unkind to their aunt, they were even in a vague way fond of her; but she was so utterly insignificant

184

a figure in their lives that they bestowed no thought whatever on her. Aunt Mehetabel did not resent this treatment; she took it quite as unconsciously as they gave it. It was to be expected when one was an old-maid dependent in a busy family. She gathered what crumbs of comfort she could from their occasional careless kindnesses and tried to hide the hurt which even yet pierced her at her brother's rough joking. In the winter when they all sat before the big hearth, roasted apples, drank mulled cider, and teased the girls about their beaux and the boys about their sweethearts, she shrank into a dusky corner with her knitting, happy if the evening passed without her brother saying, with a crude sarcasm, "Ask your Aunt Mehetabel about the beaux that used to come a-sparkin' her!" or, "Mehetabel, how was't when you was in love with Abel Cummings?" As a matter of fact, she had been the same at twenty as at sixty, a quiet, mouse-like little creature, too timid and shy for anyone to notice, or to raise her eyes for a moment and wish for a life of her own.

Her sister-in-law, a big hearty housewife, who ruled indoors with as autocratic a sway as did her husband on the farm, was rather kind in an absent, offhand way to the shrunken little old woman, and it was through her that Mehetabel was able to enjoy the one pleasure of her life. Even as a girl she had been clever with her needle in the way of patching bedquilts. More than that she could never learn to do. The garments which she made for herself were the most lamentable affairs, and she was humbly grateful for any help in the bewildering business of putting them together. But in patchwork she enjoyed a tepid importance. She could really do that as well as anyone else. During years of devotion to this one art she had accumulated a considerable store of quilting patterns. Sometimes the neighbors would send over and ask "Miss Mehetabel" for such and such a design. It was with an agreeable flutter at being able to help someone that she went to the dresser, in her bare little room under the eaves, and extracted from her crowded portfolio the pattern desired.

She never knew how her great idea came to her. Sometimes she thought she must have dreamed it, sometimes she even wondered reverently, in the phraseology of the weekly prayer-meeting, if it had not been "sent" to her. She never admitted to herself that she could have thought of it without other help; it was too great, too ambitious, too lofty a project for her humble mind to have conceived. Even when she finished drawing the design with her own fingers, she gazed at it incredulously, not daring to believe that it could indeed be her handiwork. At first it seemed to her only like a lovely but quite unreal dream. She did not think of putting it into execution. So elaborate, so complicated, so beautifully difficult a pattern could be only for the angels in heaven to quilt. But so curiously does familiarity accustom us even to very wonderful things, that as she lived with this astonishing creation of her mind, the longing grew stronger and stronger to give it material life with her nimble old fingers.

She gasped at her daring when this idea swept over her and put it away as one does a sinfully selfish notion, but she kept coming back to it again and again. Finally she said compromisingly to herself that she would make one "square," just one part of her design, to see how it would look. Accustomed to the most complete dependence on her brother and his wife, she dared not do even this without asking Sophia's permission. With a heart full of hope and fear thumping furiously against her old ribs, she approached the mistress of the house on churning-day, knowing with the innocent guile of a child that the country woman was apt to be in a good temper while working over the fragrant butter in the cool cellar.

Sophia listened absently to her sister-in-law's halting, hesitating petition. "Why, yes, Mehetabel," she said, leaning far down into the huge churn for the last golden morsels—"why, yes, start another quilt if you want to. I've got a lot of pieces from the spring sewing that will work in real good." Mehetabel tried honestly to make her see that this would be no common quilt, but her limited vocabulary and her emotion stood between her and expression. At last Sophia said, with a kindly impatience: "Oh, there! Don't bother me. I never could keep track of your quiltin' patterns, anyhow. I don't care what pattern you go by."

With this overwhelmingly, although unconsciously, generous permission, Mehetabel rushed back up the steep attic stairs to her room, and in a joyful agitation began preparations for the work of her life. It was even better than she hoped. By some heaven-sent inspiration she had invented a pattern beyond which no patchwork quilt could go.

She had but little time from her incessant round of household drudgery for this new and absorbing occupation, and she did not dare sit up late at night lest she burn too much candle. It was weeks before the little square began to take on a finished look, to show the pattern. Then Mehetabel was in a fever of impatience to bring it to completion. She was too conscientious to shirk even the smallest part of her share of the work of the house, but she rushed through it with a speed which left her panting as she climbed to the little room. This seemed like a radiant spot to her as she bent over the innumerable scraps of cloth which already in her imagination ranged themselves in the infinitely diverse pattern of her masterpiece. Finally she could wait no longer, and one evening ventured to bring her work down beside the fire where the family sat, hoping that some good fortune would give her a place near the tallow candles on the mantlepiece. She was on the last corner of the square, and her needle flew in and out with inconceivable rapidity. No one noticed her, a fact which filled her with relief, and by bedtime she had but a few more stitches to add.

As she stood up with the others, the square fluttered out of her trembling old hands and fell on the table. Sophia glanced at it carelessly. "Is that the new quilt you're beginning on?" she asked with a yawn. "It looks like a real pretty pattern. Let's see it." Up to that moment Mehetabel had labored in the purest spirit of disinterested devotion to an ideal, but as Sophia held her work toward the candle to examine it, and exclaimed in amazement and admiration, she felt an astonished joy to know that her creation would stand the test of publicity.

"Land sakes!" ejaculated her sister-in-law, looking at the many-colored square. "Why, Mehetabel Elwell, where'd you git that pattern?"

"I made it up," said Mehetabel quietly, but with unutterable pride.

"No!" exclaimed Sophia incredulously. "*Did* you! Why, I never see such a pattern in my life. Girls, come here and see what your Aunt Mehetabel is doing."

The three tall daughters turned back reluctantly from the stairs. "I don't seem to take much interest in patchwork," said one listlessly.

"No, nor I neither!" answered Sophia; "but a stone image would take an interest in this pattern. Honest, Mehetabel, did you think of it yourself? And how under the sun and stars did you ever git your courage up to start in a-making it? Land! Look at all those tiny squinchy little seams! Why the wrong side ain't a thing but seams!"

The girls echoed their mother's exclamations, and Mr. Elwell, himself came over to see what they were discussing.

"Well, I declare!" he said, looking at his sister with eyes more approving than she could ever remember. "That beats old Mis' Wightman's quilt that got the blue ribbon so many times at the county fair."

Mehetabel's heart swelled within her, and tears of joy moistened her old eyes as she lay that night in her narrow, hard bed, too proud and excited to sleep. The next day her sister-in-law amazed her by taking the huge pan of potatoes out of her lap and setting one of the younger children to peeling them. "Don't you want to go on with that quiltin' pattern?" she said; "I'd kind o' like to see how you're goin' to make the grape-vine design come out on the corner."

By the end of the summer the family interest had risen so high that Mehetabel was given a little stand in the sitting-room where she could keep her pieces, and work in odd minutes. She almost wept over such kindness, and resolved firmly not to take advantage of it by neglecting her work, which she performed with a fierce thoroughness. But the whole atmosphere of her world was changed. Things had a meaning now. Through the longest task of washing milk-pans there rose the rainbow of promise of her variegated work. She took her place by the little table and put the thimble on her knotted, hard finger with the solemnity of a priestess performing a sacred rite.

She was even able to bear with some degree of dignity the extreme honor of having the minister and the minister's wife comment admiringly on her great project. The family felt quite proud of Aunt Mehetabel as Minister Bowman had said it was work as fine as any he had ever seen, "and he didn't know but finer!" The remark was repeated verbatim to the neighbors in the following weeks when they dropped in and examined in perverse silence some astonishingly difficult tour de force which Mehetabel had just finished.

The family especially plumed themselves on the slow progress of the quilt. "Mehetabel has been to work on that corner for six weeks, come Tuesday, and she ain't half done yet," they explained to visitors. They fell out of the way of always expecting her to be the one to run errands, even for the children. "Don't bother your Aunt Mehetabel," Sophia would call. "Can't you see she's got to a ticklish place on the quilt?"

The old woman sat up straighter and looked the world in the face. She was a part of it at last. She joined in the conversation and her remarks were listened to. The children were even told to mind her when she asked them to do some service for her, although this she did but seldom, the habit of self-effacement being too strong.

One day some strangers from the next town drove up and asked if they could inspect the wonderful quilt which they had heard of, even down in their end of the valley. After that such visitations were not uncommon, making the Elwells' house a notable object. Mehetabel's quilt came to be one of the town sights, and no one was allowed to leave the town without having paid tribute to its worth. The Elwells saw to it that their aunt was better dressed than she had ever been before, and one of the girls made her a pretty little cap to wear on her thin white hair.

A year went by and a quarter of the quilt was finished; a second year passed and half was done. The third year Mehetabel had pneumonia and lay ill for weeks and weeks, overcome with terror lest she die before her work was completed. A fourth year and one could really see the grandeur of the whole design; and in September of the fifth year, the entire family watching her with eager and admiring eyes, Mehetabel quilted the last stitches in her creation. The girls held it up by the four corners, and they all looked at it in solemn silence. Then Mr. Elwell smote one horny hand within the other and exclaimed: "By ginger! That's goin' to the county fair!" Mehetabel blushed a deep red at this. It was a thought which had occurred to her in a bold moment, but she had not dared to entertain it. The family acclaimed the idea, and one of the boys was forthwith dispatched to the house of the neighbor who was chairman of the committee for their village. He returned with radiant face. "Of course he'll take it. Like's not it may git a prize, so he says; but he's got to have it right off, because all the things are goin' to-morrow morning."

Even in her swelling pride Mehetabel felt a pang of separation as the bulky package was carried out of the house. As the days went on she felt absolutely lost without her work. For years it had been her one preoccupation, and she could not bear even to look at the little stand, now quite bare of the litter of scraps which had lain on it so long. One of the neighbors, who took the long journey to the fair, reported that the quilt was hung in a place of honor in a glass case in "Agricultural Hall." But that meant little to Mehetabel's utter ignorance of all that lay outside of her brother's home. The family noticed the old woman's depression, and one day Sophia said kindly, "You feel sort o' lost without the quilt, don't you, Mehetabel?"

"They took it away so quick!" she said wistfully; "I hardly had one real good look at it myself."

Mr. Elwell made no comment, but a day or two later he asked his sister how early she could get up in the morning.

"I dun'no'. Why?" she asked.

"Well, Thomas Ralston has got to drive clear to West Oldton to see a lawyer there, and that is four miles beyond the fair. He says if you can git up so's to leave here at four in the morning he'll drive you over to the fair, leave you there for the day, and bring you back again at night."

Mehetabel looked at him with incredulity. It was as though someone had offered her a ride in a golden chariot up to the gates of heaven. "Why, you can't *mean* it!" she cried, paling with the intensity of her emotion. Her brother laughed a little uneasily. Even to his careless indifference this joy was a revelation of the narrowness of her life in his home. "Oh, 'tain't so much to go to the fair. Yes, I mean it. Go git your things ready, for he wants to start tomorrow morning."

All that night a trembling, excited old woman lay and stared at the rafters. She, who had never been more than six miles from home in her life, was going to drive thirty miles away—it was like going to another world. She who had never seen anything more exciting than a church supper was to see the county fair. To Mehetabel it was like making the tour of the world. She had never dreamed of doing it. She could not at all imagine what it would be like.

Nor did the exhortations of the family, as they bade good-by to her, throw any light on her confusion. They had all been at least once to the scene of gayety she was to visit, and as she tried to eat her breakfast they called out conflicting advice to her till her head whirled. Sophia told her to be sure and see the display of preserves. Her brother said not to miss inspecting the stock, her nieces said the fancywork was the only thing worth looking at, and her nephews said she must bring them home an account of the races. The buggy drove up to the door, she was helped in, and her wraps tucked about her. They all stood together and waved good-by to her as she drove out of the yard. She waved back, but she scarcely saw them. On her return home that evening she was very pale, and so tired and stiff that her brother had to lift her out bodily, but her lips were set in a blissful smile. They crowded around her with thronging questions, until Sophia pushed them all aside, telling them Aunt Mehetabel was too tired to speak until she had had her supper. This was eaten in an enforced silence on the part of the children, and then the old woman was helped into an easy-chair before the fire. They gathered about her, eager for news of the great world, and Sophia said, "Now, come, Mehetabel, tell us all about it!"

Mehetabel drew a long breath. "It was just perfect!" she said; "finer even than I thought. They've got it hanging up in the very middle of a sort o' closet made of glass, and one of the lower corners is ripped and turned back so's to show the seams on the wrong side."

"What?" asked Sophia, a little blankly.

"Why, the quilt!" said Mehetabel in surprise. "There are a whole lot of other ones in that room, but not one that can hold a candle to it, if I do say it who shouldn't. I heard lots of people say the same thing. You ought to have heard what the women said about that corner, Sophia. They said—well, I'd be ashamed to *tell* you what they said. I declare if I wouldn't!"

Mr. Elwell asked, "What did you think of that big ox we've heard so much about?"

"I didn't look at the stock," returned his sister indifferently. "That set of pieces you gave me, Maria, from your red waist, come out just lovely!" she assured one of her nieces. "I heard one woman say you could 'most smell the red silk roses."

"Did any of the horses in our town race?" asked young Thomas.

"I didn't see the races."

"How about the preserves?" asked Sophia.

"I didn't see the preserves," said Mehetabel calmly. "You see, I went right to the room where the quilt was, and then I didn't want to leave it. It had been so long since I'd seen it. I had to look at it first real good myself, and then I looked at the others to see if there was any that could come up to it. And then the people begun comin' in and I got so interested in hearin' what they had to say I couldn't think of goin' anywheres else. I ate my lunch right there too, and I'm as glad as can be I did, too; for what do you think?"—she gazed about her with kindling eyes—"while I stood there with a sandwich in one hand didn't the head of the hull concern come in and open the glass door and pin 'First Prize' right in the middle of the quilt!"

There was a stir of congratulation and proud exclamation. Then Sophia returned again to the attack. "Didn't you go to see anything else?" she queried.

"Why, no," said Mehetabel. "Only the quilt. Why should I?"

She fell into a reverie where she saw again the glorious creation of her hand and brain hanging before all the world with the mark of highest approval on it. She longed to make her listeners see the splendid vision with her. She struggled for words; she reached blindly after unknown superlatives. "I tell you it looked like—" she said, and paused, hesitating. Vague recollections of hymn-book phraseology came into her mind, the only form of literary expression she knew; but they were dismissed as being sacrilegious, and also not sufficiently forcible. Finally, "I tell you it looks real *well*," she assured them, and sat staring into the fire, on her tired old face the supreme content of an artist who has realized his ideal.

Paper Route

THOMAS WOLFE

*This is a passage from Thomas Wolfe's great first novel,
Look Homeward, Angel, and is about its hero's first sexual
semi-experience. It is full, exciting, compassionate, and living.*

*Altamont, they say, is Asheville, North Carolina, where
Thomas Wolfe lived. In a later book he describes their reaction to his first book. They felt they had been ruthlessly
exposed and wanted to destroy him. I was staying overnight
in Asheville on a reading tour and I found that now people
will buttonhole you on the street and say such things as,
"You know, I'm the man who sneezes on page 265 on this
very street!"*

*That's always what happens to great men. It happened to
Dickens, it happened to Rembrandt—and it has happened
to Thomas Wolfe, who is one of the great masters.*

Toward the beginning of Eugene Gant's fourteenth year, his elder
brother, Ben, got work for him as a paper carrier. He was given the
Niggertown route—the hardest and least profitable of all. He was
paid two cents a copy for weekly deliveries, given ten per cent of his
weekly collections, and ten cents for every new subscription. Thus,
he was able to earn four or five dollars a week.

From the worn central butte in Altamont round which the negro
colony swarmed, the panting voices of the Calvary Baptist Church
mounted, in an exhausting and unceasing frenzy, from seven o'clock
until two in the morning, in their wild jungle wail of sin and love
and death. The dark was hived with flesh and mystery. Rich wells of
laughter bubbled everywhere. The cat-forms slid. Everything was
immanent. Everything was far. Nothing could be touched.

In this old witch-magic of the dark, he began to know the awful
innocence of evil, the terrible youth of an ancient race; his lips slid
back across his teeth, he prowled in darkness with loose swinging
arms, and his eyes shone. Shame and terror, indefinable, surged
through him. He could not face the question in his heart.

A good part of his subscription list was solidly founded among decent and laborious darkies—barbers, tailors, grocers, pharmacists, and ginghamed black housewives, who paid him promptly on a given day each week, greeting him with warm smiles full of teeth, and titles of respect extravagant and kindly: "Mister," "Colonel," "General," "Governor," and so on. They all knew Gant.

He harried his deficient subscribers for payment, with a wild tenacity. He accepted their easy promises without question; he hunted them down in their own rooms, or in the rooms of a neighbor, he pressed so doggedly that, at length, sullenly or good-humoredly, they paid a part of their debt.

One Saturday evening, in the fading red of a summer twilight, he returned to one of these tenements, a rickety three-story shack, that dropped its two lower floors down a tall clay bank at the western ledge, near the whites. Two dozen men and women lived here. He was on the search for a woman named Ella Corpening. He had never been able to find her: she was weeks behind in her subscription. But her door stood open to-night: a warm waft of air and cooking food came up to him. He descended the rotten steps that climbed the bank.

Ella Corpening sat facing the door in a rocking chair, purring lazily in the red glow of a little kitchen range, with her big legs stretched comfortably out on the floor. She was a mulatto of twenty-six years, a handsome woman of Amazonian proportions, with smooth tawny skin.

She was dressed in the garments of some former mistress: she wore a brown woollen skirt, patent-leather shoes with high suede tops pearl-buttoned, and gray silk hose. Her long heavy arms shone darkly through the light texture of a freshly laundered white shirtwaist. A lacing of cheap blue ribbon gleamed across the heavy curve of her breasts.

There was a bubbling pot of cabbage and sliced fat pork upon the stove.

"Paper boy," said Eugene. "Come to collect."

"Is you de boy?" drawled Ella Corpening with a lazy movement of her arm. "How much does I owe?"

"$1.20," he answered. He looked meaningfully at one extended leg, where, thrust in below the knee, a wadded bank-note gleamed dully.

"Dat's my rent money," she said. "Can't give you dat. Dollah-twenty!" She brooded. "Uh! Uh!" she grunted pleasantly. "Don't seem lak it ought to be dat much."

"It is, though," he said, opening his account book.

"It mus' is," she agreed, "if de book say so."

She meditated luxuriously for a moment.

"Does you collec' Sunday mawnin'?" she asked.

"Yes," he said.

"You come roun' in de mawnin'," she said hopefully. "I'll have somethin' fo' yuh, sho. I'se waitin' fo' a white gent'man now. He's goin' gib me a dollah."

She moved her great limbs slowly, and smiled at him. Forked pulses beat against his eyes. He gulped dryly: his legs were rotten with excitement.

"What's—what's he going to give you a dollar for?" he muttered, barely audible.

"Jelly Roll," said Ella Corpening.

He moved his lips twice, unable to speak. She got up from her chair.

"What yo' want?" she asked softly. "Jelly Roll?"

"Want to see—to see!" he gasped.

She closed the door opening on the bank and locked it. The stove cast a grated glow from its open ashpan. There was a momentary rain of red cinders into the pit.

Ella Corpening opened the door beyond that, leading to another room. There were two dirty rumpled beds; the single window was bolted and covered by an old green shade. She lit a smoky little lamp, and turned the wick low.

There was a battered little dresser with a mottled glass, from which the blistered varnish was flaking. Over the screened hearth, on a low mantel, there was a Kewpie doll, sashed with pink ribbon, a vase with fluted edges and gilt flowers, won at a carnival, and a paper of pins. A calendar, also, by courtesy of the Altamount Coal and Ice Company, showing an Indian maid paddling her canoe down an alley of paved moonlight, and a religious motto in flowered scroll-work, framed in walnut: *God Loves Them Both.*

"What yo' want?" she whispered, facing him.

Far off, he listened to the ghost of his own voice.

"Take off your clothes."

Her skirt fell in a ring about her feet. She took off her starched waist. In a moment, save for her hose, she stood naked before him.

Her breath came quickly, her full tongue licked across her mouth.

"Dance!" he cried. "Dance!"

She began to moan softly, while an undulant tremor flowed through her great yellow body; her hips and her round heavy breasts writhed slowly in a sensual rhythm.

Her straight oiled hair fell across her neck in a thick shock. She extended her arms for balance, the lids closed over her large yellow eyeballs. She came near him. He felt her hot breath on his face, the smothering flood of her breasts. He was whirled like a chip in the wild torrent of her passion. Her powerful yellow hands gripped his slender arms round like bracelets. She shook him to and fro slowly, fastening him tightly against her pelt.

He strained back desperately against the door, drowning in her embrace.

"Get-'way-nigger. Get-'way," he panted thickly.

Slowly she released him: without opening her eyes, moaning, she slid back as if he had been a young tree. She sang, in a wailing minor key, with unceasing iteration:

"Jelly Roll! Je-e-e-ly Roll!"——

her voice falling each time to a low moan.

Her face, the broad column of her throat, and her deep-breasted torso were rilled with sweat. He fumbled blindly for the door, lunged across the outer room and, gasping, found his way into the air. Her chant, unbroken and undisturbed by his departure, followed him up the flimsy steps. He did not pause to get his breath until he came to the edge of the market square. Below him in the valley, across on the butte, the smoky lamps of Niggertown flared in the dusk. Faint laughter, rich, jungle-wild, welled up from hived darkness. He heard lost twangling notes, the measured thump of distant feet; beyond, above, more thin, more far than all, the rapid wail of sinners in a church.

The Flight of Betsey Lane

SARAH ORNE JEWETT

> I'm afraid "The Flight of Betsey Lane" has very much the
> same kind of plot as "The Bedquilt," by Dorothy Canfield
> Fisher. But the writing is very different. Sentimental, yes,
> but I like good slop and so do you. And Miss Jewett's style
> is brilliant. I think this story would make a beautiful motion
> picture.
>
> Sarah Orne Jewett once said to Willa Cather that her
> head was full of dear old houses and dear old women and
> when an old house and an old woman came together, she
> felt a story.
>
> Willa Cather wrote that if she were asked to name three
> American books which had the possibility of a long, long
> life, she would say at once The Scarlet Letter, Huckleberry
> Finn, and The Country of the Pointed Firs, which is the
> book from which this story comes. It is a beautiful bedside
> book, particularly when you've had an annoying day.

1   One windy morning in May, three old women sat together near
an open window in the shed chamber of Byfleet Poor-house. The
wind was from the northwest, but their window faced the southeast,
and they were only visited by an occasional pleasant waft of fresh
air. They were close together, knee to knee, picking over a bushel of
beans, and commanding a view of the dandelion-starred, green yard
below, and of the winding, sandy road that led to the village, two
miles away. Some captive bees were scolding among the cobwebs of
the rafters overhead, or thumping against the upper panes of glass;
two calves were bawling from the barnyard, where some of the men
were at work loading a dump-cart and shouting as if every one were
deaf. There was a cheerful feeling of activity, and even an air of
comfort, about the Byfleet Poor-house. Almost every one was possessed of a most interesting past, though there was less to be said
about the future. The inmates were by no means distressed or unhappy; many of them retired to this shelter only for the winter season, and would go out presently, some to begin such work as they

could still do, others to live in their own small houses; old age had impoverished most of them by limiting their power of endurance; but far from lamenting the fact that they were town charges, they rather liked the change and excitement of a winter residence on the poor-farm. There was a sharp-faced, hard-worked young widow with seven children, who was an exception to the general level of society, because she deplored the change in her fortunes. The older women regarded her with suspicion, and were apt to talk about her in moments like this, when they happened to sit together at their work.

The three bean-pickers were dressed alike in stout brown ginghams, checked by a white line, and all wore great faded aprons of blue drilling, with sufficient pockets convenient to the right hand. Miss Peggy Bond was a very small, belligerent-looking person, who wore a huge pair of steel-bowed spectacles, holding her sharp chin well up in air, as if to supplement an inadequate nose. She was more than half blind, but the spectacles seemed to face upward instead of square ahead, as if their wearer were always on the sharp lookout for birds. Miss Bond had suffered much personal damage from time to time, because she never took heed where she planted her feet, and so was always tripping and stubbing her bruised way through the world. She had fallen down hatchways and cellarways, and stepped composedly into deep ditches and pasture brooks; but she was proud of stating that she was upsighted, and so was her father before her. At the poor-house, where an unusual malady was considered a distinction, upsightedness was looked upon as a most honorable infirmity. Plain rheumatism, such as afflicted Aunt Lavina Dow, whose twisted hands found even this light work difficult and tiresome,—plain rheumatism was something of every-day occurrence, and nobody cared to hear about it. Poor Peggy was a meek and friendly soul, who never put herself forward; she was just like other folks, as she always loved to say, but Mrs. Lavina Dow was a different sort of person altogether, of great dignity and, occasionally, almost aggressive behavior. The time had been when she could do a good day's work with anybody: but for many years now she had not left the town-farm, being too badly crippled to work; she had no relations or friends to visit, but from an innate love of authority she could not submit to being one of those who are forgotten by the world. Mrs. Dow was the hostess and social lawgiver here, where she remembered every inmate and every item of interest for nearly forty years, besides an immense amount of town history and biography for three or four generations back.

She was the dear friend of the third woman, Betsey Lane; together they led thought and opinion—chiefly opinion—and held sway, not only over Byfleet Poor-farm, but also the selectmen and all others in

authority. Betsey Lane had spent most of her life as aid-in-general
to the respected household of old General Thornton. She had been
much trusted and valued, and, at the breaking up of that once large
and flourishing family, she had been left in good circumstances, what
with legacies and her own comfortable savings; but by sad misfortune
and lavish generosity everything had been scattered, and after much
illness, which ended in a stiffened arm and more uncertainty, the
good soul had sensibly decided that it was easier for the whole town
to support her than for a part of it. She had always hoped to see
something of the world before she died; she came of an adventurous,
seafaring stock, but had never made a longer journey than to the
towns of Danby and Northville, thirty miles away.

They were all old women; but Betsey Lane, who was sixty-nine,
and looked much older, was the youngest. Peggy Bond was far on in
the seventies, and Mrs. Dow was at least ten years older. She made a
great secret of her years; and as she sometimes spoke of events prior
to the Revolution with the assertion of having been an eye-witness,
she naturally wore an air of vast antiquity. Her tales were an inex-
pressible delight to Betsey Lane, who felt younger by twenty years
because her friend and comrade was so unconscious of chronological
limitations.

The bushel basket of cranberry beans was within easy reach, and
each of the pickers had filled her lap from it again and again. The
shed chamber was not an unpleasant place in which to sit at work,
with its traces of seed corn hanging from the brown crossbeams, its
spare churns, and dusty loom, and rickety wool-wheels, and a few bits
of old furniture. In one far corner was a wide board of dismal use
and suggestion, and close beside it an old cradle. There was a battered chest of drawers where the keeper of the poor-house kept his
garden-seeds, with the withered remains of three seed cucumbers
ornamenting the top. Nothing beautiful could be discovered, nothing
interesting, but there was something usable and homely about the
place. It was the favorite and untroubled bower of the bean-pickers,
to which they might retreat unmolested from the public apartments
of this rustic institution.

Betsey Lane blew away the chaff from a handful of beans. The
spring breeze blew the chaff back again, and sifted it over her face
and shoulders. She rubbed it out of her eyes impatiently, and happened to notice old Peggy holding her own handful high, as if it were
an oblation, and turning her queer, up-tilted head this way and that,
to look at the beans sharply, as if she were first cousin to a hen.

"There, Miss Bond, 't is kind of botherin' work for you, ain't it?"
Betsey inquired compassionately.

"I feel to enjoy it, anything that I can do my own way so," re-

sponded Peggy. "I like to do my part. Ain't that old Mis' Fales comin'
up the road? It sounds like her step."

The others looked, but they were not farsighted, and for a moment
Peggy had the advantage. Mrs. Fales was not a favorite.

"I hope she ain't comin' here to put up this spring. I guess she
won't now, it's gettin' so late," said Betsey Lane. "She likes to go
rovin' soon as the roads is settled."

" 'T is Mis' Fales!" said Peggy Bond, listening with solemn anxiety.
"There, do let's pray her by!"

"I guess she's headin' for her cousin's folks up Beech Hill way,"
said Betsey presently. "If she'd left her daughter's this mornin', she'd
have got just about as far as this. I kind o' wish she had stepped in
just to pass the time o' day, long's she wa'n't going to make no stop."

There was a silence as to further speech in the shed chamber; and
even the calves were quiet in the barnyard. The men had all gone
away to the field where corn-planting was going on. The beans clicked
steadily into the wooden measure of the pickers' feet. Betsey Lane
began to sing a hymn, and the others joined in as best they might,
like autumnal crickets; their voices were sharp and cracked, with now
and then a few low notes of plaintive tone. Betsey herself could sing
pretty well, but the others could only make a kind of accompani-
ment. Their voices ceased altogether at the higher notes.

"Oh my! I wish I had the means to go to the Centennial,"
mourned Betsey Lane, stopping so suddenly that the others had to
go on croaking and shrilling without her for a moment before they
could stop. "It seems to me as if I can't die happy 'less I do," she
added; "I ain't never seen nothin' of the world, an' here I be."

"What if you was as old as I be?" suggested Mrs. Dow pompously.
"You've got time enough yet, Betsey; don't you go an' despair. I
knowed of a woman that went clean round the world four times
when she was past eighty, an' enjoyed herself real well. Her folks
followed the sea; she had three sons an' a daughter married,—all
shipmasters, and she'd been with her own husband when they was
young. She was left a widder early, and fetched up her family herself,
—a real stirrin', smart woman. After they'd got married off, an' settled, an' was doing well, she come to be lonesome; and first she tried
to stick it out alone, but she wa'n't one that could; an' she got a
notion she hadn't nothin' before her but her last sickness, and she
wa'n't a person that enjoyed havin' other folks do for her. So one on
her boys—I guess 't was the oldest—said he was going to take her
to sea; there was ample room, an' he was sailin' a good time o' year
for the Cape o' Good Hope an' way up to some o' them tea-ports in
the Chiny Seas. She was all high to go, but it made a sight o' talk at
her age; an' the minister made it a subject o' prayer the last Sunday,

and all the folks took a last leave; but she said to some she'd fetch 'em home something real pritty, and so did. An' then they come home t' other way, round the Horn, an' she done so well, an' was such a sight o' company, the other child'n was jealous, an' she promised she'd go a v'y'ge long o' each on 'em. She was as sprightly a person as ever I see; an' could speak well o' what she'd seen."

"Did she die to sea?" asked Peggy with interest.

"No, she died to home between v'y'ges, or she'd gone to sea again. I was to her funeral. She liked her son George's ship the best; 't was the one she was going on to Callao. They said the men aboard all called her 'gran'ma'am,' an' she kep' 'em mended up, an' would go below and tend to 'em if they was sick. She might 'a' been alive an' enjoyin' of herself a good many years but for the kick of a cow; 't was a new cow out of a drove, a dreadful unruly beast."

Mrs. Dow stopped for breath, and reached down for a new supply of beans; her empty apron was gray with soft chaff. Betsey Lane, still pondering on the Centennial, began to sing another verse of her hymn, and again the old women joined her. At this moment some strangers came driving round into the yard from the front of the house. The turf was soft, and our friends did not hear the horses' steps. Their voices cracked and quavered; it was a funny little concert, and a lady in an open carriage just below listened with sympathy and amusement.

2   "Betsey! Betsey! Miss Lane!" a voice called eagerly at the foot of the stairs that led up from the shed. "Betsey! There's a lady here who wants to see you right away."

Betsey was dazed with excitement, like a country child who knows the rare pleasure of being called out of school. "Lor', I ain't fit to go down, be I?" she faltered, looking anxiously at her friends; but Peggy was gazing even nearer to the zenith than usual, in her excited effort to see down into the yard, and Mrs. Dow only nodded somewhat jealously, and said that she guessed 't was nobody would do her any harm. She rose ponderously, while Betsey hesitated, being, as they would have said, all of a twitter. "It is a lady, certain," Mrs. Dow assured her; " 't ain't often there's a lady comes here."

"While there was any of Mis' Gen'ral Thornton's folks left, I wa'n't without visits from the gentry," said Betsey Lane, turning back proudly at the head of the stairs, with a touch of old-world pride and sense of high station. Then she disappeared, and closed the door behind her at the stair-foot with a decision quite unwelcome to the friends above.

"She needn't 'a' been so dreadful 'fraid anybody was goin' to listen.

I guess we've got folks to ride an' see us, or had once, if we hain't now," said Miss Peggy Bond, plaintively.

"I expect 't was only the wind shoved it to," said Aunt Lavina. "Betsey is one that gits flustered easier than some. I wish 't was somebody to take her off an' give her a kind of a good time; she's young to settle down 'long of old folks like us. Betsey's got a notion o' rovin' such as ain't my natur', but I should like to see her satisfied. She'd been a very understandin' person, if she had the advantages that some does."

" 'T is so," said Peggy Bond, tilting her chin high. "I suppose you can't hear nothin' they're saying? I feel my hearin' ain't up to whar it was. I can hear things close to me well as ever; but there, hearin' ain't everything; 't ain't as if we lived where there was more goin' on to hear. Seems to me them folks is stoppin' a good while."

"They surely be," agreed Lavina Dow.

"I expect it's somethin' particular. There ain't none of the Thornton folks left, except one o' the grand'darters, an' I've often heard Betsey remark that she should never see her more, for she lives to London. Strange how folks feels contented in them strayaway places off to the ends of the airth."

The flies and bees were buzzing against the hot window-panes; the handfuls of beans were clicking into the brown wooden measure. A bird came and perched on the window-sill, and then flitted away toward the blue sky. Below, in the yard, Betsey Lane stood talking with the lady. She had put her blue drilling apron over her head, and her face was shining with delight.

"Lor', dear," she said, for at least the third time, "I remember ye when I first see ye; an awful pritty baby you was, an' they all said you looked just like the old gen'ral. Be you goin' back to foreign parts right away?"

"Yes, I'm going back; you know that all my children are there. I wish I could take you with me for a visit," said the charming young guest. "I'm going to carry over some of the pictures and furniture from the old house; I didn't care half so much for them when I was younger as I do now. Perhaps next summer we shall all come over for a while. I should like to see my girls and boys playing under the pines."

"I wish you re'lly was livin' to the old place," said Betsey Lane. Her imagination was not swift; she needed time to think over all that was being told her, and she could not fancy the two strange houses across the sea. The old Thornton house was to her mind the most delightful and elegant in the world.

"Is there anything I can do for you?" asked Mrs. Strafford kindly,

—"anything that I can do for you myself, before I go away? I shall be writing to you, and sending some pictures of the children, and you must let me know how you are getting on."

"Yes, there is one thing, darlin'. If you could stop in the village an' pick me out a pritty, little, small lookin'-glass, that I can keep for my own an' have to remember you by. 'T ain't that I want to set me above the rest o' the folks, but I was always used to havin' my own when I was to your grandma's. There's very nice folks here, some on 'em, and I'm better off than if I was able to keep house; but sence you ask me, that's the only thing I feel cropin' about. What be you goin' right back for? ain't you goin' to see the great fair to Pheladelphy, that everybody talks about?"

"No," said Mrs. Strafford, laughing at this eager and almost convicting question. "No; I'm going back next week. If I were, I believe that I should take you with me. Good-by, dear old Betsey; you make me feel as if I were a little girl again; you look just the same."

For full five minutes the old woman stood out in the sunshine, dazed with delight, and majestic with a sense of her own consequence. She held something tight in her hand, without thinking what it might be; but just as the friendly mistress of the poor-farm came out to hear the news, she tucked the roll of money into the bosom of her brown gingham dress. " 'T was my dear Mis' Katy Strafford," she turned to say proudly. "She come way over from London; she's been sick; they thought the voyage would do her good. She said most the first thing she had on her mind was to come an' find me, and see how I was, an' if I was comfortable; an' now she's goin' right back. She's got two splendid houses; an' said how she wished I was there to look after things,—she remembered I was always her gran'ma's right hand. Oh, it does so carry me back, to see her! Seems if all the rest on 'em must be there together to the old house. There, I must go right up an' tell Mis' Dow an' Peggy."

"Dinner's all ready; I was just goin' to blow the horn for the men-folks," said the keeper's wife. "They'll be right down. I expect you've got along smart with them beans,—all three of you together;" but Betsey's mind roved so high and so far at that moment that no achievements of bean-picking could lure it back.

3   The long table in the great kitchen soon gathered its company of waifs and strays,—creatures of improvidence and misfortune, and the irreparable victims of old age. The dinner was satisfactory, and there was not much delay for conversation. Peggy Bond and Mrs. Dow and Betsey Lane always sat together at one end, with an air of putting the rest of the company below the salt. Betsey was still

flushed with excitement; in fact, she could not eat as much as usual, and she looked up from time to time expectantly, as if she were likely to be asked to speak of her guest; but everybody was hungry, and even Mrs. Dow broke in upon some attempted confidences by asking inopportunely for a second potato. There were nearly twenty at the table, counting the keeper and his wife and two children, noisy little persons who had come from school with the small flock belonging to the poor widow, who sat just opposite our friends. She finished her dinner before any one else, and pushed her chair back; she always helped with the housework,—a thin, sorry, bad-tempered-looking poor soul, whom grief had sharpened instead of softening. "I expect you feel too fine to set with common folks," she said enviously to Betsey.

"Here I be a-settin'," responded Betsey calmly. "I don' know's I behave more unbecomin' than usual." Betsey prided herself upon her good and proper manners; but the rest of the company, who would have liked to hear the bit of morning news, were now defrauded of that pleasure. The wrong note had been struck; there was a silence after the clatter of knives and plates, and one by one the cheerful town charges disappeared. The bean-picking had been finished, and there was a call for any of the women who felt like planting corn; so Peggy Bond, who could follow the line of hills pretty fairly, and Betsey herself, who was still equal to anybody at that work, and Mrs. Dow, all went out to the field together. Aunt Lavina labored slowly up the yard, carrying a light splint-bottomed kitchen chair and her knitting-work, and sat near the stone wall on a gentle rise, where she could see the pond and the green country, and exchange a word with her friends as they came and went up and down the rows. Betsey vouchsafed a word now and then about Mrs. Strafford, but you would have thought that she had been suddenly elevated to Mrs. Strafford's own cares and the responsibilities attending them, and had little in common with her old associates. Mrs. Dow and Peggy knew well that these high-feeling times never lasted long, and so they waited with as much patience as they could muster. They were by no means without that true tact which is only another word for unselfish sympathy.

The strip of corn land ran along the side of a great field; at the upper end of it was a field-corner thicket of young maples and walnut saplings, the children of a great nut-tree that marked the boundary. Once, when Betsey Lane found herself alone near this shelter at the end of her row, the other planters having lagged behind the rising ground, she looked stealthily about, and then put her hand inside her gown, and for the first time took out the money that Mrs. Strafford had given her. She turned it over and over with an astonished look:

there were new bank-bills for a hundred dollars. Betsey gave a funny little shrug of her shoulders, came out of the bushes, and took a step or two on the narrow edge of turf, as if she were going to dance; then she hastily tucked away her treasure, and stepped discreetly down into the soft harrowed and hoed land, and began to drop corn again, five kernels to a hill. She had seen the top of Peggy Bond's head over the knoll, and now Peggy herself came entirely into view, gazing upward to the skies, and stumbling more or less, but counting the corn by touch and twisting her head about anxiously to gain advantage over her uncertain vision. Betsey made a friendly, inarticulate little sound as they passed; she was thinking that somebody said once that Peggy's eyesight might be remedied if she could go to Boston to the hospital; but that was so remote and impossible an undertaking that no one had ever taken the first step. Betsey Lane's brown old face suddenly worked with excitement, but in a moment more she regained her usual firm expression, and spoke carelessly to Peggy as she turned and came alongside.

The high spring wind of the morning had quite fallen; it was a lovely May afternoon. The woods about the field to the northward were full of birds, and the young leaves scarcely hid the solemn shapes of a company of crows that patiently attended the corn-planting. Two of the men had finished their hoeing, and were busy with the construction of a scarecrow; they knelt in the furrows, chuckling, and looking over some forlorn, discarded garments. It was a time-honored custom to make the scarecrow resemble one of the poor-house family; and this year they intended to have Mrs. Lavina Dow protect the field in effigy; last year it was the counterfeit of Betsey Lane who stood on guard, with an easily recognized quilted hood and the remains of a valued shawl that one of the calves had found airing on a fence and chewed to pieces. Behind the men was the foundation for this rustic attempt at statuary,—an upright stake and bar in the form of a cross. This stood on the highest part of the field; and as the men knelt near it, and the quaint figures of the corn-planters went and came, the scene gave a curious suggestion of foreign life. It was not like New England; the presence of the rude cross appealed strangely to the imagination.

4   Life flowed so smoothly, for the most part, at the Byfleet Poor-farm, that nobody knew what to make, later in the summer, of a strange disappearance. All the elder inmates were familiar with illness and death, and the poor pomp of a town-pauper's funeral. The comings and goings and the various misfortunes of those who composed this strange family, related only through its disasters, hardly served for the excitement and talk of a single day. Now that the June

days were at their longest, the old people were sure to wake earlier than ever; but one morning, to the astonishment of every one, Betsey Lane's bed was empty; the sheets and blankets, which were her own, and guarded with jealous care, were carefully folded and placed on a chair not too near the window, and Betsey had flown. Nobody had heard her go down the creaking stairs. The kitchen door was unlocked, and the old watch-dog lay on the step outside in the early sunshine, wagging his tail and looking wise, as if he were left on guard and meant to keep the fugitive's secret.

"Never knowed her to do nothin' afore 'thout talking it over a fortnight, and paradin' off when we could all see her," ventured a spiteful voice. "Guess we can wait till night to hear 'bout it."

Mrs. Dow looked sorrowful and shook her head. "Betsey had an aunt on her mother's side that went and drownded of herself; she was a pritty-appearing woman as ever you see."

"Perhaps she's gone to spend the day with Decker's folks," suggested Peggy Bond. "She always takes an extra early start; she was speakin' lately o' going up their way;" but Mrs. Dow shook her head with a most melancholy look. "I'm impressed that something's befell her," she insisted. "I heard her a-groanin' in her sleep. I was wakeful the forepart o' the night,—'t is very unusual with me, too."

" 'T wa'n't like Betsey not to leave us any word," said the other old friend, with more resentment than melancholy. They sat together almost in silence that morning in the shed chamber. Mrs. Dow was sorting and cutting rags, and Peggy braided them into long ropes, to be made into mats at a later date. If they had only known where Betsey Lane had gone, they might have talked about it until dinnertime at noon; but failing this new subject, they could take no interest in any of their old ones. Out in the field the corn was well up, and the men were hoeing. It was a hot morning in the shed chamber, and the woolen rags were dusty and hot to handle.

5   Byfleet people knew each other well, and when this mysteriously absent person did not return to the town-farm at the end of a week, public interest became much excited; and presently it was ascertained that Betsey Lane was neither making a visit to her friends the Deckers on Birch Hill, nor to any nearer acquaintances; in fact, she had disappeared altogether from her wonted haunts. Nobody remembered to have seen her pass, hers had been such an early flitting; and when somebody thought of her having gone away by train, he was laughed at for forgetting that the earliest morning train from South Byfleet, the nearest station, did not start until long after eight o'clock; and if Betsey had designed to be one of the passengers, she would have started along the road at seven, and been seen and known of all

women. There was not a kitchen in that part of Byfleet that did not have windows toward the road. Conversation rarely left the level of the neighborhood gossip: to see Betsey Lane, in her best clothes, at that hour in the morning, would have been the signal for much exercise of imagination; but as day after day went by without news, the curiosity of those who knew her best turned slowly into fear, and at last Peggy Bond again gave utterance to the belief that Betsey had either gone out in the early morning and put an end to her life, or that she had gone to the Centennial. Some of the people at table were moved to loud laughter,—it was at supper-time on a Sunday night,— but others listened with great interest.

"She never'd put on her good clothes to drownd herself," said the widow. "She might have thought 't was good as takin' 'em with her, though. Old folks has wandered off an' got lost in the woods afore now."

Mrs. Dow and Peggy resented this impertinent remark, but deigned to take no notice of the speaker. "She wouldn't have wore her best clothes to the Centennial, would she?" mildly inquired Peggy, bobbing her head toward the ceiling. " 'T would be a shame to spoil your best things in such a place. An' I don't know of her havin' any money; there's the end o' that."

"You're bad as old Mis' Bland, that used to live neighbor to our folks," said one of the old men. "She was dreadful precise; an' she so begretched to wear a good alpaca dress that was left to her, that it hung in a press forty year, an' baited the moths at last."

"I often seen Mis' Bland a-goin' in to meetin' when I was a young girl," said Peggy Bond approvingly. "She was a good-appearin' woman, an' she left property."

"Wish she'd left it to me, then," said the poor soul opposite, glancing at her pathetic row of children: but it was not good manners at the farm to deplore one's situation, and Mrs. Dow and Peggy only frowned. "Where do you suppose Betsey can be?" said Mrs. Dow, for the twentieth time. "She didn't have no money. I know she ain't gone far, if it's so that she's yet alive. She's b'en real pinched all the spring."

"Perhaps that lady that come one day give her some," the keeper's wife suggested mildly.

"Then Betsey would have told me," said Mrs. Dow, with injured dignity.

6   On the morning of her disappearance, Betsey rose even before the pewee and the English sparrow, and dressed herself quietly, though with trembling hands, and stole out of the kitchen door like a plunderless thief. The old dog licked her hand and looked at her

anxiously; the tortoise-shell cat rubbed against her best gown, and trotted away up the yard, then she turned anxiously and came after the old woman, following faithfully until she had to be driven back. Betsey was used to long country excursions afoot. She dearly loved the early morning; and finding that there was no dew to trouble her, she began to follow pasture paths and short cuts across the fields, surprising here and there a flock of sleepy sheep, or a startled calf that rustled out from the bushes. The birds were pecking their breakfast from bush and turf; and hardly any of the wild inhabitants of that rural world were enough alarmed by her presence to do more than flutter away if they chanced to be in her path. She stepped along, light-footed and eager as a girl, dressed in her neat old straw bonnet and black gown, and carrying a few belongings in her best bundle-handkerchief, one that her only brother had brought home from the East Indies fifty years before. There was an old crow perched as sentinel on a small, dead pine-tree, where he could warn friends who were pulling up the sprouted corn in a field close by; but he only gave a contemptuous caw as the adventurer appeared, and she shook her bundle at him in revenge, and laughed to see him so clumsy as he tried to keep his footing on the twigs.

"Yes, I be," she assured him. "I'm a-goin' to Pheladelphy, to the Centennial, same's other folks. I'd just as soon tell ye's not, old crow;" and Betsey laughed aloud in pleased content with herself and her daring, as she walked along. She had only two miles to go to the station at South Byfleet, and she felt for the money now and then, and found it safe enough. She took great pride in the success of her escape, and especially in the long concealment of her wealth. Not a night had passed since Mrs. Strafford's visit that she had not slept with the roll of money under her pillow by night, and buttoned safe inside her dress by day. She knew that everybody would offer advice and even commands about the spending or saving of it; and she brooked no interference.

The last mile of the foot-path to South Byfleet was along the railway track; and Betsey began to feel in haste, though it was still nearly two hours to train time. She looked anxiously forward and back along the rails every few minutes, for fear of being run over; and at last she caught sight of an engine that was apparently coming toward her, and took flight into the woods before she could gather courage to follow the path again. The freight train proved to be at a standstill, waiting at a turnout; and some of the men were straying about, eating their early breakfast comfortably in this time of leisure. As the old woman came up to them, she stopped too, for a moment of rest and conversation.

"Where be ye goin'?" she asked pleasantly; and they told her. It

was to the town where she had to change cars and take the great
through train; a point of geography which she had learned from evening talks between the men at the farm.

"What'll ye carry me there for?"

"We don't run no passenger cars," said one of the young fellows,
laughing. "What makes you in such a hurry?"

"I'm startin' for Pheladelphy, an' it's a gre't ways to go."

"So 't is; but you're consid'able early, if you're makin' for the eight-
forty train. See here! you haven't got a needle an' thread 'long of you
in that bundle, have you? If you'll sew me on a couple o' buttons,
I'll give ye a free ride. I'm in a sight o' distress, an' none o' the fellows
is provided with as much as a bent pin."

"You poor boy! I'll have you seen to, in half a minute. I'm troubled
with a stiff arm, but I'll do the best I can."

The obliging Betsey seated herself stiffly on the slope of the embankment, and found her thread and needle with utmost haste. Two
of the train-men stood by and watched the careful stitches, and even
offered her a place as spare brakeman, so that they might keep her
near; and Betsey took the offer with considerable seriousness, only
thinking it necessary to assure them that she was getting most too old
to be out in all weathers. An express went by like an earthquake, and
she was presently hoisted on board an empty box-car by two of her
new and flattering acquaintances, and found herself before noon at
the end of the first stage of her journey, without having spent a cent,
and furnished with any amount of thrifty advice. One of the young
men, being compassionate of her unprotected state as a traveler, advised her to find out the widow of an uncle of his in Philadelphia,
saying despairingly that he couldn't tell her just how to find the
house; but Miss Betsey Lane said that she had an English tongue in
her head, and should be sure to find whatever she was looking for.
This unexpected incident of the freight train was the reason why
everybody about the South Byfleet station insisted that no such
person had taken passage by the regular train that same morning,
and why there were those who persuaded themselves that Miss Betsey
Lane was probably lying at the bottom of the poor-farm pond.

7   "Land sakes!" said Miss Betsey Lane, as she watched a Turkish
person parading by in his red fez, "I call the Centennial somethin'
like the day o' judgment! I wish I was goin' to stop a month, but I
dare say 't would be the death o' my poor old bones."

She was leaning against the barrier of a patent pop-corn establish-
ment, which had given her a sudden reminder of home, and of the
winter nights when the sharp-kerneled little red and yellow ears were
brought out, and Old Uncle Eph Flanders sat by the kitchen stove,

and solemnly filled a great wooden chopping-tray for the refreshment of the company. She had wandered and loitered and looked until her eyes and head had grown numb and unreceptive; but it is only unimaginative persons who can be really astonished. The imagination can always outrun the possible and actual sights and sounds of the world; and this plain old body from Byfleet rarely found anything rich and splendid enough to surprise her. She saw the wonders of the West and the splendors of the East with equal calmness and satisfaction; she had always known that there was an amazing world outside the boundaries of Byfleet. There was a piece of paper in her pocket on which was marked, in her clumsy handwriting, "If Betsey Lane should meet with accident, notify the selectmen of Byfleet"; but having made this slight provision for the future, she had thrown herself boldly into the sea of strangers, and then had made the joyful discovery that friends were to be found at every turn.

There was something delightfully companionable about Betsey; she had a way of suddenly looking up over her big spectacles with a reassuring and expectant smile, as if you were going to speak to her, and you generally did. She must have found out where hundreds of people came from, and whom they had left at home, and what they thought of the great show, as she sat on a bench to rest, or leaned over the railings where free luncheons were afforded by the makers of hot waffles and molasses candy and fried potatoes; and there was not a night when she did not return to her lodgings with a pocket crammed with samples of spool cotton and nobody knows what. She had already collected small presents for almost everybody she knew at home, and she was such a pleasant, beaming old country body, so unmistakably appreciative and interested, that nobody ever thought of wishing that she would move on. Nearly all the busy people of the Exhibition called her either Aunty or Grandma at once, and made little pleasures for her as best they could. She was a delightful contrast to the indifferent, stupid crowd that drifted along, with eyes fixed at the same level, and seeing, even on that level, nothing for fifty feet at a time. "What be you making here, dear?" Betsey Lane would ask joyfully, and the most perfunctory guardian hastened to explain. She squandered money as she had never had the pleasure of doing before, and this hastened the day when she must return to Byfleet. She was always inquiring if there were any spectacle-sellers at hand, and received occasional directions; but it was a difficult place for her to find her way about in, and the very last day of her stay arrived before she found an exhibitor of the desired sort, an oculist and instrument-maker.

"I called to get some specs for a friend that's upsighted," she gravely informed the salesman, to his extreme amusement. "She's dreadful troubled, and jerks her head up like a hen a-drinkin'. She's got a blur a-growin' an' spreadin', an' sometimes she can see out to one side on 't, and more times she can't."

"Cataracts," said a middle-aged gentleman at her side; and Betsey Lane turned to regard him with approval and curiosity.

" 'T is Miss Peggy Bond I was mentioning, of Byfleet Poor-farm," she explained. "I count on gettin' some glasses to relieve her trouble, if there's any to be found."

"Glasses won't do her any good," said the stranger. "Suppose you come and sit down on this bench, and tell me all about it. First, where is Byfleet?" and Betsey gave the directions at length.

"I thought so," said the surgeon. "How old is this friend of yours?"

Betsey cleared her throat decisively, and smoothed her gown over her knees as if it were an apron; then she turned to take a good look at her new acquaintance as they sat on the rustic bench together. "Who be you, sir, I should like to know?" she asked, in a friendly tone.

"My name's Dunster."

"I take it you're a doctor," continued Betsey, as if they had overtaken each other walking from Byfleet to South Byfleet on a summer morning.

"I'm a doctor; part of one at least," said he. "I know more or less about eyes; and I spend my summers down on the shore at the mouth of your river; some day I'll come up and look at this person. How old is she?"

"Peggy Bond is one that never tells her age; 't ain't come quite up to where she'll begin to brag of it, you see," explained Betsey reluctantly; "but I know her to be nigh to seventy-six, one way or t' other. Her an' Mrs. Mary Ann Chick was same year's child'n, and Peggy knows I know it, an' two or three times when we've be'n in the buryin'-ground where Mary Ann lays an' has her dates right on her headstone, I couldn't bring Peggy to take no sort o' notice. I will say she makes, at times, a convenience of being upsighted. But there, I feel for her,—everybody does; it keeps her stubbin' an' trippin' against everything, beakin' and gazin' up the way she has to."

"Yes, yes," said the doctor, whose eyes were twinkling. "I'll come and look after her, with your town doctor, this summer,—some time in the last of July or first of August."

"You'll find occupation," said Betsey, not without an air of patronage. "Most of us to the Byfleet Farm has got our ails, now I tell ye. You ain't got no bitters that'll take a dozen years right off an ol' lady's shoulders?"

The busy man smiled pleasantly, and shook his head as he went away. "Dunster," said Betsey to herself, soberly committing the new name to her sound memory. "Yes, I mustn't forget to speak of him to the doctor, as he directed. I do' know now as Peggy would vally herself quite so much accordin' to, if she had her eyes fixed same as other folks. I expect there wouldn't been a smarter woman in town, though, if she'd had a proper chance. Now I've done what I set to do for her, I do believe, an' 't wa'n't glasses, neither. I'll git her a pritty little shawl with that money I laid aside. Peggy Bond ain't got a pritty shawl. I always wanted to have a real good time, an' now I'm havin' it."

8   Two or three days later, two pathetic figures might have been seen crossing the slopes of the poor-farm field, toward the low shores of Byfield pond. It was early in the morning, and the stubble of the lately mown grass was wet with rain and hindering to old feet. Peggy Bond was more blundering and liable to stray in the wrong direction than usual; it was one of the days when she could hardly see at all. Aunt Lavina Dow was unusually clumsy of movement, and stiff in the joints; she had not been so far from the house for three years. The morning breeze filled the gathers of her wide gingham skirt, and aggravated the size of her unwieldy figure. She supported herself with a stick, and trusted beside to the fragile support of Peggy's arm. They were talking together in whispers.

"Oh, my sakes!" exclaimed Peggy, moving her small head from side to side. "Hear you wheeze, Mis' Dow! This may be the death o' you; there, do go slow! You set here on the side-hill, an' le' me go try if I can see."

"It needs more eyesight than you've got," said Mrs. Dow, panting between the words. "Oh! to think how spry I was in my young days, an' here I be now, the full of a door, an' all my complaints so aggravated by my size. 'T is hard! 't is hard! but I'm a-doin' of all this for pore Betsey's sake. I know they've all laughed, but I look to see her ris' to the top o' the pond this day,—'t is just nine days since she departed; an' say what they may, I know she hove herself in. It run in her family; Betsey had an aunt that done just so, an' she ain't be'n like herself, a-broodin' an' hivin' away alone, an' nothin' to say to you an' me that was always sich good company all together. Somethin' sprung her mind, now I tell ye, Mis' Bond."

"I feel to hope we sha'n't find her, I must say," faltered Peggy. It was plain that Mrs. Dow was the captain of this doleful expedition. "I guess she ain't never thought o' drowndin' of herself, Mis' Dow; she's gone off a-visitin' way over to the other side o' South Byfleet; some thinks she's gone to the Centennial even now!"

"She hadn't no proper means, I tell ye," wheezed Mrs. Dow indignantly; "an' if you prefer that others should find her floatin' to the top this day, instid of us that's her best friends, you can step back to the house."

They walked on in aggrieved silence. Peggy Bond trembled with excitement, but her companion's firm grasp never wavered, and so they came to the narrow, gravelly margin and stood still. Peggy tried in vain to see the glittering water and the pond-lilies that starred it; she knew that they must be there; once, years ago, she had caught fleeting glimpses of them, and she never forgot what she had once seen. The clear blue sky overhead, the dark pine-woods beyond the pond, were all clearly pictured in her mind. "Can't you see nothin'?" she faltered; "I believe I'm wuss'n up-sighted this day. I'm going to be blind."

"No," said Lavina Dow solemnly; "no, there ain't nothin' whatever, Peggy. I hope to mercy she ain't"—

"Why, whoever'd expected to find you 'way out here!" exclaimed a brisk and cheerful voice. There stood Betsey Lane herself, close behind them, having just emerged from a thicket of alders that grew close by. She was following the short way homeward from the railroad.

"Why, what's the matter, Mis' Dow? You ain't over-doin', be ye? an' Peggy's all of a flutter. What in the name o' natur' ails ye?"

"There ain't nothin' the matter, as I knows on," responded the leader of this fruitless expedition. "We only thought we'd take a stroll this pleasant mornin'," she added, with sublime self-possession. "Where've you be'n, Betsey Lane?"

"To Pheladelphy, ma'am," said Betsey, looking quite young and gay, and wearing a townish and unfamiliar air that upheld her words. "All ought to go that can; why, you feel's if you'd be'n all round the world. I guess I've got enough to think of and tell ye for the rest o' my days. I've always wanted to go somewheres. I wish you'd be'n there, I do so. I've talked with folks from Chiny an' the back o' Pennsylvany; and I see folks way from Australy that 'peared as well as anybody; an' I see how they made spool cotton, an' sights o' other things; an' I spoke with a doctor that lives down to the beach in the summer, an' he offered to come up 'long in the first of August, an' see what he can do for Peggy's eyesight. There was di'monds there as big as pigeon's eggs; an' I met with Mis' Abby Fletcher from South Byfleet depot; an' there was hogs there that weighed risin' thirteen hunderd"—

"I want to know," said Mrs. Lavina Dow and Peggy Bond, together.

"Well, 't was a great exper'ence for a person," added Lavina, turning ponderously, in spite of herself, to give a last wistful look at the smiling waters of the pond.

"I don't know how soon I be goin' to settle down," proclaimed the rustic sister of Sindbad. "What's for the good o' one's for the good of all. You just wait till we're setting together up in the old shed chamber! You know, my dear Mis' Katy Strafford give me a han'-some present o' money that day she come to see me; and I'd be'n a-dreamin' by night an' day o' seein' that Centennial; and when I come to think on 't I felt sure somebody ought to go from this neighborhood, if 't was only for the good o' the rest; and I thought I'd better be the one. I wa'n't goin' to ask the selec'men neither. I've come back with one-thirty-five in money, and I see everything there, an' I fetched ye all a little somethin'; but I'm full o' dust now, an' pretty nigh beat out. I never see a place more friendly than Phela-delphy; but 't ain't natural to a Byfleet person to be always walkin' on a level. There, now, Peggy, you take my bundle-handkercher and the basket, and let Mis' Dow sag on to me. I'll git her along twice as easy."

With this the small elderly company set forth triumphant toward the poor-house, across the wide green field.

Two Science-Fiction Stories

Do not curl your lip at science fiction. In my trade it is known as "space opera," along with horse opera and soap opera. But there is some wonderful science fiction.

These two stories are by the two best science-fiction writers I know, and I knew H. G. Wells and I know Ray Bradbury. First I would like you to read a long quote from a book by H. G. Wells called Meanwhile. At the beginning of this book there is a great talk which takes place at a villa in Ventimiglia.

Once Elsa and I were his guests down at his house on Lady Warwick's estate in Essex and he gave one of his great talks after dinner in the evening. Part of this was wound up with it somehow—the part about the express train, I think.

He was talking against art. One seemed to have a sensation of sitting in an isolated capsule with the whole universe whirling around one at great speed. I did not believe afterward what he said about art—for he was proving its worthlessness—no more than I believe all of what he says in this.

H. G. Wells is, of course, Mr. Sempack—or at least H. G. Wells used to talk like Mr. Sempack. But he is and was a high and mighty magician.

I remember the talk particularly because when I was younger I used to dream of sitting in an armchair on stage and speaking this piece from Meanwhile. And then I thought of telling the Bible stories, and this has all come about except for the armchair. I stand up on the stage when I read and I have not yet done this passage from Meanwhile. I intend to.

These predictions of the future by the writers of science fiction have an uncomfortable way of coming true. One has only to mention Jules Verne to make the point. I think this kind of story is only good when we have a feeling that it may come true.

However, here we are in a villa in Ventimiglia in the south of France. Mrs. Rylands is our hostess. Among the guests is a Mr. Sempack who is a philosopher. He has a reputation of talking well. They conspire to make him talk. He does:

To many hearers the great talk that was set going in Casa Terragena by Mr. Sempack, would have seemed far less wonderful and original than it did to Mrs. Rylands and the group of young people with her that listened to him. For, after all, it was little more than a gathering together and a fitting together of the main creative suggestions for the regulation of human affairs that have accumulated so richly in the last few score years.

The ground effect of Mr. Sempack upon which all his other effects were built, was his large and unchallengeable intimation of the transitory and provisional nature of the institutions and customs and usages, the forms and appliances and resources amidst which he and his interlocutors were living. He not only had the quality of not really belonging to them himself and of reaching back before they existed and forward to when they would have gone, but he imposed the same quality of relative permanence upon the thoughts of his hearers. He had the quality less of being ephemeral than of sitting with his hearers and watching everything else go by.

The human mind discovered itself relatively immortal amidst evanescent things. This beautiful house became like a tent that would presently be folded up and taken away and the celebrated gardens like a great bouquet of flowers that had been brought from the ends of the earth, just to be looked at and to delight for a little while and then to die and be dispersed. The house was built about a Saracenic watchtower for its core; wherever its foundations had extended buried fragments of polished marble and busts and broken provincial statuary had recalled its Roman predecessor; but at the touch of Sempack these marble gods and emperors became no more than the litter of the last tenant, his torn photographs and out-of-date receipts. The Via Aurelia ran deeply through the grounds between high walls, and some one had set up, at a bridge where the gardens crossed this historical gully, a lettered-stone to recall that on this documented date or that, this emperor and that pope, Nicolo Machiavelli and Napoleon the First, had ridden past. These ghosts seemed scarcely remoter than the records of recent passages in the big leather-bound Visitors' Book in the Hall, Mr. Gladstone and King Edward the Seventh, the Austrian Empress and Mr. Keir Hardie.

Occasionally tombstones that had stood beside the high road were unearthed by changes in the garden. One inscribed quite simply "Amoena Lucina," just that and nothing more, was like a tender sigh that had scarcely passed away. Mrs. Rylands had set it up again in a little walled close of turf and purple flowers. People talked there of Lucina as though she might still hear.

Over everything hung a promise of further transformations, for the Italians had a grandiose scheme for reviving the half-obliterated tracks of the Via Aurelia as a modern motoring road to continue the Grande Corniche. Everything passed here and everything went by; fashions of life and house and people and ideas; it seemed that they passed very swiftly indeed, when one measured time by a scale that would take in those half disinterred skeletons of Cro-Magnon men and Grimaldi men who lay, under careful glass casings now, in the great cave of the Rochers Rouges just visible from the dining-room windows. That great cave was still black with the ashes of pre-historic fires, as plain almost as the traces of yesterday's picnic. Even the grisly sub-man with his rude flint-chipped stakes, was here a thing of overnight. His implements were scattered and left in the deeper layers of the silted cave, like the toys of a child that has recently been sent to bed. With a wave of his ample hand Mr. Sempack could allude to the whole span of the human story.

"Utopias, you say, deny the thing that is," said Mr. Sempack. "Why, yesterday and to-morrow deny the thing that is!"

He made Mrs. Rylands feel like some one who wakes up completely in the compartment of an express train, which between sleeping and waking she had imagined to be a house.

Colonel Bullace had to hear that his dear British Empire had hardly lasted a lifetime. "Its substantial expansion came with the steamships," said Mr. Sempack; "it is held together by the steamship. How much longer will the steamship endure?"

Before the steamship it was no more than the shrunken vestiges of the Empire of George III. Most of America was lost. Our rule in India was a trader's dominion not a third of its present extent. Canada, the Cape were coast settlements.

Now Colonel Bullace was of that variety of Englishman which believes as an article of faith that the Union Jack has "braved a thousand years the battle and the breeze" since 1800. If any one had told him that the stars and stripes was the older of the two flags he would have become homicidal. A steamship Empire! What of Nelson and our wooden walls? What of John Company? What of Raleigh? What of Agincourt? He had a momentary impulse to rise up and kill Mr. Sempack, but he was calling his hand, a rather difficult hand, just then and one must put first things first.

And while Mr. Sempack made respect for any established powerful thing seem the delusion of children still too immature to realise the reality of change, at the same time he brought the idea of the strangest and boldest innovations in the ways of human life within the range of immediately practicable things. In the past our kind had been hustled along by change: now it was being given the power to make its own changes. He did not preach the coming of the Great Age; he assumed it. He put it upon the sceptic to show why it should not arrive. He treated the advancements and extension of science as inevitable. As yet so few people do that. Science might be delayed in its progress or accelerated, but how could its process stop? And how could the fluctuating extravagances of human folly resist for ever the steady drive towards the realisations of that ever-growing and ever-strengthening body of elucidation? There was none of the prophetic visionary about the ungainly Mr. Sempack as he sat deep and low on the sofa. He made the others seem visionaries. Simply he asked them all to be reasonable.

For a time the talk had dealt with various main aspects of this Millennium which Mr. Sempack spoke of so serenely, as a probable and perhaps inevitable achievement for our distressed and confused species. He displayed a large and at times an almost exasperating patience. It was only yesterday, so to speak, that the idea of mankind controlling its own destiny had entered human thought. Were there Utopias before the days of Plato? Mr. Sempack did not know of any. And the idea of wilful and creative change was still a strange and inassimilable idea to most people. There were plenty of people who were no more capable of such an idea than a rabbit. His large grey eye had rested for a moment on Colonel Bullace and drifted pensively to the Mathisons.

"The problem is to deal with them," Mrs. Rylands had reflected, following the indication of the large grey eye.

"They will all die," said Lord Tamar.

"And plenty more get born," said Philip, following his own thoughts to the exclusion of these present applications.

"You don't consult the cat when you alter the house," said Mr. Sempack.

"But is such concealment exactly what one might call—democracy?" asked Mr. Plantagenet-Buchan in mock protest.

"You don't even turn the cat out of the room when you discuss your alterations," said Mr. Sempack, and dismissed democracy.

It was only nowadays that the plan before mankind was becoming sufficiently clear and complete for us to dream of any organised and deliberate effort to realise it. The early Utopias never pretended to be more than suggestions, too often seasoned by the deprecatory laugh. But there had been immense liberations of the human imagination in the last two centuries. Our projects grew more and more courageous and comprehensive. Every intelligent man without some sort of kink was bound to believe a political world unity not only possible but desirable. Every one who knew anything about such mat-

ters was moving towards the realisation that the world needed one
sort of money and not many currencies, and would be infinitely
richer and better if it was controlled as one economic system. These
were new ideas, just as once the idea of circumnavigating the world
had been a new idea, but they spread, they would pervade.

"But to materialise them?" said the young man from Geneva.

"That will come. The laboratory you work in is only the first of
many. The League of Nations is the mere first sketch of a pre-
liminary experiment."

Lord Tamar betrayed a partisan solicitude for his League of
Nations. He thought it was more than that.

Parliaments of Nations, said Mr. Sempack, offered no solution of
the riddle of war. Every disagreement reopened the possibility of
war. Every enduring peace in the world had been and would have
to be a peace under one government. When people spoke of the
Pax Romana and the Pax Britannica they meant one sovereignty.
Every sovereignty implied an internal peace; every permanent peace
a practical sovereignty. For the Pax Mundi there could be only one
sovereignty. It was a little hard for people who had grown up under
old traditions of nation and empire to realise that and to face its
consequences; but there was always a new generation coming along,
ready to take new ideas seriously. People were learning history in a
new spirit and their political imaginations were being born again.
The way might be long and difficult to that last Pax, but not so long
and difficult as many people, with their noses in their newspapers,
supposed.

"If one could believe that," sighed Lady Tamar.

Mr. Sempack left his politics and economics; his sure hope of the
One World State and the One World Business floating benevolently
in their mental skies; and talked of the reflection upon the individual
life of a scientific order of human affairs. It was remarkable, he
thought, how little people heeded the things that the medical and
physiological and psychological sciences were saying to them. But
these things came to them only through a haze of distortion, cari-
catured until they lost all practical significance, disguised as the
foolish fancies of a race of oddly gifted eccentrics. There was a
great gulf fixed between the scientific man and the ordinary man, the
press. So that the generality had no suspicion of the releases from
pain and fatigue, the accessions of strength, the control over this
and that embarrassing function or entangling weakness, that science
could afford even now.

Still less could it imagine the mines of power and freedom that
these first-hand specimens foretold. Contemporary psychology, all
unsuspected by the multitude, was preparing the ground for an

education that would disentangle men from a great burthen of traditional and innate self-deception; it was pointing the road to an ampler and finer social and political life. The moral atmosphere of the world, just as much as the population and hunger of the world, was a controllable thing—when men saw fit to control it. For a moment or so as Mr. Sempack talked, it seemed to Mrs. Rylands that the room was pervaded by presences, by tall, grave, friendly beings, by anticipatory ghosts of man to come, happy, wise and powerful. It was as if they were visiting the past at Casa Terragena as she had sometimes visited the sleeping bones in the caves at Rochers Rouges. Why had they come into the room? Was it because these friendly and interested visitants were the children of such thoughts as this great talk was bringing to life?

"There is no inexorable necessity for any sustained human unhappiness," said Mr. Sempack; "none at all. There is no absolute reason whatever why every child born should not be born happily into a life of activity and interest and happiness. If there is, I have never heard of it. Tell me what it is."

"Bombaccio," said Mr. Plantagenet-Buchan, glancing over his shoulder to make sure that the servants were out of the room, "is a Catholic. He believes there was a Fall."

"Do *we?*" asked Mr. Sempack.

Puppy Clarges made a furtive grimace over her cigarette at Geoffrey, but the doctrine of the Fall went by default.

"But then," asked Mrs. Bullace, "why isn't every one happy now?"

"Secondary reasons," Mr. Plantagenet-Buchan asserted. "There may be no invincible barrier to an earthly Paradise, but still we have to find the way."

"It takes a long time," said Philip.

"Everything that is longer than a lifetime is a long time," said Mr. Sempack. "But for all practical purposes, you must remember, so soon as we pass that limit, nothing is very much longer than anything else."

Mr. Plantagenet-Buchan, after an instant's thought, agreed with that as warmly as if he had met a long-lost friend, but at the first impact it reminded Mrs. Rylands rather unpleasantly of attempts to explain Einstein.

"It does not matter if it uses up six generations or six hundred," Mr. Plantagenet-Buchan endorsed.

"Except to the generations," said Philip.

"But who *wants* this world of prigs?" came the voice of Geoffrey in revolt.

"I do for one," said Mr. Sempack.

"It would bore me to death."

"Lots of us are bored almost to violence by things as they are. More will be. Progress has always been a battle of the bored against the contented and the hopeless. If you like this world with its diseases and frustrations, its toil and blind cravings and unsatisfied wants, its endless quarrellings and its pointless tyrannies and cruelties, the pettiness of its present occupations in such grotesque contrast with the hard and frightful violence to which it is so plainly heading, if you like this world, I say, defend it. But I want to push it into the past as completely as I can and as fast as I can before it turns to horror. So I shall be against you. I am for progress. I believe in progress. Work for progress is the realest thing in life to me. If some messenger came to me and said with absolute conviction to me, 'This is all. It can never be any better,' I would not go on living in it for another four and twenty hours."

Geoffrey seemed to have no retort ready. His face had assumed the mulish expression of a schoolboy being preached at. This fellow, confound him! had language. And splashed it about at dinner time!

"We have had a wonderful talk to-night, Mr. Sempack," said Mrs. Rylands. "You scatter ideas like a fir tree scatters pollen."

The Fox and the Forest

RAY BRADBURY

Let me tell you something more about Ray Bradbury. His stories have sold like hotcakes in paperback editions in America, but he has not been taken up as a writer of great consequence. It may interest you to know that he is so acknowledged in Europe, where he is very highly regarded as a constructionist and a stylist. He should be here. He will be. But he sells—that's the important thing.

There were fireworks the very first night, things that you should be afraid of perhaps, for they might remind you of other more horrible things, but these were beautiful, rockets that ascended into the ancient soft air of Mexico and shook the stars apart in blue and white fragments. Everything was good and sweet, the air was that blend of the dead and the living, of the rains and the dusts, of the incense from the church, and the brass smell of the tubas on the bandstand which pulsed out vast rhythms of "La Paloma." The church doors were thrown wide and it seemed as if a giant yellow constellation had fallen from the October sky and lay breathing fire upon the church walls; a million candles sent their color and fumes about. Newer and better fireworks scurried like tight-rope walking comets across the cool-tiled square, banged against adobe cafe walls, then rushed on hot wires to bash the high church tower, in which boys' naked feet alone could be seen kicking and re-kicking, clanging and tilting and re-tilting the monster bells into monstrous music. A flaming bull blundered about the plaza chasing laughing men and screaming children.

"The year is 1938," said William Travis, standing by his wife on the edge of the yelling crowd, smiling. "A good year."

The bull rushed upon them. Ducking, the couple ran, with fire balls pelting them, past the music and riot, the church, the band, under the stars, clutching each other, laughing. The bull passed, carried lightly on the shoulders of a charging Mexican, a framework of bamboo and sulphurous gunpowder.

"I've never enjoyed myself so much in my life." Susan Travis had stopped for her breath.

"It's amazing," said William.

"It will go on, won't it?"

"All night."

"No, I mean our trip."

He frowned and patted his breast pocket. "I've enough traveler's checks for a lifetime. Enjoy yourself. Forget it. They'll never find us."

"Never?"

"Never."

Now someone was setting off giant crackers, hurling them from the great bell-tolling tower of the church in a sputter of smoke, while the crowd below fell back under the threat and the crackers exploded in wonderful concussions among their dancing feet and flailing bodies. A wondrous smell of frying tortillas hung all about, and in the cafes men sat at tables looking out, mugs of beer in their brown hands.

The bull was dead. The fire was out of the bamboo tubes and he was expended. The laborer lifted the framework from his shoulders. Little boys clustered to touch the magnificent papier-mache head, the real horns.

"Let's examine the bull," said William.

As they walked past the cafe entrance Susan saw the man looking out at them, a white man in a salt-white suit, with a blue tie and blue shirt, and a thin, sunburned face. His hair was blond and straight and his eyes were blue, and he watched them as they walked.

She would never have noticed him if it had not been for the bottles at his immaculate elbow; a fat bottle of creme de menthe, a clear bottle of vermouth, a flagon of cognac, and seven other bottles of assorted liqueurs, and, at his fingertips, ten small half-filled glasses from which, without taking his eyes off the street, he sipped, occasionally squinting, pressing his thin mouth shut upon the savor. In his free hand a thin Havana cigar smoked, and on a chair stood twenty cartons of Turkish cigarettes, six boxes of cigars, and some packaged colognes.

"Bill—" whispered Susan.

"Take it easy," he said. "He's nobody."

"I saw him in the plaza this morning."

"Don't look back, keep walking. Examine the papier-mache bull here. That's it, ask questions."

"Do you think he's from the Searchers?"

"They couldn't follow us!"

"They might!"

"What a nice bull," said William to the man who owned it.

"He couldn't have followed us back through two hundred years, could he?"

"Watch yourself, for God's sake," said William.

She swayed. He crushed her elbow tightly, steering her away.

"Don't faint." He smiled, to make it look good. "You'll be all right. Let's go right in that cafe, drink in front of him, so if he is what we think he is, he won't suspect."

"No, I couldn't."

"We've *got* to. Come on now. And so I said to David, that's ridiculous!" This last in a loud voice as they went up the cafe steps.

We are here, thought Susan. Who are we? Where are we going? What do we fear? Start at the beginning, she told herself, holding to her sanity, as she felt the adobe floor underfoot.

My name is Ann Kristen; my husband's name is Roger. We were born in the year 2155 A.D. And we lived in a world that was evil. A world that was like a great black ship pulling away from the shore of sanity and civilization, roaring its black horn in the night, taking two billion people with it, whether they wanted to go or not, to death, to fall over the edge of the earth and the sea into radioactive flame and madness.

They walked into the cafe. The man was staring at them.

A phone rang.

The phone startled Susan. She remembered a phone ringing two hundred years in the future, on that blue April morning in 2155, and herself answering it.

"Ann, this is Rene! Have you heard? I mean about Travel in Time, Incorporated? Trips to Rome in 21 B.C., trips to Napoleon's Waterloo—any time, any place!"

"Rene, you're joking."

"No. Clinton Smith left this morning for Philadelphia in 1776. Travel in Time, Inc., arranges everything. Costs money. But, *think* —to actually see the burning of Rome, Kubla Khan, Moses and the Red Sea! You've probably got an ad in your tube mail now."

She had opened the suction mail tube and there was the metal foil advertisement:

ROME AND THE BORGIAS!
THE WRIGHT BROTHERS AT KITTY HAWK!

Travel in Time, Inc., can costume you, put you in a crowd during the assassination of Lincoln or Caesar! We guarantee to teach you any language you need to move freely in any civilization, in any year, without friction. Latin, Greek, ancient American colloquial. Take your vacation in *Time* as well as Place!

Rene's voice was buzzing on the phone. "Tom and I leave for 1492 tomorrow. They're arranging for Tom to sail with Columbus. Isn't it amazing!"

"Yes," murmured Ann, stunned. "What does the Government say about this Time Machine Company?"

"Oh, the police have an eye on it. Afraid people might evade the draft, run off and hide in the Past. Everyone has to leave a security bond behind, his house and belongings, to guarantee return. After all, the war's on."

"Yes, the war," murmured Ann. "The war."

Standing there, holding the phone, she had thought, Here is the chance my husband and I have talked and prayed over for so many years. We don't like this world of 2155. We want to run away from his work at the bomb factory, I from my position with disease-culture units. Perhaps there is a chance for us to escape, to run for centuries into a wild country of years where they will never find and bring us back to burn our books, censor our thoughts, scald our minds with fear, march us, scream at us with radios . . .

They were in Mexico in the year 1938.

She looked at the stained cafe wall.

Good workers for the Future State were allowed vacations into the Past to escape fatigue. And so she and her husband had moved back into 1938, a room in New York City, and enjoyed the theaters and the Statue of Liberty which still stood green in the harbor. And on the third day they had changed their clothes, their names, and had flown off to hide in Mexico!

"It *must* be him," whispered Susan, looking at the stranger seated at the table. "Those cigarettes, the cigars, the liquor. They give him away. Remember our first night in the Past?"

A month ago, their first night in New York, before their flight, drinking all the strange drinks, savoring and buying odd foods, perfumes, cigarettes of ten dozen rare brands, for they were rare in the Future, where war was everything. So they had made fools of themselves, rushing in and out of stores, salons, tobacconists, going up to their room to get wonderfully ill.

And now here was this stranger doing likewise, doing a thing that only a man from the Future would do who had been starved for liquors and cigarettes for many years.

Susan and William sat and ordered a drink.

The stranger was examining their clothes, their hair, their jewelry —the way they walked and sat.

"Sit easily," said William under his breath. "Look as if you've worn this clothing style all your life."

"We should never have tried to escape."

"My God!" said William, "he's coming over. Let me do the talking."

The stranger bowed before them. There was the faintest tap of heels knocking together. Susan stiffened. That military sound!—unmistakable as that certain ugly rap on your door at midnight.

"Mr. Roger Kristen," said the stranger, "you did not pull up your pant legs when you sat down."

William froze. He looked at his hands lying on either leg, innocently. Susan's heart was beating swiftly.

"You've got the wrong person," said William quickly. "My name's not Krisler."

"Kristen," corrected the stranger.

"I'm William Travis," said William. "And I don't see what my pant legs have to do with you."

"Sorry." The stranger pulled up a chair. "Let us say I thought I knew you because you did *not* pull your trousers up. *Everyone* does. If they don't the trousers bag quickly. I am a long way from home, Mr.—Travis, and in need of company. My name is Simms."

"Mr. Simms, we appreciate your loneliness, but we're tired. We're leaving for Acapulco tomorrow."

"A charming spot. I was just there, looking for some friends of mine. They are somewhere. I shall find them yet. Oh, is the lady a bit sick?"

"Good night, Mr. Simms."

They started out the door, William holding Susan's arm firmly. They did not look back when Mr. Simms called, "Oh, just one other thing." He paused and then slowly spoke the words:

"2155 A.D."

Susan shut her eyes and felt the earth falter under her. She kept going, into the fiery plaza, seeing nothing.

They locked the door of their hotel room. And then she was crying and they were standing in the dark, and the room tilted under them. Far away firecrackers exploded, and there was laughter in the plaza.

"What a damned, loud nerve," said William. "Him sitting there, looking us up and down like animals, smoking his damn cigarettes, drinking his drinks. I should have killed him then!" His voice was nearly hysterical. "He even had the nerve to use his real name to us. The Chief of the Searchers. And the thing about my pant legs. My God, I should have pulled them up when I sat. It's an automatic gesture of this day and age. When I didn't do it, it set me off from the others; it made *him* think, Here's a man who never wore pants, a man used to breech uniforms and future styles. I could kill myself for giving us away!"

"No, no, it was my walk—these high heels—that did it. Our haircuts—so new, so fresh. Everything about us odd and uneasy."

He turned on the light. "He's still testing us. He's not positive of us—not completely. We can't run out on him, then. We can't make him certain. We'll go to Acapulco leisurely."

"Maybe he *is* sure of us, but is just playing."

"I wouldn't put it past him. He's got all the time in the world. He can dally here if he wants, and bring us back to the Future sixty seconds after we left it. He might keep us wondering for days, laughing at us."

Susan sat on the bed, wiping the tears from her face, smelling the old smell of charcoal and incense.

"They won't make a scene, will they?"

"They won't dare. They'll have to get us alone to put us in that Time Machine and send us back."

"There's a solution then," she said. "We'll never be alone; we'll always be in crowds. We'll make a million friends, visit markets, sleep in the Official Palaces in each town, pay the Chief of Police to guard us until we find a way to kill Simms and escape, disguise ourselves in new clothes, perhaps as Mexicans."

Footsteps sounded outside their locked door.

They turned out the light and undressed in silence. The footsteps went away. A door closed.

Susan stood by the window looking down at the plaza in the darkness. "So that building there is a church?"

"Yes."

"I've often wondered what a church looked like. It's been so long since anyone saw one. Can we visit it tomorrow?"

"Of course. Come to bed."

They lay in the dark room.

Half an hour later their phone rang. She lifted the receiver.

"Hello?"

"The rabbits may hide in the forest," said a voice, "but a fox can always find them."

She replaced the receiver and lay back straight and cold in bed.

Outside, in the year 1938, a man played three tunes upon a guitar, one following another.

During the night she put her hand out and almost touched the year 2155. She felt her fingers slide over cool space of time, as over a corrugated surface, and she heard the insistent thump of marching feet, a million bands playing a million military tunes, and she saw the fifty thousand rows of disease cultures in their aseptic glass tubes, her hand reaching out to them at her work in that huge factory in the Future; the tubes of leprosy, bubonic, typhoid, tuberculosis, and then the great explosion. She saw her hand burned to a wrinkled plum, felt it recoil from a concussion so immense that the world was lifted and let fall and all the buildings broke and people hemorrhaged and lay silent. Great volcanoes, machines, winds, avalanches slid down to silence and she awoke, sobbing, in the bed, in Mexico, many years away....

In the early morning, drugged with the single hour's sleep they had finally been able to obtain, they awoke to the sound of loud automobiles in the street. Susan peered down from the iron balcony at a small crowd of eight people only now emerging, chattering, yelling, from trucks and cars with red lettering on them. A crowd of Mexicans had followed the trucks.

"*Que pasa?*" Susan called to a little boy.

The boy replied.

Susan turned back to her husband. "An American motion-picture company, here on location."

"Sounds interesting." William was in the shower. "Let's watch them. I don't think we'd better leave today. We'll try to lull Simms. Watch the films being made. They say the primitive film making was something. Get our minds off ourselves."

Ourselves, thought Susan. For a moment, in the bright sun, she had forgotten that somewhere in the hotel, waiting, was a man smoking a thousand cigarettes, it seemed. She saw the eight loud happy Americans below and wanted to call to them: "Save me, hide me, help me! Color my hair, my eyes; clothe me in strange clothes. I need your help. I'm from the year 2155!"

But the words stayed in her throat. The functionaries of Travel in Time, Inc., were not foolish. In your brain, before you left on your trip, they placed a psychological block. You could tell no one your true time or birthplace, nor could you reveal any of the Future to those in the Past. The Past and the Future must be protected from each other. Only with this psychological block were people allowed to travel unguarded through the ages. The Future must be protected from any change brought about by her people traveling in the Past. Even if she wanted to with all her heart, she could not tell any of those happy people below in the plaza who she was, or what her predicament had become.

"What about breakfast?" said William.

Breakfast was being served in the immense dining room. Ham and eggs for everyone. The place was full of tourists. The film people entered, all eight of them—six men and two women, giggling, shoving chairs about. And Susan sat near them, feeling the warmth and protection they offered, even when Mr. Simms came down the lobby stairs, smoking his Turkish cigarette with great intensity. He nodded at them from a distance, and Susan nodded back, smiling, because he couldn't do anything to them here, in front of eight film people and twenty other tourists.

"Those actors," said William. "Perhaps I could hire two of them, say it was a joke, dress them in our clothes, have them drive off in our car when Simms is in such a spot where he can't see their faces. If two people pretending to be us could lure him off for a few hours, we might make it to Mexico City. It'd take him years to find us there!"

"Hey!"

A fat man, with liquor on his breath, leaned on their table.

"American tourists!" he cried. "I'm so sick of seeing Mexicans, I could kiss you!" He shook their hands. "Come on, eat with us. Misery loves company. I'm Misery, this is Miss Gloom, and Mr. and Mrs. Do-We-Hate-Mexico! We all hate it. But we're here for some pre-liminary shots for a damn film. The rest of the crew arrives to-morrow. My name's Joe Melton. I'm a director. And if this ain't a hell of a country! Funerals in the streets, people dying. Come on, move over. Join the party; cheer us up!"

Susan and William were both laughing.

"Am I funny?" Mr. Melton asked the immediate world.

"Wonderful!" Susan moved over.

Mr. Simms was glaring across the dining room at them.

She made a face at him.

Mr. Simms advanced among the tables.

"Mr. and Mrs. Travis," he called. "I thought we were breakfasting together, alone."

"Sorry," said William.

"Sit down, pal," said Mr. Melton. "Any friend of theirs is a pal of mine."

Mr. Simms sat. The film people talked loudly, and while they talked, Mr. Simms said quietly, "I hope you slept well."

"Did you?"

"I'm not used to spring mattresses," replied Mr. Simms wryly. "But there are compensations. I stayed up half the night trying new cigarettes and foods. Odd, fascinating. A whole new spectrum of sensation, these ancient vices."

"We don't know what you're talking about," said Susan.

"Always the play acting," Simms laughed. "It's no use. Nor is this stratagem of crowds. I'll get you alone soon enough. I'm immensely patient."

"Say," Mr. Melton broke in, his face flushed, "is this guy giving you any trouble?"

"It's all right."

"Say the word and I'll give him the bum's rush."

Melton turned back to yell at his associates. In the laughter, Mr. Simms went on: "Let us come to the point. It took me a month of tracing you through towns and cities to find you, and all of yesterday to be sure of you. If you come with me quietly, I might be able to get you off with no punishment, if you agree to go back to work on the hydrogen-plus bomb."

"Science this guy talks at breakfast!" observed Mr. Melton, half listening.

Simms went on, imperturbably. "Think it over. You can't escape. If you kill me, others will follow you."

"We don't know what you're talking about."

"Stop it!" cried Simms irritably. "Use your intelligence! You know we can't let you get away with this escape. Other people in the year 2155 might get the same idea and do what you've done. We need people."

"To fight your wars," said William at last.

"Bill!"

"It's all right, Susan. We'll talk on his terms now. We can't escape."

"Excellent," said Simms. "Really, you've both been incredibly romantic, running away from your responsibilities."

"Running away from horror."

"Nonsense. Only a war."

"What are you guys talking about?" asked Mr. Melton.

Susan wanted to tell him. But you could only speak in generalities. The psychological block in your mind allowed that. Generalities, such as Simms and William were now discussing.

"Only the war," said William. "Half the world dead of leprosy bombs!"

"Nevertheless," Simms pointed out, "the inhabitants of the Future resent you two hiding on a tropical isle, as it were, while they drop off the cliff into hell. Death loves death, not life. Dying people love to know that others die with them. It is a comfort to learn you are not alone in the kiln, in the grave. I am the guardian of their collective resentment against you two."

"Look at the guardian of resentments!" said Mr. Melton to his companions.

"The longer you keep me waiting, the harder it will go for you. We need you on the bomb project, Mr. Travis. Return now—no torture. Later, we'll force you to work, and after you've finished the bomb, we'll try a number of complicated new devices on you, sir."

"I've a proposition," said William. "I'll come back with you if my wife stays here alive, safe, away from that war."

Mr. Simms considered it. "All right. Meet me in the plaza in ten minutes. Pick me up in your car. Drive me to a deserted country spot. I'll have the Travel Machine pick us up there."

"Bill!" Susan held his arm tightly.

"Don't argue." He looked over at her. "It's settled." To Simms: "One thing. Last night you could have gotten in our room and kidnaped us. Why didn't you?"

"Shall we say that I was enjoying myself?" replied Mr. Simms languidly, sucking his new cigar. "I hate giving up this wonderful atmosphere, this sun, this vacation. I regret leaving behind the wine and the cigarettes. Oh, how I regret it. The plaza then, in ten minutes. Your wife will be protected and may stay here as long as she wishes. Say your good-bys."

Mr. Simms arose and walked out.

"There goes Mr. Big Talk!" yelled Mr. Melton at the departing gentleman. He turned and looked at Susan. "Hey. Someone's crying. Breakfast's no time for people to cry. Now is it?"

At nine-fifteen Susan stood on the balcony of their room, gazing down at the plaza. Mr. Simms was seated there, his neat legs crossed, on a delicate bronze bench. Biting the tip from a cigar, he lit it tenderly.

Susan heard the throb of a motor, and far up the street, out of a garage and down the cobbled hill, slowly, came William in his car.

The car picked up speed. Thirty, now forty, now fifty miles an hour. Chickens scattered before it.

Mr. Simms took off his white panama hat and mopped his pink forehead, put his hat back on, and then saw the car.

It was rushing sixty miles an hour, straight on for the plaza.

"William!" screamed Susan.

The car hit the low plaza curb, thundering; it jumped up, sped across the tiles toward the green bench where Mr. Simms now dropped his cigar, shrieked, flailed his hands, and was hit by the car. His body flew up and up in the air, and down and down, crazily, into the street.

On the far side of the plaza, one front wheel broken, the car stopped. People were running.

Susan went in and closed the balcony doors.

They came down the Official Palace steps together, arm in arm, their faces pale, at twelve noon.

"*Adios, senor*," said the mayor behind them. "*Senora.*"

They stood in the plaza where the crowd was pointing at the blood.

"Will they want to see you again?" asked Susan.

"No, we went over and over it. It was an accident. I lost control of the car. I wept for them. God knows I had to get my relief out somewhere. I *felt* like weeping. I hated to kill him. I've never wanted to do anything like that in my life."

"They won't prosecute you?"

"They talked about it, but no. I talked faster. They believe me. It was an accident. It's over."

"Where will we go? Mexico City? Uruapan?"

"The car's in the repair shop. It'll be ready at four this afternoon. Then we'll get the hell out."

"Will we be followed? Was Simms working alone?"

"I don't know. We'll have a little head start on them, I think."

The film people were coming out of the hotel as they approached. Mr. Melton hurried up, scowling. "Hey, I heard what happened. Too bad. Everything okay now? Want to get your minds off it? We're doing some preliminary shots up the street. You want to watch, you're welcome. Come on, do you good."

They went.

They stood on the cobbled street while the film camera was being set up. Susan looked at the road leading down and away, and the highway going to Acapulco and the sea, past pyramids and ruins and little adobe towns with yellow walls, blue walls, purple walls and flaming bougainvillea, and she thought, We shall take the roads, travel in clusters and crowds, in markets, in lobbies, bribe police to sleep near, keep double locks, but always the crowds, never alone again, always afraid the next person who passes may be another Simms. Never knowing if we've tricked and lost the Searchers. And always up ahead, in the Future, they'll wait for us to be brought back, waiting with their bombs to burn us and disease to rot us, and their police to tell us to roll over, turn around, jump through the hoop! And so we'll keep running through the forest, and we'll never ever stop or sleep well again in our lives.

A crowd gathered to watch the film being made. And Susan watched the crowd and the streets.

"Seen anyone suspicious?"

"No. What time is it?"

"Three o'clock. The car should be almost ready."

The test film was finished at three forty-five. They all walked down to the hotel, talking. William paused at the garage. "The car'll be ready at six," he said, coming out, worried.

"But no later than that?"

"It'll be ready, don't worry."

In the hotel lobby they looked around for other men traveling alone, men who resembled Mr. Simms, men with new haircuts and too much cigarette smoke and cologne smell about them, but the lobby was empty. Going up the stairs, Mr. Melton said, "Well, it's been a long hard day. Who'd like to put a header on it? You folks? Martini? Beer?"

"Maybe one."

The whole crowd pushed into Mr. Melton's room and the drinking began.

"Watch the time," said William.

Time, thought Susan. If only they had time. All she wanted was to sit in the plaza all of a long bright day in October, with not a worry or a thought, with the sun on her face and arms, her eyes closed, smiling at the warmth, and never move. Just sleep in the Mexican sun, and sleep warmly and easily and slowly and happily for many, many days....

Mr. Melton opened the champagne.

"To a very beautiful lady, lovely enough for films," he said, toasting Susan. "I might even give you a test."

She laughed.

"I mean it," said Melton. "You're very nice. I could make you a movie star."

"And take me to Hollywood?" cried Susan.

"Get the hell out of Mexico, sure!"

Susan glanced at William and he lifted an eyebrow and nodded. It would be a change of scene, clothing, locale, name, perhaps; and they would be traveling with eight other people, a good shield against any interference from the Future.

"It sounds wonderful," said Susan.

She was feeling the champagne now. The afternoon was slipping by; the party was whirling about her. She felt safe and good and alive and truly happy for the first time in many years.

"What kind of film would my wife be good for?" asked William, refilling his glass.

Melton appraised Susan. The party stopped laughing and listened.

"Well, I'd like to do a story of suspense," said Melton. "A story of a man and wife, like yourselves."

"Go on."

"Sort of a war story, maybe," said the director, examining the color of his drink against the sunlight.

Susan and William waited.

"A story about a man and wife, who live in a little house on a little street in the year 2155, maybe," said Melton. "This is ad lib, understand. But this man and wife are faced with a terrible war, super-plus hydrogen bombs, censorship, death in that year, and—here's the gimmick—they escape into the Past, followed by a man who they think is evil, but who is only trying to show them what their duty is."

William dropped his glass to the floor.

Mr. Melton continued: "And this couple take refuge with a group of film people whom they learn to trust. Safety in numbers, they say to themselves."

Susan felt herself slip down into a chair. Everyone was watching the director. He took a little sip of wine. "Ah, that's a fine wine. Well, this man and woman, it seems, don't realize how important they are to the Future. The man, especially is the keystone to a new bomb metal. So the Searchers, let's call them, spare no trouble or expense to find, capture and take home the man and wife, once they get them totally alone, in a hotel room, where no one can see. Strategy. The Searchers work alone, or in groups of eight. One trick or another will do it. Don't you think it would make a wonderful film, Susan? Don't you, Bill?" He finished his drink.

Susan sat with her eyes straight ahead of her.

"Have a drink?" said Mr. Melton.

William's gun was out and fired three times, and one of the men fell, and the others ran forward. Susan screamed. A hand was clamped to her mouth. Now the gun was on the floor and William was struggling, held.

Mr. Melton said, "Please," standing there where he had stood, blood showing on his fingers. "Let's not make matters worse."

Someone pounded on the hall door.

"Let me in!"

"The manager," said Mr. Melton dryly. He jerked his head. "Everyone, let's move!"

"Let me in! I'll call the police!"

Susan and William looked at each other quickly, and then at the door.

"The manager wishes to come in," said Mr. Melton. "Quick!"

A camera was carried forward. From it shot a blue light which encompassed the room instantly. It widened out and the people of the party vanished, one by one.

"Quickly!"

Outside the window, in the instant before she vanished, Susan saw the green land and the purple and yellow and blue and crimson walls and the cobbles flowing down like a river, a man upon a burro riding into the warm hills, a boy drinking Orange Crush, she could feel the sweet liquid in her thirst, a man standing under a cool plaza tree with a guitar, she could feel her hand upon the strings, and, far away, the sea, the blue and tender sea, she could feel it roll her over and take her in.

And then she was gone. Her husband was gone.

The door burst wide open. The manager and his staff rushed in.

The room was empty.

"But they were just here! I saw them come in, and now—gone!" cried the manager. "The windows are covered with iron grating. They couldn't get out that way!"

In the late afternoon the priest was summoned and they opened the room again and aired it out, and had him sprinkle holy water through each corner and give it his blessing.

"What shall we do with these?" asked the charwoman.

She pointed to the closet, where there were 67 bottles of chartreuse, cognac, creme de cacao, absinthe, vermouth, tequila, 106 cartons of Turkish cigarettes, and 189 yellow boxes of fifty-cent pure Havana-filler cigars. . . .

The New Accelerator

H. G. WELLS

Certainly, if ever a man found a guinea when he was looking for a pin it is my good friend Professor Gibberne. I have heard before of investigators overshooting the mark, but never quite to the extent that he has done. He has really, this time at any rate, without any touch of exaggeration in the phrase, found something to revolutionise human life. And that when he was simply seeking an all-round nervous stimulant to bring languid people up to the stresses of these pushful days. I have tasted the stuff now several times, and I cannot do better than describe the effect the thing had on me. That there are astonishing experiences in store for all in search of new sensations will become apparent enough.

Professor Gibberne, as many people know, is my neighbour in Folkstone. Unless my memory plays me a trick, his portrait at various ages has already appeared in *The Strand Magazine*—I think late in 1899; but I am unable to look it up because I have lent that volume to someone who has never sent it back. The reader may, perhaps, recall the high forehead and the singularly long black eyebrows that give such a Mephistophelian touch to his face. He occupies one of those pleasant detached houses in the mixed style that make the western end of the Upper Sandgate Road so interesting. His is the one with the Flemish gables and the Moorish portico, and it is in the room with the mullioned bay window that he works when he is down here, and in which of an evening we have so often smoked and talked together. He is a mighty jester, but, besides, he likes to talk to me about his work; he is one of those men who find a help and stimulus in talking, and so I have been able to follow the conception of the New Accelerator right up from a very early stage. Of course, the greater portion of his experimental work is not done in Folkstone, but in Gower Street, in the fine new laboratory next to the hospital that he has been the first to use.

As everyone knows, or at least as all intelligent people know, the special department in which Gibberne has gained so great and deserved a reputation among physiologists is the action of drugs upon the nervous system. Upon soporifics, sedatives, and anæsthetics he is, I am told, unequalled. He is also a chemist of considerable eminence, and I suppose in the subtle and complex jungle of riddles that centres about the ganglion cell and the axis fibre there are little cleared places of his making, glades of illumination, that, until he sees fit to publish his results, are inaccessible to every other living man. And in the last few years he has been particularly assiduous upon this question of nervous stimulants, and already, before the discovery of the New Accelerator, very successful with them. Medical science has to thank him for at least three distinct and absolutely safe invigorators of unrivalled value to practising men. In cases of exhaustion the preparation known as Gibberne's B Syrup has, I suppose, saved more lives already than any lifeboat round the coast.

"But none of these things begin to satisfy me yet," he told me nearly a year ago. "Either they increase the central energy without affecting the nerves or they simply increase the available energy by lowering the nervous conductivity; and all of them are unequal and local in their operation. One wakes up the heart and viscera and leaves the brain stupefied, one gets at the brain champagne fashion and does nothing good for the solar plexus, and what I want—and what, if it's an earthly possibility, I mean to have—is a stimulant that stimulates all round, that wakes you up for a time from the crown of your head to the tip of your great toe, and makes you go two—or even three to everybody else's one. Eh? That's the thing I'm after."

"It would tire a man," I said.

"Not a doubt of it. And you'd eat double or treble—and all that. But just think what the thing would mean. Imagine yourself with a little phial like this"—he held up a bottle of green glass and marked his points with it—"and in this precious phial is the power to think twice as fast, move twice as quickly, do twice as much work in a given time as you could otherwise do."

"But is such a thing possible?"

"I believe so. If it isn't, I've wasted my time for a year. These various preparations of the hypophosphites, for example, seem to show that something of the sort.... Even if it was only one and a half times as fast it would do."

"It *would* do," I said.

"If you were a statesman in a corner, for example, time rushing up against you, something urgent to be done, eh?"

"He could dose his private secretary," I said.

"And gain—double time. And think if *you*, for example, wanted to finish a book."

"Usually," I said, "I wish I'd never begun 'em."

"Or a doctor, driven to death, wants to sit down and think out a case. Or a barrister—or a man cramming for an examination."

"Worth a guinea a drop," said I, "and more—to men like that."

"And in a duel again," said Gibberne, "where it all depends on your quickness in pulling the trigger."

"Or in fencing," I echoed.

"You see," said Gibberne, "if I get it as an all-round thing it will really do you no harm at all—except perhaps to an infinitesimal degree it brings you nearer old age. You will just have lived twice to other people's once—"

"I suppose," I meditated, "in a duel—it would be fair?"

"That's a question for the seconds," said Gibberne.

I harked back further. "And you really think such a thing *is* possible?" I said.

"As possible," said Gibberne, and glanced at something that went throbbing by the window, "as a motor-bus. As a matter of fact—"

He paused and smiled at me deeply, and tapped slowly on the edge of his desk with the green phial. "I think I know the stuff.... Already I've got something coming." The nervous smile upon his face betrayed the gravity of his revelation. He rarely talked of his actual experimental work unless things were very near the end. "And it may be, it may be—I shouldn't be surprised—it may even do the thing at a greater rate than twice."

"It will be rather a big thing," I hazarded.

"It will be, I think, rather a big thing."

But I don't think he quite knew what a big thing it was to be, for all that.

I remember we had several subsequent talks about the stuff. "The New Accelerator" he called it, and his tone about it grew more confident on each occasion. Sometimes he talked nervously of unexpected physiological results its use might have, and then he would get a bit unhappy; at others he was frankly mercenary, and we debated long and anxiously how the preparation might be turned to commercial account. "It's a good thing," said Gibberne, "a tremendous thing. I know I'm giving the world something, and I think it only reasonable we should expect the world to pay. The dignity of science is all very well, but I think somehow I must have the monopoly of the stuff for, say, ten years. I don't see why *all* the fun in life should go to the dealers in ham."

My own interest in the coming drug certainly did not wane in the time. I have always had a queer twist towards metaphysics in my mind. I have always been given to paradoxes about space and time, and it seemed to me that Gibberne was really preparing no less than the absolute acceleration of life. Suppose a man repeatedly dosed with such a preparation: he would live an active and record life indeed, but he would be an adult at eleven, middle-aged at twenty-five, and by thirty well on the road to senile decay. It seemed to me that so far Gibberne was only going to do for anyone who took this drug exactly what Nature has done for the Jews and Orientals, who are men in their teens and aged by fifty, and quicker in thought and act than we are all the time. The marvel of drugs has always been great to my mind; you can madden a man, calm a man, make him incredibly strong and alert or a helpless log, quicken this passion and allay that, all by means of drugs, and here was a new miracle to be added to this strange armoury of phials the doctors use! But Gibberne was far too eager upon his technical points to enter very keenly into my aspect of the question.

It was the 7th or 8th of August when he told me the distillation that would decide his failure or success for a time was going forward as we talked, and it was on the 10th that he told me the thing was done and the New Accelerator a tangible reality in the world. I met him as I was going up the Sandgate Hill towards Folkestone—I think I was going to get my hair cut; and he came hurrying down to meet me—I suppose he was coming to my house to tell me at once of his success. I remember that his eyes were unusually bright and his face flushed, and I noted even then the swift alacrity of his step.

"It's done," he cried, and gripped my hand, speaking very fast; "it's more than done. Come up to my house and see."

"Really?"

"Really!" he shouted. "Incredibly! Come up and see."

"And it does—twice?"

"It does more, much more. It scares me. Come up and see the stuff. Taste it! Try it! It's the most amazing stuff on earth. He gripped my arm and, walking at such a pace that he forced me into a trot, went shouting with me up the hill. A whole charabancful of people turned and stared at us in unison after the manner of people in charabancs. It was one of those hot, clear days that Folkestone sees so much of, every colour incredibly bright and every outline hard. There was a breeze, of course, but not so much breeze as sufficed under these conditions to keep me cool and dry. I panted for mercy.

"I'm not walking fast, am I?" cried Gibberne, and slackened his pace to a quick march.

"You've been taking some of this stuff," I puffed.

"No," he said. "At the utmost a drop of water that stood in a beaker from which I had washed out the last traces of the stuff. I took some last night, you know. But that is ancient history, now."

"And it goes twice?" I said, nearing his doorway in a grateful perspiration.

"It goes a thousand times, many thousand times!" cried Gibberne, with a dramatic gesture, flinging open his Early English carved oak gate.

"Phew!" said I, and followed him to the door.

"I don't know how many times it goes," he said, with his latch-key in his hand.

"And you—"

"It throws all sorts of light on nervous physiology, it kicks the theory of vision into a perfectly new shape! ... Heaven knows how many thousand times. We'll try all that after— The thing is to try the stuff now."

"Try the stuff?" I said, as we went along the passage.

"Rather," said Gibberne, turning on me in his study. "There it is in that little green phial there! Unless you happen to be afraid?"

I am a careful man by nature, and only theoretically adventurous. I *was* afraid. But on the other hand there is pride.

"Well," I haggled. "You say you've tried it?"

"I've tried it," he said, "and I don't look hurt by it, do I? I don't even look livery and I *feel*—"

I sat down. "Give me the potion," I said. "If the worst comes to the worst it will save having my hair cut, and that I think is one of the most hateful duties of a civilised man. How do you take the mixture?"

"With water," said Gibberne, whacking down a carafe.

He stood up in front of his desk and regarded me in his easy chair; his manner was suddenly reflected by a touch of the Harley Street specialist. "It's rum stuff, you know," he said.

I made a gesture with my hand.

"I must warn you in the first place as soon as you've got it down to shut your eyes, and open them very cautiously in a minute or so's time. One still sees. The sense of vision is a question of length of vibration, and not of multitude of impacts; but there's a kind of shock to the retina, a nasty giddy confusion just at the time if the eyes are open. Keep 'em shut."

"Shut," I said. "Good!"

"And the next thing is, keep still. Don't begin to whack about. You may fetch something a nasty rap if you do. Remember you will be going several thousand times faster than you ever did before, heart, lungs, muscles, brain—everything—and you will hit hard without knowing it. You won't know it, you know. You'll feel just as you do now. Only everything in the world will seem to be going ever so many thousand times slower than it ever went before. That's what makes it so deuced queer."

"Lor'," I said. "And you mean—"

"You'll see," said he, and took up a measure. He glanced at the material on his desk. "Glasses," he said, "water. All here. Mustn't take too much for the first attempt."

The little phial glucked out its precious contents. "Don't forget what I told you," he said, turning the contents of the measure into a glass in the manner of an Italian waiter measuring whisky. "Sit with the eyes tighly shut and in absolute stillness for two minutes," he said. "Then you will hear me speak."

He added an inch or so of water to the dose in each glass.

"By-the-bye," he said, "don't put your glass down. Keep it in your hand and rest your hand on your knee. Yes—so. And now—"

He raised his glass.

"The New Accelerator," I said.

"The New Accelerator," he answered, and we touched glasses and drank, and instantly I closed my eyes.

You know that blank non-existence into which one drops when one has taken "gas." For an indefinite interval it was like that. Then I heard Gibberne telling me to wake up, and I stirred and opened my eyes. There he stood as he had been standing, glass still in hand. It was empty, that was all the difference.

"Well?" said I.

"Nothing out of the way?"

"Nothing. A slight feeling of exhilaration, perhaps. Nothing more."

"Sounds?"

"Things are still," I said. "By Jove! yes! They *are* still. Except the sort of faint pat, patter, like rain falling on different things. What is it?"

"Analysed sounds," I think he said, but I am not sure. He glanced at the window. "Have you ever seen a curtain before a window fixed in that way before?"

I followed his eyes, and there was the end of the curtain, frozen, as it were, corner high, in the act of flapping briskly in the breeze.

"No," said I; "that's odd."

"And here," he said, and opened the hand that held the glass. Naturally I winced, expecting the glass to smash. But so far from smashing it did not even seem to stir; it hung in mid-air—motionless. "Roughly speaking," said Gibberne, "an object in these latitudes falls 16 feet in the first second. This glass is falling 16 feet in a second now. Only, you see, it hasn't been falling yet for the hundredth part of a second. That gives you some idea of the pace of my Accelerator." And he waved his hand round and round, over and over the slowly sinking glass. Finally he took it by the bottom, pulled it down and placed it very carefully on the table. "Eh?" he said to me, and laughed.

"That seems all right," I said, and began very gingerly to raise myself from my chair. I felt perfectly well, very light and comfortable, and quite confident in my mind. I was going fast all over. My heart, for example, was beating a thousand times a second, but that caused me no discomfort at all. I looked out of the window. An immovable cyclist, head down and with a frozen puff of dust behind his driving-wheel, scorched to overtake a galloping charabanc that did not stir. I gaped in amazement at this incredible spectacle. "Gibberne," I cried, "how long will this confounded stuff last?"

"Heaven knows!" he answered. "Last time I took it I went to bed and slept it off. I tell you, I was frightened. It must have lasted some minutes, I think—it seemed like hours. But after a bit it slows down rather suddenly, I believe."

I was proud to observe that I did not feel frightened—I suppose because there were two of us. "Why shouldn't we go out?" I asked.

"Why not?"

"They'll see us."

"Not they. Goodness, no! Why, we shall be going a thousand times faster than the quickest conjuring trick that was ever done. Come along! Which way shall we go? Window, or door?"

And out by the window we went.

Assuredly of all the strange experiences that I have ever had, or imagined, or read of other people having or imagining, that little raid I made with Gibberne on the Folkestone Leas, under the influence of the New Accelerator, was the strangest and maddest of all. We went out by his gate into the road, and there we made a minute examination of the statuesque passing traffic. The tops of the wheels and some of the legs of the horses of this charabanc, the end of the whip-lash and the lower jaw of the conductor—who was just begin-ning to yawn—were perceptibly in motion, but all the rest of the lumbering conveyance seemed still. And quite noiseless except for a faint rattling that came from one man's throat! And as parts of this frozen edifice there were a driver, you know, and a conductor, and eleven people! The effect as we walked about the thing began by being madly queer and ended by being—disagreeable. There they were, people like ourselves and yet not like ourselves, frozen in care-less attitudes, caught in mid-gesture. A girl and a man smiled at one another, a leering smile that threatened to last for evermore; a woman in a floppy capelline rested her arm on the rail and stared at Gib-berne's house with the unwinking stare of eternity; a man stroked his moustache like a figure of wax, and another stretched a tiresome stiff hand with extended fingers towards his loosened hat. We stared at them, we laughed at them, we made faces at them, and then a sort of disgust of them came upon us, and we turned away and walked round in front of the cyclist towards the Leas.

"Goodness!" cried Gibberne, suddenly; "look there!"

He pointed, and there at the tip of his finger and sliding down the air with wings flapping slowly and at the speed of an exceptionally languid snail—was a bee.

And so we came out upon the Leas. There the thing seemed madder than ever. The band was playing in the upper stand, though all the sound it made for us was a low-pitched, wheezy rattle, a sort of prolonged last sigh that passed at times into a sound like the slow muffled ticking of some monstrous clock. Frozen people stood erect; strange, silent, self-conscious-looking dummies hung unstably in midstride, promenading upon the grass. I passed close to a poodle dog suspended in the act of leaping, and watched the slow movement of his legs as he sank to earth. "Lord, look *here!*" cried Gibberne, and we halted for a moment before a magnificent person in white faint-striped flannels, white shoes, and a Panama hat, who turned back to wink at two gaily dressed ladies he had passed. A wink, studied with such leisurely deliberation as we could afford, is an unattractive thing. It loses any quality of alert gaiety, and one remarks that the winking eye does not completely close, that under its drooping lid appears the lower edge of an eyeball and a line of white. "Heaven give me memory," said I, "and I will never wink again."

"Or smile," said Gibberne, with his eye on the lady's answering teeth.

"It's infernally hot, somehow," said I. "Let's go slower."

"Oh, come along!" said Gibberne.

We picked our way among the bath-chairs in the path. Many of the people sitting in the chairs seemed almost natural in their passive poses, but the contorted scarlet of the bandsmen was not a restful thing to see. A purple-faced gentleman was frozen in the midst of a violent struggle to refold his newspaper against the wind; there were many evidences that all these people in their sluggish way were exposed to a considerable breeze, a breeze that had no existence so far as our sensations went. We came out and walked a little way from the crowd, and turned and regarded it. To see all that multitude changed to a picture, smitten rigid, as it were, into the semblance of realistic wax, was impossibly wonderful. It was absurd, of course; but it filled me with an irrational, an exultant sense of superior advantage. Consider the wonder of it! All that I had said and thought and done since the stuff had begun to work in my veins had happened, so far as those people, so far as the world in general went, in the twinkling of an eye. "The New Accelerator—" I began, but Gibberne interrupted me.

"There's that infernal old woman!" he said.

"What old woman?"

"Lives next door to me," said Gibberne. "Has a lapdog that yaps. Gods! The temptation is strong!"

There is something very boyish and impulsive about Gibberne at times. Before I could expostulate with him he had dashed forward, snatched the unfortunate animal out of visible existence, and was running violently with it towards the cliff of the Leas. It was most extraordinary. The little brute, you know, didn't bark or wiggle or make the slightest sign of vitality. It kept quite stiffly in an attitude of somnolent repose, and Gibberne held it by the neck. It was like running about with a dog of wood. "Gibberne," I cried, "put it down!" Then I said something else. "If you run like that, Gibberne," I cried, "you'll set your clothes on fire. Your linen trousers are going brown as it is!"

He clapped his hand on his thigh and stood hesitating on the verge. "Gibberne," I cried, coming up, "put it down. This heat is too much! It's our running so! Two or three miles a second! Friction of the air!"

"What?" he said, glancing at the dog.

"Friction of the air," I shouted. "Friction of the air. Going too fast. Like meteorites and things. Too hot. And, Gibberne! Gibberne! I'm all over pricking and a sort of perspiration. You can see people stirring slightly. I believe the stuff's working off! Put that dog down."

"Eh?" he said.

"It's working off," I repeated. "We're too hot and the stuff's working off! I'm wet through."

He stared at me. Then at the band, the wheezy rattle of whose performance was certainly going faster. Then with a tremendous sweep of the arm he hurled the dog away from him and it went spinning upward, still inanimate and hung at last over the grouped parasols of a knot of chattering people. Gibberne was gripping my elbow. "By Jove!" he cried. "I believe it is! A sort of hot pricking and—yes. That man's moving his pocket-handkerchief! Perceptibly. We must get out of this sharp."

But we could not get out of it sharply enough. Luckily perhaps! For we might have run, and if we had run we should, I believe, have burst into flames. Almost certainly we should have burst into flames! You know we had neither of us thought of that. . . . But before we could even begin to run the action of the drug had ceased. It was the business of a minute fraction of a second. The effect of the New Accelerator passed like the drawing of a curtain, vanished in the movement of a hand. I heard Gibberne's voice in infinite alarm. "Sit down," he said, and flop, down upon the turf at the edge of the Leas I sat—scorching as I sat. There is a patch of burnt grass there still where I sat down. The whole stagnation seemed to wake up as

I did so, the disarticulated vibration of the band rushed together into a blast of music, the promenaders put their feet down and walked their ways, the papers and flags began flapping, smiles passed into words, the winker finished his wink and went on his way complacently, and all the seated people moved and spoke.

The whole world had come alive again, was going as fast as we were, or rather we were going no faster than the rest of the world. It was like slowing down as one comes into a railway station. Everything seemed to spin round for a second or two, I had the most transient feeling of nausea, and that was all. And the little dog which had seemed to hang for a moment when the force of Gibberne's arm was expended fell with a swift acceleration clean through a lady's parasol!

That was the saving of us. Unless it was for one corpulent old gentleman in a bath-chair, who certainly did start at the sight of us and afterwards regarded us at intervals with a darkly suspicious eye, and finally, I believe, said something to his nurse about us, I doubt if a solitary person remarked our sudden appearance among them. Plop! We must have appeared abruptly. We ceased to smoulder almost at once, though the turf beneath me was uncomfortably hot. The attention of everyone—including even the Amusements' Association band, which on this occasion, for the only time in its history, got out of tune —was arrested by the amazing fact, and the still more amazing yapping and uproar caused by the fact, that a respectable, over-fed lapdog sleeping quietly to the east of the bandstand should suddenly fall through the parasol of a lady on the west—in a slightly singed condition due to the extreme velocity of its movements through the air. In these absurd days, too, when we are all trying to be as psychic and silly and superstitious as possible! People got up and trod on other people, chairs were overturned, the Leas policeman ran. How the matter settled itself I do not know—we were much too anxious to disentangle ourselves from the affair and get out of range of the eye of the old gentleman in the bath-chair to make minute inquiries. As soon as we were sufficiently cool and sufficiently recovered from our giddiness and nausea and confusion of mind to do so we stood up and, skirting the crowd, directed our steps back along the road below the Metropole towards Gibberne's house. But amidst the din I heard very distinctly the gentleman who had been sitting beside the lady of the ruptured sunshade using quite unjustifiable threats and language to one of those chair-attendants who have "Inspector" written on their caps. "If you didn't throw the dog," he said, "who *did?*"

The sudden return of movement and familiar noises, and our natural anxiety about ourselves (our clothes were still dreadfully hot, and the fronts of the thighs of Gibberne's white trousers were scorched a drabbish brown), prevented the minute observations I should have liked to make on all these things. Indeed, I really made no observations of any scientific value on that return. The bee, of course, had gone. I looked for that cyclist, but he was already out of sight as we came into the Upper Sandgate Road or hidden from us by traffic; the charabanc, however, with its people now all alive and stirring, was clattering along at a spanking pace almost abreast of the nearer church.

We noted, however, that the window-sill on which we had stepped in getting out of the house was slightly singed, and that the impressions of our feet on the gravel of the path were unusually deep.

So it was I had my first experience of the New Accelerator. Practically we had been running about and saying and doing all sorts of things in the space of a second or so of time. We had lived half an hour while the band had played, perhaps, two bars. But the effect it had upon us was that the whole world had stopped for our convenient inspection. Considering all things, and particularly considering our rashness in venturing out of the house, the experience might certainly have been much more disagreeable than it was. It showed, no doubt, that Gibberne has still much to learn before his preparation is a manageable convenience, but its practicability it certainly demonstrated beyond all cavil.

Since that adventure he has been steadily bringing its use under control, and I have several times, and without the slightest bad result, taken measured doses under his direction; though I must confess I have not yet ventured abroad again while under its influence. I may mention, for example, that this story has been written at one sitting and without interruption, except for the nibbling of some chocolate, by its means. I began at 6.25, and my watch is now very nearly at the minute past the half-hour. The convenience of securing a long, uninterrupted spell of work in the midst of a day full of engagements cannot be exaggerated. Gibberne is now working at the quantitative handling of his preparation, with especial reference to its distinctive effects upon different types of constitution. He then hopes to find a Retarder with which to dilute its present rather excessive potency. The Retarder will, of course, have the reverse effect to the Accelerator; used alone it should enable the patient to spread a few seconds over many hours of ordinary time, and so to maintain an apathetic inaction, a glacierlike absence of alacrity, amidst the most animated or irritating surroundings. The two things together must necessarily work an entire revolution in civilised existence. It is the beginning of our escape from that Time Garment of which Carlyle speaks. While this Accelerator will enable us to concentrate ourselves with tremendous impact upon any moment or occasion that demands our utmost sense and vigour, the Retarder will enable us to pass in passive tranquillity through infinite hardship and tedium. Perhaps I am a little optimistic about the Retarder, which has indeed still to be discovered, but about the Accelerator there is no possible sort of doubt whatever. Its appearance upon the market in a convenient, controllable, and assimilable form is a matter of the next few months. It will be obtainable of all chemists and druggists, in small green bottles, at a high but, considering its extraordinary qualities, by no means excessive price. Gibberne's Nervous Accelerator it will be called, and he hopes to be able to supply it in three strengths: one in 200, one in 900, and one in 2000, distinguished by yellow, pink, and white labels respectively.

No doubt its use renders a great number of very extraordinary things possible; for, of course, the most remarkable and, possibly, even criminal proceedings may be effected with impunity by thus dodging, as it were, into the interstices of time. Like all potent preparations it will be liable to abuse. We have, however, discussed this aspect of the question very thoroughly, and we have decided that this is purely a matter of medical jurisprudence and altogether outside our province. We shall manufacture and sell the Accelerator, and, as for the consequences—we shall see.

Tales of Derring-Do

What male child in his early days has not played the game of knights on horseback and ladies and dragons? You know the sort of thing: "Gadzooks, Sir Cuthbert, I will e'en spindle your gizzard with my trusty Excalibur if you but touch one hair on the head of this beauteous damsel riding on yonder palfrey!"

David and Goliath

THE FIRST BOOK OF SAMUEL
Chapter 17, verses 1–54, extracts

"David and Goliath" from the Old Testament is the first, I suppose, of the big-bully-and-brave-little-kid stories, and it must be the best. The building up of the giant so that you long for him to fall right on his face, the lightly sketched background on David before he sets out on his journey, the charming scene between Saul the king and the little boy telling fibs—for fibs they surely are—Saul the king being overpowered by the little boy's faith, the device of David choosing a boyish and small weapon, the bad behavior of the giant, David's triumph, the behavior of the crowd, and the final touch of David putting the trophy of his victory in his tent—are incomparable storytelling.

Of course, being an actor, when I read the story I try to make a noise something like a Damon Runyon person for Goliath, and to characterize the little boy and David's father and his brother and King Saul. I think it comes out much more clearly that way, but it's a superb narrative anyhow.

Now the Philistines gathered together their armies to battle. And Saul and the men of Israel were gathered together. And the Philistines stood on a mountain on the one side, and Israel stood on a mountain on the other side: and there was a valley between them.

And there went out a champion of the camp of the Philistines, named Goliath, of Gath, whose height was six cubits and a span. And he had a helmet of brass upon his head, and he was armed with a coat of mail; and the weight of the coat was five thousand shekels of brass. And he had greaves of brass upon his legs, and a target of brass between his shoulders. And the staff of his spear was like a weaver's beam; and his spear's head weighed six hundred shekels of iron: and one bearing a shield went before him. And he stood and cried unto the armies of Israel, and said unto them:

"Why are ye come out to set your battle in array? Am not I a Philistine, and ye servants to Saul? Choose you a man for you and let him come down to me. If he be able to fight with me, and to kill me, then will we be your servants: but if I prevail against him, and kill him, then shall ye be our servants, and serve us."

When Saul and all Israel heard those words of the Philistine, they were dismayed and greatly afraid.

Now David was the son of that Ephrathite of Bethlehem-judah, whose name was Jesse; and he had eight sons. And David was the youngest; and the three eldest followed Saul. But David went and returned from Saul to feed his father's sheep at Beth-lehem.

And Jesse said unto David his son, "Take now for thy brethren an ephah of this parched corn, and these ten loaves, and run to the camp to thy brethren; and carry these ten cheeses unto the captain of their thousand, and look how thy brethren fare, and take their pledge."

And David rose up early in the morning, and left the sheep with a keeper, and took, and went, as Jesse had commanded him; and he came to the trench, as the host was going forth to the fight, and shouted for the battle. And David left his carriage in the hand of the keeper of the carriage, and ran into the army, and came and saluted his brethren. And as he talked with them, behold, there came up the champion, the Philistine of Gath, Goliath by name, out of the armies of the Philistines, and spoke according to the same words: and David heard them. And all the men of Israel, when they saw the man, fled from him, and were sore afraid.

And the men of Israel said, "Have ye seen this man that is come up? Surely to defy Israel is he come up: and it shall be that the man who killeth him, the king will enrich him with great riches, and will give him his daughter, and make his father's house free in Israel."

And David spoke to the men that stood by him, saying, "What shall be done to the man that killeth this Philistine, and taketh away the reproach from Israel? For who is this uncircumcised Philistine, that he should defy the armies of the living God?"

And Eliab his eldest brother heard when he spoke unto the men; and Eliab's anger was kindled against David, and he said, "Why camest thou down hither? And with whom hast thou left those few sheep in the wilderness? I know thy pride, and the naughtiness of thine heart; for thou art come down that thou mightest see the battle."

And David said, "What have I now done? Is there not a cause?"

And he turned from him toward another, and spoke after the same manner; and the people answered him again after the former manner. And when the words were heard which David spoke, they rehearsed them before Saul: and he sent for him.

And David said to Saul, "Let no man's heart fail because of him; thy servant will go and fight with this Philistine."

And Saul said to David, "Thou art not able to go against this Philistine to fight with him: for thou art but a youth, and he a man of war from his youth."

And David said unto Saul, "Thy servant kept his father's sheep, and there came a lion, and a bear, and took a lamb out of the flock: and I went out after him, and smote him, and delivered it out of his mouth and when he arose against me, I caught him by his beard, and smote him, and slew him. Thy servant slew both the lion and the bear: and this uncircumcised Philistine shall be as one of them, seeing he hath defied the armies of the living God."

David said moreover, "The Lord that delivered me out of the paw of the lion, and out of the paw of the bear, he will deliver me out of the hand of this Philistine."

And Saul said unto David, "Go, and the Lord be with thee."

And Saul armed David with his armour, and he put a helmet of brass upon his head; also he armed him with a coat of mail. And David said unto Saul, "I cannot go with these; for I have not proved them."

And David put them off him. And he took his staff in his hand, and chose him five smooth stones out of the brook, and put them in a shepherd's bag, which he had, even in a scrip; and his sling was in his hand: and he drew near unto the Philistine. And the Philistine came on and drew near unto David; and the man that bore the shield went before him. And when the Philistine looked about, and saw David, he disdained him: for he was but a youth, and ruddy, and of a fair countenance. And the Philistine said unto David, "Am I a dog that thou comest to me with staves?"

And the Philistine cursed David by his gods. And the Philistine said to David, "Come to me, and I will give thy flesh unto the fowls of the air, and to the beasts of the field."

Then said David to the Philistine, "Thou comest to me with a sword and with a spear, and with a shield: but I come to thee in the name of the Lord of hosts, the God of the armies of Israel, whom thou hast defied. This day will the Lord deliver thee into mine hand; and I will smite thee, and take thy head from thee; and I will give the carcases of the host of the Philistines this day unto the fowls of the air, and to the wild beasts of the earth; that all the earth may know that there is a God in Israel. And all this assembly shall know that the Lord saveth not with sword and spear: for the battle is the Lord's, and he will give you into our hands."

And it came to pass, when the Philistine arose, and came and drew nigh to meet David, that David hastened, and ran toward the army to meet the Philistine. And David put his hand in his bag, and took thence a stone, and slung it, and smote the Philistine in his forehead, that the stone sunk into his forehead; and he fell upon his face to the earth. So David prevailed over the Philistine with a sling and with a stone, and smote the Philistine, and slew him; but there was no sword in the hand of David. Therefore David ran and stood upon the Philistine, and took his sword, and drew it out of the sheath thereof, and slew him, and cut off his head therewith. And when the Philistines saw their champion was dead, they fled.

And the men of Israel and of Judah arose, and shouted, and pursued the Philistines, until they came to the valley, and to the gates of Ekron. And the wounded of the Philistines fell down by the way to Shaaraim, even unto Gath, and unto Ekron. And the children of Israel returned from chasing after the Philistines and they spoiled their tents. And David took the head of the Philistine, and brought it to Jerusalem: but he put his armour in his tent.

The Sunday Zeppelin

WILLIAM SAROYAN

> This is a beautifully observed story of Saroyan's. I put it next
> to "David and Goliath" because it seemed to me that the
> children telling fibs about why they shouldn't like the
> movies is very similar to David's fibbing about what he did
> with the lion and the bear. We feel the children's brave
> imaginings of what the dollar zeppelin is going to be like
> —and we can see the ad calculated to deceive them. The
> same thing happened to me, only in my case it was a
> bicycle lamp, a carbide bicycle lamp. I expected the beam
> to shine from Scarborough across the North Sea so that I
> could see the coast of Germany. In fact, it smelt horrible,
> was made of very thin tin of some kind, and blew up and
> made a mess of the cellar floor. I remember the name of
> the firm I ordered it from and I can still see its picture in
> the catalogue.
>
> And the secret language. We used to have one of those
> even as late as the days when we were shooting Mutiny on
> the Bounty. This was a cast and crew of men and we got
> swearing and so on because there were no girls around and
> we were out in the open. And when newspaperwomen
> came on board the ship we invented a new language, be-
> cause we didn't want to stop swearing. I remember my
> secret glee in watching the expression on the face of a lady
> who didn't know what we were saying.

Luke was holding my hand and I was holding Margaret's. We had
a nickel each for collection, and Luke said to me, Don't forget,
Mark, drop the nickel: don't keep it like last time and buy ice-cream.

You too, I said.

Last time Luke didn't drop his nickel and I saw him. I bought an
ice-cream cone in the afternoon when it was very hot. Schultz gave
me two scoops. Luke saw me eating the ice-cream cone under the
china-ball trees of Emerson School.

He acted like Hawkshaw the detective.

Ah-ha, he said.

Where'd you get the money, Mark?

You know where, I said.

No, he said. Where? Tell me.

Sunday School, I said. I didn't drop it.

That's a sin, Luke said.

I know it, I said. You didn't either.

I did too, Luke said.

No, you didn't, I said. I saw you pass the basket without dropping the nickel.

I'm saving, Luke said.

Saving for what? I said.

For a zeppelin, he said.

How much is a zeppelin? I said.

There's one in Boys' World, he said, that costs a dollar. It comes from Chicago.

A real zeppelin? I said.

Two people can go up in it, he said. Me and Ernest West.

I swallowed the last mouthful of ice-cream.

How about me? I said.

You can't go up, Luke said. You're too small. You're a baby. Ernest West is my age.

I ain't a baby, I said. I'm eight and you're ten. Let me go up in the zeppelin with you, Luke.

No, Luke said.

I didn't cry, but I felt sad. Then Luke got me sore.

You like Alice Small, he said. You're just a baby.

This was true. I did like Alice Small, but the way Luke said it made me sore.

I felt sad and alone. I liked Alice Small all right, but did I ever do any of the things I wanted to do? Did I ever walk with her? Did I ever hold her hand and tell her how much I liked her? Did I ever say her name to her the way I wanted to, so she'd know how much she meant to me? No. I was too scared. I wasn't even brave enough to look at her long. She scared me because she was so pretty, and when Luke talked that way I got sore.

You're a son of a bitch, Luke, I said. You're a dirty bastard, I said. I couldn't think of any of the other bad words I had heard big boys saying, so I started to cry.

I felt very bad about calling my own brother these names. In the evening I told him I was sorry.

Don't try to fool me, Luke said. Sticks and stones can break my bones, but names can never hurt me.

I never threw sticks and stones at you, Luke, I said.

You called me those names, he said.

I didn't mean to, Luke, I said. Honest I didn't. You said I like Alice Small.

Well, you do, Luke said. You know you do. The whole world knows you do.

I don't, I said. I don't like anybody.

You like Alice Small, Luke said.

You're a son of a bitch, I said.

Pa heard me.

He was sitting in the parlor reading a book. He jumped up and came into our room, Luke's and mine. I started to cry.

What was that, young man? he said. What was that you just called your brother?

Sticks and stones, Luke started to say.

Never mind that, Pa said. Why are you always teasing Mark?

I wasn't teasing him, Luke said.

He was, I cried. He said I like Alice Small.

Alice Small? Pa said.

He hadn't even heard of Alice Small. He didn't even know she was alive.

Who in the world is Alice Small? he said.

She's in my class at school, I said. Her father's the preacher at our church. She's going to be a missionary when she grows up. She told us in front of the whole class.

Pa said:

Tell Luke you're sorry you called him a bad name.

I'm sorry I called you a bad name, Luke, I said.

Luke, said Pa, tell Mark you're sorry you teased him about Alice Small.

I'm sorry I teased you about Alice Small, Luke said. Only I knew he wasn't sorry. I was sorry when I told him I was sorry, but I knew he wasn't sorry when he told me he was sorry. He was only saying it because Pa told him to.

Pa went back to his chair in the parlor. Just before he sat down he said:

I want you boys to occupy yourselves intelligently and not get on one another's nerves. Do you understand?

Yes, sir, Luke said.

So we got a copy each of The Saturday Evening Post and started looking at the pictures. Luke wouldn't talk to me.

Can I go up in the zeppelin? I said.

He just turned the pages of the magazine and wouldn't talk.

Just once? I said.

I woke up in the middle of the night and started thinking about being up in the zeppelin.

Luke, I said.

Finally he woke up.

What do you want? he said.

Luke, I said, let me go up in the zeppelin with you when it comes from Chicago.

No, he said.

That was last week.

Now we were on our way to Sunday School.

Luke said: Don't forget, Mark. Drop the nickel.

You too, I said.

You do what you're told to do, Luke said.

I want a zeppelin too, I said.

Who said anything about a zeppelin? Luke said.

If you don't drop your nickel, I said, neither will I.

It looked like Margaret didn't even hear us. She just walked along while me and Luke argued about the zeppelin.

I'll give half, Luke, I said, if you let me go up.

Ernest West is giving the other half, Luke said. We're partners.

Eight more weeks, Luke said, and the zeppelin will come from Chicago.

All right for you, I said. Don't let me go up. I'll get even with you some day. You'll be sorry when you see me going around the world in my own boat.

Go ahead, Luke said.

Please, Luke, I said, let me go up in the zeppelin. I'll let you go around the world with me in my boat.

No, Luke said. You go alone.

Ernest West and his sister Dorothy were standing in front of the church when we got there. Margaret and Ernest's sister went into the churchyard together, and me and Luke and Ernest stayed on the sidewalk.

Palka eskos, Ernest said to Luke.

Immel, said Luke.

What's that mean, Luke? I said.

Can't tell you, Luke said. That's our secret language.

Tell me what it means, Luke, I said. I won't tell anybody.

No, said Ernest.

Effin ontur, he said to Luke.

Garic hopin, Luke said, and then they busted out laughing.

Garic hopin, Ernest laughed.

Tell me, Luke, I said. I promise never to let anybody else know what it means.

No, said Luke. Invent your own secret language, he said. Nobody's stopping you.

I don't know how, I said.

The church bell rang, so we went inside and sat down. Luke and Ernest sat together. Luke told me to go away from them. I sat in the row behind them, the last row. In the first row was Alice Small. Her father, our preacher, walked down the aisle and then went upstairs to his private study. That's where he made up his sermons. He was a tall man who smiled at everybody before and after the sermon. During the sermon he never smiled at all.

We sang some songs, then Ernest West called for *At the Cross*, only he and Luke sang, *At the bar, at the bar, where I smoked my last cigar, and the nickels and the dimes rolled away, rolled away.*

I felt jealous of Luke and Ernest West. They knew how to have fun. Even at church. Once in a while Ernest would look at Luke and say arkel ropper, and Luke would answer haggid ossum, and then both of them would try to keep from laughing. They would hold themselves in with all their might until the loud singing began, then they would bust loose with all the laughter that was part of their secret language. I felt miserable being out of all that fine stuff.

Arkel ropper, I said and tried to feel how funny it was, but it wasn't. It was terrible not knowing what arkel ropper meant. I could imagine it meant something funnier than anything else in the world, but I didn't know what it was. Haggid ossum, I said, only it made me feel sad. Some day I would invent the funniest language in the world and not let Luke or Ernest West know what the words meant. Every word would make me feel happy and I would talk no other language. Only me and one other person in the world would know my secret language. Alice Small. Only Alice and me. Ohber linten, I would say to Alice, and she would know what a beautiful thing that meant, and she would look at me and smile and I would hold her hand and maybe kiss her.

Then Harvey Gillis, our superintendent, got up on the platform and told us about the Presbyterian missionary work we were helping to pay for in many foreign and heathen countries of the world.

In Northern Africa, my dear young people, he said in a high-pitched voice, our shepherds of the Lord are performing miracles every day in the name of Jesus. The native savage is being taught the holy gospel and the pious life, and the light of our Lord is penetrating the darkest depths of ignorance. We can well rejoice and pray.

Umper gamper Harvey Gillis, Luke said to Ernest.

Luke could barely keep from laughing.

I felt all alone.

If I only knew what they knew. Umper gamper Harvey Gillis. That could mean so many things about our superintendent. He was a sissy and he talked in a high-pitched voice. I don't think anybody, except maybe Alice Small, believed a word of what he said.

Our noble heroes in the field are healing the sick, he said. They are sacrificing life and limb to prepare the world for the Lord's second coming. They are spreading His truth to the far corners of the earth. Let us pray for them. Will Miss Valentine pray?

Would she? She'd been waiting all week for a chance to pray.

Miss Valentine got up from the organ bench and took off her glasses and wiped her eyes. She was a skinny woman of forty or so who played the organ at our church. She played it as if she were sore at somebody and wanted to get even, pounding the keys and turning around every once in a while to take a quick look at the congregation. It seemed as if she hated everybody. I only stayed for the sermon twice in my life, but both times she did those things, and once in a while she nodded very wisely at something our preacher said, as if she was the only person in the whole church who knew what he meant.

Now she got up to pray for our heroic missionaries in dark Africa and other heathen places of the world.

Exel sorga, Ernest said to Luke.

You said it, Luke answered, and more besides.

Almighty and merciful Father, she prayed. We have erred and strayed from Thy ways like lost sheep.

And a lot of other stuff.

I thought it was supposed to be for our noble workers in the field, but all she talked about was straying away and doing wrong things, instead of right ones. She prayed too long too.

For a while I thought Harvey Gillis was going to touch her arm and make her open her eyes and tell her, That will be enough for this morning, Miss Valentine. But he didn't. I opened my eyes the minute she started to pray. You were supposed to keep your eyes shut, but I always opened mine to see what was going on in the church.

Nothing was going on. All the heads were bowed except Luke's and Ernest's and mine, and Luke and Ernest were still whispering funny things to one another in their secret language. I could see Alice Small with her head bowed lower than anybody else's, and I said, O God, some day let me talk to Alice Small in our own secret language that nobody else in the world will understand.

Amen.

Miss Valentine finally stopped praying and we went to the corner of the church where boys between seven and twelve studied the stories in The Bible and dropped their Sunday offering in the basket.

Luke and Ernest sat together again and told me to get away from them. I sat right behind them to see if Luke would drop his nickel. Every Sunday they gave each of us one copy of a little Sunday School paper called Boys' World. It told about little boys doing kind things for old people and the blind and the crippled, and it had advice on how to make things. Me and Luke tried to make a wheel-barrow once, but we didn't have a wheel. After that we didn't try to make anything. On the back page were the advertisements with pictures.

Our teacher was Henry Parker. He was a fellow who wore thick glasses and had some red pimples around his mouth. He looked sick and nobody liked him. I guess nobody liked going to Sunday School at all. We had to go because Pa said it would certainly do less harm than good. Later on, he said, when you get to be older you can stop going or keep on going, as you choose. Right now, he said, it's good discipline.

Ma said, That's right.

So we went. Maybe we got used to it because we never asked not to go. There wasn't much else to do Sunday morning anyway. Ernest West had to go too, and I guess that's why Luke never tried to get out of it. He could always talk their secret language with Ernest West and laugh about everybody.

The story was the story of Joseph and his brothers, Joseph with the brightly-colored coat, and then all of a sudden the whole class started talking about the movies.

Ah-ha, Luke said to Ernest West.

Now, said Henry Parker, I want each of you to give me one good reason why no one should go to the movies.

There were seven of us in the class.

The movies, said Pat Carrico, show us naked women dancing. That's why we shouldn't go.

Well, said Henry Parker, yes, that's a good reason.

They show us robbers killing people, said Tommy Cesar, and that's a sin.

Very good, said our teacher.

Yes, said Ernest West, but the robbers always get killed by the police, don't they? The robbers always get theirs in the end, don't they? That's no reason.

Is too, said Tommy Cesar. It teaches us how to steal.

I would be inclined to agree with Mr. Cesar, said Henry Parker. Yes, he said, it sets a bad example for us.

Oh, all right, Ernest West said.

He looked at Luke wisely and was about to say something in the secret language, only this time he didn't need to because Luke laughed out loud anyway, and then Ernest laughed with him. It seemed as if Luke knew what Ernest was going to say and it must have been something very funny because they laughed like anything.

What's this? said our teacher. Laughing in Sunday School? What are you two laughing about?

I'll tell on them, I thought. I'll tell him they've got a secret language. Then I decided not to. That would spoil it. It was such a funny language. I didn't want to spoil it, even if I couldn't understand any of the words.

Nothing, Luke said. Can't a fellow laugh?

Then it was Jacob Hyland's turn. Jacob was the dumbest boy in the world. He couldn't think up anything. He couldn't make up any kind of an answer. He couldn't even guess.

Now, said Mr. Parker, you tell us why we shouldn't go to the movies.

I don't know why, Jacob said.

Come now, Mr. Parker said, surely you know one good reason why we shouldn't.

Jacob started to think. I mean, he started to look around the room, then down at his feet, then up at the ceiling, while all of us waited to hear what he'd think up.

He thought a long time. Then he said:

I guess I don't know why, Mr. Parker. Why? he said.

I'm asking you, our teacher said. I know why, but I want you to know why for yourself. Now, come, give me one reason, Mr. Hyland.

So Jacob started thinking all over again, and all of us felt sore at him. Anybody could make up some small reason, anybody but a dumb boy like Jacob. Nobody knew what made him so dumb. He was older than anybody else in our class. He kept squirming around in his chair and then he started picking his nose and scratching his head and looking at Mr. Parker like a dog looks at somebody it wants to be friends with.

Well? said our teacher.

Honest, said Jacob. I don't know why. I don't go to the movies much.

You've been to the movies once, haven't you? said our teacher.

Yes, sir, he said. More than once, but I forget quick. I don't remember.

Surely, said our teacher, you remember one little thing you saw in the movies that was a bad example, and a good reason why we should never go.

All of a sudden Jacob's face lighted up with a big smile.

I know, he said.

Yes? said our teacher.

It teaches us to throw custard pies at our enemies and kick ladies and run.

Is that all you remember? said Mr. Parker.

Yes, sir, Jacob said.

That's no reason, Ernest West said. What's wrong about throwing a custard pie?

It gets all over you, Jacob said, and he busted out laughing. You remember, he said, how it drips down a man's face.

It is certainly wrong to kick a lady, said Mr. Parker. Very fine, Mr. Hyland, he said. I knew you would remember a good reason if you thought carefully enough.

Then it was Nelson Holgum's turn.

It's expensive, he said. It costs too much.

Only a nickel at the Bijou, I said. That's no reason.

You can buy a loaf of bread with a nickel, Nelson said. A nickel is a lot of money these days.

True, said Mr. Parker. A very good reason indeed. There are much nobler ways for us to spend our money. If our young people would stop going to movies and give their money to missionary work, think of the tremendous progress we would make in only one year. Why, we could convert the whole world to Christianity in one year on the money spent annually for frivolous amusements like the movies.

Mr. Parker nodded at Ernest West.

The movies teach us to be dissatisfied with what we've got, Ernest said. We see people riding around in big automobiles and living in big houses and we get jealous.

Envious, said Mr. Parker.

We start wanting all them things, Ernest said, and we know we can't have them because we haven't got the money to buy them with, so we feel bad.

A splendid reason, said Mr. Parker.

It was Luke's turn, and next it would be mine.

The music is bad, Luke said.

Not at the Liberty, Tommy Cesar said. Not even at the Kinema. That's no reason.

It's bad at the Bijou, Luke said. They play one song over and over again on the player-piano, he said. It gets monotonous. *Wedding of the Winds.*

That's not true, Tommy Cesar said. Sometimes they play another song. I don't know the name. Sometimes they play six or seven songs.

They all sound alike, Luke said. It gives you a headache.

Now we're getting somewhere, said our teacher. It gives us head-
aches. It harms our health. And we shouldn't do anything that is
harmful to the health. Health is our most precious possession. We
must do those things which improve our health rather than those
which harm it.

I said we shouldn't go to the movies because when we got out of
the theater we didn't like our town.

Everything seems silly in our town, I said. We want to go away.

Then it was time to pass the basket around. Mr. Parker made a
little speech about how urgently money was needed and how much
better it was to give than to receive.

Tommy Cesar dropped two pennies, Pat Carrico three, Nelson
Holgum one, Jacob Hyland a nickel, and then the basket reached
Ernest West. He handed it to Luke and Luke handed it to me and I
handed it back to Mr. Parker. We didn't drop anything. Mr. Parker
took a purse from his pocket, jingled some coins, picked out a
quarter so all of us could see it, and dropped it among the other
coins. He looked very noble. Everybody hated him for the way he
looked, even a dumb boy like Jacob Hyland. He looked as if he was
saving the whole world with that quarter.

Then he gave each of us a copy of Boys' World, and class ended.

Everybody jumped up and ran out to the sidewalk.

Well, said Ernest West to Luke, aplica till we meet again.

Aplica, said Luke. Then my little sister Margaret came out of the
church and we started walking home.

I turned to the last page of Boys' World and saw the advertisement
of the zeppelin. The picture showed two boys high in the sky, standing in the basket of the zeppelin. Both of the boys looked sad; they
were waving good-bye.

We went home and had Sunday dinner. Pa and Ma were very
cheerful at the table and we ate till we couldn't get any more down.
Pa said, What was the lesson, Luke?

Evils of the movies, Luke said.

What are they? Pa said.

Naked women dancing, Luke said. Robbers killing police. Expensive. Teaches us to throw custard pies.

I see, said Pa. Very evil.

After dinner I couldn't think of anything to do. If I wasn't so
scared I would go to Alice Small's house and tell her I liked her.
Alice, I would say, I like you. But I was scared. If I had my boat
I would go around the world in it. Then I thought of the zeppelin.
Luke was in the yard, nailing two pieces of wood together.

What are you making? I said.

Nothing, Luke said. I'm just nailing.

Luke, I said, here's my nickel. When the zeppelin comes let me go up with you.

I tried to give him the nickel but he wouldn't take it.

No, he said. The zeppelin's for me and Ernest West.

All right for you, I said. I'll get even.

Go ahead, he said.

It was very hot. I sat on the cool grass under our sycamore tree and watched Luke nail the boards together. The way he was hitting the nails you'd think he was making something, and I couldn't believe he wasn't until he was all through. He nailed about ten boards together, and that was all. They were just nailed together. They didn't make anything.

Pa heard all the hammering and came out smoking his pipe.

What do you call that? he said.

That? Luke said.

Yes, said Pa. What is it?

Nothing, Luke said.

Splendid, Pa said, and he turned around and went right back in.

Splendid? Luke said.

It ain't anything, I said. Why don't you *make* something?

I could hear Pa singing inside. I guess he was drying the dishes for Ma. He sang very loud, and after a while Ma started singing with him.

Then Luke stopped nailing and threw the boards over the garage.

He ran around the garage and came back with the boards and threw them over again and went and got them again.

What are you playing? I said.

Nothing, Luke said.

Luke, I said, let's go to the Bijou together.

Me and *you?* Luke said.

Sure, I said. You got your nickel and I got mine. Let's go see Tarzan.

I got to save up for the zeppelin, Luke said. I got a dime now. Eight more weeks and it'll be here, and then good-bye.

Good-bye? I said.

Yes, said Luke, good-bye.

You ain't going away, are you, Luke? I said.

Sure, he said. What did you think I wanted it for?

You mean never to come back again, Luke?

I'll come back all right, he said. I'll go away for a month or two, but I'll come back.

Where will you go, Luke? I said.

Klondike, he said. North.

Up there in that cold country, Luke?

Sure, Luke said. Me and my partner Ernest West. Palka eskos, he said.

What's it mean, Luke? I said. Tell me, please. What's palka eskos mean?

Only me and my partner know, Luke said.

I won't tell anybody, Luke. Honest I won't.

You'll go and tell somebody, Luke said.

Cross my heart, I said. Hope to die.

Needles through your tongue, if you do?

Yes, I said, needles and hot irons too, Luke.

On your word of honor?

Yes, Luke. What does it mean?

Palka eskos? he said.

Yes, Luke. Palka eskos.

Good morning, he said. It means good morning.

I couldn't believe it.

Is that all, Luke?

That's all palka eskos means. We got a whole language, though.

Palka eskos, Luke, I said.

Immel, he said.

What's immel mean, Luke?

Immel?

Yes, Luke.

You won't tell?

Same as before, I said. Hot irons through my tongue.

Hello, said Luke. Immel means hello.

Let's go to the Bijou, Luke, I said. We got a nickel each.

All right, he said. The music doesn't really give you a headache. I just said that.

Tell Ma, I said.

Maybe she won't let us go, Luke said.

Maybe she will. Maybe Pa will tell her to.

Luke and me went inside. Pa was drying the dishes and Ma was washing them.

Can we go to the Bijou, Ma? Luke said.

What's that? Pa said. I thought the lesson was the evils of the movies.

Yes, sir, Luke said.

Well, is your conscience clear? Pa said.

Oh, what's playing? Ma said.

Tarzan, I said. Can we go, Ma? We didn't drop our nickels. Luke is saving up for a zeppelin, but he won't let me go up with him.

Didn't drop your nickels? Pa said. What kind of religion do you call that? First thing you know them Presbyterian missionaries will be packing up and leaving Africa if you boys don't keep them supplied with nickels.

I guess so, Luke said, but me and Ernest West are saving up for a zeppelin. We *had* to do it.

What kind of a zeppelin? Pa said.

A *real* one, Luke said. It travels eighty miles an hour and carries two people, me and Ernest West.

How much does it cost? Pa said.

One dollar, Luke said. It comes from Chicago.

I'll tell you what, Pa said. If you clean out the garage and keep the yard in order next week, I'll give you a dollar Saturday. All right?

I'll say, Luke said.

Provided, Pa said, you let Mark go up.

If he'll help me with the work, Luke said.

He'll help, Pa said. Won't you, Mark?

I'll do more than Luke, I said.

Pa gave us ten cents more each and said to go to the movies. We went to the Bijou and saw Tarzan, chapter eighteen. Two more chapters and it would be all over. Tommy Cesar was there with Pat Carrico. They made more noise when Tarzan was cornered by the tiger than all the rest of us put together.

Me and Luke cleaned out the garage and kept the yard in order all week, and Saturday night Pa gave Luke a dollar bill. Luke sat down and wrote a nice letter to the people in Chicago who sold zeppelins. He put the dollar bill in an envelope and dropped the letter in the mailbox on the corner. I went to the mailbox with him.

Now, he said, all we got to do is wait.

We waited ten days. We talked about all the strange and faraway places we would go to in the zeppelin.

Then it came. It was a small flat package with the same picture we saw in Boys' World stamped on the box. It didn't weigh a pound, not even half a pound. Luke's hands shook when he opened the box. I felt sick because I knew something was wrong. There was a slip of paper with some writing on it in the box. It said:

Dear Boys: Here is your zeppelin, with instructions on how to operate it. If every direction is carefully followed this toy will ascend and stay aloft for as long as twenty seconds.

And a lot more like that.

Luke followed every direction carefully, and blew into the tissue-paper sack until it was almost full and almost the shape of a zeppelin. Then the paper tore and the whole shape collapsed, the way a rubber balloon does.

That was all. That was our zeppelin. Luke couldn't figure it out.

He said, The picture shows two boys standing in the basket. I thought the zeppelin was coming out in a freight train.

Then he started talking in his secret language.

What are you saying, Luke? I said.

Good thing you can't understand, he said.

He smashed what was left of the zeppelin and tore the tissue-paper to pieces, then went out to the barn and got a lot of boards and nails and the hammer and started nailing the boards together. All I could do was say to myself, Them people in Chicago are sons of bitches, that's what they are.

The Sword in the Stone

SIR THOMAS MALORY

Here is an extract from that great book Morte d'Arthur *which is a complete story.* Morte d'Arthur *is the main source of our tales of chivalry. You know—King Arthur, Queen Guinevere, Sir Lancelot, Sir Galahad, and the rest of the Knights of the Round Table.*

This is the story of how it was found out that young Arthur was the son of the King of England and how he himself became King.

Again the little boy is beautifully and touchingly characterized. Notice his relationship to his brother, which is very similar to the relationship of David and his brother.

By the way, though this book is the source of so many children's stories, don't leave it around the house. There are some pretty lurid incidents between Sir Lancelot and Queen Guinevere and you will have to answer a great many awkward questions to any children who pick it up.

Then stood the realm in great jeopardy long while, for every lord that was might of men made him strong, and many weened to have been king. Then Merlin went to the Archbishop of Canterbury, and counselled him for to send for all the lords of the realm, and all the gentlemen of arms, that they should to London come by Christmas, upon pain of cursing; and for this cause, that Jesus, that was born on that night, that he would of his great mercy show some miracle, as he was come to be king of mankind, for to show some miracle who should be rightways king of this realm. So the Archbishop, by the advice of Merlin, sent for all the lords and gentlemen of arms that they should come by Christmas even unto London. And many of them made them clean of their life, that their prayer might be the more acceptable unto God. So in the greatest church of London, whether it were Paul's or not the French book maketh no mention, all the estates were long in the church for to pray. And when matins and the first mass was done, there was seen in the churchyard, against the high altar, a great stone four square, like unto a marble stone, and in midst thereof was like an anvil of steel a foot on high, and therein stuck a fair sword naked by the point, and letters there were written in gold about the sword that said thus:—Whoso pulleth out this sword of this stone and anvil, is rightwise king born of all England. Then the people marvelled, and told it to the Archbishop. I command, said the Archbishop, that he keep you within your church, and pray unto God still; that no man touch the sword till the high mass be all done. So when all masses were done all the lords went to behold the stone and the sword. And when they saw the scripture, some assayed; such as would have been king. But none might stir the sword nor move it. He is not here, said the Archbishop, that shall achieve the sword, but doubt not God will make him known. But this is my counsel, said the Archbishop, that we let purvey ten knights, men of good fame, and they to keep this sword. So it was ordained, and then there was made a cry, that every man should essay that would, for to win the sword. And upon New Year's Day the barons let make a jousts and a tournament, that all knights that would joust or tourney there might play, and all this was ordained for to keep the lords and the commons together, for the Archbishop trusted that God would make him known that should win the sword. So upon New Year's Day, when the service was done, the barons rode unto the field, some to joust and some to tourney, and so it happened that Sir Ector, that had great livelihood about London, rode unto the jousts, and with him rode Sir Kay his son, and young Arthur that was his nourished brother; and Sir Kay was made knight at All Hallowmass afore. So as they rode to the joustsward, Sir Kay had lost his sword, for he had left it at his father's lodging, and so he prayed young Arthur for to ride for his sword. I will well, said Arthur, and rode fast after the sword, and when he came home, the lady and all were out to see the jousting. Then was Arthur wroth, and said to himself, I will ride to the churchyard, and take the sword with me that sticketh in the stone, for my brother Sir Kay shall not be without a sword this day. So when he came to the churchyard, Sir Arthur alit and tied his horse to the stile, and so he went to the tent, and found no knights there, for they were at jousting; and so he handled the sword by the handles, and lightly and fiercely pulled it out of the stone, and took his horse and rode his way until he came to his brother Sir Kay, and delivered him the sword. As soon as Sir Kay saw the sword he wist well it was the sword of the stone, and so he rode to his father Sir Ector, and said: Sir, lo here is the sword of the stone, wherefore I must be king of this land. When Sir Ector beheld the sword, he returned again and came to the church, and there they alit all three, and went into the church. And anon he made Sir Kay to swear upon a book how he came to that sword. Sir, said Sir Kay, by my brother Arthur, for he brought it to me. How gat ye this sword? said Sir Ector to Arthur. Sir, I will tell you. When I came home for my brother's sword, I found nobody at home to deliver me his sword, and so I thought my brother Sir Kay should not be swordless, and so I came hither eagerly and pulled it out of the stone without any pain. Found ye any knights about this sword? said Sir Ector. Nay, said Arthur. Now, said Sir Ector to Arthur, I understand ye must be king of this land. Wherefor I, said Arthur, and for what cause? Sir, said Ector, for God will have it so, for there should never man have drawn out this sword, but he that shall be rightways king of this land. Now let me see whether ye can put the sword there as it was, and pull it out again. That is no mastery, said Arthur, and so he put it in the stone, therewithal Sir Ector essayed to pull out the sword and failed.

Now essay, said Sir Ector unto Sir Kay. And anon he pulled at the sword with all his might, but it would not be. Now shall ye essay, said Sir Ector to Arthur. I will well, said Arthur, and pulled it out easily. And therewithal Sir Ector knelt down to the earth, and Sir Kay. Alas, said Arthur, my own dear father and brother, why kneel ye to me? Nay, nay, my lord Arthur, it is not so, I was never your father nor of your blood, but I wot well ye are of an higher blood than I weened ye were. And then Sir Ector told him all, how he was bitaken him for to nourish him, and by whose commandment, and by Merlin's deliverance. Then Arthur made great doole when he understood that Sir Ector was not his father. Sir, said Ector unto Arthur, will ye be my good and gracious lord when ye are king? Else were I to blame, said Arthur, for ye are the man in the world that I am most beholden to, and my good lady and mother your wife, that as well as her own hath fostered me and kept. And if ever it be God's will that I be king as ye say, ye shall desire of me what I may do, and I shall not fail you, God forbid I should fail you. Sir, said Sir Ector, I will ask no more of you, but that ye will make my son, your foster brother, Sir Kay, seneschal of all your lands. That shall be done, said Arthur, and more, by the faith of my body, that never man shall have that office but he, while he and I live. Therewithal they went unto the Archbishop, and told him how the sword was achieved, and by whom; and on Twelfth-day all the barons came thither, and to essay to take the sword, who that would essay. But there afore them all, there might none take it out but Arthur; wherefore there were many lords wroth, and said it was great shame unto them all and the realm, to be over-governed with a boy of no high blood born, and so they fell out at that time that it was put off till Candlemas, and then all the barons should meet there again; but always the ten knights were ordained to watch the sword day and night, and so they set a pavilion over the stone and the sword, and five always watched. So at Candlemas many more great lords came thither for to have won the sword, but there might none prevail. And right as Arthur did at Christmas, he did at Candlemas, and pulled out the sword easily, whereof the barons were sore aggrieved and put it off in delay till the high feast of Easter. And as Arthur sped before, so did he at Easter, yet there were some of the great lords had indignation that Arthur should be king, and put it off in delay till the feast of Pentecost.

And at the feast of Pentecost all manner of men essayed to pull at the sword that would essay, but none might prevail but Arthur, and pulled it out afore all the lords and commons that were there, wherefore all the commons cried at once, We will have Arthur unto our king, we will put him no more in delay, for we all see that it is God's will that he shall be our king, and who that holdeth against it, we will slay him. And therewith they all kneeled at once, both rich and poor, and cried Arthur mercy because they had delayed him so long, and Arthur forgave them, and took the sword between both his hands, and offered it upon the altar where the Archbishop was, and so was he made knight of the best man that was there. And so anon was the coronation made. And there was he sworn unto his lords and the commons for to be a true king, to stand with true justice from thenceforth the days of this life.

Tales of Folly

From the beginning people have told stories of human folly. There are stories of folly in the Bible. Perhaps the simplest example I can think of is the old fairy story where a fairy gives the man and his wife three wishes. The first thing the man wishes for is a pudding and his wife is so mad at him wishing for so simple a thing when he might have wished for wealth or a new house or what not that she snaps out at the table, "I wish it on the end of your nose." And there is the man with the pudding on his nose. And in order to get rid of the inconvenience the man has to wish it off the end of his nose, and the three wishes are used up.

The Search for the Right House and How Mrs. Jump Had Her Annual Attack

GEORGE ADE

George Ade appears to be against women who are always moving the furniture around and changing the drapes. I had a row with Elsa last year over a hole in a large carpet in our living room in Hollywood which she wanted to replace. In the end we put a small rug over the hole. But the rug was expensive, anyhow.

Once there was a Family called Jump that had sampled every Ward within the Corporation Limits.

The Jumps did a Caravan Speciality every time the Frost went out of the Ground.

When the Sarsaparilly Ads began to blossom, and the Peach Crop had been ruined by the late Cold Snap and the Kids were batting up Flies in the Lot back of the Universalist Church, and a Barrel-Organ down Street was tearing the Soul out of "Trovatore"—these were the Cues for Mrs. Jump to get her Nose into the Air and begin to champ at the Bit.

Mother was a House-Hunter from away back. She claimed to be an Invalid eleven months out of the Year and took Nerve Medicine that cost $2.00 a Bottle. Just the same when April hove into view and Dame Nature began to stretch herself, then Mother put on her Short Skirt and a pair of Shoes intended for a Man and did a tall Prance.

She was good for 12 hours a Day on any kind of Pavements. With her Reticule loaded full of "To Let" Clippings, she hot-footed from Street to Street. Every time she struck a Fresh Trail she broke into a Run.

Mother was looking for a House that had twice as many Closets as Rooms and a Southern Exposure on all four sides.

She had conned herself into the Belief that some day she would run down a Queen Anne Shack that would be O.K. in all Particulars.

In the Magazine that came every Month she had seen these Dream-Pictures of Palaces that can be put up for $1,500 if you steal your Materials.

She had gazed at the Bunco Illustration of the swell Structure with bushy trees dotting the Lawn and a little Girl rolling a Hoop along the Cement Side-Walk and she had set her Heart on that kind of a Home.

Mother loved to study the Plans and count the Bathrooms and figure on Window Seats and what kind of Curtains to put in the Guest Chamber.

Every Spring she found the Place she had been seeking and gave a Grand Signal for the whole Outfit to begin packing up. Those were the bright vernal Days when Mr. Jump got all that was coming to him. Mr. Jump was a Man, therefore any old kind of a Hut suited him. For eight years before starting on his continuous Tour with Mother, he had roomed over a Drug Store.

His Apartment had been one of those delectable Man-Joints where Women never butted in to hide things and give the whole Place a Soapy Smell.

The Sweepings went under the Bed, so as not to litter up the Hallway.

Once a Year he had a House-Cleaning. That is to say, he employed a Colored Man to beat the Rugs, which had to be separated from the Floor by means of a Shovel.

Inasmuch as Women never came in to straighten up, he knew where to find everything. He knew it was somewhere in the Room and all he had to do was to excavate until he found it.

Then he hooked up with Laura so as to get a real Home and she gave him a new one every Year.

Mr. Jump soon discovered that, although every Man is the Architect of his own Fortune, the Wife usually superintends the Construction.

When Mrs. Jump made her Spring Announcement that they would move to another House, he did a deal of Kicking, but he always went into the Wood Shed to do it. He sassed her inwardly, but not so that she could hear.

She was a Wonder at framing up Reasons for hurling the Lease back at the Landlord.

One Year she quit because the Owner papered the Upstairs with a Jay Pattern that cost only 15 cents a Bolt. Another time the Family next door kept Chickens. Usually the Children across the Alley were not fit Associates for their own little Brood.

One Time she quit on account of a Cockroach. She saw it scoot across the Pantry and that afternoon she headed for a Renting Agency.

Father suggested that instead of vacating in favor of the Cockroach, they offer a reward of $100 for its Capture, dead or alive, and thereby save a little Money, but she refused to listen.

If the Plumbing wasn't out of Whack, the Furnace required too much Coal or else the Woman across the Street had been divorced too many times.

If they squatted in a low-down Neighborhood, Mrs. Jump was ashamed to give her Address to Friends in the Congregation.

If they got into a Nest of the New Rich, then Laura had the freeze-out worked on her, because Mr. Jump was on a Salary and she had to ride on the Trolleys. So she began looking for a Street in which Intellect would successfully stack up against the good, old Collateral. And, of course, that meant a long Search.

Therefore, every May 1st, something Red and about the size of a Caboose backed up to the Jumps'. Several husky Boys began throwing Things out of the Windows.

Father did a Vanishing Act. When it came to lifting one corner of a Piano or hanging Pictures he was a sad Bluff and he knew it.

"How about Paradise?" he asked one day. "I understand that inside of the Pearly Gates, each Family has Permanent Quarters. There are no Folding Beds to juggle down Back Stairways, no Picture Cords to Shorten, no Curtain Poles to saw off, no Book Cases to get jammed in Stairways. I am sure there will be no Piano Movers, for I have heard their Language. Do you think you can be happy in the Promised Land?"

"It will depend entirely on whether or not the Rugs fit," she replied.

"Let us hope for the Best," said Mr. Jump.

MORAL: *The Queen of the May is usually a Woman.*

The Truth about Pyecraft

H. G. WELLS

> *H. G. Wells's tale of folly is unfortunately about the folly of being fat. I used to say that I was fat because there was something wrong with my pituitary gland. A lot of people do that sort of thing but it is always because we eat too much.*
>
> *I don't know why I eat too much. I was told the other day it was because I must have some deep, basic unhappiness and that I ought to go to a psychoanalyst to find out what it is. But I'm not going to a psychoanalyst. I am not that much interested in myself. I'll go on a diet instead —sometime next month!*

He sits not a dozen yards away. If I glance over my shoulder I can see him. And if I catch his eye—and usually I catch his eye—it meets me with an expression—

It is mainly an imploring look—and yet with suspicion in it.

Confound his suspicion! If I wanted to tell on him I should have told long ago. I don't tell and I don't tell, and he ought to feel at his ease. As if anything so gross and fat as he could feel at ease! Who would believe me if I did tell?

Poor old Pyecraft! Great, uneasy jelly of substance! The fattest clubman in London.

He sits at one of the little club tables in the huge bay by the fire, stuffing. What is he stuffing? I glance judiciously and catch him biting at the round of hot buttered teacake, with his eyes on me. Confound him!—with his eyes on me!

That settles it, Pyecraft! Since you *will* be abject, since you *will* behave as though I was not a man of honour, here, right under your embedded eyes, I write the thing down—the plain truth about Pyecraft. The man I helped, the man I shielded, and who has requited me by making my club unendurable, absolutely unendurable, with his liquid appeal, with the perpetual "don't tell" of his looks.

And, besides, why does he keep on eternally eating?

Well, here goes for the truth, the whole truth, and nothing but the truth!

Pyecraft— I made the acquaintance of Pyecraft in this very smoking-room. I was a young, nervous new member, and he saw it. I was sitting all alone, wishing I knew more of the members, and suddenly he came, a great rolling front of chins and abdomina, towards me, and grunted and sat down in a chair close by me, and wheezed for a space, and scraped for a space with a match and lit a cigar, and then addressed me. I forget what he said—something about the matches not lighting properly, and afterwards as he talked he kept stopping the waiters one by one as they went by, and telling them about the matches in that thin, fluty voice he has. But, anyhow, it was in some such way we began our talking.

He talked about various things and came round to games. And thence to my figure and complexion. "You ought to be a good cricketer," he said. I suppose I am slender, slender to what some people would call lean, and I suppose I am rather dark, still— I am not ashamed of having a Hindu great-grandmother, but, for all that, I don't want casual strangers to see through me at a glance to *her*. So that I was set against Pyecraft from the beginning.

But he only talked about me in order to get to himself.

"I expect," he said, "you take no more exercise than I do, and probably you eat no less." (Like all excessively obese people he fancied he ate nothing.) "Yet"—and he smiled an oblique smile—"we differ."

And then he began to talk about his fatness and his fatness; all he did for his fatness and all he was going to do for his fatness; what people had advised him to do for his fatness and what he had heard of people doing for fatness similar to his. "A *priori*," he said, "one would think a question of nutrition could be answered by dietary and a question of assimilation by drugs." It was stifling. It was dumpling talk. It made me feel swelled to hear him.

One stands that sort of thing once in a way at a club, but a time came when I fancied I was standing too much. He took to me altogether too conspicuously. I could never go into the smoking-room but he would come wallowing towards me, and sometimes he came and gormandised round and about me while I had my lunch. He seemed at times almost to be clinging to me. He was a bore, but not so fearful a bore as to be limited to me; and from the first there was something in his manner—almost as though he knew, almost as though he penetrated to the fact that I *might*—that there was a remote, exceptional chance in me that no one else presented.

"I'd give anything to get it down," he would say—"anything," and peer at me over his vast cheeks and pant.

Poor old Pyecraft! He has just gonged, no doubt to order another buttered teacake!

He came to the actual thing one day. "Our Pharmacopœia," he said, "our Western Pharmacopœia, is anything but the last word of medical science. In the East, I've been told—"

He stopped and stared at me. It was like being at an aquarium.

I was quite suddenly angry with him. "Look here," I said, "who told you about my great-grandmother's recipes?"

"Well," he fenced.

"Every time we've met for a week," I said—"and we've met pretty often—you've given me a broad hint or so about that little secret of mine."

"Well," he said, "now the cat's out of the bag, I'll admit, yes, it is so. I had it—"

"From Pattison?"

"Indirectly," he said, which I believe was lying, "yes."

"Pattison," I said, "took that stuff at his own risk."

He pursed his mouth and bowed.

"My great-grandmother's recipes," I said, "are queer things to handle. My father was near making me promise—"

"He didn't?"

"No. But he warned me. He himself used one—once."

"Ah! . . . But do you think—? Suppose—suppose there did happen to be one—"

"The things are curious documents," I said. "Even the smell of 'em. . . . No!"

But after going so far Pyecraft was resolved I should go farther. I was always a little afraid if I tried his patience too much he would fall on me suddenly and smother me. I own I was weak. But I was also annoyed with Pyecraft. I had got to that state of feeling for him that disposed me to say, "Well, *take* the risk!" The little affair of Pattison to which I have alluded was a different matter altogether. What it was doesn't concern us now, but I knew, anyhow, that the particular recipe I used then was safe. The rest I didn't know so much about, and, on the whole, I was inclined to doubt their safety pretty completely.

Yet even if Pyecraft got poisoned—

I must confess the poisoning of Pyecraft struck me as an immense undertaking.

That evening I took that queer, odd-scented sandalwood box out of my safe and turned the rustling skins over. The gentleman who wrote the recipes for my great-grandmother evidently had a weakness for skins of a miscellaneous origin, and his handwriting was cramped to the last degree. Some of the things are quite unreadable to me—though my family, with its Indian Civil Service associations, has kept up a knowledge of Hindustani from generation to generation—and none are absolutely plain sailing. But I found the one that I knew was there soon enough, and sat on the floor by my safe for some time looking at it.

"Look here," said I to Pyecraft next day, and snatched the slip away from his eager grasp.

"So far as I can make it out, this is a recipe for Loss of Weight. ("Ah!" said Pyecraft.) I'm not absolutely sure, but I think it's that. And if you take my advice you'll leave it alone. Because, you know— I blacken my blood in your interest, Pyecraft—my ancestors on that side were, so far as I can gather, a jolly queer lot. See?"

"Let me try it," said Pyecraft.

I leant back in my chair. My imagination made one mighty effort and fell flat within me. "What in Heaven's name, Pyecraft," I asked, "do you think you'll look like when you get thin?"

He was impervious to reason. I made him promise never to say a word to me about his disgusting fatness again what ever happened —never, and then I handed him that little piece of skin.

"It's nasty stuff," I said.

"No matter," he said, and took it.

He goggled at it. "But—but—" he said.

He had just discovered that it wasn't English.

"To the best of my ability," I said, "I will do you a translation."

I did my best. After that we didn't speak for a fortnight. Whenever he approached me I frowned and motioned him away, and he respected our compact, but at the end of the fortnight he was as fat as ever. And then he got a word in.

"I must speak," he said. "It isn't fair. There's something wrong. It's done me no good. You're not doing your great-grandmother justice."

"Where's the recipe?"

He produced it gingerly from his pocket-book.

I ran my eye over the items. "Was the egg addled?" I asked.

"No. Ought it to have been?"

"That," I said, "goes without saying in all my poor dear great-grandmother's recipes. When condition or quality is not specified you must get the worst. She was drastic or nothing. . . . And there's one or two possible alternatives to some of these other things. You got *fresh* rattlesnake venom?"

"I got rattlesnake from Jamrach's. It cost—it cost—"

"That's your affair, anyhow. This last item—"

"I know a man who—"

"Yes. H'm. Well, I'll write the alternatives down. So far as I know the language, the spelling of this recipe is particularly atrocious. By-the-bye, dog here probably means pariah dog."

For a month after that I saw Pyecraft constantly at the club and as fat and anxious as ever. He kept our treaty, but at times he broke the spirit of it by shaking his head despondently. Then one day in the cloak-room he said, "Your great-grandmother—"

"Not a word against her," I said: and he held his peace.

I could have fancied he had desisted, and I saw him one day talking to three new members about his fatness as though he was in search of other recipes. And then, quite unexpectedly his telegram came.

"Mr. Formalyn!" bawled a page-boy under my nose and I took the telegram and opened it at once.

"For Heaven's sake come.—Pyecraft."

"H'm," said I, and to tell the truth I was so pleased at the rehabilitation of my great-grandmother's reputation this evidently promised that I made a most excellent lunch.

I got Pyecraft's address from the hall porter. Pyecraft inhabited the upper half of a house in Bloomsbury, and I went there as soon as I had done my coffee and Trappistine. I did not wait to finish my cigar.

"Mr. Pyecraft?" said I, at the front door.

They believed he was ill; he hadn't been out for two days.

"He expects me," said I, and they sent me up.

I rang the bell at the lattice-door upon the landing.

"He shouldn't have tried it, anyhow," I said to myself. "A man who eats like a pig ought to look like a pig."

An obviously worthy woman, with an anxious face and a carelessly placed cap, came and surveyed me through the lattice.

I gave my name and she opened his door for me in a dubious fashion.

"Well?" said I, as we stood together inside Pyecraft's piece of the landing.

" 'E said you was to come in if you came," she said, and regarded me, making no motion to show me anywhere. And then, confidentially, " 'E's locked in, sir."

"Locked in?"

"Locked himself in yesterday morning and 'asn't let anyone in since, sir. And ever and again *swearing*. Oh, my!"

I stared at the door she indicated by her glances. "In there?" I said.

"Yes, sir."

"What's up?"

She shook her head sadly. " 'E keeps on calling for vittles, sir. 'E*avy* vittles 'e wants. I get 'im what I can. Pork 'e's 'ad, sooit puddin', sossiges, noo bread. Everythink like that. Left outside, if you please, and me go away. 'E's eatin' sir, somethink *awful*."

There came a piping bawl from inside the door: "That Formalyn?"
"That you, Pyecraft?" I shouted, and went and banged the door.
"Tell her to go away."

I did.

Then I could hear a curious pattering upon the door, almost like someone feeling for the handle in the dark, and Pyecraft's familiar grunts.

"It's all right," I said, "she's gone."

But for a long time the door didn't open.

I heard the key turn. Then Pyecraft's voice said, "Come in."

I turned the handle and opened the door. Naturally I expected to see Pyecraft.

Well, you know, he wasn't there!

I never had such a shock in my life. There was his sitting-room in a state of untidy disorder, plates and dishes among the books and writing things, and several chairs overturned, but Pyecraft—

"It's all right, o' man; shut the door," he said, and then I discovered him.

There he was right up close to the cornice in the corner by the door, as though someone had glued him to the ceiling. His face was anxious and angry. He panted and gesticulated. "Shut the door," he said. "If that woman gets hold of it—"

I shut the door, and went and stood away from him and stared.

"If anything gives way and you tumble down," I said, "you'll break your neck, Pyecraft."

"I wish I could," he wheezed.

"A man of your age and weight getting up to kiddish gymnastics—"

"Don't," he said, and looked agonized. "Your damned great-grandmother—"

"Be careful," I warned him.

"I'll tell you," he said, and gesticulated.

"How the deuce," said I, "are you holding on up there?"

And then abruptly I realized that he was not holding on at all, that he was floating up there—just as a gas-filled bladder might have floated in the same position. He began a struggle to thrust himself away from the ceiling and to clamber down the wall to me. "It's that prescription," he panted, as he did so. "Your great-gran—"

"No!" I cried.

He took hold of a framed engraving rather carelessly as he spoke and it gave way, and he flew back to the ceiling again, while the picture smashed on to the sofa. Bump he went against the ceiling, and I knew then why he was all over white on the more salient curves and angles of his person. He tried again more carefully, coming down by way of the mantel.

It was really a most extraordinary spectacle, that great, fat, apoplectic-looking man upside down and trying to get from the ceiling to the floor. "That prescription," he said. "Too successful."

"How?"

"Loss of weight—almost complete."

And then, of course, I understood.

"By Jove, Pyecraft," said I, "what you wanted was a cure for fatness! But you always called it weight. You would call it weight."

Somehow I was extremely delighted. I quite liked Pyecraft for the time. "Let me help you!" I said, and took his hand and pulled him down. He kicked about, trying to get foothold somewhere. It was very like holding a flag on a windy day.

"That table," he said, pointing, "is solid mahogany and very heavy. If you can put me under that—"

I did, and there he wallowed about like a captive balloon, while I stood on his hearthrug and talked to him.

I lit a cigar. "Tell me," I said, "what happened?"

"I took it," he said.

"How did it taste?"

"Oh, *beastly!*"

I should fancy they all did. Whether one regards the ingredients or the probable compound or the possible results, almost all my great-grandmother's remedies appear to me at least to be extraordinarily uninviting. For my own part—

"I took a little sip first."

"Yes?"

"And as I felt lighter and better after an hour, I decided to take the draught."

"My dear Pyecraft!"

"I held my nose," he explained. "And then I kept on getting lighter and lighter—and helpless, you know."

He gave way suddenly to a burst of passion. "What the goodness am I to *do?*" he said.

"There's one thing pretty evident," I said, "that you mustn't do. If you go out of doors you'll go up and up." I waved an arm upward. "They'd have to send Santos-Dumont after you to bring you down again."

"I suppose it will wear off?"

I shook my head. "I don't think you can count on that," I said.

And then there was another burst of passion, and he kicked out at adjacent chairs and banged the floor. He behaved just as I should have expected a great, fat, self-indulgent man to behave under trying circumstances—that is to say, very badly. He spoke of me and of my great-grandmother with an utter want of discretion.

"I never asked you to take the stuff," I said.

And generously disregarding the insults he was putting upon me, I sat down in his armchair and began to talk to him in a sober, friendly fashion.

I pointed out to him that this was a trouble he had brought upon himself, and that it had almost an air of poetical justice. He had eaten too much. This he disputed, and for a time we argued the point.

He became noisy and violent, so I desisted from this aspect of his lesson. "And then," said I, "you committed the sin of euphuism. You called it, not Fat, which is just and inglorious, but Weight. You—"

He interrupted to say that he recognised all that. What was he to *do?*

I suggested he should adapt himself to his new conditions. So we came to the really sensible part of the business. I suggested that it would not be difficult for him to learn to walk about on the ceiling with his hands—

"I can't sleep," he said.

But that was no great difficulty. It was quite possible, I pointed out, to make a shake-up under a wire mattress, fasten the under things on with tapes, and have a blanket, sheet, and coverlid to button at the side. He would have to confide in his housekeeper, I said; and after some squabbling he agreed to that. (Afterwards it was quite delightful to see the beautifully matter-of-fact way with which the good lady took all these amazing inversions.) He could have a library ladder in his room, and all his meals could be laid on the top of his bookcase. We also hit on an ingenious device by which he could get to the floor whenever he wanted, which was simply to put the *British Encyclopædia* (tenth edition) on the top of his open shelves. He just pulled out a couple of volumes and held on, and down he came. And we agreed there must be iron staples along the skirting, so that he could cling to those whenever he wanted to get about the room on the lower level.

As we got on with the thing I found myself almost keenly interested. It was I who called in the housekeeper and broke matters to her, and it was I chiefly who fixed up the inverted bed. In fact, I spent two whole days at his flat. I am a handy, interfering sort of man with a screwdriver, and I made all sorts of ingenious adaptations for him—ran a wire to bring his bells within reach, turned all his electric lights up instead of down, and so on. The whole affair was extremely curious and interesting to me, and it was delightful to think of Pyecraft like some great, fat blow-fly, crawling about on his ceiling and clambering round the lintel of his doors from one room to another, and never, never, never coming to the club any more. . . .

Then, you know, my fatal ingenuity got the better of me. I was sitting by his fire drinking his whisky, and he was up in his favourite corner by the cornice, tacking a Turkey carpet to the ceiling, when the idea struck me. "By Jove, Pyecraft!" I said, "all this is totally unnecessary."

And before I could calculate the complete consequences of my notion I blurted it out. "Lead underclothing," said I, and the mischief was done.

Pyecraft received the thing almost in tears. "To be right ways up again—" he said.

I gave him the whole secret before I saw where it would take me. "Buy sheet lead," I said, "stamp it into discs. Sew 'em all over your underclothes until you have enough. Have lead-soled boots, carry a bag of solid lead, and the thing is done! Instead of being a prisoner here you may go abroad again, Pyecraft! you may travel—"

A still happier idea came to me. "You need never fear a shipwreck. All you need do is just slip off some or all of your clothes, take the necessary amount of luggage in your hand, and float up in the air—"

In his emotion he dropped the tack-hammer within an ace of my head. "By Jove!" he said, "I shall be able to come back to the club again."

The thing pulled me up short. "By Jove!" I said, faintly. "Yes. Of course—you will."

He did. He does. There he sits behind me now stuffing—as I live! —a third go of buttered teacake. And no one in the whole world knows—except his housekeeper and me—that he weighs practically nothing; that he is a mere boring mass of assimilatory matters, mere clouds in clothing, *niente, nefas*, and most inconsiderable of men. There he sits watching until I have done this writing. Then, if he can, he will waylay me. He will come billowing up to me....

He will tell me over again all about it, how it feels, how it doesn't feel, how he sometimes hopes it is passing off a little. And always somewhere in that fat, abundant discourse he will say, "The secret's keeping, eh? If anyone knew of it—I should be so ashamed.... Makes a fellow look such a fool, you know. Crawling about on a ceiling and all that...."

And now to elude Pyecraft, occupying, as he does, an admirable strategic position between me and the door.

The Happy Family

HANS CHRISTIAN ANDERSEN

This is a story of some snails who thought it was the height of chic to be cooked and served on a silver platter at the big house—just as some people think it is the height of something or other to be cooked in a room with a chandelier and served up in evening clothes and attend the social "party of the year."

The largest green leaf here in the country is certainly the burdock leaf: if you put it round your little waist it is like an apron; and if you lay it upon your head when it rains, it is almost as good as an umbrella, for it is extremely large. One burdock never grows alone; where one grows there are several more, making quite a splendid sight. And all this splendour is food for snails. Of these large white snails, which lived on burdock leaves, the grand people in olden times used to have fricassee made, and when they had eaten it they would say, "Dear me!—how nice it is"; for they really belived it tasted excellent. And that is why burdocks were sown.

Now there was an old country-seat, where snails were no longer eaten. They had died out, but the burdocks had not died out. They grew and grew in all the paths, on all the beds; there was no stopping them any more—it was quite a forest of burdocks. Here and there stood an apple or plum tree; otherwise one would never have thought that it was a garden. Everything was burdock, and among it all lived the two last ancient snails.

They did not know themselves how old they were, but they could very well remember that there had been a great many more of them, that they came from a foreign family, and that the forest had been planted for them and theirs. They had never been out of it, but it was known to them that there was something in the world besides, which was called "the Castle"; there one was boiled, became black, and was laid upon a silver dish—but what happened after that they did not know. They could not imagine what it was like to be boiled and laid upon a silver dish, but it was said to be very fine and particularly grand. Neither the cockchafer, nor the toad, nor the earth-

worm, all of whom they questioned, could give them any information about it; for none of their kind had ever been boiled or laid upon
a silver dish.

The old white snails were the grandest in the world: that they
knew. The forest was there on their account, and the castle too, so
that they might be boiled and laid upon a silver dish.

They lived very retired and happy, and as they themselves were
childless, they had adopted a common little snail, which they
brought up as their own child. But the little one would not grow,
for it was only a common snail; the old people, however, particularly
the mother-snail, declared that it was easy to see how it grew. And
she said that if the father could not see that, he was only just to feel
the little shell, and on doing so, he found that the mother was right.

One day it rained very hard.

"Listen how it drums upon the burdock-leaves—rum-a-dum-dum,
rum-a-dum-dum!" said the father-snail.

"Those are what I call drops!" said the mother-snail. "It is running
down the stalk. You see it will get wet here. I'm only glad that we
have our good houses, and that the little one has his too. More has
really been done for us than for other creatures; it is very plainly to be
seen that we are the lords of the world. We have houses from our
birth, and the burdock forest was planted for our sakes. I should
like to know how far it extends, and what lies outside it."

"There is nothing," said the father-snail, "that could be better than
it is with us: I have nothing to wish for."

"Yes," said the mother. "I should like to be taken up to the Castle,
boiled and laid upon a silver dish; that is what happened to all our
ancestors, and you may believe that it is something uncommon."

"The Castle has perhaps fallen in," said the father-snail; "or the
burdock forest has grown over it, so that the people cannot come
out. But there's not the slightest hurry about it. You're always in too
great a hurry, and the little one is beginning to be just the same. Has
he not been crawling up that stalk for already three days? It really
gives me a headache to look up at him."

"You must not scold him," said the mother-snail. "He crawls
along very deliberately: we shall certainly live to have great joy of
him, and we old ones have really nothing else to live for. But have
you ever thought of where we shall get a wife for him? Don't you
think that there are some of our kind still living farther in the
burdock forest?"

"I daresay there are some black snails there," said the old man;
"black snails without houses; but they are too vulgar, and yet they
fancy themselves somebody. But we can give the ants the commis-

sion; they run to and fro, as though they had some business to do; they will certainly know of a wife for our little one."

"I certainly know the most beautiful one you could have," said one of the ants; "but I am afraid the proposal is of no use; for she is a queen."

"That doesn't matter!" said the old people. "Has she a house?"

"She has a castle," answered the ant; "a most beautiful anthill with seven hundred passages."

"Many thanks!" said the mother-snail. "Our son shall not go into an ant-hill. If you know of nothing better than that, we will give the white gnats the commission; they fly far around in rain and sunshine; they know the burdock forest in and out."

"We have a wife for him," said the gnats. "A hundred man's paces from here there is a little snail with a house sitting on a gooseberry-bush; she is all alone, and old enough to marry. It is only a hundred man's paces from here."

"Well, let her come to him," said the old people. "He has a burdock forest; she has only a bush."

And so they fetched the little maiden snail. She took eight days in coming; but that was the beauty of it, for by that one could see that she was of the right kind.

Then they had the wedding. Six glow-worms gave as much light as they could; for the rest, things went very quietly, for the old people could not bear much feasting and dissipation. A beautiful speech was, however, made by the mother-snail. The father could not speak; he was too deeply moved. Then they gave the young couple the whole burdock forest as an inheritance, and said what they had always said: that it was the best in the world, and that if they lived honest and upright lives, and multiplied, they and their children would one day be taken to the Castle, boiled black, and laid upon a silver dish. And after this speech had been made, the old people crept back into their houses and never came out again; they slept. The young couple now ruled in the forest and had a numerous progeny. But as they were never boiled and laid upon the silver dish, they concluded that the Castle must have fallen in, and that all the people in the world had died out. And as nobody contradicted them, they knew they were right. The rain fell upon the burdock leaves to play the drum for them, and the sun shone to colour the burdock forest for their sake. They were very happy, and the whole family was happy— infinitely happy!

Tall Stories

Tall stories are mostly sympathetic stories told of the exaggerated prowess of an admired human being or an insect or a bull or something or other. Tall stories were invented about Paul Bunyan, the logging giant, about Pantagruel by Rabelais, and so on. Tall stories are told today about the exaggerated strength of a champ. I've heard lonely men in their cups tell tall stories of the kindnesses of their mothers.

In other words, a tall story is a story that you accept as untrue, but you accept it because its exaggerations make it amusing to hear and amusing to repeat.

The Ruined Man Who Became
Rich Again Through a Dream

THE ARABIAN NIGHTS

*This first is a tall story, but of another kind. I don't believe
a word of it but it still makes me laugh. I find myself repeating it again and again to my friends. It is about a thousand years old, but don't let that put you off.*

There lived once in Baghdad a wealthy man and made of money,
who lost all his substance and became so destitute that he could earn
his living only by hard labour. One night, he lay down to sleep, de-
jected and heavy hearted, and saw in a dream a Speaker who said to
him, "Verily thy fortune is in Cairo; go thither and seek it." So he set
out for Cairo; but when he arrived there, evening overtook him and
he lay down to sleep in a mosque. Presently, by decree of Allah Almighty, a band of bandits entered the mosque and made their way
thence into an adjoining house; but the owners, being aroused by
the noise of the thieves, awoke and cried out; whereupon the Chief
of Police came to their aid with his officers. The robbers made off;
but the Wali entered the mosque and, finding the man from Baghdad
asleep there, laid hold of him and beat him with palm-rods so
grievous a beating that he was well-nigh dead. Then they cast him
into jail, where he abode three days; after which the Chief of Police
sent for him and asked him, "Whence art thou?"; and he answered,
"From Baghdad." Quoth the Wali, "And what brought thee to
Cairo?"; and quoth the Baghdadi, "I saw in a dream One who said
to me, Thy fortune is in Cairo; go thither to it. But when I came to
Cairo the fortune which he promised me proved to be the palm-rods
thou so generously gavest to me." The Wali laughed till he showed
his wisdom-teeth and said, "O man of little wit, thrice have I seen
in a dream one who said to me:—There is in Baghdad a house in
such a district and of such a fashion and its courtyard is laid out
gardenwise, at the lower end whereof is a jetting-fountain and under
the same a great sum of money lieth buried. Go thither and take it.
Yet I went not; but thou, of the briefness of thy wit, hast journeyed

from place to place, on the faith of a dream, which was but an idle galimatias of sleep." Then he gave him money saying, "Help thee back herewith to thine own country;" and he took the money and set out upon his homewards march. Now the house the Wali had described was the man's own house in Baghdad; so the wayfarer returned thither and, digging underneath the fountain in his garden, discovered a great treasure. And thus Allah gave him abundant fortune; and a marvellous coincidence occurred.

The Celebrated Sassage Factory

CHARLES DICKENS

The Pickwick Papers *is one of my favorite books.* "The Celebrated Sassage Factory" *is a story invented by Sam Weller, who was himself invented by Charles Dickens.*

Sam Weller, Mr. Pickwick's servant, is trying to cheer him up after Mr. Pickwick has visited his lawyers. (We all need cheering up after we have visited our lawyers.)

It will put you off sausages for the moment, but you'll get over that.

I have changed some of Dickens's spelling because the phonetic spelling of the Cockney of his day makes Sam Weller's story almost unreadable to me.

They had walked some distance, Mr. Pickwick trotting on before, plunged in profound meditation, and Sam following behind, with a countenance expressive of the most enviable and easy defiance of everything and everybody, when the latter, who was always especially anxious to impart to his master any exclusive information he possessed, quickened his pace until he was close at Mr. Pickwick's heels; and, pointing up at a house they were passing, said,

"Very nice pork-shop that there, Sir."

"Yes, it seems so," said Mr. Pickwick.

"Celebrated Sassage factory," said Sam.

"Is it?" said Mr. Pickwick.

"Is it!" reiterated Sam with some indignation: "I should rather think it was. Why sir, bless your innocent eyebrows, that's where the mysterious disappearance of a respectable tradesman took place, four years ago."

"You don't mean to say he was burked,* Sam?" said Mr. Pickwick, looking hastily round.

"No I don't indeed, Sir," replied Mr. Weller, "I wish I did; far worse than that. He was the master of that there shop, Sir, and the

---

* Murdered by strangling or suffocation with no marks of violence so that the corpse could be sold to hospitals as a specimen, after the method of William Burke, the Edinburgh murderer hanged in 1829.

inventor of the patent-never-leavin'-off sassage steam ingine, as would swallow up a paving stone if you put it too near, and grind it into sassages as easy as if it was a tender young babby. Very proud of that machine he was, as it was nat'ral he should be; and he'd stand down in the cellar a-lookin' at it, when it was in full play, till he got quite melancholy with joy. A very happy man he'd have been, Sir, in the procession of that there ingine and two more lovely infants be-sides, if it hadn't been for his wife, who was a most ow-dacious vixen. She was always a followin' him about, and dinnin' in his ears till at last he couldn't stand it no longer.

" 'I'll tell you what it is, my dear,' he says one day: 'If you persevere in this here sort of amusement,' he says, 'I'm blessed if I don't go away to 'Merica; and that's all about it.'

" 'You're an idle villain,' says she, 'and I wish the 'Mericans joy of their bargain.'

"After which she keeps on abusin' him for half an hour, and then runs into the little parlour behind the shop, sets to a screamin', says he'll be the death on her, and falls in a fit, which lasts for three good hours—one of them fits which is all screamin' and kickin'. Well, next mornin', the husband was missin'. He hadn't taken nothin' from the till,—hadn't even put on his great coat, so it was quite clear he warn't gone to 'Merica. Didn't come back next day, didn't come back next week; the Missis had bills printed sayin' that, if he'd come back, he should be forgiven everythin', (which was very liberal, seein' that he hadn't done nothin' at all,) all the canals was dragged, and for two months afterwards whenever a body turned up, it was carried, as a reg'lar thing, straight off to the sassage shop. Howsoever none of 'em answered, so they gave out that he'd run away, and she kept on the bis'ness. One Saturday night, a little thin old gen'lman comes into the shop in a great passion and says,

" 'Are you the missis of this here shop?'

" 'Yes I am,' says she.

" 'Well Ma'am,' says he, 'then I've just looked in to say, that me and my family ain't a goin' to be choked for nothin'; and more than that Ma'am,' he says, 'you'll allow me to observe, that as you don't use the primest parts of the meat in the manufacture of sassages, I think you'd find beef come nearly as cheap as buttons.'

" 'Buttons, Sir!' says she.

" 'Buttons, Ma'am,' says the little old gentleman, unfolding a bit of paper, and showin' twenty or thirty halves of buttons. 'Nice seasonin' for sassages, is trousers' buttons, Ma'am.'

" 'They're my husband's buttons,' says the widder, beginning to faint.

" 'What!' screams the little old gen'lman, turnin' very pale.

" 'I see it all,' says the widder; 'in a fit of temporary insanity he rashly converted his-self into sassages!'

"And so he had, Sir," said Mr. Weller, looking steadily into Mr. Pickwick's horror-stricken countenance, "or else he'd been draw'd into the ingine, but however that might have been the little old gen'lman, who had been remarkably partial to sassages all his life, rushed out of the shop in a wild state, and was never heard of afterwards!"

Big Trees

WALTER FRY AND J. R. WHITE

Here is a tall story indeed, but it is a true story. I have seen it with my own eyes many times, and I look forward to seeing it again very soon.

I came across this little book years ago when I first visited Yosemite National Park, at a time when I was losing my soul to the West of the United States of America.

The book was written by a man who was the first United States Commissioner of Sequoia National Park, and by a former Sequoia superintendent. They had a great deal to do with the preservation of this wonder of nature for us in perpetuity.

I have never felt such a feeling of awe and wonder before any work of nature as before the great trees. I used to stay in the Big Tree Lodge, which is in the Mariposa Grove at Yosemite, and clear out on a picnic during the daytime because there were a lot of people around. But in the evening and the early morning there was no one, and the dwarfed little lodge was in the middle of those gigantic pillars, and the animals are tame, for it is not allowed to kill animals in Yosemite. And to see the deer, standing unafraid among the great trees, is something that moves me, as Wordsworth once said, "too deep for tears."

First I would like to quote from various places in the book:

Size and Age

Let us consider a tree. And while we are about it let us consider a big tree. Better still, let us consider the largest tree on earth—General Sherman in the Sequoia National Park in California and in the very heart of the Giant Forest.

The total volume of wood in the trunk of the General Sherman as well as of the General Grant and other trees was calculated by several engineers employed in 1931 by the Fresno County Chamber of Commerce. The figures obtained were:

General Sherman, volume of trunk   600,120 board feet
General Grant, volume of trunk   542,784 board feet

So the old General Sherman is shown to be 57,336 board feet bigger than his nearest competitor, General Grant. To reduce these figures within the layman's comprehension: the average five-room bungalow contains about 17,000 board feet of lumber. General Sherman is therefore approximately 3½ bungalows bigger than his nearest competitor, General Grant.

If you cannot visit the Big Trees, try an experiment at home. Pace out thirty-seven feet on the lawn in front of your house or actually make a circle of that diameter, and reflect that there is a tree that large. In 1921, we built of lumber and bark a half-section of the trunk of the General Sherman and installed it at the fair in Visalia. I had told the workmen to be sure not to exaggerate the measurements. But when I inspected the work on the ground, alongside the city auditorium, I could not believe that it was a replica, for it dwarfed the surrounding buildings and other objects. In the forest all is so harmonious, Nature has balanced all so carefully, and one is led so gradually toward the largest tree in the world that it is difficult to appreciate its bulk. If you could see the General Sherman out on a plain, or could place it in an average city street, where it would completely block traffic, then you would realize that it is truly large.

It is difficult to say whether the age or the size of the Big Trees has excited greater wonderment.

The oldest tree that I have found was cut in the Millwood Grove, near General Grant National Park, and was 3,126 years by careful ring count. This tree was 26½ feet in diameter six feet above the ground.

John Muir states that he found a tree in the Converse Basin Grove 4,000 years old.

Statements of the age of such trees as the Grizzly Giant, the General Sherman, the General Grant, and the Boole must be conjectures. These trees are probably all over 3,500 years of age.

The age limit of the Big Tree is unknown, because we have no record of one dying of old age.

The Death of a Giant

Now all this I have seen.
The following I have not seen; I have only seen its results.
This chapter in the book called Big Trees I read again and
again. I find it more exciting and cleansing than most any-
thing I can name.

A forest fire of any intensity is death to all trees except the Big Tree.
He lives through fire after fire. The debris-littered forest may flame
around him for hours or for days; scores or hundreds of fires may
flicker and roar through the centuries over his thick asbestos bark, but
almost in vain; nine-tenths or more of that bark may finally be
charred away; two hundred feet of his vitals may be eaten out so
that he stands a mere shell—a chimney or a window tree—and yet
he lives on! Not until the last strip of bark is burned away, or repeated fires have cooked the wood and entirely stopped the running
sap, not until the massive column has become a lacy black shroud
full of holes, not until then does the Big Tree die. And even in
death he stands for epochs or for eons, a black monument presiding
over his descendants in the groves and forest aisles.

Nevertheless, forest fires are the deadliest, almost the only enemy
of the Big Trees—excepting man. Rarely does a single fire kill a Big
Tree or even destroy a portion of it. Many fires are needed to accomplish the deed, so that a thousand or more years may be consumed
in destroying even a part of one Big Tree. Scores of attacks by fire
over a thousand years to injure or to kill one tree!

A tree which for thousands of years towers above the forest canopy
must eventually be struck by lightning. Scarcely any mature Big
Tree has escaped a Jovial bolt.

Although lightning is responsible for setting most of the fires in
the Big Tree groves, nevertheless few sequoias are killed directly by
the lightning. No ordinary bolt even seriously injures a Big Tree. In
all my mountain experience I have known it to kill outright only two.

Lightning, though rare in the California lowlands, occurs occasionally in the High Sierra during the summer months. Thunderstorms are more frequent over the higher portions of the range and
more rare over and among the Big Tree groves. Although these
storms seldom last more than an hour, they are usually intense in
their proportions of rain and electricity.

The Big Tree groves are all situated on the western slopes of the Sierra Nevada, chiefly between 5,000 and 7,000 feet elevation, with a drop off almost to sea-level in the valley a few miles to the westward and an ascent to 13,000 or 14,000 feet a few miles to the eastward. Owing to these conditions, thunderstorms vary in formation. The thunderheads usually gather above the groves, but sometimes below, and occasionally right in the groves. The clouds range in depth from one hundred feet to five hundred feet, and they shroud the area of the storm with fog, mist, and rain.

Because of these storm conditions, there are three different kinds of lightning strokes in the Big Tree groves:

First there is the vertical stroke, which is the most common. The explosion takes place in the clouds high above, and sends one tongue of lightning straight downward through the tree. This kind of a stroke seldom seriously injures the tree, for if the tree is a perfect one, only a few boughs in the path of the lightning are slivered; and these soon fall off and are replaced by new growth.

Second is the horizontal or side stroke, which is very rare. This occurs when the clouds drift heavily for from one to three hundred feet along the mountainside and parallel, or nearly so, to the trees. When the explosion takes place, a single tongue of lightning shoots out horizontally and hits the tree on one side. A stroke of this character always cuts the tree off at the point of first contact by knocking out ten or twenty feet of its brittle trunk on the other side from the stroke, thus leaving the top to tumble to the ground. It also sometimes splits a sequoia open in two halves, and the portion of the tree above the split may fall in and be wedged.

One of these stands in Putnam Canyon, Sequoia National Park, and Ranger C. W. Blossom and I saw the lightning hit that tree. It is a unique experience to see such a battle of the gods as a thunderbolt striking a Big Tree. One sunny day in late October 1905 we were headed on horseback down the South Fork Kaweah River canyon from Hockett Meadow to Three Rivers, a distance of twenty-five miles, and a drop downward of almost eight thousand feet. When we were near the 6,500-foot level in the Garfield Grove, to our surprise and amazement we were suddenly confronted with a vast blue-black V-shaped cloud, pointing up the canyon. We were just on a level with the top of the cloud and could see both above and beneath it. The cloud appeared to be about three hundred feet in thickness, and in thousands of places the lower current of air was continually breaking upward through the black blanket, giving the appearance of so many miniature volcanoes erupting in succession. Each of these apparent eruptions lasted only a few moments and scattered in all directions small fragments of cloud, which soon settled back to the main body. As yet no rain had begun to fall.

While we were silently watching this wonderful phenomenon and awaiting the approach of the V point of the cloud, which was moving slowly eastward up the center of the canyon toward us but not touching the canyon walls by some two hundred feet on either side, a tremendous explosion took place on the south side of the pointed cloud about two or three hundred yards from us. Three tongues of lightning darted out. One went up, one down, and one horizontally. This horizontal tongue hit a sequoia about sixteen feet in base diameter and three hundred feet high. The lightning struck over halfway up, cut the tree right in half by knocking out about twenty feet of its trunk and splitting the remainder in two almost to the ground.

Never shall I forget that sight. For when the lightning hit the tree we could see clear daylight through the opening of the cut, and broken chunks of tree scattering everywhere; and while the two split portions of the tree gaped wide apart, the cut-off top of the tree was for a moment poised erect in the air above. Only for a moment was this strange spectral tree top suspended in midair. Then it dropped straight downward between the two open slabs, which clamped tightly upon it. There it is held to this day, giving the appearance of a very peculiar tree. Of course, the cut-off portion is dead, but the mutilated trunk lives and is setting out new growth.

The third kind of lightning stroke is what, for lack of a better name, I call the crushing or compressive stroke. This is most uncommon and occurs only when the thunder clouds float through the trees. Of all the freakish pranks ever performed by lightning this is the most difficult for me to understand or even attempt to explain.

In this tremendously powerful stroke, the explosion seems to occur on the trunk of the tree, as if it were a case of spontaneous combustion, except that the pressure comes from without rather than from within the tree. The trunk is crushed into small pieces and falls in one piled-up mass, while the top of the tree topples over in any direction. Chunks of wood are not thrown off in every direction, as is the case with the vertical and horizontal strokes.

I have only seen two sequoia trees that were destroyed in this fashion. Each was from nine to twelve feet in diameter, and each had about fifty feet of its lower trunk crushed. One of the trees stood in the Kings River grove, the other in the Coffee Pot Canyon grove, in the Sequoia National Park.

I witnessed the destruction of the latter tree. It was in August 1895 while I was looking for my cattle in this Big Tree grove, elevation 7,000 feet, that a cloud began to form on top of Castle Crags, Sequoia National Park, five miles to the north and a thousand feet or so higher. The cloud built up rapidly and soon spread over an area of about two miles by four miles; from it came a downpour of rain with peals of thunder and flashes of lightning.

In a few minutes the cloud had crossed the canyon and the upper part hit the mountainside near me, to drift on up through the trees. A torrential rain fell and I took shelter under a rock ledge. Straight out in front of me, about four hundred feet away, stood a sequoia about twelve feet in diameter and nearly three hundred feet high. The tree was partly veiled by the cloud. All of a sudden, about fifty feet of the lower part of the tree seemed one solid cylinder of fire, while instantaneously there occurred a deafening clap of thunder and the crash of the falling tree. There were no tongues of lightning— just one pillar of fire, and then the crash.

Such wreckage of a tree I have never seen before or since. About fifty feet of the lower trunk of the twelve-foot tree was crushed to kindling and heaped in one circular, sloping pile about fifty feet across and twenty feet in depth in the center. The upper part of the tree was sprawled down the canyon. I examined the wreck carefully, but could find no evidence that lightning had struck the tree in a particular spot, nor were fragments thrown from the tree as is the case in the more common types of lightning attack. This tree looked as though it had been passed through a gigantic rock crusher and the product symmetrically piled.

I have never yet found any sequoia tree that had been killed by insect attack, fungus, or disease.

It may be said that the noble sequoia yields its life only when overpowered by the still more noble force of lightning. When passing a Big Tree, therefore, of whatever age, it would be almost fitting for one to give the biblical salute: "O King, live forever!"

Life with a Capital "L"

When I was a child all the grownups around me had a joke; that is to say, all the women grownups. If we passed a pair of lovers spooning on a park bench my mother would look significantly at my Auntie Winnie, and Auntie Winnie would say, "Life with a capital L," and they would both laugh secretly and I would feel uncomfortable.

If we passed a gaudy lady on the street my Auntie Winnie would look significantly at my mother, and my mother would say, "Life with a capital L," and they would both laugh and I would look at the lady and my mother would say, "Don't look, Charlie. She's a theatrical!"

I remember this incident because the gaudy lady was dressed in white, with a white parasol lined in green and pink roses on her hat, and my mother nearly yanked my arm out of its socket and I became an actor.

I suppose by now you've got the idea.

Dusky Ruth

A. E. COPPARD

"Dusky Ruth" is about the Cotswolds. I think the two
loveliest parts of England are the Cotswolds, which are
near Stratford on Avon, and the Yorkshire moors. I put
this story in because in the moorland village where we had
a farmhouse all the houses are of stone with red-tiled roofs.

There was an inn and there was Elsie the barmaid, who
was the landlord's daughter. (Elsie is not to be confused
with Elsa. I dreamed about Elsie at the age of fourteen; I
married Elsa when I was twenty-nine.) Elsie had sandy hair
and blue eyes and a fine slappable shape. My father had
some grouse shooting up there, and Elsie serving the foam-
ing tankards of beer was quite a sight.

When I read this story I thought of Elsie, so here it is.

At the close of an April day, chilly and wet, the traveller came to
a country town. In the Cotswolds, though the towns are small and
sweet and the inns snug, the general habit of the land is bleak and
bare. He had newly come upon upland roads so void of human affairs,
so lonely, that they might have been made for some forgotten uses
by departed men, and left to the unwitting passage of such strangers
as himself. Even the unending walls, built of old rough laminated
rock, that detailed the far-spreading fields, had grown very old
again in their courses; there were dabs of darkness, buttons of moss,
and fossils on every stone. He had passed a few neighbourhoods,
sometimes at the crook of a stream, or at the cross of debouching
roads, where old habitations, their gangrenated thatch riddled with
bird holes, had been not so much erected as just spattered about the
places. Beyond these signs an odd lark or blackbird, the ruckle of
partridges, or the nifty gallop of a hare had been the only mitigation
of the living loneliness that was almost as profound by day as by
night. But the traveller had a care for such times and places. There
are men who love to gaze with the mind at things that can never
be seen, feel at least the throb of a beauty that will never be known,
and hear over immense bleak reaches the echo of that which is no

celestial music, but only their own hearts' vain cries; and though his garments clung to him like clay it was with deliberate questing step that the traveller trod the single street of the town, and at last entered the inn, shuffling his shoes in the doorway for a moment and striking the raindrops from his hat. Then he turned into a small smoking-room. Leather-lined benches, much worn, were fixed to the wall under the window and in other odd corners and nooks behind mahogany tables. One wall was furnished with all the congenial gear of a bar, but without any intervening counter. Opposite, a bright fire was burning, and a neatly dressed young woman sat before it in a Windsor chair, staring at the flames. There was no other inmate of the room, and as he entered, the girl rose up and greeted him. He found that he could be accommodated for the night, and in a few moments his hat and scarf were removed and placed inside the fender, his wet overcoat was taken to the kitchen, the landlord, an old fellow, was lending him a roomy pair of slippers, and a maid was setting supper in an adjoining room.

He sat while this was doing and talked to the barmaid. She had a beautiful but rather mournful face as it was lit by the firelight, and when her glance was turned away from it her eyes had a piercing brightness. Friendly and well spoken as she was, the melancholy in her aspect was noticeable—perhaps it was the dim room, or the wet day, or the long hours ministering a multitude of cocktails to thirsty gallantry.

When he went to his supper he found cheering food and drink, with pleasant garniture of silver and mahogany. There were no other visitors, he was to be alone; blinds were drawn, lamps lit, and the fire at his back was comforting. So he sat long about his meal until a white-faced maid came to clear the table, discoursing to him about country things as she busied about the room. It was a long, narrow room, with a sideboard and the door at one end and the fireplace at the other. A bookshelf, almost devoid of books, contained a number of plates; the long wall that faced the windows was almost destitute of pictures, but there were hung upon it, for some inscrutable but doubtless sufficient reason, many dish-covers, solidly shaped, of the kind held in such mysterious regard and known as "willow pattern"; one was even hung upon the face of a map. Two musty prints were mixed with them, presentments of horses having a stilted extravagant physique and bestridden by images of inhuman and incommunicable dignity, clothed in whiskers, coloured jackets, and tight white breeches.

He took down the books from the shelf, but his interest was speedily exhausted, and the almanacs, the county directory, and various guide-books were exchanged for the *Cotswold Chronicle*. With this, having drawn the deep chair to the hearth, he whiled away the time. The newspaper amused him with its advertisements of stock shows, farm auctions, travelling quacks and conjurers, and there was a lengthy account of the execution of a local felon, one Timothy Bridger, who had murdered an infant in some shameful circumstances. This dazzling crescendo proved rather trying to the traveller; he threw down the paper.

The town was all as quiet as the hills, and he could hear no sounds in the house. He got up and went across the hall to the smoke-room. The door was shut, but there was light within, and he entered. The girl sat there much as he had seen her on his arrival, still alone, with feet on fender. He shut the door behind him, sat down, and crossing his legs puffed at his pipe, admired the snug little room and the pretty figure of the girl, which he could do without embarrassment, as her meditative head, slightly bowed, was turned away from him. He could see something of her, too, in the mirror at the bar, which repeated also the agreeable contours of bottles of coloured wines and rich liqueurs—so entrancing in form and aspect that they seemed destined to charming histories, even in disuse—and those of familiar outline containing mere spirits or small beer, for which are reserved the harsher destinies of base oils, horse medicines, disinfectants, and cold tea. There were coloured glasses for bitter wines, white glasses for sweet, a tiny leaden sink beneath them, and the four black handles of the beer engines.

The girl wore a light blouse of silk, a short skirt of black velvet, and a pair of very thin silk stockings that showed the flesh of instep and shin so plainly that he could see they were reddened by the warmth of the fire. She had on a pair of dainty cloth shoes with high heels, but what was wonderful about her was the heap of rich black hair piled at the back of her head and shadowing the dusky neck. He sat puffing his pipe and letting the loud tick of the clock fill the quiet room. She did not stir and he could move silently. That, he felt now, had been his desire all the evening; and here, in her presence, he was more strangely stirred in a few short minutes than by any event he could remember.

In youth he had viewed women as futile, pitiable things that grew long hair, wore stays and garters, and prayed incomprehensible prayers. Viewing them in the stalls of the theatre from his vantage point in the gallery, he always disliked the articulation of their naked shoulders. But still, there was a god in the sky, a god with flowing hair and exquisite eyes, whose one stride with an ardour grandly rendered took him across the whole round hemisphere to which his buoyant limbs were bound like spokes to the eternal rim and axle, his bright hair burning in the pity of the sunsets and tossing in the anger of the dawns.

Master traveller had indeed come into this room to be with this woman, and she as surely desired him, and for all its accidental occasion it was as if he, walking the ways of the world, had suddenly come upon what, what so imaginable with all permitted reverence as, well, just a shrine; and he, admirably humble, bowed the instant head.

Were there no other people within? The clock indicated a few minutes to nine. He sat on, still as stone, and the woman might have been of wax for all the movement or sound she made. There was allurement in the air between them; he had forborne his smoking, the pipe grew cold between his teeth. He waited for a look from her, a movement to break the trance of silence. No footfall in street or house, no voice in the inn but the clock, beating away as if pronouncing a doom. Suddenly it rasped out nine large notes, a bell in the town repeated them dolefully, and a cuckoo no farther than the kitchen mocked them with three times three. After that came the weak steps of the old landlord along the hall, the slam of doors, the clatter of lock and bolt, and then the silence returning unendurably upon them.

He rose and stood behind her; he touched the black hair. She made no movement or sign. He pulled out two or three combs and, dropping them into her lap, let the whole mass tumble about his hands. It had a curious harsh touch in the unravelling, but was so full and shining; black as a rook's wings it was. He slid his palms through it. His fingers searched it and fought with its fine strangeness; into his mind there travelled a serious thought, stilling his wayward fancy—this was no wayward fancy, but a rite accomplishing itself! (*Run, run, silly man, y'are lost!*) But having got so far, he burnt his boats, leaned over, and drew her face back to him. And at that, seizing his wrists, she gave him back ardour for ardour, pressing his hands to her bosom, while the kiss was sealed and sealed again. Then she sprang up and picking his scarf and hat from the fender said:

"I have been drying them for you, but the hat has shrunk a bit, I'm sure—I tried it on."

He took them from her and put them behind him; he leaned lightly back upon the table, holding it with both his hands behind him; he could not speak.

"Aren't you going to thank me for drying them?" she asked, picking her combs from the rug and repinning her hair.

"I wonder why we did that?" he asked, shamedly.

"It is what I'm thinking too," she said.

"You were so beautiful about—about it, you know."

She made no rejoinder, but continued to bind her hair, looking brightly at him under her brows. When she had finished she went close to him.

"Will that do?"

"I'll take it down again."

"No, no, the old man or the old woman will be coming in."

"What of that?" he said, taking her into his arms. "Tell me your name."

She shook her head, but she returned his kisses and stroked his hair and shoulders with beautifully melting gestures.

"What is your name? I want to call you by your name," he said. "I can't keep calling you Lovely Woman, Lovely Woman."

Again she shook her head and was dumb.

"I'll call you Ruth, then, Dusky Ruth, Ruth of the black, beautiful hair."

"That is a nice-sounding name— I knew a deaf and dumb girl named Ruth; she went to Nottingham and married an organ-grinder —but I should like it for my name."

"Then I give it to you."

"Mine is so ugly."

"What is it?"

Again the shaken head and the burning caress.

"Then you shall be Ruth; will you keep that name?"

"Yes, if you give me the name I will keep it for you."

Time had indeed taken them by the forelock, and they looked upon a ruddled world.

"I stake my one talent," he said jestingly, "and behold it returns me fortyfold; I feel like the boy who catches three mice with one piece of cheese."

At ten o'clock the girl said:

"I must go and see how *they* are getting on," and she went to the door.

"Are we keeping them up?"

She nodded.

"Are you tired?"

"No, I am not tired." She looked at him doubtfully.

"We ought not to stay in here; go into the coffee room and I'll come there in a few minutes."

"Right," he whispered gaily, "we'll sit up all night."

She stood at the door for him to pass out, and he crossed the hall to the other room. It was in darkness except for the flash of the fire. Standing at the hearth he lit a match for the lamp, but paused at the globe; then he extinguished the match.

"No, it's better to sit in the firelight."

He heard voices at the other end of the house that seemed to have a chiding note in them.

"Lord," he thought, "is she getting into a row?"

Then her steps came echoing over the stone floor of the hall; she opened the door and stood there with a lighted candle in her hand; he stood at the other end of the room, smiling.

"Good night," she said.

"Oh, no, no!—come along," he protested, but not moving from the hearth.

"Got to go to bed," she answered.

"Are they angry with you?"

"No."

"Well, then, come over here and sit down."

"Got to go to bed," she said again, but she had meanwhile put her candlestick upon the little sideboard and was trimming the wick with a burnt match.

"Oh, come along, just half an hour," he protested. She did not answer, but went on prodding the wick of the candle.

"Ten minutes, then," he said, still not going towards her.

"Five minutes," he begged.

She shook her head and, picking up the candlestick, turned to the door. He did not move, he just called her name: "Ruth!"

She came back then, put down the candlestick, and tiptoed across the room until he met her. The bliss of the embrace was so poignant that he was almost glad when she stood up again and said with affected steadiness, though he heard the tremor in her voice:

"I must get you your candle."

She brought one from the hall, set it on the table in front of him, and struck the match.

"What is my number?" he asked.

"Number six room," she answered, prodding the wick vaguely with her match, while a slip of white wax dropped over the shoulder of the new candle. "Number six ... next to mine."

The match burnt out; she said abruptly: "Good night," took up her own candle, and left him there.

In a few moments he ascended the stairs and went into his room. He fastened the door, removed his coat, collar, and slippers, but the rack of passion had seized him and he moved about with no inclination to sleep. He sat down, but there was no medium of distraction. He tried to read the newspaper that he had carried up with him, and without realizing a single phrase he forced himself to read again the whole account of the execution of the miscreant Bridger. When he had finished this he carefully folded the paper and stood up, listening. He went to the parting wall and tapped thereon with his fingertips. He waited half a minute, one minute, two minutes; there was no answering sign. He tapped again, more loudly, with his knuckles, but there was no response, and he tapped many times. He opened his door as noiselessly as possible; along the dark passage there were slips of light under the other doors, the one next his own, and the one beyond that. He stood in the corridor listening to the rumble of old voices in the farther room, the old man and his wife going to their rest. Holding his breath fearfully, he stepped to *her* door and tapped gently upon it. There was no answer, but he could somehow divine her awareness of him; he tapped again; she moved to the door and whispered: "No, no, go away." He turned the handle, the door was locked.

"Let me in," he pleaded. He knew she was standing there an inch or two beyond him.

"Hush," she called softly. "Go away, the old woman has ears like a fox."

He stood silent for a moment.

"Unlock it," he urged; but he got no further reply, and feeling foolish and baffled he moved back to his own room, cast his clothes from him, doused the candle and crept into the bed with soul as wild as a storm-swept forest, his heart beating a vagrant summons. The room filled with strange heat, there was no composure for mind or limb, nothing but flaming visions and furious embraces.

"Morality . . . what is it but agreement with your own soul?"

So he lay for two hours—the clocks chimed twelve—listening with foolish persistency for *her* step along the corridor, fancying every light sound—and the night was full of them—was her hand upon the door.

Suddenly then—and it seemed as if his very heart would abash the house with its thunder—he could hear distinctly someone knocking on the wall. He got quickly from his bed and stood at his door, listening. Again the knocking was heard, and having half-clothed himself he crept into the passage, which was now in utter darkness, trailing his hand along the wall until he felt her door; it was standing open. He entered her room and closed the door behind him. There was not the faintest gleam of light, he could see nothing. He whispered: "Ruth!" and she was standing there. She touched him, but not speaking. He put out his hands, and they met round her neck; her hair was flowing in its great wave about her; he put his lips to her face and found that her eyes were streaming with tears, salt and strange and disturbing. In the close darkness he put his arms about her with no thought but to comfort her; one hand had plunged through the long harsh tresses and the other across her hips before he realized that she was ungowned; then he was aware of the softness of her breasts and the cold naked sleekness of her shoulders. But she was crying there, crying silently with great tears, her strange sorrow stifling his desire.

"Ruth, Ruth, my beautiful dear!" he murmured soothingly. He felt for the bed with one hand, and turning back the quilt and sheets, he lifted her in as easily as a mother does her child, replaced the bedding, and, in his clothes, he lay stretched beside her, comforting her. They lay so, innocent as children, for an hour, when she seemed to have gone to sleep. He rose then and went silently to his room, full of weariness.

In the morning he breakfasted without seeing her, but as he had business in the world that gave him just an hour longer at the inn before he left it for good and all, he went into the smokeroom and found her. She greeted him with a curious gaze, but merrily enough, for there were other men there now—farmers, a butcher, a registrar, an old, old man. The hour passed, but not these men, and at length he donned his coat, took up his stick, and said good-bye. Her shining glances followed him to the door, and from the window as far as they could view him.

David and Bathsheba

THE SECOND BOOK OF SAMUEL
Chapter 11, verses 2–27; Chapter 12, verses 1–24

What is to be said about this magnificent tale? I printed it in this form because that is the form I read it from when I read it in public. I hope you will find it easier to read this way than in the two-column-and-verse business in the regular edition of the Bible.

And it came to pass in an eveningtide
That David arose from off his bed, and walked upon the roof of
    the king's house
And from the roof he saw a woman washing herself;
And the woman was very beautiful to look upon.
And David sent and enquired after the woman.
And one said,
"Is not this Bath-sheba,
The wife of Uriah the Hittite?"

And David sent messengers, and took her;
And she came in unto him,
And he lay with her;
And she returned unto her house.
And the woman conceived,
And sent and told David, and said,
"I am with child."

And David sent to Joab, saying,
"Send me Uriah the Hittite."
And Joab sent Uriah to David.
And when Uriah was come unto him,
David demanded of him how Joab did,
And how the people did,
And how the war prospered.
And David said to Uriah,
"Go down to thy house, and wash thy feet."

And Uriah departed out of the king's house,
And there followed him a mess of meat from the king.
But Uriah slept at the door of the king's house with all the servants
     of his lord,
And went not down to his house.

And when they had told David, saying,
"Uriah went not down unto his house,"
David said unto Uriah,
"Camest thou not from thy journey?
Why then didst thou not go down unto thine house?"

And Uriah said unto David,
"The ark, and Israel, and Judah, abide in tents;
And my lord Joab, and the servants of my lord,
Are encamped in the open fields,
Shall I then go into mine house,
To eat and to drink, and to lie with my wife?
As thou livest, and as thy soul liveth,
I will not do this thing."

And David said to Uriah,
"Tarry here to-day also,
And tomorrow I will let thee depart."

So Uriah abode in Jerusalem that day, and the morrow.
And when David had called him, he did eat and drink before him,
And he made him drunk:
And at even he went out to lie on his bed with the servants of his
     lord,
But went not down to his house.

And it came to pass in the morning
That David wrote a letter to Joab, and sent it by the hand of Uriah.
And he wrote in the letter, saying,
"Set ye Uriah in the forefront of the hottest battle,
And retire ye from him,
That he may be smitten, and die."

And it came to pass,
When Joab observed the city,
That he assigned Uriah unto a place where he knew that valiant
     men were.

And the men of the city went out, and fought with Joab:
And there fell some of the people of the servants of David;
And Uriah the Hittite died also.
Then Joab sent and told David all the things concerning the war;
And charged the messenger, saying,
"When thou hast made an end of telling the matters of the war
          unto the king.
And if so be that the king's wrath arise, and he say unto thee,
'Wherefore approached he so nigh unto the city when ye did fight?
Knew ye not that they would shoot from the wall?
Why went ye nigh the wall?' then say thou,
'Thy servant Uriah the Hittite is dead also.' "

So the messenger went,
And came and showed David all that Joab had sent him for.
And the messenger said unto David,
"Surely the men prevailed against us.
We were upon them even unto the entering of the gate.
And the shooters shot from off the wall upon thy servants;
And some of the king's servants be dead,
And thy servant Uriah the Hittite is dead also."

Then David said unto the messenger.
"Thus shalt thou say unto Joab,
'Let not this thing displease thee, for the sword devoureth one as
          well as another;
Make thy battle more strong against the city, and overthrow it':
And encourage thou him."

And when the wife of Uriah heard that Uriah her husband was dead,
She mourned for her husband.
And when the mourning was past,
David sent and fetched her to his house,
And she became his wife, and bore him a son.
But the thing that David had done
Displeased the Lord.
And the Lord sent Nathan unto David.
And he came unto him, and said unto him.

"There were two men in one city;
The one rich, and the other poor.
The rich man had exceeding many flocks and herds;
But the poor man had nothing,

Save one little ewe lamb, which he had bought and nourished up:
And it grew up together with him, and with his children;
It did eat of his own meat,
And drank of his own cup,
And lay in his bosom,
And was unto him as a daughter.

"And there came a traveller unto the rich man,
And he spared to take of his own flock and of his own herd,
To dress for the wayfaring man that was come unto him;
But took the poor man's lamb,
And dressed it for the man that was come to him."
And David's anger was greatly kindled against the man; and he said
    to Nathan,
"As the Lord liveth, the man that hath done this thing shall surely
    die;
And he shall restore the lamb four-fold, because he did this thing,
And because he had no pity."

And Nathan said to David,
"Thou art the man.
Thus saith the Lord God of Israel,
I anointed thee king over Israel,
And I delivered thee out of the hand of Saul;
And I gave thee thy master's house, and thy master's wives unto thy
    bosom,
And if that had been too little, I would moreover have given unto
    thee such and such things.
Wherefore hast thou despised the commandment of the Lord,
To do evil in his sight?
Thou hast killed Uriah the Hittite with the sword, and hast taken
    his wife to be thy wife.
Now therefore the sword shall never depart from thine house;
Because thou hast despised me,
And hast taken the wife of Uriah the Hittite to be thy wife.
Thus saith the Lord,
Behold,
I will raise up evil against thee out of thine own house,
And I will take thy wives before thine eyes, and give them unto thy
    neighbour,
And he shall lie with thy wives in the sight of this sun.
For thou didst it secretly:
But I will do this before all Israel,
And before the sun."

And David said unto Nathan,
"I have sinned against the Lord."

And Nathan said unto David,
"The Lord also hath put away thy sin;
Thou shalt not die.
Howbeit, because by this deed thou hast given great occasion to the
        enemies of the Lord to blaspheme,
The child also that is born unto thee
Shall surely die."

And Nathan departed unto his house.
And the Lord struck the child that Uriah's wife bore unto David,
And it was very sick.
David therefore besought God for the child;
And David fasted, and went in, and lay all night upon the earth.
And the elders of his house arose, and went to him, to raise him up
        from the earth but he would not,
Neither did he eat bread with them.

And it came to pass on the seventh day that the child died.
And the servants of David feared to tell him that the child was
        dead:
For they said,
"Behold, while the child was yet alive, we spoke unto him, and he
        would not hearken unto our voice:
How will he then vex himself, if we tell him that the child is dead?"

But when David saw that his servants whispered,
David perceived that the child was dead:
Therefore David said unto his servants,
"Is the child dead?"
And they said,
"He is dead."

Then David arose from the earth, and washed; and anointed
        himself, and changed his apparel, and came into the house
        of the Lord, and worshipped:
Then he came to his own house; and when he required, they set
        bread before him, and he did eat.
Then said his servants unto him,
"What thing is this that thou hast done?
Thou didst fast and weep for the child, while it was alive;
But when the child was dead, thou didst rise and eat bread."

And he said,
"While the child was yet alive, I fasted and wept: for I said,
'Who can tell whether God will be gracious to me, that the child
        may live?'
But now he is dead, wherefore should I fast?
Can I bring him back again?
I shall go to him, but he shall not return to me."

And David comforted Bath-sheba his wife,
And went in unto her,
And lay with her:
And she bore a son,
And he called his name Solomon:
And the Lord loved him.

Just Like Little Dogs

DYLAN THOMAS

*Dylan Thomas lived in a seaside town in Wales. I lived in
a seaside town in Yorkshire. We were in the hotel business,
and in England every time you want to have a dance in
your hotel you have to apply for an extension of the liquor
license until midnight or what have you, and it was always
my job to make the application.*

*I hated doing it because I always felt like a criminal. I
remember the chief of police had a particularly straight back.
I have never liked straight backs since.*

*Dylan Thomas has captured exactly my own youthful
feelings. Whether or not anything of the sort happened to
me that is related in the story, I ain't telling.*

Standing alone under a railway arch out of the wind, I was looking
at the miles of sands, long and dirty in the early dark, with only a
few boys on the edge of the sea and one or two hurrying couples
with their mackintoshes blown around them like balloons, when two
young men joined me, it seemed out of nowhere, and struck matches
for their cigarettes and illuminated their faces under bright-checked
caps.

One had a pleasant face; his eyebrows slanted comically towards
his temples, his eyes were warm, brown, deep, and guileless, and his
mouth was full and weak. The other man had a boxer's nose and a
weighted chin ginger with bristles.

We watched the boys returning from the oily sea; they shouted
under the echoing arch, then their voices faded. Soon there was not
a couple in sight; the lovers had disappeared among the sandhills and
were lying down there with the broken tins and bottles of the summer past, old paper blowing by them, and nobody with any sense was
about. The strangers, huddled against the wall, their hands deep in
their pockets, their cigarettes sparkling, stared, I thought, at the
thickening of the dark over the empty sands, but their eyes may have
been closed. A train raced over us, and the arch shook. Over the
shore, behind the vanishing train, smoke clouds flew together, rags of

wings and hollow bodies of great birds black as tunnels, and broke up lazily; cinders fell through a sieve in the air, and the sparks were put out by the wet dark before they reached the sand. The night before, little quick scarecrows had bent and picked at the track-line and a solitary dignified scavenger wandered three miles by the edge with a crumpled coal sack and a park-keeper's steel-tipped stick. Now they were tucked up in sacks, asleep in a siding, their heads in bins, their beards in straw, in coal-trucks thinking of fires, or lying beyond pickings on Jack Stiff's slab near the pub in the Fishguard Alley, where the methylated-spirit drinkers danced into the policemen's arms and women like lumps of clothes in a pool waited, in doorways and holes in the soaking wall, for vampires of firemen. Night was properly down on us now. The wind changed. Thin rain began. The sands themselves went out. We stood in the scooped, windy room of the arch, listening to the noises from the muffled town, a goods train shunting, a siren in the docks, the hoarse trams in the street far behind, one bark of a dog, unplaceable sounds, iron being beaten, the distant creaking of wood, doors slamming where there were no houses, an engine coughing like a sheep on a hill.

The two young men were statues smoking, tough-capped and collarless watchers and witnesses carved out of the stone of the blowing room where they stood at my side with nowhere to go, nothing to do, and all the raining, almost winter, night before them. I cupped a match to let them see my face in a dramatic shadow, my eyes mysteriously sunk, perhaps, in a startling white face, my young looks savage in the sudden flicker of light, to make them wonder who I was as I puffed my last butt and puzzled about them. Why was the soft-faced young man, with his tame devil's eyebrows, standing like a stone figure with a glow-worm in it? He should have a nice girl to bully him gently and take him to cry in the pictures, or kids to bounce in a kitchen in Rodney Street. There was no sense in standing silent for hours under a railway arch on a hell of a night at the end of a bad summer when girls were waiting, ready to be hot and friendly, in chip-shops and shop-doorways and Rabbiotti's all-night café, when the public bar of the "Bay View" at the corner had a fire and skittles and a swarthy, sensuous girl with different coloured eyes, when the billiard saloons were open, except the one in High Street you couldn't go into without a collar and tie, when the closed parks had empty, covered bandstands and the railings were easy to climb.

A church clock somewhere struck a lot, faintly from the night on the right, but I didn't count.

The other young man, less than two feet from me, should be shouting with the boys, boasting in lanes, propping counters, prancing and clouting in the Mannesman Hall, or whispering around a bucket in a ring-corner. Why was he humped here with a moody man and myself, listening to our breathing, to the sea, the wind scattering sand through the archway, a chained dog and a foghorn and the rumble of trams a dozen streets away, watching a match strike, a boy's fresh face spying in a shadow, the lighthouse beams, the movement of a hand to a fag, when the sprawling town in a drizzle, the pubs and the clubs and the coffeeshops, the prowlers' streets, the arches near the promenade, were full of friends and enemies? He could be playing nap by a candle in a shed in a wood-yard.

Families sat down to supper in rows of short houses, the wireless sets were on, the daughters' young men sat in the front rooms. In neighbouring houses they read the news off the table-cloth, and the potatoes from dinner were fried up. Cards were played in the front rooms of houses on the hills. In the houses on tops of the hills families were entertaining friends, and the blinds of the front rooms were not quite drawn. I heard the sea in a cold bit of the cheery night.

One of the strangers said suddenly, in a high, clear voice: "What are we all doing then?"

"Standing under a bloody arch," said the other one.

"And it's cold," I said.

"It isn't very cosy," said the high voice of the young man with the pleasant face, now invisible. "I've been in better hotels than this."

"What about that night in the Majestic?" said the other voice.

There was a long silence.

"Do you often stand here?" said the pleasant man. His voice might never have broken.

"No, this is the first time here," I said. "Sometimes I stand in the Brynmill arch."

"Ever tried the old pier?"

"It's no good in the rain, is it?"

"Underneath the pier, I mean, in the girders."

"No, I haven't been there."

"Tom spends every Sunday under the pier," the pug-faced young man said bitterly. "I got to take him his dinner in a piece of paper."

"There's another train coming," I said. It tore over us, the arch bellowed, the wheels screamed through our heads, we were deafened and spark-blinded and crushed under the fiery weight and we rose again, like battered black men, in the grave of the arch. No noise at all from the swallowed town. The trams had rattled themselves dumb. A pressure of the hidden sea rubbed away the smudge of the docks. Only three young men were alive.

One said: "It's a sad life, without a home."

"Haven't you got a home then?" I said.

"Oh, yes, I've got a home all right."

"I got one, too."

"And I live near Cwndonkin Park," I said.

"That's another place Tom sits in in the dark. He says he listens to the owls."

"I knew a chap once who lived in the country, near Bridgend," said Tom, "and they had a munition works there in the War and it spoiled all the birds. The chap I know says you can always tell a cuckoo from Bridgend, it goes: 'Cuckbloodyoo! cuckbloodyoo!' "

"Cuckbloodyoo!" echoed the arch.

"Why are you standing under the arch then?" asked Tom. "It's warm at home. You can draw the curtains and sit by the fire, snug as a bug. Gracie's on the wireless to-night. No shananacking in the old moonlight."

"I don't want to be home, I don't want to sit by the fire. I've got nothing to do when I'm in and I don't want to go to bed. I like standing about like this with nothing to do, in the dark all by myself," I said.

And I did, too. I was a lonely night-walker and a steady stander-at-corners. I liked to walk through the wet town after midnight, when the streets were deserted and the window lights out, alone and alive on the glistening tram-lines in dead and empty High Street under the moon, gigantically sad in the damp streets by ghostly Ebenezer Chapel. And I never felt more a part of the remote and overpressing world, or more full of love and arrogance and pity and humility, not for myself alone, but for the living earth I suffered on and for the unfeeling systems in the upper air, Mars and Venus and Brazell and Skully, men in China and St Thomas, scorning girls and ready girls, soldiers and bullies and policemen and sharp, suspicious buyers of second-hand books, bad, ragged women who'd pretend against the museum wall for a cup of tea, and perfect, unapproachable women out of the fashion magazines, seven feet high, sailing slowly in their flat, glazed creations through steel and glass and velvet. I leant against the wall of a derelict house in the residential areas or wandered in the empty rooms, stood terrified on the stairs or gazing through the smashed windows at the sea or at nothing, and the lights going out one by one in the avenues. Or I mooched in a half-built house, with the sky stuck in the roof and cats on the ladders and a wind shaking through the bare bones of the bedrooms.

"And you can talk," I said. "Why aren't you at home?"

"I don't want to be home," said Tom.

"I'm not particular," said his friend.

When a match flared, their heads rocked and spread on the wall, and shapes of winged bulls and buckets grew bigger and smaller. Tom began to tell a story. I thought of a new stranger walking on the sands past the arch and hearing all of a sudden that high voice out of a hole.

I missed the beginning of the story as I thought of the man on the sands listening in a panic or dodging, like a footballer, in and out among the jumping dark towards the lights behind the railway line, and remembered Tom's voice in the middle of a sentence.

"... went up to them and said it was a lovely night. It wasn't a lovely night at all. The sands were empty. We asked them what their names were and they asked us what ours were. We were walking along by this time. Walter here was telling them about the glee party in the Melba and what went on in the ladies' cloakroom. You had to drag the tenors away like ferrets."

"What were their names?" I asked.

"Doris and Norma," Walter said.

"So we walked along the sands towards the dunes," Tom said, "and Walter was with Doris and I was with Norma. Norma worked in the steam laundry. We hadn't been walking and talking for more than a few minutes when, by God, I knew I was head over heels in love with the girl, and she wasn't the pretty one, either."

He described her. I saw her clearly. Her plump, kind face, jolly brown eyes, warm wide mouth, thick bobbed hair, rough body, bottle legs, broad bum, grew from a few words right out of Tom's story, and I saw her ambling solidly along the sands in a spotted frock in a showering autumn evening with fancy gloves on her hard hands, a gold bangle, with a voile handkerchief tucked in it, round her wrist, and a navy-blue handbag with letters and outing snaps, a compact, a bus ticket, and a shilling.

"Doris was the pretty one," said Tom, "smart and touched-up and sharp as a knife. I was twenty-six years old and I'd never been in love, and there I was, gawking at Norma in the middle of Tawe sands, too frightened to put my finger on her gloves. Walter had his arm round Doris then."

They sheltered behind a dune. The night dropped down on them quickly. Walter was a caution with Doris, hugging and larking, and Tom sat close to Norma, brave enough to hold her hand in its cold glove and tell her all his secrets. He told her his age and his job. He liked staying in in the evenings with a good book. Norma liked dances. He liked dances, too. Norma and Doris were sisters. "I'd never have thought that," Tom said, "you're beautiful, I love you."

Now the story-telling night in the arch gave place to the loving night in the dunes. The arch was as high as the sky. The faint town noises died. I lay like a pimp in a bush by Tom's side and squinted through to see him round his hands on Norma's breast. "Don't you dare!" Walter and Doris lay quietly near them. You could have heard a safety-pin fall.

"And the curious thing was," said Tom, "that after a time we all sat up on the sand and smiled at each other. And then we all moved softly about on the sand in the dark, without saying a word. And Doris was lying with me, and Norma was with Walter."

"But why did you change over, if you loved her?" I asked.

"I never understood why," said Tom. "I think about it every night."

"That was in October," Walter said.

And Tom continued: "We didn't see much of the girls until July. I couldn't face Norma. Then they brought two paternity orders against us, and Mr. Lewis, the magistrate, was eighty years old, and stone deaf, too. He put a little trumpet by his ear and Norma and Doris gave evidence. Then we gave evidence, and he couldn't decide whose was which. And at the end he shook his head back and fore and pointed his trumpet and said: 'Just like little dogs!' "

All at once I remembered how cold it was. I rubbed my numb hands together. Fancy standing all night in the cold. Fancy listening, I thought, to a long, unsatisfactory story in the frost-bite night in a polar arch. "What happened then?" I asked.

Walter answered: "I married Norma and Tom married Doris. We had to do the right thing by them, didn't we? That's why Tom won't go home. He never goes home till the early morning. I've got to keep him company. He's my brother."

It would take me ten minutes to run home. I put up my coat collar and pulled my cap down.

"And the curious thing is," said Tom, "that I love Norma and Walter doesn't love Norma or Doris. We've two nice little boys. I call mine Norman."

We all shook hands.

"See you again," said Walter.

"I'm always hanging about," said Tom.

"Abyssinia!"

I walked out of the arch, crossed Trafalgar Terrace, and pelted up the steep streets.

Stained Glass and Stone

There are three buildings which have moved me profoundly: Mont St. Michel and Chartres cathedral in France, which are medieval, and Frank Lloyd Wright's ranch, Taliesin, in Phoenix, Arizona.

I am proud to say that I know Frank Lloyd Wright quite well and I enjoy his company. One day we were walking in front of Taliesin —which seems as if it had flowed from the desert mountains—and he waved his stick at it in a wide arc and said, "I have given Arizona a voice."

He has. After I had seen this beautiful creation, everywhere the desert landscape seemed more lovely and I regretted all the other things that have been built on it.

I saw Mont St. Michel only once, many years ago (it must be over thirty years ago), and it is stamped on my memory.

Chartres I have seen many times. Those of you who have not had the good fortune to see these buildings might read—if you have the time—Henry Adams's Mont St. Michel and Chartres.

The first time I went to Chartres cathedral it was a sunny, warm day in June. The streets were decorated and at the moment we drove into the place in front of the cathedral the great doors opened and one could see the sunlight coming through the stained-glass windows at the back of the altar. It was Corpus Christi.

I will never forget walking around the great windows for the first time. While I was looking at one window a stooped little man of about fifty or so walked in front of me in a black alpaca coat and one of those funny oval black alpaca hats. I asked him if the window I was looking at was a twelfth- or thirteenth-century window. He said, "That is a curious question for a young man." (I was twenty-three years old.)

He told me that it was a twelfth-century window, an especially fine one. It was a wonderful blue window with a madonna and child in the central panel, and he started to show me the difference between twelfth-century, fourteenth- and fifteenth-century art in the great cathedral. At the end of his explanations he said that if I would come back at three o'clock he would show me how the light struck some pillars from a particular window. I came back at three and I stayed in Chartres for three days.

He would have me come back at different times of the day and the sunset and the dawn to show me the statuary and the windows and the pillars in different lights.

I didn't know who he was at the time. I found out later that he was Étienne Houvet and was famous indeed—an academician, I believe— and had written the monograph on Chartres.

Much later, in the late forties, I was making a film in Paris and had taken two of the actors, Bill Phipps and Bill Cottrell, to show them the cathedral. I wanted to see it myself again and I wanted company. I went up to the place where they sell photographs and fearfully asked if M. Houvet was still alive. I was told he was—and out he came.

He was over eighty years old now and he looked at me and said, "Where have you been for twenty-five years? What did you become? I remember I thought you must be an artist."

"I became an actor," I said.

"Indeed," he said. "Are you successful?"

"Yes," I said.

I introduced the two Bills as young American actors, and he said, "I will show them what I showed you."

It was fortunately quite early in the morning and a shining day, and round he took us to the main points of view in the different lights he had shown me so many years before. As we left he said, "Well, in another twenty-five years I shall be dead, but no doubt they will give me a cathedral up there to show you when you die."

I went back two years later and his daughter told me that he had died.

Étienne Houvet, by the way, was responsible for all those beautiful photographs you see of the statuary of Chartres. He would set up his camera on a composition and wait for two weeks or more until the light was exactly right before he shot his picture. He was probably the best still photographer in the world.

So, these three stories remind me of all that.

(One interesting point: the two little stories of St. Francis were translated by Thomas Arnold, who was the father of Matthew Arnold, the English poet, and was the headmaster of Rugby school in England. I have heard that the portrait of the headmaster in Tom Brown's School Days, by Thomas Hughes, is a portrait of Thomas Arnold.)

The Little Flowers of St. Francis

ST. FRANCIS

How Saint Francis preached unto the birds,
and made the swallows hold their peace

The humble servant of Christ, Saint Francis, a short while after
his conversion, having already gathered together many companions
and received them into the order, rose up with fervour exceeding
great, and said: "Let us be going in the name of God"; and he
took for his companions Brother Masseo and Brother Agnolo,
holy men. And setting forth with fervent zeal of spirit, taking no
thought for road or way, they came unto a little town that was called
Savurniano, and Saint Francis set himself to preach, but first he
bade the swallows that were twittering keep silence till such time
as he had done the preaching; and the swallows were obedient to
his word, and he preached there with such fervour that all the
men and women of that town minded through their devotion to
come after him and leave the town, but Saint Francis suffered them
not, saying: "Make not ill haste nor leave your homes; and I will
ordain for you what ye should do for the salvation of your souls":
and therewith he resolved to found the third Order, for the salvation of all the world. And so leaving them much comforted and
with minds firm set on penitence, he departed thence and came
unto a place between Cannaio and Bevagno. And as with great
fervour he was going on the way, he lifted up his eyes and beheld
some trees hard by the road whereon sat a great company of birds
well-nigh without number; whereat Saint Francis marvelled, and
said to his companions: "Ye shall wait for me here upon the way and
I will go to preach unto my little sisters, the birds." And he went
unto the field and began to preach unto the birds that were on the
ground; and immediately those that were on the trees flew down
to him, and they all of them remained still and quiet together, until
Saint Francis made an end of preaching: and not even then did
they depart, until he had given them his blessing. And according to
what Brother Masseo afterwards related unto Brother Jacques da
Massa, Saint Francis went among them touching them with his

329

cloak, howbeit none moved from out his place. The sermon that Saint Francis preached unto them was after this fashion: "My little sisters, the birds, much bounden are ye unto God, your Creator, and alway in every place ought ye to praise Him, for that He hath given you liberty to fly about everywhere, and hath also given you double and triple raiment; moreover He preserved your seed in the ark of Noah, that your race might not perish out of the world; still more are ye beholden to Him for the element of the air which He hath appointed for you; beyond all this, ye sow not, neither do you reap; and God feedeth you, and giveth you the streams and fountains for your drink; the mountains and the valleys for your refuge and the high trees whereon to make your nests; and because ye know not how to spin or sew, God clotheth you, you and your children; wherefore your Creator loveth you much, seeing that He hath bestowed on you so many benefits; and therefore, my little sisters, beware of the sin of ingratitude, and study always to give praises unto God." Whereas Saint Francis spake these words to them, those birds began all of them to open their beaks, and stretch their necks, and spread their wings, and reverently bend their heads down to the ground, and by their acts and by their songs to show that the holy Father gave them joy exceeding great. And Saint Francis rejoiced with them, and was glad, and marvelled much at so great a company of birds and their most beautiful diversity and their good heed and sweet friendliness, for the which cause he devoutly praised their Creator in them. At the last, having ended the preaching, Saint Francis made over them the sign of the cross, and gave them leave to go away; and thereby all the birds with wondrous singing rose up in the air; and then, in the fashion of the cross that Saint Francis had made over them, divided themselves into four parts; and the one part flew towards the East, and the other towards the West, and the other towards the South, and the fourth towards the North, and each flight went on its way singing wondrous songs; signifying thereby that even as Saint Francis, the standard-bearer of the Cross of Christ, had preached unto them, and made over them the sign of the cross, after the pattern of which they separated themselves unto the four parts of the world: even so the preaching of the Cross of Christ, renewed by Saint Francis, would be carried by him and the brothers throughout the world; the which brothers, after the fashion of the birds, possessing nothing of their own in this world, commit their lives wholly unto the providence of God.

Of the most holy miracle that Saint Francis wrought
when he converted the fierce wolf of Agobio

What time Saint Francis abode in the city of Agobio, there appeared in the country of Agobio an exceeding great wolf, terrible and
fierce, the which not only devoured animals, but also men, in so
much that all the city folk stood in great fear, sith oft-times he
came near to the city, and all men when they went out arrayed them
in arms as it were for the battle, and yet withal they might not
avail to defend them against him whensoe'er any chanced on him
alone; for fear of this wolf they were come to such a pass that none
durst go forth of that place. For the which matter, Saint Francis
having compassion on the people of that land, wished to go forth
unto that wolf, albeit the townsfolk all gave counsel against it: and
making the sign of the most holy cross he went forth from that
place with his companions, putting all his trust in God. And the
others misdoubting to go further, Saint Francis took the road to
the place where the wolf lay. And lo! in the sight of many of the
townsfolk that had come out to see this miracle, the said wolf
made at Saint Francis with open mouth: and coming up to him,
Saint Francis made over him the sign of the most holy cross, and
called him to him, and bespake him thus: "Come hither, brother
wolf: I command thee in the name of Christ that thou do no
harm, nor to me nor to any one." O wondrous thing! Whenas
Saint Francis had made the sign of the cross, right so the terrible
wolf shut his jaws and stayed his running: and when he was bid,
came gently as a lamb and lay him down at the feet of Saint Francis.
Thereat Saint Francis thus bespake him: "Brother wolf, much
harm hast thou wrought in these parts and done grievous ill, spoiling and slaying the creatures of God, without His leave: and not
alone hast thou slain and devoured the brute beasts, but hast dared
to slay men, made in the image of God; for the which cause thou
art deserving of the gibbet as a thief and a most base murderer;
and all men cry out and murmur against thee and all this land is
thine enemy. But I would fain, brother wolf, make peace between
thee and these; so that thou mayest no more offend them, and they
may forgive thee all thy past offences, and nor men nor dogs pursue
thee any more." At these words the wolf with movements of body,
tail, and eyes, and by the bending of his head, gave sign of his as-
sent to what Saint Francis said, and of his will to abide thereby.
Then spake Saint Francis again: "Brother wolf, sith it pleaseth
thee to make and hold this peace, I promise thee that I will see
to it that the folk of this place give thee food alway so long as
thou shalt live, so that thou suffer not hunger any more; for that

I wot well that through hunger hast thou wrought all this ill. But sith I win for thee this grace, I will, brother wolf, that thou promise me to do none hurt to any more, be he man or beast; dost promise me this?" And the wolf gave clear token by the bowing of his head that he promised. Then quoth Saint Francis: "Brother wolf, I will that thou plight me troth for this promise, that I may trust thee full well." And Saint Francis stretching forth his hand to take pledge of his troth, the wolf lifted up his right paw before him and laid it gently on the hand of Saint Francis, giving thereby such sign of good faith as he was able. Then quoth Saint Francis: "Brother wolf, I bid thee in the name of Jesu Christ come now with me, nothing doubting, and let us go stablish this peace in God's name." And the wolf obedient set forth with him, in fashion as a gentle lamb; whereat the townsfolk made mighty marvel, beholding. And straightway the bruit of it was spread through all the city, so that all the people, men-folk and women-folk, great and small, young and old, gat them to the market place for to see the wolf with Saint Francis. And the people being gathered all together, Saint Francis rose up to preach, avizing them among other matters how for their sins God suffered such things to be, and pestilences also: and how far more parlous is the flame of hell, ᵗhe which must vex the damned eternally, than is the fury of the wolf that can but slay the body; how much then should men fear the jaws of hell, when such a multitude stands sore adread of the jaws of one so small a beast? Then turn ye, beloved, unto God, and work out a fit repentance for your sins; and God will set you free from the wolf in this present time, and in time to come from out the fires of hell. And done the preaching, Saint Francis, said: "Give ear, my brothers: brother wolf, who standeth here before ye, hath promised me and plighted troth to make his peace with you, and to offend no more in any thing; and do ye promise him to give him every day whate'er he needs: and I am made his surety unto you that he will keep this pact of peace right steadfastly." Then promised all the folk with one accord to give him food abidingly. Then quoth Saint Francis to the wolf before them all: "And thou, brother wolf, dost thou make promise to keep firm this pact of peace, that thou offend not man nor beast nor any creature?" And the wolf knelt him down and bowed his head: and with gentle movements of his body, tail, and eyes, gave sign as best he could that he would keep their pact entire. Quoth Saint Francis: "Brother wolf, I wish that as thou hast pledged me thy faith to this promise without the gate, even so shouldest thou pledge me thy faith to thy promise before all the people, and that thou play me not false for my promise, and the surety that I have given for thee." Then the wolf lifting up his right paw, laid it in the hand of Saint Francis. Therewith, this act, and the others set forth above, wrought such great joy and marvel in all the people, both through devotion to the saint, and through the newness of the miracle, and through the peace with the wolf, that all began to lift up their voices unto heaven praising and blessing God, that had sent Saint Francis unto them, who by his merits had set them free from the jaws of the cruel beast. And thereafter this same wolf lived two years in Agobio; and went like a tame beast in and out the houses, from door to door, without doing hurt to any or any doing hurt to him, and was courteously nourished by the people; and as he passed thuswise through the country and the houses, never did any dog bark behind him. At length, after a two years' space, brother wolf died of old age: whereat the townsfolk sorely grieved, sith marking him pass so gently through the city, they minded them the better of the virtue and the sanctity of Saint Francis.

The Divided Horsecloth

FROM THE MEDIEVAL FRENCH

Have you ever read a medieval recipe? They did things like stuffing oxen with squids and then pouring rose water over the whole thing. Brrrh!

But the professional storytellers of the time, who were called troubadours, certainly told good stories. So you can imagine yourself in a baronial banquet hall—reeds on the floor, rush light, dogs under the table, the swells at the upper table on a dais, the riffraff below, and a rank odor pervading over all because of the overripe food and the lack of plumbing facilities.

"The Divided Horsecloth" is a version of King Lear with a happy ending.

Each owes it to his fellows to tell as best he may, or better still, to write with fair enticing words, such deeds and adventures as are good and profitable for us to know. For as men come and go about their business in the world, many things are told them which it is seemly to keep in remembrance. Therefore, it becomes those who say and relate, diligently and with fair intent to keep such matters in thought and study, even as did our fathers before us. Theirs is the school to which we all should pass, and he who would prove an apt scholar, and live beyond his day, must not be idle at his task. But the world dims our fine gold: the minstrel is slothful, and singers forget to sing, because of the pain and travail which go to the finding of their songs. So without waiting for any tomorrow, I will bring before you a certain adventure which chanced, even as it was told to me.

Some seven years ago it befell that a rich burgess of Abbeville departed from the town, together with his wife, his only son, and all his wealth, his goods and plenishing. This he did like a prudent man, since he found himself at enmity with men who were stronger and of more substance than he. So, fearing lest a worse thing should bechance him, from Abbeville he went up to Paris. There he sought a shop and dwelling, and paying his service, made himself vassal and burgess of the King. The merchant was diligent and courteous, his wife smiling and gracious, and their son was not given over to folly, but went soberly, even as his parents taught him. Much were they praised of their neighbours, and those who lived in the same street often set foot in their dwelling. For very greatly are those loved and esteemed by their fellows who are courteous in speech and address. He who has fair words in his mouth receives again sweet words in his ear, and foul words and foul deeds bring naught but bitterness and railing. Thus was it with this prudent merchant. For more than seven years he went about his business, buying and selling, concerning himself with matters of which he had full knowledge, putting by of his earnings a little every day, like a wise and worthy citizen. So this wealthy merchant lived a happy blameless life, till, by the will of God, his wife was taken from him, who had been his companion for some thirty years. Now these parents had but one only child, a son, even as I have told you before. Very grievously did he mourn the death of her who had cherished him so softly, and lamented his mother with many tears, till he came nigh to swoon. Then, to put a little comfort in his heart, his father said to him—

"Fair son, thy mother is dead, and we will pray to God that He grant her mercy in that day. But dry now thine eyes and thy face, for tears can profit thee nothing. By that road we all must go, neither can any man pass Death upon the way, nor return to bring us any word. Fair son, for thee there is goodly comfort. Thou art a young bachelor, and it is time to take thee a wife. I am full of years, and so I may find thee a fair marriage in an honourable house I will endow thee with my substance. I will now seek a bride for thee of birth and breeding—one of family and descent, one come of ancient race, with relations and friends a gracious company, a wife from honest folk and from an honest home. There, where it is good and profitable to be, I will set thee gladly, nor of wealth and moneys shalt thou find a lack."

Now in that place were three brethren, knights of high lineage, cousins to mighty lords of peerage, bearing rich and honourable blazons on their shields. But these knights had no heritage, since they had pawned all that they owned of woods and houses and lands, the better to take their pleasure at the tourney. Passing heavy and tormented were these brethren because in no wise might they redeem their pledge. The eldest of these brothers had a daughter, but the mother of the maid was dead. Now this damsel owned in Paris a certain fair house, over against the mansion of the wealthy merchant. The house was not of her father's heritage, but came to her from her mother, who had put the maid in ward to guardians, so that the house was free from pledge. She received in rent therefrom the sum of twenty Paris pounds every year, and her dues were paid

her right willingly. So the merchant, esteeming her a lady of family
and estate, demanded her hand in marriage of her father and of all
her friends. The knight inquired in his turn of the means and substance of the merchant, who answered very frankly—

"In merchandise and in moneys I have near upon fifteen hundred
pounds. Should I tell you that I had more, I should lie, and speak not
the truth. I have besides one hundred Paris pounds, which I have
gained in honest dealings. Of all this I will give my son the half."

"Fair sir," made answer the knight, "in no wise can this be agreed
to. Had you become a Templar, or a White or a Black monk you
would have granted the whole of your wealth either to the Temple
or your Abbey. By my faith, we cannot consent to so grudging an
offer, certes, sir merchant, no."

"Tell me then what you would have me do."

"Very willingly, fair, dear sir. We would that you grant to your
son the sum and total of your substance, so that he be seised of all
your wealth, and this in such fashion that neither you, nor any in
your name, may claim return of any part thereof. If you consent to
this the marriage can be made, but otherwise he shall never wed our
child and niece."

The merchant turned this over for a while, now looking upon his
son, now deep in thought. But very badly he was served of all his
thought and pondering. For at the last he made reply to him and
said—

"Lord, it shall even be done according to your will. This is our
covenant and bargain, that so your daughter is given to my son I will
grant him all that I have of worth. I take this company as witness
that here I strip myself of everything I own, so that naught is mine,
but all is his, of what I once was seised and possessed."

Thus before the witnesses he divested himself utterly of all his
wealth, and became naked as a peeled wand in the eyes of the world,
for this merchant now had neither purse nor penny, nor wherewithal
to break his fast, save it were given him by his son. So when the
words were spoken and the merchant altogether spoiled, then the
knight took his daughter by the hand and handfasted her with
the bachelor, and she became his wife.

For two years after this marriage the husband and the dame lived
a quiet and peaceful life. Then a fair son was born to the bachelor,
and the lady cherished and guarded him fondly. With them dwelt
the merchant in the same lodging, but very soon he perceived that
he had given himself a mortal blow in despoiling himself of his
substance to live on the charity of others. But perforce he remained
of their household for more than twelve years, until the lad had
grown up tall, and began to take notice, and to remember that which

often he heard of the making of his father's marriage. And well he promised himself that it should never go from mind.

The merchant was full of years. He leaned upon his staff, and went bent with age, as one who searches for his lost youth. His son was weary of his presence, and would gladly have paid for the spinning of his shroud. The dame, who was proud and disdainful, held him in utter despite, for greatly he was against her heart. Never was she silent, but always was she saying to her lord—

"Husband, for love of me, send your father upon his business. I lose all appetite just for the sight of him about the house."

"Wife," answered he, "this shall be done according to your wish."

So because of his wife's anger and importunity, he sought out his father straightway, and said—

"Father, father, get you gone from here. I tell you that you must do the best you can, for we may no longer concern ourselves with you and your lodging. For twelve years and more we have given you food and raiment in our house. Now all is done, so rise and depart forthwith, and fend for yourself, as fend you must."

When the father heard these words he wept bitterly, and often he cursed the day and the hour in which he found he had lived too long.

"Ah, fair, sweet son, what is this thou sayest to me! For the love of God turn me not from thy door. I lie so close that thou canst not want my room. I require of thee neither seat in the chimney corner, nor soft bed of feathers, no, nor carpet on the floor; but only the attic, where I may bide on a little straw. Throw me not from thy house because I eat of thy bread, but feed me without grudging for the short while I have to live. In the eyes of God this charity will cover all thy sins better than if thou went in haircloth next the flesh."

"Fair father," replied the bachelor, "preach me no preachings, but get you forth at once, for reason that my wife would have you gone."

"Fair son, where then shall I go, who am esteemed of nothing worth?"

"Get you gone to the town, for amongst ten thousand others very easily you may light on good fortune. Very unlucky you will be if there you cannot find a way to live. Seek your fortune bravely. Perchance some of your friends and acquaintances will receive you into their houses."

"Son, how then shall men take me to their lodging, when you turn me from the house which I have given you? Why should the stranger welcome that guest whom the son chases from his door? Why should I be received gladly by him to whom I have given naught, when I am evilly entreated of the rich man for whose sake I go naked?"

"Father," said he, "right or wrong, I take the blame upon my own head; but go you must because it is according to my will."

Then the father grieved so bitterly that for a little his very heart would have broken. Weak as he was, he raised himself to his feet and went forth from the house, weeping.

"Son," said he, "I commend thee to God; but since thou wilt that I go, for the love of Him give me at least a portion of packing cloth to shelter me against the wind. I am asking no great matter; nothing but a little cloth to wrap about me, because I am but lightly clad, and fear to die for reason of the cold."

Then he who shrank from any grace of charity made reply—

"Father, I have no cloth, so neither can I bestow, nor have it taken from me."

"Fair, sweet son, my heart trembles within me, so greatly do I dread the cold. Give me, then, the cloth you spread upon your horse, so that I come to no evil."

So, he, seeing that he might not rid himself of his father save by the granting of a gift, and being desirous above all that he should part, bade his son to fetch this horsecloth. When the lad heard his father's call he sprang to him, saying—

"Father, what is your pleasure?"

"Fair son," said he, "get you to the stable, and if you find it open give my father the covering that is upon my horse. Give him the best cloth in the stable, so that he may make himself a mantle or a habit, or any other sort of cloak that pleases him."

Then the lad, who was thoughtful beyond his years, made answer—

"Grandsire, come now with me."

So the merchant went with him to the stable, exceedingly heavy and wrathful. The lad chose the best horsecloth he might find in the stable, the newest, the largest, and the most fair; this he folded in two, and drawing forth his knife, divided the cloth into two portions. Then he bestowed on his grandfather one half of the sundered horsecloth.

"Fair child," said the old man, "what have you done? Why have you cut the cloth that your father has given me? Very cruelly have you treated me, for you were bidden to give me the horsecloth whole. I shall return and complain to my son thereof."

"Go where you will," replied the boy, "for certainly you shall have nothing more from me."

The merchant went forth from the stable.

"Son," said he, "chastise now thy child, since he counts thy word as nothing but an idle tale, and fears not to disobey thy commandment. Dost thou not see that he keeps one half of the horsecloth?"

"Plague take thee!" cried the father; "give him all the cloth."

"Certes," replied the boy, "that will I never do, for how then shall ·
you be paid? Rather will I keep the half until I am grown a man,
and then give it to you. For just as you have chased him from your
house, so I will put you from my door. Even as he has bestowed on
you all his wealth, so, in my turn, will I require of you all your substance. Naught from me shall you carry away, save that only which
you have granted to him. If you leave him to die in his misery, I wait
my day, and surely will leave you to perish in yours."

The father listened to these words, and at the end sighed heavily.
He repented him of the evil that he purposed, and from the parable
that his child had spoken took heed and warning. Turning himself
about towards the merchant, he said—

"Father, return to my house. Sin and the Enemy thought to have
caught me in the snare, but, please God, I have escaped from the
fowler. You are master and lord, and I render all that I have received
into your hands. If my wife cannot live with you in quiet, then you
shall be served and cherished elsewhere. Chimney corner, and carpet,
pillow and bed of feathers, at your ease you shall have pleasure in
them all. I take St. Martin to witness that never will I drink stoup
of wine, never carve morsel from dish, but that yours shall be the
richer portion. Henceforth you shall live softly in the ceiled chamber,
near by a blazing fire, clad warmly in your furred robe, even as I. And
all this is not of charity, but of your right, for, fair sweet father, if I
am rich it is because of your substance."

Thus the brave witness and the open remonstrance of a child freed
his father from the bad thoughts that he harboured. And deeply
should this adventure be considered of those who are about to marry
their children. Let them not strip themselves so bare as to have
nothing left. For he who gives all, and depends upon the charity of
others, prepares a rod for his own back.

After-dinner Stories

There is an old custom, still observed in some houses, that after a dinner party the ladies excuse themselves and go to the drawing room, for it is not nice for the gentlemen to see the ladies going one by one to the bathroom; and the gentlemen stay around the dinner table, for it is not nice for the ladies to see the gentlemen going one by one to the bathroom.

And the convention is that the gentlemen tell each other smoking-room stories, as they feel obliged to be lewd when the ladies are not present; and I have always assumed that the ladies upstairs tell each other boudoir stories for the same reasons.

So here are two after-dinner stories, one for the gentlemen and one for the ladies.

Sun and Shadow

RAY BRADBURY

*"Sun and Shadow" is not only a good story, but it also
teaches a lesson.*

*I have included it in this book because I have always
wanted to know what to do in front of press photographers
by whom I do not want to be photographed.*

The camera clicked like an insect. It was blue and metallic, like a
great fat beetle held in the man's precious and tenderly exploiting
hands. It winked in the flashing sunlight.

"Hsst, Ricardo, come away!"

"You down there!" cried Ricardo out the window.

"Ricardo, stop!"

He turned to his wife. "Don't tell me to stop, tell them to stop.
Go down and tell them, or are you afraid?"

"They aren't hurting anything," said his wife patiently.

He shook her off and leaned out the window and looked down
into the alley. "You there!" he cried.

The man with the black camera in the alley glanced up, then went
on focusing his machine at the lady in the salt-white beach pants,
the white bra, and the green checkered scarf. She leaned against the
cracked plaster of the building. Behind her a dark boy smiled, his
hand to his mouth.

"Tomás!" yelled Ricardo. He turned to his wife. "Oh, Jesus the
Blessed, Tomás is in the street, my own son laughing there." Ricardo
started out the door.

"Don't do anything!" said his wife.

"I'll cut off their heads!" said Ricardo, and was gone.

In the street the lazy woman was lounging now against the peeling
blue paint of a banister. Ricardo emerged in time to see her doing
this. "That's my banister!" he said.

The cameraman hurried up. "No, no, we're taking pictures. Everything's all right. We'll be moving on."

"Everything's not all right," said Ricardo, his brown eyes flashing.
He waved a wrinkled hand. "She's on my house."

"We're taking fashion pictures," smiled the photographer.

"*Now* what am I to do?" said Ricardo to the blue sky. "Go mad with this news? Dance around like an epileptic saint?"

"If it's money, well, here's a five-peso bill," smiled the photographer.

Ricardo pushed the hand away. "I *work* for my money. You don't understand. Please go."

The photographer was bewildered. "Wait ..."

"Tomás, get in the house!"

"But, Papa ..."

"Gahh!" bellowed Ricardo.

The boy vanished.

"This has *never* happened before," said the photographer.

"It is long past time! What are we? Cowards?" Ricardo asked the world.

A crowd was gathering. They murmured and smiled and nudged each other's elbows. The photographer with irritable good will snapped his camera shut, said over his shoulder to the model, "All right, we'll use that other street. I saw a nice cracked wall there and some nice deep shadows. If we hurry ..."

The girl, who had stood during this exchange nervously twisting her scarf, now seized her make-up kit and darted by Ricardo, but not before he touched at her arm. "Do not misunderstand," he said quickly. She stopped, blinked at him. He went on. "It is not you I am mad at. Or you." He addressed the photographer.

"Then why—" said the photographer.

Ricardo waved his hand. "You are employed; I am employed. We are all people employed. We must understand each other. But when you come to my house with your camera that looks like the complex eye of a black horsefly, then the understanding is over. I will not have my alley used because of its pretty shadows, or my sky used because of its sun, or my house used because there is an interesting crack in the wall, here! You *see!* Ah, how beautiful! Lean here! Stand there! Sit here! Crouch there! Hold it! Oh, I *heard* you. Do you think I am stupid? I have books up in my room. You see that window? Maria!"

His wife's head popped out. "Show them my books!" he cried.

She fussed and muttered, but a moment later she held out one, then two, then half a dozen books, eyes shut, head turned away, as if they were old fish.

"And two dozen more like them upstairs!" cried Ricardo. "You're not talking to some cow in the forest, you're talking to a man!"

"Look," said the photographer, packing his plates swiftly. "We're going. Thanks for nothing."

"Before you go, you must see what I am getting at," said Ricardo. "I am not a mean man. But I *can* be a very angry man. Do I look like a cardboard cutout?"

"Nobody said anybody looked like anything." The photographer hefted his case and started off.

"There is a photographer two blocks over," said Ricardo, pacing him. "They have cutouts. You stand in front of them. It says GRAND HOTEL. They take a picture of you and it looks like you are in the Grand Hotel. Do you see what I mean? My alley is my alley, my life is my life, my son is my son. My son is not cardboard! I saw you putting my son against the wall, so, and thus, in the background. What do you call it—for the correct air? To make the whole attractive, and the lovely lady in front of him?"

"It's getting late," said the photographer, sweating. The model trotted along on the other side of him.

"We are poor people," said Ricardo. "Our doors peel paint, our walls are chipped and cracked, our gutters fume in the street, the alleys are all cobbles. But it fills me with a terrible rage when I see you make over these things as if I had *planned* it this way, as if I had years ago induced the wall to crack. Did you think I knew you were coming and aged the paint? Or that I knew you were coming and put my boy in his dirtiest clothes? We are *not* a studio! We are people and must be given attention as people. Have I made it clear?"

"With abundant detail," said the photographer, not looking at him, hurrying.

"Now that you know my wishes and my reasoning, you will do the friendly thing and go home?"

"You are a hilarious man," said the photographer. "Hey!" They had joined a group of five other models and a second photographer at the base of a vast stone stairway which in layers, like a bridal cake, led up to the white town square. "How you doing, Joe?"

"We got some beautiful shots near the Church of the Virgin, some statuary without any noses, lovely stuff," said Joe. "What's the commotion?"

"Pancho here got in an uproar. Seems we leaned against his house and knocked it down."

"My name is Ricardo. My house is completely intact."

"We'll shoot it *here*, dear," said the first photographer. "Stand by the archway of that store. There's a nice antique wall going up there." He peered into the mysteries of his camera.

"So!" A dreadful quiet came upon Ricardo. He watched them prepare. When they were ready to take the picture he hurried forward, calling to a man in a doorway. "Jorge! What are you *doing*?"

"I'm standing here," said the man.

"Well," said Ricardo, "isn't that *your* archway? Are you going to let them *use* it?"

"I'm not bothered," said Jorge.

Ricardo shook his arm. "They're treating your property like a movie actor's place. Aren't you insulted?"

"I haven't thought about it." Jorge picked his nose.

"Jesus upon earth, man, *think!*"

"I can't see any harm," said Jorge.

"Am I the *only* one in the world with a tongue in my mouth?" said Ricardo to his empty hands. "And taste on my tongue? Is this a town of backdrops and picture sets? Won't *anyone* do something about this except me?"

The crowd had followed them down the street, gathering others to it as it came; now it was of a fair size and more were coming, drawn by Ricardo's bullish shouts. He stomped his feet. He made fists. He spat. The cameraman and the models watched him nervously. "Do you want a *quaint* man in the background?" he said wildly to the cameraman. "I'll pose back here. Do you want me near this wall, my hat *so*, my feet *so*, the light so and thus on my sandals which I made myself? Do you want me to rip this hole in my shirt a bit larger, eh, like *this? So!* Is my face smeared with enough perspiration? Is my hair long enough, kind sir?"

"Stand there if you want," said the photographer.

"I won't look in the camera," Ricardo assured him.

The photographer smiled and lifted his machine. "Over to your left one step, dear." The model moved. "Now turn your right leg. That's fine. Fine, fine. *Hold* it!"

The model froze, chin tilted up.

Ricardo dropped his pants.

"Oh, my God!" said the photographer,

Some of the models squealed. The crowd laughed and pummeled each other a bit. Ricardo quietly raised his pants and leaned against the wall.

"Was that quaint enough?" he said.

"Oh, my God!" muttered the photographer.

"Let's go down to the docks," said his assistant.

"I think *I'll* go there too," Ricardo smiled.

"Good God, what can we do with the idiot?" whispered the photographer.

"Buy him off!"

"I *tried* that!"

"You didn't go high enough."

"Listen, you run get a policeman. I'll put a stop to this."

The assistant ran. Everyone stood around smoking cigarettes

nervously, eying Ricardo. A dog came by and briefly made water against the wall.

"Look at that!" cried Ricardo. "What art! What a pattern! Quick, before the sun dries it!"

The cameraman turned his back and looked out to sea.

The assistant came rushing along the street. Behind him, a native policeman strolled quietly. The assistant had to stop and run back to urge the policeman to hurry. The policeman assured him with a gesture, at a distance, that the day was not yet over and in time they would arrive at the scene of whatever disaster lay ahead.

The policeman took up a position behind the two cameramen. "What seems to be the trouble?"

"That man up there. We want him removed."

"That man up there seems only to be leaning against a wall," said the officer.

"No, no, it's not the leaning, he— Oh hell," said the cameraman. "The only way to explain is to show you. Take your pose, dear."

The girl posed. Ricardo posed, smiling casually.

"Hold it!"

The girl froze.

Ricardo dropped his pants.

Click went the camera.

"Ah," said the policeman.

"Got the evidence right in this old camera if you need it!" said the cameraman.

"Ah," said the policeman, not moving, hand to chin. "So." He surveyed the scene like an amateur photographer himself. He saw the model with the flushed, nervous marble face, the cobbles, the wall, and Ricardo. Ricardo magnificently smoking a cigarette there in the noon sunlight under the blue sky, his pants where a man's pants rarely are.

"Well, officer?" said the cameraman, waiting.

"Just what," said the policeman, taking off his cap and wiping his dark brow, "do you want me to do?"

"Arrest that man! Indecent exposure!"

"Ah," said the policeman.

"Well?" said the cameraman.

The crowd murmured. All the nice lady models were looking out at the sea gulls and the ocean.

"That man up there against the wall," said the officer, "I know him. His name is Ricardo Reyes."

"Hello, Esteban!" called Ricardo.

The officer called back at him, "Hello, Ricardo."

They waved at each other.

"He's not doing anything *I* can see," said the officer.

"What do you mean?" asked the cameraman. "He's as naked as a rock. It's immoral!"

"That man is doing nothing immoral. He's just standing there," said the policeman. "Now if he were *doing* something with his hands or body, something terrible to view, I would act upon the instant. However, since he is simply leaning against the wall, not moving a single limb or muscle, there *is* nothing wrong."

"He's naked, *naked!*" screamed the cameraman.

"I don't understand." The officer blinked.

"You just don't go around naked, that's all!"

"There are naked people and naked people," said the officer. "Good and bad. Sober and with drink in them. I judge this one to be a man with no drink in him, a good man by reputation; naked, yes, but doing nothing with this nakedness in any way to offend the community."

"What *are* you, his *brother?* What are you, his confederate?" said the cameraman. It seemed that at any moment he might snap and bite and bark and woof and race around in circles under the blazing sun. "Where's the justice? What's going *on* here? Come on, girls, we'll go somewhere else!"

"France," said Ricardo.

"What!" The photographer whirled.

"I said France, or Spain," suggested Ricardo. "Or Sweden. I have seen some nice pictures of walls in Sweden. But not many cracks in them. Forgive my suggestion."

"We'll get pictures in spite of you!" The cameraman shook his camera, his fist.

"I will be there," said Ricardo. "Tomorrow, the next day, at the bullfights, at the market, anywhere, everywhere you go I go, quietly, with grace. With dignity, to perform my necessary task."

Looking at him, they knew it was true.

"Who are you—who in hell do you think you are?" cried the photographer.

"I have been waiting for you to ask me," said Ricardo. "Consider me. Go home and think of me. As long as there is one man like me in a town of ten thousand, the world will go on. Without me, all would be chaos."

"Good night, nurse," said the photographer, and the entire swarm of ladies, hatboxes, cameras, and make-up kits retreated down the street toward the docks. "Time out for lunch, dears. We'll figure something later!"

Ricardo watched them go, quietly. He had not moved from his position. The crowd still looked upon him and smiled.

Now, Ricardo thought, I will walk up the street to my house, which has paint peeling from the door where I have brushed it a thousand times in passing, and I shall walk over the stones I have worn down in forty-six years of walking, and I shall run my hand over the crack in the wall of my own house, which is the crack made by the earthquake in 1930. I remember well the night, us all in bed, Tomás as yet unborn, and Maria and I much in love, and thinking it was our love which moved the house, warm and great in the night; but it was the earth trembling, and in the morning, that crack in the wall. And I shall climb the steps to the lacework-grille balcony of my father's house, which grillwork he made with his own hands, and I shall eat the food my wife serves me on the balcony, with the books near at hand. And my son Tomás, whom I created out of whole cloth, yes, bed sheets, let us admit it, with my good wife. And we shall sit eating and talking, not photographs, not backdrops, not paintings, not stage furniture, any of us. But actors, all of us, very fine actors indeed.

As if to second this last thought, a sound startled his ear. He was in the midst of solemnly, with great dignity and grace, lifting his pants to belt them around his waist, when he heard this lovely sound. It was like the winging of soft doves in the air. It was applause.

The small crowd, looking up at him, enacting the final scene of the play before the intermission for lunch, saw with what beauty and gentlemanly decorum he was elevating his trousers. The applause broke like a brief wave upon the shore of the nearby sea.

Ricardo gestured and smiled to them all.

On his way home up the hill he shook hands with the dog that had watered the wall.

Rose

GUY DE MAUPASSANT

If ladies do not tell stories like this after dinner to each other, I hope they will forgive me. There is no way of finding out unless there happens to have been a Rose in their midst.

The two young women had the appearance of being buried in a bed of flowers. They were alone in an immense landau filled with bouquets like a giant basket. Upon the seat before them were two small hampers full of Nice violets, and upon the bearskin which covered their knees was a heap of roses, gillyflowers, marguerites, tuberoses and orange flowers, bound together with silk ribbons, which seemed to crush the two delicate bodies, only allowing to appear above the spreadout, perfumed bed the shoulders, arms and a little of their bodices, one of which was blue and the other lilac.

The coachman's whip bore a sheath of anemones; the horses' heads were decorated with wallflowers; the spokes of the wheels were clothed in mignonette, and in place of lanterns, there were two round, enormous bouquets, which seemed like the two eyes of this strange, rolling, flowery beast.

The landau went along Antibes Street at a brisk trot, preceded, followed and accompanied by a crowd of other garlanded carriages full of women concealed under a billow of violets. For it was the Flower Festival at Cannes.

They arrived at the Foncière Boulevard, where the battle took place. The whole length of the immense avenue, a double line of bedecked equipages was going and coming, like a ribbon without end. They threw flowers from one to the other. Flowers passed in the air like balls, hit the fair faces, hovered and fell in the dust where an army of street urchins gathered them.

A compact crowd, clamorous but orderly, looked on, standing in rows upon the sidewalks and held in place by policemen on horseback who passed along, pushing back the curious brutally with their feet, in order that the villains might not mingle with the rich.

Now the people in the carriages recognized each other, called to each other and bombarded one another with roses. A chariot full of pretty young women, clothed in red like devils, attracted and held all eyes. One gentleman, who resembled the portraits of Henry IV, threw repeatedly, with joyous ardor, a huge bouquet retained by an elastic. At the threat of the blow the women lowered their heads and hid their eyes, but the gracious projectile only described a curve and again returned to its master, who immediately threw it again to a new face.

The two young women emptied their arsenal with full hands and received a shower of bouquets; then after an hour of battle, a little wearied at the last, they ordered the coachman to take the road to the Juan Gulf, which skirts the sea.

The sun disappeared behind the Esterel, outlining in black upon a background of fire the lacy silhouette of the stretched-out mountain. The calm sea was spread out blue and clear as far as the horizon, where it mingled with the sky and with the squadron anchored in the middle of the gulf, having the appearance of a troop of monstrous beasts, immovable upon the water, apocalyptic animals, humpbacked and clothed in coats of mail, capped with thin masts like plumes and with eyes that lighted up when night came on.

The young women, stretched out under the fur robe, looked upon it languidly. Finally one of them said:

"How delicious these evenings are! Everything seems good. Is it not so, Margot?"

The other replied: "Yes, it is good. But there is always something lacking."

"What is it? For my part, I am completely happy. I have need of nothing."

"Yes? You think so, perhaps. But whatever well-being surrounds our bodies, we always desire something more—for the heart."

Said the other smiling: "A little love?"

"Yes."

They were silent, looking straight before them; then the one called Marguerite said: "Life does not seem supportable to me without that. I need to be loved, if only by a dog. And we are all so, whatever you may say, Simone."

"No, no, my dear. I prefer not to be loved at all than to be loved by no one of importance. Do you think, for example, that it would be agreeable to me to be loved by—by—"

She looked for someone by whom she could possibly be loved, casting her eyes over the neighboring country. Her eyes, after having made the tour of the whole horizon, fell upon the two metal buttons shining on the coachman's back, and she continued, laughing, "By my coachman?"

Mlle. Marguerite scarcely smiled as she replied:

"I can assure you it is very amusing to be loved by a domestic. This has happened to me two or three times. They roll their eyes so queerly that one is dying to laugh. Naturally, the more one is loved, the more severe she becomes, since otherwise, one puts herself in the way of being made ridiculous for some very slight cause, if anyone happened to observe it."

Mlle. Simone listened, her look fixed straight before her; then she declared:

"No, decidedly, the heart of my valet at my feet would not appear to me sufficient. But tell me how you perceived that you were loved."

"I perceived it in them as I do in other men; they become so stupid!"

"But others do not appear so stupid to me when they are in love."

"Idiots, my dear, incapable of chatting, of answering, of comprehending anything."

"And you? What effect did it have on you to be loved by a domestic? Were you moved—flattered?"

"Moved? No. Flattered? Yes, a little. One is always flattered by the love of a man, whoever he may be."

"Oh, now, Margot!"

"Yes, my dear. Wait! I will tell you a singular adventure that happened to me. You will see what curious things take place among us in such cases.

"It was four years ago in the autumn, when I found myself without a maid. I had tried five or six, one after the other, all of them incompetent, and almost despaired of finding one, when I read in the advertisements of a newspaper of a young girl knowing how to sew, embroider and dress hair, who was seeking a place and could furnish the best of references. She could also speak English.

"I wrote to the address given, and the next day the person in question presented herself. She was rather tall, thin, a little pale, with a very timid air. She had beautiful black eyes, a charming color, and she pleased me at once. I asked for her references; she gave me one written in English, because she had come, she said, from the house of Lady Ryswell, where she had been for ten years.

"The certificate attested that the girl was returning to France of her own will and that she had nothing to reproach her for during her long service with her, except a little of the *French coquettishness.*

"The modest turn of the English phrase made me smile a little, and I engaged the maid immediately. She came to my house the same day; she called herself Rose.

"At the end of a month I adored her. She was a treasure, a pearl, a phenomenon.

"She could dress my hair with exquisite taste; she could flute the lace of a cap better than the best of the professionals, and she could make frocks. I was amazed at her ability. Never had I been so well served.

"She dressed me rapidly with an astonishing lightness of hand. I never felt her fingers upon my skin, and nothing is more disagreeable to me than contact with a maid's hand. I immediately got into excessively idle habits, so pleasant was it to let her dress me from head to foot, from chemise to gloves—this tall, timid girl, always blushing a little and never speaking. After my bath she would rub me and massage me while I slept a little while on my divan; indeed, I came to look upon her more as a friend in poorer circumstances than a servant.

"One morning the concierge, with some show of mystery, said he wished to speak to me. I was surprised but let him enter. He was an old soldier, once orderly for my husband.

"He appeared to hesitate at what he was going to say. Finally he said stammeringly: 'Madame, the police captain for this district is downstairs.'

"I asked: 'What does he want?'

" 'He wants to search the house.'

"Certainly the police are necessary, but I do detest them. I never can make it seem a noble profession. And I answered, irritated as well as wounded:

" 'Why search here? For what purpose? There has been no burglary?'

"He answered:

" 'He thinks that a criminal is concealed somewhere here.'

"I began to be a little afraid and ordered the police captain to be brought that I might have some explanation. He was a man rather well brought up and decorated with the Legion of Honor. He excused himself, asked my pardon, then asserted that I had among my servants a convict!

"I was thunderstruck and answered that I could vouch for every one of them and that I would make a review of them for his satisfaction.

" 'There is Peter Courtin, an old soldier.'

"It was not he.

" 'The coachman, Francis Pingau, a peasant, son of my father's farmer.'

"It was not he.

" 'A stableboy, also from Champagne and also a son of peasants I had known, and no more except the footman, whom you have seen.'

"It was not any of them.

" 'Then, sir, you see that you have been deceived.'

" 'Pardon me, madame, but I am sure I am not deceived. As he has not at all the appearance of a criminal, will you have the goodness to have all your servants appear here before you and me, all of them?'

"I hesitated at first, then I yielded, summoning all my people, men and women.

"He looked at them all for an instant, then declared:

" 'This is not all.'

" 'Your pardon, sir,' I replied; 'this is all, except my own maid who could not possibly be confounded with a convict.'

"He asked: 'Could I see her too?'

" 'Certainly.'

"I rang, and Rose appeared immediately. Scarcely had she entered when he gave a signal, and two men, whom I had not seen, concealed behind the door, threw themselves upon her, seized her hands and bound them with cords.

"I uttered a cry of fury and was going to try and defend her. The captain stopped me:

" 'This girl, madame, is a man who calls himself John Nicholas Lecapet, condemned to death in 1879 for assassination preceded by violation. His sentence was changed to life imprisonment. He escaped four months ago. We have been on the search for him ever since.'

"I was dismayed, struck dumb. I could not believe it. The policeman continued, laughing:

" 'I can only give you one proof. His right arm is tattooed.'

"His sleeve was rolled up. It was true. The policeman continued, certainly in bad taste:

" 'Doubtless you will be satisfied without the other proofs.'

"And he led away my maid!

"Well, if you will believe it, the feeling which was uppermost in me was that of anger at having been played with in this way, deceived and made ridiculous; it was not shame at having been dressed, undressed, handled and touched by this man, but—a—profound humiliation—the humiliation of a woman. Do you understand?"

"No, not exactly."

"Let me see. Think a minute. He had been condemned—for violation, this young man—and that—that humiliated me—there! Now do you understand?"

And Mlle. Simone did not reply. She looked straight before her, with her eyes singularly fixed upon the two shining buttons of the livery and with that sphinx's smile that women have sometimes.

In the Beginning

One day a friend of mine who was the president of a college made me a bet. We had talked about reading aloud quite a lot, and he said that I couldn't keep a bunch of children quiet with the Bible and Shakespeare for an hour and a half or so, and I said I could if he'd let me read one other story first.

So along we went to a school in Pasadena. I think I'm right in saying that the children's ages varied from about five to fourteen, so after a little joshing around I read them Rudyard Kipling's "The Elephant's Child," which, as you will read, is how the elephant got its trunk.

They were very pleased because you can make all sorts of funny noises reading that story. I read the Bi-Coloured-Python-Rock-Snake with a "veddy, veddy" English accent, and the crocodile with a sinister, quiet, gangster accent. They enjoyed it hugely and felt the evening was going to be all right.

Afterward I read them the Garden of Eden story, which is basically the same story in form—how it happened that the snake has to crawl on its belly, why Mother has pains when she has a baby, and why Father has to work for a living. In the light of "The Elephant's Child" they enjoyed that hugely too and were impressed by its more solemn side.

However, when I had finished reading it, one little girl stood up, blushing, and said, "O-o-o-oh," with a rising inflection.

"What is it, dear?" I said.

"Oh," she said, "it's a sto-o-o-ry!"

And after that I read them other things from the Bible and A Midsummer Night's Dream and the teacher told me afterward that they wanted to hear more of the Bible and more of Shakespeare.

Mission accomplished.

My good friend, the president of the college, laughed all the way home.

The Elephant's Child

RUDYARD KIPLING

In the High and Far-Off Times the Elephant, O Best Beloved, had no trunk. He had only a blackish, bulgy nose, as big as a boot, that he could wriggle about from side to side; but he couldn't pick up things with it. But there was one Elephant—a new Elephant—an Elephant's Child—who was full of 'satiable curtiosity, and that means he asked ever so many questions. *And* he lived in Africa, and he filled all Africa with his 'satiable curtiosities. He asked his tall aunt, the Ostrich, why her tail-feathers grew just so, and his tall aunt the Ostrich spanked him with her hard, hard claw. He asked his tall uncle, the Giraffe, what made his skin spotty, and his tall uncle, the Giraffe, spanked him with his hard, hard hoof. And still he was full of 'satiable curtiosity! He asked his broad aunt, the Hippopotamus, why her eyes were red, and his broad aunt, the Hippopotamus, spanked him with her broad, broad hoof; and he asked his hairy uncle, the Baboon, why melons tasted just so, and his hairy uncle, the Baboon, spanked him with his hairy, hairy paw. And *still* he was full of 'satiable curtiosity! He asked questions about everything that he saw, or heard, or felt, or smelt, or touched, and all his uncles and his aunts spanked him. And still he was full of 'satiable curtiosity!

One fine morning in the middle of the Precession of the Equinoxes this 'satiable Elephant's Child asked a new fine question that he had never asked before. He asked, "What does the Crocodile have for dinner?" Then everybody said, "Hush!" in a loud and dretful tone, and they spanked him immediately and directly, without stopping, for a long time.

By and by, when that was finished, he came upon Kolokolo Bird sitting in the middle of a wait-a-bit thorn-bush, and he said, "My father has spanked me, and my mother has spanked me; all my aunts and uncles have spanked me for my 'satiable curtiosity; and *still* I want to know what the Crocodile has for dinner!"

Then Kolokolo Bird said, with a mournful cry, "Go to the banks of the great grey-green, greasy Limpopo River, all set about with fever-trees, and find out."

That very next morning, when there was nothing left of the Equi-

357

noxes, because the Precession had preceded according to precedent, this 'satiable Elephant's Child took a hundred pounds of bananas (the little short red kind), and a hundred pounds of sugar-cane (the long purple kind), and seventeen melons (the greeny-crackly kind), and said to all his dear families, "Good-bye. I am going to the great grey-green, greasy Limpopo River, all set about with fever-trees, to find out what the Crocodile has for dinner." And they all spanked him once more for luck, though he asked them most politely to stop.

Then he went away, a little warm, but not at all astonished, eating melons, and throwing the rind about, because he could not pick it up.

He went from Graham's Town to Kimberley, and from Kimberley to Khama's Country, and from Khama's Country he went east by north, eating melons all the time, till at last he came to the banks of the great grey-green, greasy Limpopo River, all set about with fever-trees, precisely as Kolokolo Bird had said.

Now you must know and understand, O Best Beloved, that till that very week, and day, and hour, and minute, this 'satiable Elephant's Child had never seen a Crocodile, and did not know what one was like. It was all his 'satiable curiosity.

The first thing that he found was a Bi-Coloured-Python-Rock-Snake curled round a rock.

"'Scuse me," said the Elephant's Child most politely, "but have you seen such a thing as a Crocodile in these promiscuous parts?"

"Have I seen a Crocodile?" said the Bi-Coloured-Python-Rock-Snake, in a voice of dretful scorn. "What will you ask me next?"

"'Scuse me," said the Elephant's Child, "but could you kindly tell me what he has for dinner?"

Then the Bi-Coloured-Python-Rock-Snake uncoiled himself very quickly from the rock, and spanked the Elephant's Child with his scalesome, flailsome tail.

"That is odd," said the Elephant's Child, "because my father and my mother, and my uncle and my aunt, not to mention my other aunt, the Hippopotamus, and my other uncle, the Baboon, have all spanked me for my 'satiable curtiosity—and I suppose this is the same thing."

So he said good-bye very politely to the Bi-Coloured-Python-Rock-Snake, and helped to coil him up on the rock again, and went on, a little warm, but not at all astonished, eating melons, and throwing the rind about, because he could not pick it up, till he trod on what he thought was a log of wood at the very edge of the great grey-green, greasy Limpopo River, all set about with fever-trees.

But it really was the Crocodile, O Best Beloved, and the Crocodile winked one eye—like this!

" 'Scuse me," said the Elephant's Child most politely, "but do you happen to have seen a Crocodile in these promiscuous parts?"

Then the Crocodile winked the other eye, and lifted half his tail out of the mud; and the Elephant's Child stepped back most politely, because he did not wish to be spanked again.

"Come hither, Little One," said the Crocodile. "Why do you ask such things?"

" 'Scuse me," said the Elephant's Child most politely, "but my father has spanked me, my mother has spanked me, not to mention my tall aunt, the Ostrich, and my tall uncle, the Giraffe, who can kick ever so hard, as well as my broad aunt, the Hippopotamus, and my hairy uncle, the Baboon, *and* including the Bi-Coloured-Python-Rock-Snake, with the scalesome, flailsome tail, just up the bank, who spanks harder than any of them; and *so*, if it's quite all the same to you, I don't want to be spanked any more."

"Come hither, Little One," said the Crocodile, "for I am the Crocodile," and he wept crocodile-tears to show it was quite true.

Then the Elephant's Child grew all breathless, and panted, and kneeled down on the bank and said, "You are the very person I have been looking for all these long days. Will you please tell me what you have for dinner?"

"Come hither, Little One," said the Crocodile, "and I'll whisper."

Then the Elephant's Child put his head down close to the Crocodile's musky, tusky mouth, and the Crocodile caught him by his little nose, which up to that very week, day, hour, and minute, had been no bigger than a boot, though much more useful.

"I think," said the Crocodile—and he said it between his teeth, like this—"I think to-day I will begin with Elephant's Child!"

At this, O Best Beloved, the Elephant's Child was much annoyed, and he said, speaking through his nose, like this, "Led go! You are hurtig be!"

Then the Bi-Coloured-Python-Rock-Snake scuffled down from the bank and said, "My young friend, if you do not now, immediately and instantly, pull as hard as ever you can, it is my opinion that your acquaintance in the large-pattern leather ulster" (and by this he meant the Crocodile) "will jerk you into yonder limpid stream before you can say Jack Robinson."

This is the way Bi-Coloured-Python-Rock-Snakes always talk.

Then the Elephant's Child sat back on his little haunches, and pulled, and pulled, and pulled, and his nose began to stretch. And the Crocodile floundered into the water, making it all creamy with great sweeps of his tail, and *he* pulled, and pulled, and pulled.

The Elephant's Child's nose kept on stretching; and the Elephant's Child spread all his little four legs and pulled, and pulled, and pulled, and his nose kept on stretching; and the Crocodile threshed his tail like an oar, and *he* pulled, and pulled, and pulled, and at each pull the Elephant's Child's nose grew longer and longer—and it hurt him hijjus!

Then the Elephant's Child felt his legs slipping, and he said through his nose, which was now nearly five feet long, "This is too butch for be!"

Then the Bi-Coloured-Python-Rock-Snake came down from the bank, and knotted himself in a double-clove-hitch round the Elephant's Child's hind legs, and said, "Rash and inexperienced traveller, we will now seriously devote ourselves to a little high tension, because if we do not, it is my impression that yonder self-propelling man-of-war with the armour-plated upper deck" (and by this, O Best Beloved, he meant the Crocodile), "will permanently vitiate your future career."

That is the way all Bi-Coloured-Python-Rock-Snakes always talk.

So he pulled, and the Elephant's Child pulled, and the Crocodile pulled; but the Elephant's Child and the Bi-Coloured-Python-Rock-Snake pulled hardest; and at last the Crocodile let go of the Elephant's Child's nose with a plop that you could hear all up and down the Limpopo.

Then the Elephant's Child sat down most hard and sudden; but first he was careful to say "Thank you" to the Bi-Coloured-Python-Rock-Snake; and next he was kind to his poor pulled nose, and wrapped it all up in cool banana leaves, and hung it in the great grey-green, greasy Limpopo to cool.

"What are you doing that for?" said the Bi-Coloured-Python-Rock-Snake.

" 'Scuse me," said the Elephant's Child, "but my nose is badly out of shape, and I am waiting for it to shrink."

"Then you will have to wait a long time," said the Bi-Coloured-Python-Rock-Snake. "Some people do not know what is good for them."

The Elephant's Child sat there for three days waiting for his nose to shrink. But it never grew any shorter, and, besides, it made him squint. For, O Best Beloved, you will see and understand that the Crocodile had pulled it out into a really truly trunk same as all Elephants have to-day.

At the end of the third day a fly came and stung him on the shoulder, and before he knew what he was doing he lifted up his trunk and hit that fly dead with the end of it.

" 'Vantage number one!" said the Bi-Coloured-Python-Rock-Snake. "You couldn't have done that with a mere-smear nose. Try and eat a little now."

Before he thought what he was doing the Elephant's Child put out his trunk and plucked a large bundle of grass, dusted it clean against his fore-legs, and stuffed it into his own mouth.

" 'Vantage number two!" said the Bi-Coloured-Python-Rock-Snake. "You couldn't have done that with a mere-smear nose. Don't you think the sun is very hot here?"

"It is," said the Elephant's Child, and before he thought what he was doing he schlooped up a schloop of mud from the banks of the great grey-green, greasy Limpopo, and slapped it on his head, where it made a cool schloopy-sloshy mud-cap all trickly behind his ears.

" 'Vantage number three!" said the Bi-Coloured-Python-Rock-Snake. "You couldn't have done that with a mere-smear nose. Now how do you feel about being spanked again?"

" 'Scuse me," said the Elephant's Child, "but I should not like it at all."

"How would you like to spank somebody?" said the Bi-Coloured-Python-Rock-Snake.

"I should like it very much indeed," said the Elephant's Child.

"Well," said the Bi-Coloured-Python-Rock-Snake, "you will find that new nose of yours very useful to spank people with."

"Thank you," said the Elephant's Child, "I'll remember that; and now I think I'll go home to all my dear families and try."

So the Elephant's Child went home across Africa frisking and whisking his trunk. When he wanted fruit to eat he pulled fruit down from a tree, instead of waiting for it to fall as he used to do. When he wanted grass he plucked grass up from the ground, instead of going on his knees as he used to do. When the flies bit him he broke off the branch of a tree and used it as a fly-whisk; and he made himself a new, cool, slushy-squshy mud-cap whenever the sun was hot. When he felt lonely walking through Africa he sang to himself down his trunk, and the noise was louder than several brass bands. He went especially out of his way to find a broad Hippopotamus (she was no relation of his), and he spanked her very hard, to make sure that the Bi-Coloured-Python-Rock-Snake had spoken the truth about his new trunk. The rest of the time he picked up the melon rinds that he had dropped on his way to the Limpopo—for he was a Tidy Pachyderm.

One dark evening he came back to all his dear families, and he coiled up his trunk and said, "How do you do?" They were very glad to see him, and immediately said, "Come here and be spanked for your 'satiable curtiosity."

"Poh," said the Elephant's Child. "I don't think you peoples know anything about spanking; but *I* do, and I'll show you."

Then he uncurled his trunk and knocked two of his dear brothers head over heels.

"O Bananas!" said they, "where did you learn that trick, and what have you done to your nose?"

"I got a new one from the Crocodile on the banks of the great grey-green, greasy Limpopo River," said the Elephant's Child. "I asked him what he had for dinner, and he gave me this to keep."

"It looks very ugly," said his hairy uncle, the Baboon.

"It does," said the Elephant's Child. "But it's very useful," and he picked up his hairy uncle, the Baboon, by one hairy leg, and hove him into a hornets' nest.

Then that bad Elephant's Child spanked all his dear families for a long time, till they were very warm and greatly astonished. He pulled out his tall Ostrich aunt's tail-feathers; and he caught his tall uncle, the Giraffe, by the hind-leg, and dragged him through a thorn-bush; and he shouted at his broad aunt, the Hippopotamus, and blew bubbles into her ear when she was sleeping in the water after meals; but he never let any one touch Kolokolo Bird.

At last things grew so exciting that his dear families went off one by one in a hurry to the banks of the great grey-green, greasy Limpopo River, all set about with fever-trees, to borrow new noses from the Crocodile. When they came back nobody spanked anybody any more; and ever since that day, O Best Beloved, all the Elephants you will ever see, besides all those that you won't, have trunks precisely like the trunk of the 'satiable Elephant's Child.

The Garden of Eden

THE BOOK OF GENESIS
Chapter 2, verses 4–25; Chapter 3

The Fall of Man

In the day that the Lord God made the earth and the heavens and every plant of the field before it was in the earth, and every herb of the field before it grew (for the Lord God had not caused it to rain upon the earth, and there was not a man to till the ground) there went up a mist from the earth, and watered the whole face of the ground. And the Lord God formed man of the dust of the ground, and breathed into his nostrils the breath of life; and man became a living soul.

And the Lord God planted a garden eastward in Eden; and there he put the man whom he had formed. And out of the ground made the Lord God to grow every tree that is pleasant to the sight, and good for food; the tree of life also in the midst of the garden, and the tree of knowledge of good and evil. And a river went out of Eden to water the garden.

And the Lord God took the man, and put him into the garden of Eden to dress it and to keep it. And the Lord God commanded the man, saying, "Of every tree of the garden thou mayest freely eat: but of the tree of the knowledge of good and evil, thou shalt not eat of it; for in the day that thou eatest thereof thou shalt surely die."

And the Lord God said,

"It is not good that the man should be alone; I will make him an help meet for him." And out of the ground the Lord God formed every beast of the field, and every fowl of the air; and brought them unto Adam to see what he would call them: and whatsoever Adam called every living creature, that was the name thereof. And Adam gave names to all cattle, and to the fowl of the air, and to every beast of the field; but for Adam there was not found an help meet for him.

And the Lord God caused a deep sleep to fall upon Adam, and he slept: and he took one of his ribs, and closed up the flesh instead thereof; and the rib, which the Lord God had taken from man, made he a woman, and brought her unto the man.

And Adam said,

"This is now bone of my bones,
And flesh of my flesh;
She shall be called Woman
Because she was taken out of Man."

Therefore shall a man leave his father and his mother, and shall cleave unto his wife: and they shall be one flesh. And they were both naked, the man and his wife, and were not ashamed.

Now the serpent was more subtil than any beast of the field which the Lord God had made.

And he said unto the woman,

"Yea, hath God said, 'Ye shall not eat of every tree of the garden'?"

And the woman said unto the serpent,

"We may eat of the fruit of the trees of the garden: but of the fruit of the tree which is in the midst of the garden, God hath said, 'Ye shall not eat of it, neither shall ye touch it, lest ye die.' "

And the serpent said unto the woman,

"Ye shall not surely die: for God doth know that in the day ye eat thereof, then your eyes shall be opened, and ye shall be as gods, knowing good and evil."

And when the woman saw that the tree was good for food, and that it was pleasant to the eyes, and a tree to be desired to make one wise, she took of the fruit thereof, and did eat, and gave also unto her husband with her; and he did eat. And the eyes of them both were opened, and they knew that they were naked; and they sewed fig leaves together, and made themselves aprons.

And they heard the voice of the Lord God walking in the garden in the cool of the day: and Adam and his wife hid themselves from the presence of the Lord God amongst the trees of the garden.

And the Lord God called unto Adam, and said unto him,

"Where art thou?"

And he said,

"I heard thy voice in the garden, and I was afraid, because I was naked: and I hid myself."

And he said,

"Who told thee that thou wast naked? Hast thou eaten of the tree, whereof I commanded thee that thou shouldest not eat?"

And the man said,

"The woman whom thou gavest to be with me, she gave me of the tree, and I did eat."

And the Lord God said unto the woman,

"What is this that thou hast done?"

And the woman said, "The serpent beguiled me, and I did eat."

And the Lord God said unto the serpent,

"Because thou hast done this,
Thou art cursed above all cattle,
And above every beast of the field;
Upon thy belly shalt thou go,
And dust shalt thou eat
All the days of thy life:
And I will put enmity between thee and the woman,
And between thy seed and her seed;
It shall bruise thy head,
And thou shalt bruise his heel."

Unto the woman he said,

"I will greatly multiply thy sorrow and thy conception;
In sorrow thou shalt bring forth children;
And thy desire shall be to thy husband,
And he shall rule over thee."

And unto Adam he said,

"Because thou hast hearkened unto the voice of thy wife, and hast eaten of the tree, of which I commanded thee, saying, 'Thou shalt not eat of it':

"Cursed is the ground for thy sake;
In sorrow shalt thou eat of it all the days of thy life.
Thorns also and thistles shall it bring forth to thee
And thou shalt eat the herb of the field;
In the sweat of thy face shalt thou eat bread,
Till thou return unto the ground;
For out of it wast thou taken:
For dust thou art,
And unto dust shalt thou return."

And Adam called his wife's name Eve; because she was the mother of all living. Unto Adam also and to his wife did the Lord God make coats of skins, and clothed them.

And the Lord God said,

"Behold, the man is become as one of us, to know good and evil: and now, lest he put forth his hand, and take also of the tree of life, and eat, and live for ever"; therefore the Lord God sent him forth from the garden of Eden, to till the ground from whence he was taken. So he drove out the man; and he placed at the east of the garden of Eden Cherubims, and a flaming sword which turned every way, to keep the way of the tree of life.

Stories of Belief

You may believe or not believe but there is one thing that mankind has always persisted in believing. Races which could not possibly have had contact with one another have always believed in a higher power.

I knew a man once and he was a sculptor and he was old. His name was Carl Milles. There are statues of his and fountains all over the United States. He loved to build fountains. He was a great builder of fountains. One of his fountains is outside the depot in St. Louis, another outside the Art Institute in Des Moines. There is a great fountain of his in Stockholm, Sweden, and there is another fountain at the Art Institute in Chicago, and there is a great statue of an Indian by him in the Town Hall in St. Paul.

I used to go and visit him when I was reading anywhere around Detroit. He lived near Detroit, and I would go and read to Mr. and Mrs. Milles of an evening. (That's how I always seemed to spend my time in between reading dates, reading to friends.)

One day he asked me if he could read something he had written. Apparently the editor of an educational publication wrote to him asking, as a great artist, for a statement of his faith, something the editor could print for young people.

I was apprehensive about his reading; good sculptors do not necessarily read well. The English is written with a Swedish accent, but I haven't touched it. I knew that if I did, I would take the bloom off it.

Milles read it beautifully, and here it is for you.

May 1949

Dear Mr. Arthur Sherrill:

In answer to your letter of February 24, 1949. I can tell you the following:

As a boy in school it was hard for me to follow the lessons in Christianity.

That time already—as still today—I was more interested in Nature —the Earth—the Planets—the stars etc.—in Animals, plants and in arts.

In school they said I was thinking too much.

I think all that came from my Father and also Mother, but she died when I was 4 of age.

Our Father introduced us children in Nature, Astronomy, Arts, different religions and he did it in a way that we just got it in our thinking without knowing it.

I remember the time when I at 6 of age already studied the stars with him using his glasses—or at daytime I looked at insects, animals, birds—all a tremendous riddle to me—who has made all that? where I turned—always the same question—Who? Why?

I studied bacteriological world, where I had the opportunity to see the smallest invisible animals enlarged in a drop of water—where we saw how they organized themselves in groups to save one of them who was in danger to be eaten by another bigger animal. And I studied Life of Ants and Bees. Where I turned—same question appeared to me—who has created us and all that, why, it must be someone??? I wondered why we think, why we can feel so much for someone else, why I felt so much for my dog and he for me, same with birds and other animals. Who has created These Feelings???

Why are we here? What is Talent? Who has created Talent even by the most primitive?

Where do we go when we die? From where did we come? When I asked someone, who should know—I thought—he could not find words to express his Faith.

As an old man now I know that no one can answer, and no one will. We have not the capacity to do it. As artist I often ask—why this longing for art—for sculpture, for painting, music, buildings, literature? Why are we attracted to beauty?

The Philosophers try to explain and still their capacity is suddenly just closed—as the Tree cannot grow bigger than it is allowed to grow—as everything—the animals, insects, flowers and we selves. We build churches to glorify that which we do not know. The *one*, we feel in everything—which we—thanks to our senses—see and feel and listen to—the one we call GOD. In the wonderful churches on which mankind have worked on and beautified in centuries—on one single cathedral 5, 6, 800 years—all to honor God and pray to him—who is the master of everything, the greatest men on earth have prayed—to Lord or God. In Rome is still to be seen a greek altar—about 3000 years old—upon this is written

"AGNOSTO DEO"

—to the unknown God.

We feel him, we hear him, we see him in that we love, but we cannot come further in our life than to that, Abraham Lincoln prayed, Pasteur prayed, the hardest man can pray, the worst murderer can pray.

I can pray in any place—churches or Nature or in my studio. When I was a child and Grandmother died, first time I saw someone die, I felt so strange—what has happened? Why is she not more talking? not moving? When she was buried, I put a little letter to her in her grave, asking her to pray Lord to help me to become a great artist. Later I stepped a snowy day in the newly made steps of an old sculptor who I admired so much—praying Lord to make me as good an artist as he was. I saw once in Europe a poor man pray the Lord for his sick horse. I prayed once for my dying dog.

Now I am old, in reality I do not think I know more now than when I was newborn. But I recognize that there must be someone, who is interested in everything we know of Life and still more than we know big or small.

Isn't this enough—that we feel it in that way? I think so. Life is grand—young People—if we only have that as background—that Life is created for some purpose—it cannot be created for nothing.

We do not know what "Nothing" is—therefore it must be something—just this something we have to think about. This something we call GOD.

I never forget the old Song a Negro once sang in radio—"Lord—the old time Religion of my Fathers and Mothers—is good enough for me. . . ."

How modest—how wonderful.

Yours
Carl Milles

The Fiery Furnace

THE BOOK OF DANIEL
Chapter 3, verses 1–30

The story of Shadrach, Meshach, and Abednego is one of the most perfectly formed of all stories. Reading it, this might be rather hard to understand, for it is much better spoken.

"The Fiery Furnace" depends on the use of repetitions for its dramatic effect. Before I was first conscious of its drama, I started to cut them and found that I had cut the story's heart out. It is tremendous fun to speak. Each time you repeat one of those lists of musical instruments it becomes funnier and funnier. You can yell like the dickens when Nebuchadnezzar goes up to the mouth of the fiery furnace and you can be very oily as the counsellors and very healthy as Shadrach, Meshach, and Abednego. I'm afraid I did Nebuchadnezzar in a tired Oscar Wilde sort of way. It works, but maybe you have other ideas.

I do not know any other story in which so much is told in such a small space: the landscape, the crowds, the court, the idol, the dramatization of the flames, and the story of the miracle. Try it sometime. However, it looks deceptively simple. I recommend you to try something easier first.

Nebuchadnezzar the king made an image of gold, whose height
    was threescore cubits, and the breadth thereof six cubits:
He set it up in the plain of Dura,
In the province of Babylon.
Then Nebuchadnezzar the king sent to gather together
The princes,
The governors
And the captains,
The judges,
The treasurers,
The counsellors,

The sheriffs,
And all the rulers of the provinces,
To come to the dedication of the image which Nebuchadnezzar
        the king had set up. Then
The princes,
The governors,
And captains,
The judges,
The treasurers,
The counsellors,
The sheriffs,
And all the rulers of the provinces,
Were gathered together unto the dedication of the image that
        Nebuchadnezzar the king had set up;
And they stood before the image that Nebuchadnezzar had set up.

Then a herald cried aloud,
"To you it is commanded, O people, nations and languages, that at
        what time ye hear the sound of the
Cornet,
Flute,
Harp,
Sackbut,
Psaltery,
Dulcimer,
And all kinds of music,
Ye fall down and worship the golden image that Nebuchadnezzar
        the king hath set up: and whoso falleth not down and
        worshippeth shall the same hour be cast into the midst of a
Burning fiery furnace."

Therefore at that time,
When all the people heard the sound of the
Cornet,
Flute,
Harp,
Sackbut,
Psaltery,
And all kinds of music,
All the people, the nations, and the languages
Fell down
And worshipped the golden image that Nebuchadnezzar the king
        had set up.

Wherefore at that time
Certain Chaldeans came near, and accused the Jews.
They spoke and said to the king Nebuchadnezzar,

"O king, live for ever. Thou, O king, hast made a decree, that every
    man that shall hear the sound of the
Cornet,
Flute,
Harp,
Sackbut,
Psaltery,
And dulcimer,
And all kinds of music,
Shall fall down and worship the golden image:
And whoso falleth not down and worshippeth, that he should be
    cast into the midst of a
Burning fiery furnace. There are certain
Jews
Whom thou hast set over the affairs of the province of Babylon,
Shadrach, Meshach, and Abed-nego;
These men,
O king,
Have not regarded thee: they serve not thy gods, nor worship the
    golden image which thou hast set up."

Then Nebuchadnezzar in his rage and fury commanded to bring
Shadrach, Meshach, and Abed-nego.
Then they brought these men before the king.

Nebuchadnezzar spoke and said unto them,
"Is it true,
O Shadrach, Meshach, and Abed-nego,
Do not ye serve my gods, nor worship the golden image which I
    have set up?
Now
If ye be ready that at what time ye hear the sound of the
Cornet,
Flute,
Harp,
Sackbut,
Psaltery,
And dulcimer,
And all kinds of music,

Ye fall down and worship the image which I have made:
Well;
But
If ye worship not, ye shall be cast the same hour into the midst of a
Burning fiery furnace;
And who is that God
That shall deliver you out of my hands?"

Shadrach, Meshach, and Abed-nego
Answered and said to the king,
"O Nebuchadnezzar, we are not careful to answer thee in this matter.
  If it be so, our God whom we serve is able to deliver us from
  the burning fiery furnace, and he will deliver us out of thine
  hand,
O king.
But if not, be it known unto thee,
O king,
That we will not serve thy gods, nor worship the golden image
  which thou hast set up."

Then was Nebuchadnezzar full of fury, and the form of his visage
  was changed against
Shadrach, Meshach, and Abed-nego:
Therefore he spoke,
And commanded that they should heat the furnace one seven
  times more than it was wont to be heated.
And he commanded the most mighty men that were in his army
  to bind
Shadrach, Meshach, and Abed-nego,
And to cast them into the
Burning fiery furnace.
Then these men were bound in
Their coats,
Their hosen,
And their hats,
And their other garments,
And were cast into the midst of the
Burning fiery furnace.
Therefore because the king's commandment was urgent,
And the furnace exceedingly hot,
The flame of the fire slew those men that took up
Shadrach, Meshach, and Abed-nego.
And these three men,
Shadrach, Meshach, and Abed-nego,

Fell down bound into the midst of the
Burning fiery furnace.

Then Nebuchadnezzar the king was astonished,
And rose up in haste, and spoke, and said unto his counsellors,
"Did not we cast three men bound into the midst of the fire?"
They answered and said unto the king,
"True, O king."
He answered and said,
"Lo,
I see four men
Loose,
Walking in the midst of the fire,
And they have no hurt;
And the form of the fourth is like the Son of God."

Then Nebuchadnezzar came near to the mouth of the burning fiery
        furnace, and spoke, and said,
"Shadrach,
Meshach,
And Abed-nego,
Ye servants of the most high God,
Come forth,
And
Come hither."

Then
Shadrach, Meshach, and Abed-nego
Came forth of the midst of the fire. And the
Princes,
Governors,
And captains,
And the king's counsellors,
Being gathered together,
Saw these men upon whose bodies
The fire had no power,
Nor was a hair of their head singed,
Neither were their coats changed,
Nor the smell of fire had passed on them.

Then Nebuchadnezzar spoke, and said,
"Blessed be the God of
Shadrach, Meshach, and Abed-nego,
Who hath sent his angel,

And delivered his servants that trusted in him.
Therefore I make a decree,
That every people, nation, and language,
Which speak any thing amiss against the God of Shadrach, Meshach,
       and Abed-nego,
Shall be cut in pieces,
And their houses shall be made a dunghill:
Because there is no other God
That can deliver after this sort."

Then the king promoted
Shadrach, Meshach, and Abed-nego,
In the province of Babylon.

The Three Hermits

An Old Legend Current in the Vólga District

LEO TOLSTOY

*We all love stories about simple faith as against formal
teaching. This one even succeeds in being funny and is written with understanding, for the Bishop is likable and you
feel you have shared his revelation with him.*

*"And in praying use not vain repetitions, as the Gentiles do: for they
think that they shall be heard for their much speaking. Be not therefore
like unto them: for your Father knoweth what things ye have need of,
before ye ask Him."*—Matthew 6:7, 8

A Bishop was sailing from Archangel to the Solovétsk Monastery,
and on the same vessel were a number of pilgrims on their way to
visit the shrines at that place. The voyage was a smooth one. The
wind favorable and the weather fair. The pilgrims lay on deck, eating,
or sat in groups talking to one another. The Bishop, too, came on
deck, and as he was pacing up and down he noticed a group of men
standing near the prow and listening to a fisherman, who was pointing to the sea and telling them something. The Bishop stopped, and
looked in the direction in which the man was pointing. He could see
nothing, however, but the sea glistening in the sunshine. He drew
nearer to listen, but when the man saw him, he took off his cap and
was silent. The rest of the people also took off their caps and bowed.

"Do not let me disturb you, friends," said the Bishop. "I came to
hear what this good man was saying."

"The fisherman was telling us about the hermits," replied one, a
tradesman, rather bolder than the rest.

"What hermits?" asked the Bishop, going to the side of the vessel
and seating himself on a box. "Tell me about them. I should like to
hear. What were you pointing at?"

"Why, that little island you can just see over there," answered
the man, pointing to a spot ahead and a little to the right. "That
is the island where the hermits live for the salvation of their souls."

"Where is the island?" asked the Bishop. "I see nothing."

"There, in the distance, if you will please look along my hand. Do you see that little cloud? Below it, and a bit to the left, there is just a faint streak. That is the island."

The Bishop looked carefully, but his unaccustomed eyes could make out nothing but the water shimmering in the sun.

"I cannot see it," he said. "But who are the hermits that live there?"

"They are holy men," answered the fisherman. "I had long heard tell of them, but never chanced to see them myself till the year before last."

And the fisherman related how once, when he was out fishing, he had been stranded at night upon that island, not knowing where he was. In the morning, as he wandered about the island, he came across an earth hut, and met an old man standing near it. Presently two others came out, and after having fed him and dried his things, they helped him mend his boat.

"And what are they like?" asked the Bishop.

"One is a small man and his back is bent. He wears a priest's cassock and is very old; he must be more than a hundred, I should say. He is so old that the white of his beard is taking a greenish tinge, but he is always smiling, and his face is as bright as an angel's from heaven. The second is taller, but he also is very old. He wears a tattered peasant coat. His beard is broad, and of a yellowish grey color. He is a strong man. Before I had time to help him, he turned my boat over as if it were only a pail. He too is kindly and cheerful. The third is tall, and has a beard as white as snow and reaching to his knees. He is stern, with overhanging eyebrows; and he wears nothing but a piece of matting tied round his waist."

"And did they speak to you?" asked the Bishop.

"For the most part they did everything in silence, and spoke but little even to one another. One of them would just give a glance, and the others would understand him. I asked the tallest whether they had lived there long. He frowned, and muttered something as if he were angry; but the oldest one took his hand and smiled, and then the tall one was quiet. The oldest one only said: 'Have mercy upon us,' and smiled."

While the fisherman was talking, the ship had drawn nearer to the island.

"There, now you can see it plainly, if your Lordship will please to look," said the tradesman, pointing with his hand.

The Bishop looked, and now he really saw a dark streak—which was the island. Having looked at it a while, he left the prow of the vessel, and going to the stern, asked the helmsman:

"What island is that?"

"That one," replied the man, "has no name. There are many such in this sea."

"Is it true that there are hermits who live there for the salvation of their souls?"

"So it is said, your Lordship, but I don't know if it's true. Fishermen say they have seen them; but of course they may only be spinning yarns."

"I should like to land on the island and see these men," said the Bishop. "How could I manage it?"

"The ship cannot get close to the island," replied the helmsman, "but you might be rowed there in a boat. You had better speak to the captain."

The captain was sent for and came.

"I should like to see these hermits," said the Bishop. "Could I not be rowed ashore?"

The captain tried to dissuade him.

"Of course it could be done," said he, "but we should lose much time. And if I might venture to say to your Lordship, the old men are not worth your pains. I have heard say that they are foolish old fellows, who understand nothing, and never speak a word, any more than the fish in the sea."

"I wish to see them," said the Bishop, "and I will pay you for your trouble and loss of time. Please let me have the boat."

There was no help for it; so the order was given. The sailors trimmed the sails, the steersman put up the helm, and the ship's course was set for the island. A chair was placed at the prow for the Bishop, and he sat there, looking ahead. The passengers all collected at the prow, and gazed at the island. Those who had the sharpest eyes could presently make out the rocks on it, and then a mud hut was seen. At last one man saw the hermits themselves. The captain brought a telescope and, after looking through it, handed it to the Bishop.

"It's right enough. There are three men standing on the shore. There, a little to the right of that big rock."

The Bishop took the telescope, got it into position, and he saw the three men: a tall one, a shorter one, and one very small and bent, standing on the shore and holding each other by the hand.

The captain turned to the Bishop.

"The vessel can get no nearer in than this, your Lordship. If you wish to go ashore, we must ask you to go in the boat, while we anchor here."

The cable was quickly let out; the anchor cast, and the sails furled. There was a jerk, and the vessel shook. Then, a boat having been lowered, the oarsmen jumped in, and the Bishop descended the ladder and took his seat. The men pulled at their oars and the boat moved rapidly towards the island. When they came within a stone's throw, they saw three old men: a tall one with only a piece of matting tied round his waist: a shorter one in a tattered peasant coat, and a very old one bent with age and wearing an old cassock—all three standing hand in hand.

The oarsmen pulled in to the shore, and held on with the boathook while the Bishop got out.

The old men bowed to him, and he gave them his blessing, at which they bowed still lower. Then the Bishop began to speak to them.

"I have heard," he said, "that you, godly men, live here saving your own souls and praying to our Lord Christ for your fellow men. I, an unworthy servant of Christ, am called, by God's mercy, to keep and teach His flock. I wished to see you, servants of God, and to do what I can to teach you, also."

The old men looked at each other smiling, but remained silent.

"Tell me," said the Bishop, "what you are doing to save your souls, and how you serve God on this island."

The second hermit sighed, and looked at the oldest, the very ancient one. The latter smiled, and said:

"We do not know how to serve God. We only serve and support ourselves, servant of God."

"But how do you pray to God?" asked the Bishop.

"We pray in this way," replied the hermit. "Three are ye, three are we, have mercy upon us."

And when the old man said this, all three raised their eyes to heaven, and repeated:

"Three are ye, three are we, have mercy upon us!"

The Bishop smiled.

"You have evidently heard something about the Holy Trinity," said he. "But you do not pray aright. You have won my affection, godly men. I see you wish to please the Lord, but you do not know how to serve Him. That is not the way to pray; but listen to me, and I will teach you. I will teach you, not a way of my own, but the way in which God in the Holy Scriptures has commanded all men to pray to Him."

And the Bishop began explaining to the hermits how God had revealed Himself to men; telling them of God the Father, and God the Son, and God the Holy Ghost.

"God the Son came down on earth," said he, "to save men, and this is how He taught us all to pray. Listen, and repeat after me: 'Our Father.' "

And the first old man repeated after him, "Our Father," and the second said, "Our Father," and the third said, "Our Father."

"Which art in heaven," continued the Bishop.

The first hermit repeated, "Which art in heaven," but the second blundered over the words, and the tall hermit could not say them properly. His hair had grown over his mouth so that he could not speak plainly. The very old hermit, having no teeth, also mumbled indistinctly.

The Bishop repeated the words again, and the old men repeated them after him. The Bishop sat down on a stone, and the old men stood before him, watching his mouth, and repeating the words as he uttered them. And all day long the Bishop labored, saying a word twenty, thirty, a hundred times over, and the old men repeated it after him. They blundered, and he corrected them, and made them begin again.

The Bishop did not leave off till he had taught them the whole of the Lord's Prayer so that they could not only repeat it after him, but could say it by themselves. The middle one was the first to know it, and to repeat the whole of it alone. The Bishop made him say it again and again, and at last the others could say it too.

It was getting dark and the moon was appearing over the water, before the Bishop rose to return to the vessel. When he took leave of the old men they all bowed down to the ground before him. He raised them, and kissed each of them, telling them to pray as he had taught them. Then he got into the boat and returned to the ship.

As he sat in the boat and was rowed to the ship he could hear the three voices of the hermits loudly repeating the Lord's Prayer. As the boat drew near the vessel their voices could no longer be heard, but they could still be seen in the moonlight, standing as he had left them on the shore, the shortest in the middle, the tallest on the right, the middle one on the left. As soon as the Bishop had reached the vessel and got on board, the anchor was weighed and the sails unfurled. The wind filled them and the ship sailed away, and the Bishop took a seat in the stern and watched the island they had left. For a time he could still see the hermits, but presently they disappeared from sight, though the island was still visible. At last it too vanished, and only the sea was to be seen, rippling in the moonlight.

The pilgrims lay down to sleep, and all was quiet on deck. The Bishop did not wish to sleep, but sat alone at the stern, gazing at the sea where the island was no longer visible, and thinking of the good old men. He thought how pleased they had been to learn the Lord's Prayer; and he thanked God for having sent him to teach and help such godly men.

So the Bishop sat, thinking, and gazing at the sea where the island had disappeared. And the moonlight flickered before his eyes, sparkling, now here, now there, upon the waves. Suddenly he saw something white and shining, on the bright path which the moon cast across the sea. Was it a seagull, or the little gleaming sail of some small boat? The Bishop fixed his eyes on it, wondering.

"It must be a boat sailing after us," thought he, "but it is overtaking us very rapidly. It was far, far away a minute ago, but now it is much nearer. It cannot be a boat, for I can see no sail; but whatever it may be, it is following us and catching us up."

And he could not make out what it was. Not a boat, nor a bird, nor a fish! It was too large for a man, and besides a man could not be out there in the midst of the sea. The Bishop rose, and said to the helmsman:

"Look there, what is that, my friend? What is it?" the Bishop repeated, though he could now see plainly what it was—the three hermits running upon the water, all gleaming white, their grey beards shining, and approaching the ship as quickly as though it were not moving.

The steersman looked, and let go the helm in terror.

"Oh, Lord! The hermits are running after us on the water as though it were dry land!"

The passengers, hearing him, jumped up and crowded to the stern. They saw the hermits coming along hand in hand, and the two outer ones beckoning the ship to stop. All three were gliding along upon the water without moving their feet. Before the ship could be stopped, the hermits had reached it, and raising their heads, all three as with one voice, began to say:

"We have forgotten your teaching, servant of God. As long as we kept repeating it we remembered, but when we stopped saying it for a time, a word dropped out, and now it has all gone to pieces. We can remember nothing of it. Teach us again."

The Bishop crossed himself, and leaning over the ship's side, said:

"Your own prayer will reach the Lord, men of God. It is not for me to teach you. Pray for us sinners."

And the Bishop bowed low before the old men; and they turned and went back across the sea. And a light shone until daybreak on the spot where they were lost to sight.

The Pool of Siloam

THE GOSPEL ACCORDING TO ST. JOHN
Chapter 9, verses 1–38

> *It would be impertinent on my part to make any comment on a story from the life of Jesus. I have included this one because it is a story that I go back to frequently when I am angry or blue or discontented.*
>
> *It was brought to my attention by Bertolt Brecht, the dramatist, when I was working with him on a translation of his play, Galileo, as the most compassionate story he knew.*

And as Jesus passed by, he saw a man which was blind from his birth. And his disciples asked him, saying, "Master, who did sin, this man, or his parents, that he was born blind?"

Jesus answered, "Neither hath this man sinned, nor his parents: but that the works of God should be made manifest in him. I must work the works of him that sent me, while it is day: the night cometh, when no man can work. As long as I am in the world, I am the light of the world."

When he had thus spoken, he spat on the ground, and made clay of the spittle, and he anointed the eyes of the blind man with the clay, and said unto him, "Go, wash in the pool of Siloam."

He went his way therefore, and washed, and came seeing. The neighbours therefore, and they which before had seen him that he was blind, said, "Is not this he that sat and begged?"

Some said, "This is he": others said, "He is like him": but he said, "I am he."

Therefore said they unto him, "How were thine eyes opened?"

He answered and said, "A man that is called Jesus made clay, and anointed mine eyes, and said unto me, 'Go to the pool of Siloam, and wash': and I went and washed, and I received sight."

Then said they unto him, "Where is he?"

He said, "I know not."

They brought to the Pharisees him that aforetime was blind. And it was the sabbath day when Jesus made the clay, and opened his eyes.

Then again the Pharisees also asked him how he had received his sight. He said unto them, "He put clay upon mine eyes, and I washed, and do see."

Therefore said some of the Pharisees, "This man is not of God, because he keepeth not the sabbath day."

Others said, "How can a man that is a sinner do such miracles?" And there was a division among them. They say unto the blind man again, "What sayest thou of him, that he hath opened thine eyes?"

He said, "He is a prophet."

But the Jews did not believe concerning him, that he had been blind, and received his sight, until they called the parents of him that had received his sight. And they asked them, saying, "Is this your son, who ye say was born blind? how then doth he now see?"

His parents answered them and said, "We know that this is our son, and that he was born blind: but by what means he now seeth, we know not; or who hath opened his eyes, we know not: he is of age; ask him: he shall speak for himself."

These words spoke his parents, because they feared the Jews: for the Jews had agreed already, that if any man did confess that he was Christ, he should be put out of the synagogue. Therefore said his parents, "He is of age; ask him."

Then again called they the man that was blind, and said unto him, "Give God the praise: we know that this man is a sinner."

He answered and said, "Whether he be a sinner or no, I know not: one thing I know, that, whereas I was blind, now I see."

Then said they to him again, "What did he to thee? how opened he thine eyes?"

He answered them, "I have told you already, and ye did not hear: wherefore would ye hear it again? will ye also be his disciples?"

Then they reviled him, and said, "Thou art his disciple; but we are Moses' disciples. We know that God spoke unto Moses: as for this fellow, we know not from whence he is."

The man answered and said unto them, "Why herein is a marvellous thing, that ye know not from whence he is, and yet he hath opened mine eyes. Now we know that God heareth not sinners: but if any man be a worshipper of God, and doeth his will, him he heareth. Since the world began was it not heard that any man opened the eyes of one that was born blind. If this man were not of God, he could do nothing."

They answered and said unto him, "Thou wast altogether born in sins, and dost thou teach us?" And they cast him out.

Jesus heard that they had cast him out; and when he had found him, he said unto him, "Dost thou believe on the Son of God?"

He answered and said, "Who is he, Lord, that I might believe on him?"

And Jesus said unto him, "Thou hast both seen him, and it is he that talketh with thee."

And he said, "Lord, I believe." And he worshipped him.

Endpiece

When I am on the stage doing a reading I always finish up with something patriotic. This is an old stage tradition—waving the flag as the final curtain comes down—and it has been mocked at. But I think that it is a good thing to do something about your country at the end of a show (and I think of a book in terms of a show) so that you and your audience feel warm and hopeful together.

Burning in the Night

THOMAS WOLFE

> *This is an extract from Thomas Wolfe's last book,* You
> Can't Go Home Again. *The book has many wonderful
> things in it. Here he is speaking of the young students all
> over the map of this vast country, burning in the night.*

The desire for fame is rooted in the hearts of men. It is one of the
most powerful of all human desires.

And we?

O brothers, like our fathers in their time, we are burning,

burning,

burning in the night.

Go, seeker, if you will, throughout the land and you will find us
burning in the night.

There where the hackles of the Rocky Mountains blaze in the
blank and naked radiance of the moon, go make your resting stool
upon the highest peak.

Can you not see us now?

The continental wall juts sheer and flat, its huge black shadow
on the plain, and the plain sweeps out against the East, two thousand miles away.

The great snake that you see there is the Mississippi River.

Behold the gem-strung towns and cities of the good, green East,
flung like star-dust through the field of night.

That spreading constellation to the north is called Chicago, and
that giant wink that blazes in the moon is the pendant lake that it
is built upon.

Beyond, close-set and dense as a clenched fist, are all the jeweled
cities of the eastern seaboard.

There's Boston, ringed with the bracelet of its shining little towns,
and all the lights that sparkle on the rocky indentations of New
England.

Here, southward and a little to the west, and yet still coasted to
the sea, is our intensest ray, the splintered firmament of the towered

island of Manhattan. Round about her, sown thick as grain, is the glitter of a hundred towns and cities. The long chain of lights there is the necklace of Long Island and the Jersey shore.

Southward and inland, by a foot or two, behold the duller glare of Philadelphia.

Southward further still, the twin constellations—Baltimore and Washington.

Westward, but still within the borders of the good, green East, that nighttime glow and smolder of hell-fire is Pittsburgh.

Here, St. Louis, hot and humid in the cornfield belly of the land, and bedded on the mid-length coil and fringes of the snake.

There at the snake's mouth, southward six hundred miles or so, you see the jeweled crescent of old New Orleans.

Here, west and south again, you see the gemmy glitter of the cities on the Texas border.

Turn now, seeker, on your resting stool atop the Rocky Mountains, and look another thousand miles or so across moon-blazing fiend-worlds of the Painted Desert and beyond Sierras' ridge.

That magic congeries of lights there to the west, ringed like a studded belt around the magic setting of its lovely harbor, is the fabled town of San Francisco.

Below it, Los Angeles and all the cities of the California shore.

A thousand miles to north and west, the sparkling towns of Oregon and Washington.

Observe the whole of it, survey it as you might survey a field.

Make it your garden, seeker, or your backyard patch.

Be at ease in it.

It's your oyster—yours to open if you will. Don't be frightened, it's not so big now, when your footstool is the Rocky Mountains.

Reach out and dip a hatful of cold water from Lake Michigan.

Drink it—we've tried it—you'll not find it bad.

Take your shoes off and work your toes down in the river oozes of the Mississippi bottom—it's very refreshing on a hot night in the summertime.

Help yourself to a bunch of Concord grapes up there in northern New York State—they're getting good now.

Or raid that watermelon patch down there in Georgia.

Or, if you like, you can try the Rockyfords here at your elbow, in Colorado.

Just make yourself at home, refresh yourself, get the feel of things, adjust your sights, and get the scale. It's your pasture now, and it's not so big—only three thousand miles from east to west, only two thousand miles from north to south—

but all between, where ten thousand points of light prick out the
cities, towns, and villages, there, seeker, you will find us
    burning in the night.

Here, as you pass through the brutal sprawl, the twenty miles of
rails and rickets, of the South Chicago slums—here, in an unpainted
shack, is a Negro boy, and, seeker, he is burning in the night. Behind him is a memory of the cotton fields, the flat and mournful
pineland barrens of the lost and buried South, and at the fringes of
the pine another nigger shack, with mammy and eleven little niggers.
Farther still behind, the slave-driver's whip, the slave ship, and, far
off, the jungle dirge of Africa. And before him, what? A roped-in
ring, a blaze of lights, across from him a white champion; the bell,
the opening, and all around the vast sea-roaring of the crowd. Then
the lightning feint and stroke, the black panther's paw—the hot,
rotating presses, and the rivers of sheeted print. O seeker, where is
the slave ship now?

Or there, in the clay-baked piedmont of the South, that lean and
tan-faced boy who sprawls there in the creaking chair among admiring cronies before the open doorways of the fire department, and
tells them how he pitched the team to shut-out victory today. What
visions burn, what dreams possess him, seeker of the night? The
packed stands of the stadium, the bleachers sweltering with their
unshaded hordes, the faultless velvet of the diamond, unlike the
clay-baked outfields down in Georgia. The mounting roar of eighty
thousand voices and Gehrig coming up to bat, the boy himself upon
the pitching mound, the lean face steady as a hound's; then the
nod, the signal, and the wind-up, the rawhide arm that snaps and
crackles like a whip, the small white bullet of the blazing ball, its
loud report in the oiled pocket of the catcher's mitt, the umpire's
thumb jerked upward, the clean strike.

Or there again, in the East-Side Ghetto of Manhattan, two blocks
away from the East River, a block away from the gas-house district
and its thuggery, there in the swarming tenement, shut in his sweltering cell, breathing the sun-baked air through opened window at the
fire escape, celled there away into a little semblance of privacy and
solitude from all the brawling and vociferous life and argument of
his family and the seething hive around him, the Jew boy sits and
pores upon his book. In shirt-sleeves, bent above his table to meet
the hard glare of a naked bulb, he sits with gaunt, starved face con-
verging to his huge beaked nose, the weak eyes squinting painfully
through his thick-lens glasses, his greasy hair roached back in oily

scrolls above the slanting cage of his painful and constricted brow. And for what? For what this agony of concentration? For what this hell of effort? For what this intense withdrawal from the poverty and squalor of dirty brick and rusty fire escapes, from the raucous cries and violence and never-ending noise? For what? Because, brother, he is burning in the night. He sees the class, the lecture room, the shining apparatus of gigantic laboratories, the open field of scholarship and pure research, certain knowledge, and the world distinction of an Einstein name.

So, then, to every man his chance—

to every man, regardless of his birth, his shining, golden opportunity

—to every man the right to live, to work, to be himself, and to become whatever thing his manhood and his vision can combine to make him

—this, seeker, is the promise of America.